Chantecoq and the Aubry Affair

This work is dedicated to the inspirational

Melanie A.L.

ARTHUR BERNÈDE

Chantecoq and the Aubry Affair

TRANSLATED INTO ENGLISH FOR THE FIRST TIME BY

ANDREW K. LAWSTON

Contents

CHAPTER ONE:

The Combat Aircraft

In Paris's Saint-Mandé, towards the end of a glorious October afternoon, the tram leading from the fortifications was just stopping at the junction of Cours de Vincennes and Rue de la République.

Passengers were hastily disembarking, forcing their way between the people who were crowding around the tram's step, when the conductor shouted out in a loud, gruff voice, addressing a traveller who had just reached the pavement.

"Hey, you there, sir, you've forgotten something!"

Instinctively the man turned and, seeing the tram driver holding a briefcase full of files out to him, he replied, with a slightly distracted air,

"Thank you so much, friend," then, as if he were talking to himself, he added, "it's official, I'm losing my mind!"

Crossing the track, he set off down Avenue de la Tourelle, shoulders hunched, head down, walking with a weary, dragging step, and stopping every so often as though he were reluctant to reach his home.

Finally, he turned on to Rue du Parc, pushed open an iron-grilled gate, crossed a garden strewn with yellowed leaves which were starting to fall from the trees, and without knocking he entered a small villa whose walls were garnished with a green trellis, from which hung a barren vine whose golden brown tones signalled the end of summer's finest days.

"Has Miss Germaine come home?" he asked the housekeeper who had run to meet him, her waist encircled by a thick blue canvas apron.

"Not yet, Mr. Aubry." The brave woman, whose own beaming face radiated health and candour, noted her master's sombre, pre-occupied mood, and added immediately, "Has something happened, sir? You're not ill?"

"Why would you ask me that?"

"Because sir is in a funny mood."

"That's your own notion that you've got into your head, my good Victoire."

"And yet, sir . . ."

"It's all right. Leave me," the master of the house interrupted nervously, marching into his study, and closing the door brusquely.

Throwing his briefcase dejectedly on to the table in the middle of the room, he let himself fall into a leather armchair; burying his head in his hands, he broke down in tears.

Jean Aubry looked about fifty years old. Of tall stature; grey hair, brushed neatly, a burning gaze under his bushy eyebrows, his mouth topped with a Gallic moustache, forehead creased by premature wrinkles, he seemed to be prey to a violent torment that he had long held within himself, but which he could no longer contain.

From time to time, fragments of sentences escaped his lips. "There's no more to be done . . . nothing . . . it's fatal . . . If they'd only listened to me . . . but they didn't want to . . . they'll never want to . . . it's all hopeless!"

The door opened. A young girl aged twenty, whose very simple black clothes brought out her impeccable figure and whose bonnet of dark velvet, carelessly thrown on her magnificent brown tresses, further heightened her enchanting beauty, rushed into Jean Aubry's arms saying, "Good evening, father!"

"Good evening, my dear!" said the inventor while trying to hide the chagrin which gripped him.

Fixing her father with her very blue, very clear eyes, where there was nothing to read but intelligence, tenderness and pride, Germaine replied, with a gently reproachful tone, "I'm sure you've given yourself more wicked ideas?"

"Oh no, my child."

"Oh yes. Poor dear father!"

As Jean Aubry turned away, Germaine, taking his hands and gently forcing him to sit near her on the couch, spoke to him in a voice full of inflections that were both wheedling and profound.

"I can see that for some time you have been discouraged. You mustn't be. A genius such as yourself will naturally overcome any obstacles."

"I believed that once," replied the inventor in a dull voice, "but today . . ."

"Today, who's to say that we're not on the verge of success?"

"This afternoon I went to the Ministry of War again."

"Oh. Well?"

"He wouldn't even see me. And I'm not surprised; last time I had a meeting with the president of the Commission, he laughed in my face and virtually treated me like a madman, assuring me my combat aircraft was an unrealistic daydream. So, what do you want me to do? Who do you want me to speak to?"

"What about Captain Evrard?"

"Hah! Captain Evrard!"

"You know how much, he too, believes in you."

"Yes, I know. But what do you want him to do against the inertia of some, and the malevolence of others?"

"Captain Evrard," Germaine declared with conviction, "is not only an aviator of incomparable audacity who displays perfect composure at every challenge; but, as an enthusiast of your work, he will defend it to the end. His aerial exploits have won him the admiration of the highest in France. He promised to go and plead your cause to the Minister. He will do it, and he will win."

"That would be too perfect!" sighed the inventor, completely despondent.

And as, silently, new tears fell from his eyes, Germaine, leaning her head on his shoulder, murmured to him with an expression of infinite tenderness.

"My father, my dear father, you can't imagine how much it pains me to see you so dejected, when I've known you to be so strong, so valiant. The good days will come, I'm certain of it."

The brave man shook his head. The young girl added. "You're frightening me, I fear that you've not told me the whole truth."

"I have."

"No, father, you're hiding something from me! Since the death of my dear mother, I have always been your confidante, your companion. So speak! I beg of you . . ."

"My poor dear . . ."

"Yes, speak!"

"I didn't want to tell you," revealed Jean Aubry, "and yet you must know, my last resources are spent. I have no more money, and I'm asking myself what will become of us."

"Am I not here?" replied Germaine simply.

"You, my dear!" exclaimed the father, giving the young girl a look full of paternal sadness.

"Yes, me!" affirmed Germaine. "When I was a child, you made heavy sacrifices in order to give me a superior education. You sent me to England for two years, then to Berlin for three years to help me in my studies of the German language. Thanks to that, on my return to France, not only have I been made a teacher at the Lycée Fénelon, but I could still easily find private lessons."

"No, I don't want that."

"Why?"

"Because I couldn't forgive myself if you fell ill."

"Don't worry, I'm robust."

"And then, my child, I have another problem."

His voice trembling, anguished, the professor added. "Why don't you want to marry the captain?"

At these words, the young girl started. She got up suddenly, trembling, while a vivid blush spread over her face.

"He loves you," continued the inventor, "I don't need to sing his praises to you. You know him better than I. He's a true hero."

"Father!" stammered Germaine, in the grip of her emotions.

"Certainly, I'm not ignorant of how dreadful it must sometimes be to be the wife of an aviator who, each day, risks adding his name to the glorious list of martyrs where are inscribed in letters of gold and blood the names of Ferber, Caumont, and such others. But it seemed to me, my dear child that, you too, you felt for our friend Evrard some sentiments-"

"My dear father," Jean Aubry's daughter interrupted brusquely, "I have great respect for the captain. I admire his audacity. I am infinitely grateful for all that he wants to do for us; but I can't be his wife."

And lowering her head, she added in a whisper, her voice breaking, "I don't love him . . ."

She stopped herself, hesitated, as though the words were caught in her throat.

Finally, in one breath, she managed, "And I feel sure that I will never love him."

In one bound, as though he had regained all his energy, Jean Aubry was on his feet.

"So!" he cried, "What do you want to become of me?"

"We will struggle on."

"I've had enough! I'm heartbroken, disillusioned, I want no more of this abominable existence of daily battles and incessant defeats. A convict, do you hear me? A convict is happier than I. He, at least, can hope for his escape or his pardon. While I, I am the eternally condemned wretch who can do nothing more than bang his skull against the walls of his prison!"

And, seizing the briefcase which was lying on the table, mad with despair and rage, he returned to his daughter, declaiming to her, "You know what's in there. All my plans. All my secrets. All the fruits of my work. All the output of my brain. You who are initiated, you also know that in there is the material to build an invincible army. Well, just now, I left all that in the tram. Without the conductor who called me back, well, where would it have gone? I have no idea. Perhaps to make paper bags for a grocer. Or for a tobacconist. At least that would have been more useful!"

Shaking the two pockets of the briefcase whose files were scattered over the table, the inventor added with a sinister sneer, "To the winds, beautiful ideas! Get out, great projects! My combat aircraft will finally float in the skies, because I'm going to throw it all out of the window."

"Oh, father!" Germaine cried, rushing towards the inventor.

"Stop. My dear Mr. Aubry," a deep male voice said suddenly, resonating through the room.

The soberly elegant silhouette of an artillery officer loomed on the threshold!

"Captain Evrard!" cried the young girl, growing pale.

Then with eyes full of joy, his face illuminated, with a glee that flowed from his whole being, the young aviator replied. "Yes, Captain Evrard, who brings you great news."

CHAPTER TWO:

The Traitor

The father and the daughter remained where they stood, speechless.

The officer stepped forward, holding out his hands and, seizing those of Jean Aubry and Germaine together:

"Yes, good news!" he emphasised.

The military aviator was a man of around thirty, with martial features, open, with a clear, penetrating gaze.

"The bad times are finished," he explained in a voice vibrant with joy. "I have just seen the Minister of War; he charged me to tell you, my dear Mr. Aubry, that he awaits you tomorrow morning at ten o'clock in his office."

"Is this possible?" the inventor interrupted, staggered.

"Wait, I've not finished," continued the captain. "As I promised you, I explained to the Minister the whole mechanism of your marvellous combat aircraft."

"And what did he say?" Germaine asked feverishly.

"After having listened to me with the greatest attention, he posed numerous questions which proved to me the extent to which I had succeeded in interesting him. I responded as best I could and I ended up convincing him, because he decided that from tomorrow he will put at the disposal of Mr. Aubry all the necessary funds for the construction of a prototype, which I am charged to test in his presence. And he added that if, as he wished with all his heart, this machine fulfils in practice all the hopes that it raises in theory, he was ready not only to buy your patent from you for five hundred thousand francs, but also to name you as director of the factory that he will have built for the construction of a fleet of combat aircraft whose command will be entrusted to me."

"Father!" Germaine cried, "You see I was right when I told you not to give up hope."

"So! My dear Mr. Aubry, are you pleased?" the officer asked.

"That's to say . . ." replied the inventor, dazed by this news which was so unexpected and which he could still hardly believe. "That's to say that I can find no words to express to you my gratitude . . ."

Comforted, transfigured, he shook the aviation officer's hands effusively, while he cried, addressing his daughter in particular who, breathless, could not take her eyes off the young captain.

"Finally, I have justice! I wish that in a few months, France might possess a fourth army which will be a guarantee of victory for her for a long time, and I have instantly forgotten all my disappointments and all my suffering. I'm drunk with joy. I don't know . . . I'm laughing . . . I'm weeping . . . I'm too happy . . . yes, too happy!"

In fact, some tears now moistened the eyes of that excellent man who continued, his heart overflowing with emotion and gratitude. "My dear friend, we thank you with all our heart, my daughter and I. Without you, I would never have succeeded in reaching the Minister. Without you, my work would never have seen daylight."

"Ah, captain!" Germaine said in a trembling voice, "My poor father was desperate. Also I . . . I . . ."

Her throat caught; and pale, she staggered, ready to fall.

"Dear child!" said Jean Aubry, catching her in his arms.

And, crying, the inventor's daughter leaned her head on her father's shoulder. Her father replied. "Why do you weep? You should be as happy as I am now."

"Yes, father. I am happy, very happy . . ." stammered the beautiful creature through her tears, "but . . ."

"What, then, my dear?"

"I daren't . . . I can't . . ."

"Speak. Let's see."

"All right! There is mixed in my joy a great bitterness, caused by regret, that I have irritated the captain."

"Me, miss?" the officer asked, moved.

Calling on all her energy, the young girl, improved by the expression of celestial purity which spread over her face, continued. "Before you arrived, Mr. Evrard, my father told me how my refusal to be your wife had caused you pain."

"In fact, miss," said the aviator, whose energetic voice began to tremble, "this refusal was more than an irritation for me. It was truly agony. But, profoundly respectful of your will, never would I have allowed myself to make the slightest allusion to a despair which must have no other confidant than myself.

"However, since you give me the right to break my silence, let me tell you that, more than ever, my heart is yours. Forever."

"And so, in spite of my disdain," Germaine cried, "you continued to defend my father. You succeeded in bringing to light his idea, and you are ready to risk your life to guarantee the triumph of his work!"

"I have only done my soldier's duty. However, I love you too much to bear any rancour towards you. A soul can't be forced. And then, there is a genius, an admirable man whose sacred cause I made my own. And finally, overriding all the human considerations, above all, there is the nation, for which everyone must be ready to sacrifice their existence, their dreams!"

"Ah! Pardon me, captain. Pardon me!" the noble child cried, giving way to the irresistible impulse which seized her.

"Pardon you? Why?"

"Because just now, I swore to my father that I didn't love you, that I would never love you. Well, I lied. Yes, I lied."

"Germaine!" the two men cried simultaneously.

"I had to give a reason for my refusal," she explained to the inventor, "because I didn't want to leave you at the moment where everything was crumbling around you. I wanted to stay to support your courage, to rekindle your faith, and above all to warm your heart."

"Ah, my poor children," exclaimed Mr Aubry, "When I think that it was I who has delayed your happiness!"

"It's only more complete today!" said the young girl, holding out her hand to the officer who hastened to seize it and to raise it to his lips with respectful fervour.

"You understand the sacred motive which imposed this conduct upon me," continued Germaine, "You do understand, don't you? I couldn't have acted otherwise."

"Don't defend yourself." said the officer, "The pure sentiment which dictated your attitude merely increases again my tenderness which dates not from yesterday, but from last year."

"From last year?"

"Yes, from the day where, for the first time, I climbed above the clouds. Over there . . ."

"At the Vincennes airfield!" Germaine finished, radiant at this memory. "I was there too, lost in the crowd, leaning on my father's arm, and neither of us took our eyes from a little black dot, almost the size of a swallow and which shrank quickly, so quickly, soon to disappear completely. Oh! How long seemed to me those minutes where nothing could be seen. Nothing! And how joyfully I cried when I saw again the little black dot, the tiny little swallow which returned, growing and regaining bit by bit its true shape, of a dragonfly with huge wings. Finally the descending aircraft landed, full of grace and majesty in the middle of the strip, while applause, shouts, cheers, succeeded the anguished silence which grasped us all and how, from everywhere, people swarmed from the stands to run towards you."

"And how a young girl, adorably beautiful, reached Captain Evrard, hurried, tearing a flower from her corsage to give to the aviator, a simple rose whose scent I still keep in my heart."

"Now, to dinner!" said Jean Aubry, more moved than he wanted to appear, seeing Victoire, the cook, hovering impatiently. "Because you will stay and dine with us, captain."

"Oh, of course!" insisted the young girl, seeing the officer attempt a gesture of protest. This will be our engagement party."

"Beware," warned Jean Aubry, "you will be getting a poor meal."

"Of course!" said Victoire who was already setting an extra place, "Everything is overcooked, not only do you arrive late, but then you start arguing . . ."

"We'll make up for it on the day of the wedding!"

And, as he sat down, the inventor could not resist saying, "It's all the same. The president of the Technical Commission will pull a strange face when he learns that the Minister has accepted my aircraft."

"He won't be the only one," said the officer.

"But I know one of them, at least, who will be very happy; that's our friend Jacques Müller."

"Oh yes, the young man from Alsace who has such affection and regard for you."

"A brave boy," Germaine stressed.

"He told me recently how much the two of you showered him with affection and care when he was ill."

"He was a child from Alsace, with no family," Jean Aubry revealed, "no resources, no moral support, somewhat lost in Paris. I met him in the class that I teach each week at Saint-Antoine university. Straight away I distinguished him from the others by virtue of his careful attention and his good manners. He seemed happy to learn through the intelligent questions which he asked me. When I heard that he'd fallen ill in a nasty hostel bedroom, I went to see him. He was alone there, abandoned. I sent a doctor to him and I ensured that he lacked nothing.

"I see that I have not indulged an ungrateful wretch. He will come this evening, because he's still in the area and he comes to see me each time I go to my class."

"I'll be very happy to meet him," the officer declared. "Which town is he from, then?"

"From Strasbourg. He comes from an old family there. His grandfather was shot in 1870, as a rebel, by the Prussians. As to his father and his mother, ruined by German speculators, they died, some years ago, from sorrow and misery."

"Mr Müller is here!" Victoire announced as she returned to the room.

"I am a little late this evening," said Jean Aubry, looking at the clock.

And, addressing the housekeeper, he added, "Let him enter! He will join us in a toast, eh, captain?"

"Gladly!"

A tall young man stepped forward, with a silky moustache and blond hair with an impeccable centre parting, keeping a natural elegance under the simplicity of his outfit, his hat in his hand, at ease and at home.

"We have just been speaking ill of you," the inventor said, holding out his hand to him.

"Captain Maurice Evrard," he continued, as the young man exchanged a salute with the officer. "As I know that you are truly our friend, I have the pleasure of informing you that he is my daughter's fiancé."

"Oh, my dear captain!" Jacques Müller cried with spontaneous force, "I congratulate you with all my heart. And you too, miss. Believe that I have for you the most ardent good wishes."

"But that's not all!" the radiant inventor continued, "My combat aircraft, of which I've spoken to you so often . . ."

"Ah! Yes?" the newcomer demanded quickly.

"It has been accepted in principle, and tomorrow I shall resubmit the plans to the Minister of War, who is expecting me."

"What did you say?" the man from Alsace started, as he struggled to control the reaction which had escaped him.

"I said," replied Jean Aubry, becoming animated, "that in one year, France will possess a true high-altitude force from which we will be able, thanks to an engine of my invention, that is to say with the help of a small projectile and a prodigiously expansive force, not only destroy our adversaries' entire defensive lines in a matter of hours, but also wipe out their armies on the march."

And as the Alsatian remained silent, Germaine's father added, "That must make your patriotic heart rejoice, eh? My dear Müller, what magnificent revenge!"

"Yes, what magnificent revenge . . ." repeated the man with the blond moustache dully.

And, his voice anguished, he continued. "Forgive me, Mr Aubry, if I don't express all the emotions that are stirring me as I want to, but the word you just pronounced reminds me of such memories, over there, my family, all those tombs . . ."

"I understand, my dear friend," said the patriot.

"Away, Victoire," he ordered the cook joyously, "Bring us that bottle of champagne, my last remaining one, so that we can drain it drinking to the happiness of these children and to the health of the Minister who will finally bring me justice!"

Jacques Müller had taken a place between Aubry and Germaine, opposite the captain who, while the champagne was being uncorked, spoke with him of the Alsace, which he knew well.

The filled glasses were clinked.

"To the combat aircraft," said Maurice Evrard.

"To military aviation! And to your happiness, my dear children," said Jean Aubry.

Jacques Müller seemed to have chased from his soul the saddening memories that the inventor's enthusiastic declarations had awakened there, and he drank with joy.

But in an instant, a swift cloud passed over his face; an uneasy expression darkened his eyes, and a bitter crease contorted his mouth. All lost in joy, the inventor, Germaine and the captain could not notice the unease which escaped the Alsatian from time to time, and which he managed to master almost immediately.

"Eh! But time has flown!" Jean Aubry cried suddenly, raising his eyes to the clock. "Hell! And my class!"

Rising, he added, "I would not like to keep these brave people waiting who forego their rest in order to learn."

Müller stood up as well, getting ready to accompany the professor.

"For my part," said the officer, "It's getting late to announce our engagement to my dear mother. I want her to hear the good news this evening as well."

"Give her a kiss for me," murmured the inventor's daughter while leaning towards her fiancé.

"I promise."

"Off we go!" the inventor cried.

"Don't forget, dear Mr Aubry," the captain observed, "that you are expected tomorrow morning at the Ministry at ten o'clock."

"Relax. I'll be there on the dot," replied the inventor of the combat aircraft.

And addressing his daughter, he asked, "Put all my files and my briefcase away in the bureau, so that I'll have everything ready tomorrow morning."

Then taking a little nickel key from the pocket of his waistcoat, he handed it to Germaine while telling her, "Above all, don't lose this."

"Don't worry!" agreed the young girl, threading the key on a gold chain that she wore round her neck and which held a locket containing a lock of her mother's hair.

Then kissing his child, Jean Aubry said to her: "I'll get back between eleven o'clock and midnight, as usual. Don't feel you have to wait for me. Let's be off then! Good night, my dear."

"Good night, father."

Germaine accompanied the three men as far as the iron-grilled gate, squeezed her fiancé's hand tenderly once more and watched them walk away down the street until their shadows, and then their footsteps, were lost in the night.

Back in the house, while Victoire cleared the table and washed the dishes, she went into the office and carefully locked the briefcase and her father's precious files in the bureau.

As the housekeeper, her work done, came to ask if she needed anything before retiring, the young girl thanked her kindly, and asked her to be there early the next morning, as Mr Aubry would have to go out on his business.

Left alone, Germaine locked the house's front door; then, returning to her father's office, she took a book from the library, sat in an armchair near the table, on which a green-shaded lamp was lit, and began to leaf through the book's pages distractedly.

But Captain Evrard's fiancée's thoughts were elsewhere, her mind was absorbed by the happiness that this unforgettable day had brought her. The forthcoming success assured for her father's invention, through which glory and fortune would soon crown all the tireless labour. Love, that love hidden so deep within her all these months, and finally allowed space in her heart!

For a long time, Germaine remained in this dreamy state. A happy smile illuminated her adorable face.

Her whole being overflowed with a superhuman, almost divine joy. Standing up, she went over to the portrait of a pretty young girl leaning on a vase full of blooming roses. She grasped the image and raised it to her lips, saying:

"My dear mother, why are you no longer here to share our happiness?"

But suddenly Germaine stopped.

It sounded as though someone was knocking gently at the pavilion gate.

"That can't be my father coming home," she said to herself, "It's too early. Anyway, he has his key."

Almost instantly, a louder knock echoed through the house.

Germaine hadn't been wrong, then. There was someone at the gate.

From the vestibule, she asked, "Who's there?"

"It's me, Miss Germaine," replied the familiar voice of Jacques Müller.

Germaine hurried across the garden.

"Is my father . . . ?" she asked, suddenly anxious.

"Calm yourself. Nothing bad has happened to Mr Aubry," replied the Alsatian, entering as soon as the grille was opened.

"Truly?" asked the young girl as she accompanied him into the ante-chamber. "Nothing's happened to my father?"

"I assure you."

"So . . .?"

"Mr Aubry has forgotten some notes which are important for his conference," Jacques Müller explained, "He wanted to come back, but he was already running late, and I wanted to save him this trouble by coming instead."

"Oh, that's all right! I was frightened!"

"It's just a few notes he left in his briefcase," added the young man, pointing at the bureau.

But if Germaine, still alarmed, had not been put on guard by Jacques Müller's agitated voice, the light that she saw burn in his eyes the moment his gaze locked on the desk inspired sudden defiance in her.

She raised her hand instinctively to her neck, where the little key hung.

The young man believed she was going to use it to open the bureau, and with a too eager gesture, he held out his hand, saying, "Give it to me. I know where the papers are."

Germaine took a step backward.

"Hurry, miss," the Alsatian insisted, "I must rejoin Mr Aubry, he's waiting for me."

Overcome suddenly by dreadful unease, Germaine shrank back, stammering, "I assure you my father had the documents with him, and I don't understand . . ."

She didn't finish.

In one brutal, swift, unexpected gesture, Jacques Müller had flung himself on her, suddenly seizing the gold chain that the young girl wore on her neck; with his left hand, he tore it violently, breaking it and leaving a painful red groove on the unfortunate girl's neck.

Germaine froze for an instant as though petrified, staring with haggard eyes at this man that she had until now considered as a friend, this man who was the protégé of, and indebted to, her father and who now, wild, hateful, terrifying, held her with a gaze full of threats and death!

"Wretch!" she shouted with a cry of rage and pain.

"Not one word, or I'll strangle you!" roared the traitor while a criminal flame flickered in his eyes.

"The key. Give me the key!" Germaine demanded in a furious voice, having already guessed the false Alsatian's criminal intent.

Put under pressure by the danger that the young girl's cry rendered imminent, Jacques Müller threw himself at her throat and was going to crush it, implacably, when he suddenly felt Germaine's body slip between his hands, while her head fell back and her eyelids, after having blinked two or three times, closed heavily over her eyes.

"Fainted!" the bandit murmured, while coldly considering the young teacher who lay inanimate on the parquet floor. And cynically he added. "That's preferable!"

Then, running to Jean Aubry's bureau, he thrust into the lock the key that he had just stolen in such a cowardly fashion from a defenceless young girl, opened the desk, and set to rummaging through the files he found there.

In an instant his face took on a triumphant expression. "Combat aircraft," he muttered, "there it is. My work is done!"

And slipping the inventor's secret plans in his jacket's large inside pocket, he headed outside.

CHAPTER THREE:

The Revolt

It was almost midnight when Jean Aubry, his class finished, reached his home.

Apparently rejuvenated by ten years, he walked with a joyful step, rolling a thousand new projects around in his boiling mind when, arriving before the villa and noticing the light in the windows, he said. "She will have insisted on waiting for me, the soft, stubborn . . . Ah! I'm not about to scold her tonight!"

But he stopped, surprised. The garden gate was ajar.

He was astonished. "And yet I closed it properly when leaving."

Quickening his step, he crossed the garden. The villa door was similarly open.

This time Jean Aubry felt doubt take hold of him. He hurried into the vestibule, calling in a loud voice. "Germaine! Germaine!"

No one responded.

His heart gripped with anxiety, he went to enter his office, when he stopped, glued to the threshold. He had just seen his daughter lying on the parquet.

"Dead!" the father yelled with a despairing cry. "She's been murdered!"

Then, flinging himself on the young girl, he saw the bloody groove on her neck, then, on the ground, the broken gold chain.

Instinctively, the inventor's eyes darted to the bureau and noticing that it was open and that the files had disappeared, he let out a wail of unspeakable pain. "They've stolen everything and they've killed my daughter!"

Falling back to his knees beside Germaine, he leaned over her, took her in his arms, tried to make out whether she was still breathing. Then, after several seconds of dreadful waiting, he murmured. "Alive! She's alive!"

And, carrying her on to a sofa, he sought to bring her to her senses.

"Germaine, my beloved daughter. Wake up. I'm here, to defend you."

As he spoke, Jean Aubry covered his child's face with kisses and, little by little, insensibly, she opened her eyelids, breathed more freely and gave some painful groans, all while trying, with jerky movements, to remove from her eyes a terrible vision which returned to haunt her as soon as she recovered her senses.

"Father? Is it you?" she soon asked in a flat voice.

"Yes, my darling."

Then, raising her head, she asked. "He's left, hasn't he?"

"Who has?"

"Jacques Müller."

"Jacques Müller!" the inventor repeated, taken aback.

"Yes. The thief, the bandit, the traitor!" Germaine revealed, hissing. "It was he who took everything, stole everything."

"Him? You've gone mad!"

"No, no. It was him, I'm telling you. He returned earlier. I, unsuspecting, let him in. He seemed troubled. He pretended that you had sent him to fetch some notes that you'd forgotten. But he could see that I didn't believe him, he realised I was suspicious of him, and he threw himself on me. He tore the key to your bureau from my neck. I believed he was going to kill me. He grabbed me, grabbed me by the throat. A cloud covered my eyes and I thought I would die."

"Then," continued Jean Aubry in a muffled voice, "this man would be . . .? No, no, it's not possible. Jacques Müller left me, excusing himself from my class because he was fatigued. You're mistaken. An Alsatian, a patriot . . ."

"An Alsatian, a patriot, him!" cried the young girl who, little by little, was finding all her strength and energy. "No, father, he's a wretch who, knowing the importance of your secrets, introduced himself to us in order to discover them, gambling on our generosity, betraying our trust, and betraying the friendship which he knew how to inspire in us with such treacherous skill."

"But this is abominable!"

"This evening, he learned that you were on the point of resubmitting your plan for your combat aircraft to the Minister of War, and he told himself, 'Time to act! Tomorrow will be too late!' He made an excuse to leave you. He returned here, knowing I was alone, and look what he has done."

"My God! To be so betrayed! And you believe that Jacques Müller is . . .?"

"A Prussian spy, I'm sure of it!" said the young girl, whose eyes sparkled with indignation and rage.

"A spy!" said the inventor with a heartbreaking sadness in his tone. "So, not only is all my work lost for me, but it will still serve them over there. And that superiority that I was going to give to my country, will profit the enemy, to crush us forever. The wretch! How he duped me by exulting his hatred of the conqueror and his desire for revenge! How he toyed with me by talking about his grandfather the rebel. Ah! If I got hold of him, I would beat him, I would strangle him. Yes, I would kill this bandit! But he is already long gone, and he carries away my stolen thoughts, my dream destroyed, all that was going to be my life, my pride, my glory!"

"Father," proposed Germaine who had regained her composure. "We must run to the police and provide a description of this man. By telephoning in every direction, maybe someone will manage to arrest him."

"A useless effort!" said Jean Aubry, shaking his head, "A scoundrel of this magnitude will have taken every precaution. Remember that it's past midnight! Before we've put the police in motion, the traitor will have crossed the border. And all that at the exact moment I reached my goal, at the moment we were celebrating a success for which I no longer dared hope! What will the Minister say, tomorrow, when I tell him that a German spy introduced himself to my home and stole my plans? Who knows if he'll believe me? Who knows if he might not accuse me of having sold my invention to foreigners?"

"Father!"

Then, gripped by a sudden hallucination, the inventor shouted: "Oh! I see them, engines of war engendered by my own brain. They no longer soar over our heads, precursors of sacred revenge. But they advance, dark birds of the night, sowing our territory with devastation, carnage and death!"

"Oh no!" Germaine cried suddenly, in a sublime and impetuous outpouring of filial love and exalted patriotism, "No, that will never be. I know what I have to do. I'm going to leave!"

"Leave?"

"Yes, not only to try and snatch back your secrets from our enemies, but also to discover their own!"

"What madness, my poor child!"

"No, father, because I know how to overcome all obstacles. I'll travel everywhere. I'll penetrate the hearts of strongholds, citadels, inventors' workshops, all the way up to generals and ministers, and I swear to you that I shall bring back to France ten times that which has been stolen from her!"

"An insane project, which will destroy you."

"A noble task, which I shall realise."

"What will you do alone, out there?"

"I lived in Berlin for three years. I speak German as well as my mother tongue. The love of my country and your dear thoughts will guide me and will give me the necessary strength."

"And your fiancé?"

At this evocation, the heroic young girl gave a painful shudder; but she mastered her emotion immediately; and superbly she replied. "You will bid him farewell, or rather *au revoir* for me. Because I shall return. Yes, I'm sure of it. I shall return! But it would be better for me to leave without seeing him again. That would be too cruel. He will approve of my action, I'm sure. Yes, he'll approve!"

Then Jean Aubry shouted, "But what about me? I don't want you to leave. No, I don't want that! I repeat, this would be folly. You would be discovered by the police immediately, arrested as a spy, and locked up in some fortress from which you would never get out. It will be enough, in fact, for it to be known over there that you are my daughter in order for you to be suspected straight away."

"Over there, I won't be your daughter," replied Germaine, whose resolve had already hardened. "Tomorrow morning, first thing, I'll go and find the director of General Security; I will tell him who I am and what I want to do, he'll take on the task of procuring identity papers for me, thanks to which I'll be able to travel wherever I want without being recognised."

"No, I don't want . . . I don't want this," her father still rejected the idea. "You could find yourself face to face with this spy, this wretch who will denounce you like a coward."

"He will not denounce me. I'll kill him first!" Germaine pronounced with implacable energy, "I must leave, father! Now I have my mission just as you have your own, and just as yesterday I had no right to leave you, today you have no right to keep me! When the nation is in danger, a Frenchman can not prevent his child from going to fight!"

Spreading his arms wide to the heroic creature, Jean Aubry cried in a tragic sob, "So be it! Go, my daughter! Go."

CHAPTER FOUR:

The Ambush

Dawn. A new day begins.

A long-bodied grey car, runs at top speed on the road from Lunéville to Avricourt.

The man driving it is alone. An oil and grease-stained duster covers his clothes; a helmet is jammed on his head down to his ears; thick black goggles hide half his face. His nervous hands clench on the wheel. From time to time Jacques Müller, completely transformed with his hair cut short and moustache entirely shaved, murmurs in a twitchy voice.

"Finally, I have them, these plans, these files that my bosses wanted at any price! I'll bring them back to my country! What a master-stroke! What triumph awaits me there!"

But suddenly, a cry escapes the spy's chest. In the new dawn light he has just seen, blocking the road fifty metres ahead, a cart full of manure, such as peasants often leave in fields.

Müller grasps his brake immediately; the car obeys, slows, and stops a few centimetres from the obstacle. At that moment, five identically-dressed men jump on the driver, who has not had time to prepare to defend himself, so brusque and unexpected has the attack been.

"Not one shout or you're dead!" one of the bandits threatens, a revolver in his hand.

But the Prussian spy gets away with one leap. He jumps from the other side of the car, draws a Browning from his pocket and fires on his attackers three times. Two men fall, the others have already returned fire.

Müller, struck full in the chest, throws up his hands and collapses on the road. The three bandits, rushing to him, stamp on his face with their boots, growling, "You killed two of ours, but at least you have your reckoning."

Without wasting a moment, the three car thieves then pick up the bodies of their comrades and dump them in the car. After pushing the cart which is obstructing the road to the kerb, they jump in the car, packed tightly with their accomplices, one groaning and the other expired, and they set off at top speed, soon turning off to the left in the direction of Nancy.

Jacques Müller has stayed motionless on the road, in the middle of a puddle of blood.

A fine stabbing rain begins to fall on the deserted countryside.

Soon a light shiver shakes the wounded man, who seems to revive. His eyelids open for an instant. A pained cry dies on his lips. He has one instinct. He puts his hand on his chest that the bullet hit; but he is not looking for his wound. His fingers tremble, palpate, fumble, ferret; suddenly a cry of joy rises to his lips.

"The papers are there!" he murmurs. "They didn't steal them from me. But how to save them, as I'm still in France? If I die here, they will be found on my corpse, and I don't want them to be taken from me! They're mine, mine!"

So, stiffening, appealing to all his remaining strength and energy, the spy drags himself towards a pile of freshly broken rocks whose whiteness stands out on the damp grass.

He only has a few metres to travel. Yet he stops three times and, in spite of all his efforts to control the pain, groans escape from him.

"I'm sick. I'm suffering. This is horrible! Provided I don't die before . . ."

But he gathers himself. He crawls again, on his elbows and knees. He moves forward, he reaches the goal, he is there, leaning over the ditch. His groping hands take out a knife, which he opens with his teeth. In the middle of the mud, in the sodden earth, he digs a hole, his wound bleeds; blood flows over his hands; his ears buzz. He digs some more, he carries on digging, and when the hiding place seems large enough for his purposes, he unbuttons his coat and draws from his reddened chest a thin blood-stained envelope that he buries in the earth. These are the plans for the combat aircraft stolen from Jean Aubry.

Only half the task is done. He must fill the hole. The spy is running out of strength.

Far away, a bugle sounds. Soldiers are arriving on the scene.

"All is lost!" groans the injured man.

With a supreme effort, however, he gathers himself and kneels; he takes some stones from the pile by the road; he piles them on top of the treasure. He still has enough strength to pick up more earth, brushwood, tufts of grass, hiding the place where the combat aircraft plans are buried.

Then, a terrible grimace contorts his dying, disfigured face, and he lets out one last groan which is like a sigh of relaxation and joy.

While the French bugle music approaches, the spy goes back and rolls in the wet ditch, in the middle of the tall ferns, in which he disappears, suddenly buried.

CHAPTER FIVE:

Bertha Stegel

In a vast, sumptuous lounge, whose high windows, garnished with gold-fringed brocade drapes, look out over Wilhelmstrasse, a young girl dressed in a very simple black dress and wearing a hat decorated with lace was waiting, standing, letting her eyes wander over the portraits hanging on the walls which represented Prussian officers of all ranks, including Cuirassiers, Uhlans, Death Hussars and other uniforms, from Frederick the Great to the present day.

Among all these severe figures some imposing warriors stood out, such as a couple of great lords lost in the middle of a camp of riders, two beautiful oval canvasses from the 17th Century, surrounded by a frame of golden oak. One showed a gentleman with regular features, an energetic look and an attitude full of nobility and dignity. The other depicted a woman of a rare beauty enhanced by her court dress, but whose melancholic and gentle gaze inspired, without quite being able to say why, a feeling of kindness not far removed from pity.

"It's extraordinary," the young girl murmured, "It could be said that these two portraits were made rather to be hung on the walls of the palace of Versailles rather than those of the Chief of Military Staff of the German army."

Approaching them again, looking for the signatures, she managed to make them out, declaring, surprised, "But this is a Rigaud, Louis XIV's great painter."

Instinctively, her eyes went to the neighbouring canvas – a marshal from the time of Frederick – and she noticed with astonishment that he greatly resembled, in his powder and under his armour, the great lord and also the beautiful French lady.

The following portrait, a hussar colonel, resembled them too, but to a lesser extent, and the type so clearly distinguished continued in this way across the line, always transforming, to be erased completely and then to reappear again in the final frame, that of a young officer in the Guards of Wilhelm II, King of Prussia and Emperor of Germany.

"Could it be, perhaps, that General von Talberg could be of French origin?" reflected the stranger whose curiosity had been awakened at the sight of all these Rhineland soldiers who seemed to look at her with a sort of wild hatred.

But a door opened and a messenger, a huge Uhlan wearing his chapka and casting his tall shadow over the threshold of a double door, announced in a hoarse voice, "The general will see you."

The young girl followed the soldier who took her into a large office furnished in the Gothic style and at the end of which, before a table piled with papers and files organised meticulously, a general was sitting.

At the sight of the young girl, von Talberg stood up in one motion, automatically, in the German style.

He was a magnificent man, in every sense of the word; if his shape and stature were those of a colossus, his fine and regular features, framed by a brown beard that was barely greying, his clear and loyal gaze, and his high untroubled forehead, all revealed aristocratic origins and an elite intelligence.

"Miss Bertha Stegel, is it not?" Von Talberg asked in a resonant voice.

"Yes, general."

"You come on behalf of the Friedmann agency?"

"Yes, general."

"Welcome."

Indicating an armchair placed opposite him, the Chief of Staff added, "Do take a seat, please."

The young girl obeyed.

Reaching into her leather handbag, she drew out a bundle of papers, secured with a blue ribbon that she untied, placed it on the desk; and in the purest

German, nuanced with a clear accent from the northern provinces, said:

"General, if you would like to take a look, these are my identity papers and certificates."

With the most careful attention, the general looked over the papers that the young girl had just given him; then, after a moment, replied. "You were born at Rostock, in the Grand Duchy of Mecklenbourg, and you are twenty-two years old. You have already been a tutor for several families . . ."

"In just two, general," the stranger corrected, "One in Danzig, the other in Thorn."

"I see that they were very satisfied with you. What gave you the idea to come to Berlin?"

"The hope of finding myself a better position than in the provinces."

"Are you an orphan?"

"Yes, general."

"But doubtless you still have some family?"

"Some distant relatives with whom I have lost touch."

"The Friedmann house, in which I have the highest confidence, recommended you to me most particularly. The positive things they told me about you, combined, I won't hide it, with the excellent impression you have made on me, have persuaded me to take you on here."

"I thank you, general," the young girl replied, "and I dare to hope that you will only have cause to commend my services."

Von Talberg, completely conquered by the distinguished manners and the thoroughly proper way with which the young tutor expressed herself, continued benevolently. "Before introducing you to my daughter, it is essential that you know her character, her tastes and her aptitudes. She is a very sweet child, but highly impressionable.

"She is often prey to long periods of melancholy which I attribute to her mother's death, which occurred only five years ago in tragic circumstances, a terrible automobile accident. So she locks herself into a mute state from which nothing can rouse her; she takes refuge in her bedroom and cries for hours at a time.

"The immense work which occupies my time prevents me from taking care of this dear child as much as I would like to.

"The grandparents who could compensate for me remain in Hamburg, and in Dresden, and Frida, who is not naturally sociable, doesn't seem able to make friends.

"She's a little savage who you will have trouble taming. I entrust her to you. There is nothing left for me now but to introduce you to your pupil."

The Chief of Staff pressed the button of an electric bell, and the colossal Uhlan appeared immediately, looming immobile in the door frame.

"Ulrich," the general commanded, "Go and warn Miss von Talberg that I wish to speak to her."

The messenger raised his hand, turned on the spot and disappeared.

A few moments later, the door opened again.

A sweet, frail creature wearing a white dress, her face framed with silky blond hair, emerged like a divine apparition.

"My child," said the general, "I present Miss Bertha Stegel who I have chosen to be your tutor."

The young girl advanced towards Frida, a smile on her lips when, bursting into the room like a gust of wind, an officer wearing the uniform of a colonel in the Saxon infantry, whose smooth face, shaved in the style of Moltke, bore traces of great astonishment, ran up to the Chief of Staff crying. "I beg your pardon, general."

"What is it, Colonel Hoffmann, that you allow yourself . . ."

The newcomer's voice trembled with both emotion and anger as he explained. "General, Lieutenant Wilhelm Ansbach has disappeared and . . ."

"Shut up, idiot," von Talberg interrupted, glancing at the tutor and her pupil.

But hardly had he spoken this sentence than a jarring cry resounded through the room.

Frida had just fainted in the arms of Bertha Stegel.

Already General von Talberg had hurried to his child; he helped the young girl to place her in an armchair.

Impatient, Colonel Hoffmann rolled his frightened eyes.

With marvellous composure, the tutor had taken hold of a jug of water and, dampening her handkerchief, she applied it to the young girl's temples. Little by little the girl returned to her senses and murmured, forcing herself to react.

"It's nothing, a simple dizzy spell."

"Of course, do you feel better?" the tutor asked kindly.

Before responding, Frida gave her a long questioning look, as though she wanted straight away to know what lay in the heart of her future companion.

Then, while her head fell back languishing on her shoulder, she said in a weak voice.

"I would like to retire to my bedroom."

"Frida!" the general cried, visibly anxious.

"Yes," repeated the young girl, "I would like to go, all alone."

Her eyes full of tears, the young Berliner stood up and took a few shaky steps towards the door, when Bertha Stegel, approaching her, spoke to her in a very soft voice and offered her arm. "Lean on me, miss, and allow me to accompany you."

The general's daughter stopped and cast a look of worried curiosity towards this woman who had just spoken to her with such bounteous affection. As a strange melancholic smile wandered across her pale lips, she said simply, "Come on, miss."

And these two improvised sisters, Bertha and Frida, went away, already closer by this kind of mysterious link that certain pains seem to create so well between certain souls.

Astonished and reassured all at the same time, von Talberg followed them with his eyes until the moment when the heavy door closed behind them. Then, as if he spoke to himself, he murmured. "They must understand each other, they no longer have mothers!"

Returning to Colonel Hoffmann, whose bright, sparkling, glowing eyes formed a striking contrast with his stiff, stuffy, almost mechanical gait, he said in a tone of violent reproach, "I have never seen such clumsiness!

"How is that you, the Chief of our intelligence bureau, who, without worrying yourself if there was anyone with me, comes to announce to me in such brutal fashion a piece of news which, until further ordered, must remain unknown to all!

"That surprises me on your part, Colonel Hoffmann. You ought to be used to having more tact and composure!"

"Excuse me, general," stammered the officer, as sheepish as a schoolboy caught misbehaving, "but never had I felt such emotion. Think, general, at the moment of achieving our goal, because he had them, the papers, he held them, the plans."

Then the Chief of Staff, striking the table hard with a massive bronze paperweight, interrupted him with a cutting, acerbic tone. "Colonel Hoffmann, I would ask you to put your thoughts in order and to explain to me methodically the event which leads you here."

"On your orders, general," the Colonel obeyed.

Immediately taming his over-excited nerves, the uniformed policeman explained briefly.

"General, ten days ago, I received an encrypted telegram from Lieutenant Wilhelm Ansbach, who left six months ago on an extraordinary mission.

"This telegram, sent and dated last September 8th at ten-thirty in the evening, at the Bourse in Paris, announced to me with no further details that Wilhelm Ansbach had succeeded in getting his hands on the plan for a combat aircraft, on the eve of it being accepted by the French Minister for War.

"The lieutenant added that he would be in Berlin by the day after next at the latest, in my office with the precious documents.

"After three days, and nothing happening, I began to worry. I sent a first telegram, in plain language, to the lieutenant's address, that is to say Mr Jacques Müller, in Vincennes.

"Receiving no response, I addressed myself to Emma Lückner who runs our counter-espionage so

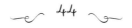

skilfully in Paris, and with whom Wilhelm Ansbach was in contact.

"I learned that this officer, as he had telegrammed to me, really had seized the plans in question; that he had left, that same night, in an excellent racing car which Emma Lückner had provided, and that he set off at top speed towards the border.

"Since then, nothing!

"So, general, before referring this to you, I sent one of our best bloodhounds to make enquiries on the scene and I have just learned that after following the tracks of the automobile driven by Lieutenant Ansbach as far as Lunéville, he had lost them completely."

Colonel Hoffmann concluded. "In my opinion, the young officer has been assassinated. By whom and in what circumstances? I don't know what to tell you. But now I estimate that there is no more hope of finding him and that we must bear the grief of this brave man who died in the service of his country."

"My word!" shouted General von Talberg, who had listened to his subordinate with the greatest attention, "I presume that we will have to continue our own enquiries until the shadows which surround this mysterious affair are completely exposed. Wilhelm Ansbach must be found, dead or alive!

"Do you hear me, Colonel Hoffmann? Dead or alive!"

While his eyes glowed with a light made at once of ardent hatred and energetic defiance the Intelligence

Chief, standing up straight and raising his hand to the visor of his helmet, said,

"As you order, general!"

CHAPTER SIX:

Frida

Seeing the blonde and gentle Frida faint suddenly in her arms, Germaine Aubry, our reader will have recognised her, had completely forgotten her mission in the spontaneous outpouring of her generous heart, to show touching compassion to this delicate and charming creature who seemed so painfully wounded.

The young teacher had read at once, on this pure face and through her clear gaze, the most unspeakable sorrow.

She had already guessed that, in this melancholy which enveloped the general's daughter like a dark and almost impenetrable fog, there was something other than the real and profound sorrow caused by the premature death of a dear mother.

When she found herself alone with Frida, in a bedroom decorated in soft blues and which, by its plain tasteful furnishings gave the impression of the elegant interior of a young Parisian lady from Avenue du Bois rather than that of a Berliner from Wilhelmstrasse, Germaine asked her, completely naturally, completely sincerely, "Miss, do you want me to be your friend?"

And the little 'savage' who, to that point, had seemed so opposed to all friendly effusion, had held out a kindly hand to her, saying,

"I would like that a lot, because you seem to me to be a good person."

"You too, miss."

"I don't know," Frida declared, shaking her head.

"It's so very sad," the inventor's daughter sighed, "losing a mother."

"Ah! You too!" Miss von Talberg exclaimed.

"Alas! It was over six years ago."

"It's been five years for me."

"But you," replied the false Bertha Stegel, "at least you have the consolation – what am I saying? – the joy of staying close to your father."

"I see so little of him," Frida declared. "His responsibilities as Chief of Staff absorb him to the point that he barely has time to give me a furtive kiss in the morning, and not much longer in the evening.

"Almost every day, I breakfast and dine alone. My father often leaves for inspections, on missions, on manoeuvres. So I'm isolated in this huge house."

"But do you have any distractions?"

The general's daughter sighed. "Distractions! Some official receptions where my father has taken me along with him, and where everyone is pretending somehow, those bloody men in their gala uniforms or frozen in their black suits, and the women are haughty and even aggressive in their gaudy and pretentious costumes.

"Oh! When I remember my travels in France, to Paris, and above all the month I spent in a small corner of the Cote d'Azur, at Beaulieu, next to the Mediterranean and at the foot of the White Alps!"

Interrupting herself suddenly, Frida demanded. "Don't you know France?"

"No, miss…" Germaine Aubry replied, as she controlled the reaction which had escaped her as soon as the name of her country was mentioned.

"It's such a beautiful country!" continued the young Berliner, becoming dreamy.

The inventor's daughter probed further. "You love it well, then?"

"Oh, yes!" the blonde creature cried with a strange vivacity. "I love everything that comes from France, its writers, its poets, its musicians, its artists, its fashions and even its tasty fruits which could never ripen under the grey skies of our Germany.

"But there's nothing shocking about that, because I am originally French."

"Really!"

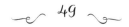

"Yes. My ancestors, who still live in the Cevennes, had to take refuge in Prussia in the 17th Century, to avoid the persecution which Louis XIV had ordered against Protestants after the revocation of the Edict of Nantes."

"I had an idea," Germaine let slip.

"How so?" Frida asked, surprised.

"Just now, while awaiting the honour of being received by sir your father, I had a few moments to look at the beautiful portraits which decorate your salon, and my attention was held particularly by that of a lady with a gaze full of melancholy."

"It is said that I resemble her," said the general's daughter quietly.

"Indeed," Germaine agreed, "you resemble her greatly."

"Yes, it's dear granny, the Frenchwoman!" Lowering her voice, Frida continued. "Ah! How many times have I contemplated that portrait. She too must have had much sorrow, my poor granny! She is my soul's confidant. When I feel my heart grows too heavy, I go to see her and it seems to me when I speak to her quietly, very quietly, that she bows her head and that she weeps with me."

"You must not sadden yourself so," advised Jean Aubry's daughter. "You are young, you are pretty, very pretty. You bear an illustrious name, you are wealthy. One day, soon perhaps, a heart will cross your path which will beat gently close to your own."

"Oh! Don't tell me that!" Frida cried, growing pale.

Captain Evrard's fiancée was astonished. "Don't you want to be loved, or to love yourself?"

Then, in a spontaneous movement, the pretty Berliner, taking her hands from her tutor, said, "Miss, I have only known you for the shortest time, and strangely, it seems to me that I already have a friend in you. No. I won't hide it from you, you who are a stranger to me, you inspire me to share a confidence that I have never been able to grant to anyone.

"I who have always locked my thoughts away in a chest that I hide from the world, and to which I jealously guard the key, I feel an irresistible need to lay all my suffering before you."

"Your suffering?"

"Yes, my suffering! You're surprised to hear me speak to you like this! My father, just now, had to introduce me to you as a savage little being, stubborn against all effusion. Indeed, I am completely astonished, totally stupefied. I no longer recognise myself! Why am I behaving like this with you? I wonder. Is it because you speak to me with a kindness, a generosity and above all a tact to which I am not accustomed to encountering in those around me?"

And while her voice broke into a sob, the general's daughter continued. "In the end, is it because you arrived at the moment where I was going to learn…"

Frida did not finish.

This time, overcome by a pain that she sought vainly to contain, the young girl let her head fall back on her tutor's shoulder; and, incapable of pronouncing a word, she started to cry like a child.

"Let's see. What is it?" asked the inventor's daughter affectionately. Faced with the touching distress of her gracious pupil, she had completely forgotten the mission that she had assigned herself.

And she continued, caressing Frida's silky blonde curls with her delicate hand. "Calm down, dear lady. As you feel attracted to me by a very real bond, why not tell me all your sorrows, the secret of which, however, I believe I have already guessed?"

"Truly!" Frida murmured, raising her head. "You guessed?"

"Perhaps!"

"Tell me then, that will help me a lot."

The young Frenchwoman, gazing into the eyes of the gentle German, spoke slowly. "Was it not the news that the officer came to announce to your father just now which has plunged you into such an emotional state?"

"Yes," confessed Frida as she began to sob again.

"You love this lieutenant?"

The young Berliner gave a simple nod of the head which said much more than any verbal admission.

"And doubtless he loves you too?" the Frenchwoman insisted.

Deciding to speak, the general's daughter replied, interrupting herself almost at every sentence to control the sobs which rose in her throat. "We met last year in France, at Beaulieu, with friends, in a villa whose beautiful garden was completely shaded by exotic trees. Perfumed with mimosas and roses, it naturally seemed to appeal to the sharing of confidences. Like two school children on holidays, we walked together on a path looking out over the sea, whose murmur gently fed our dreaming.

"We held each other by the hand, we were silent. Only our souls spoke. We were in love."

More and more won over by these touching revelations, Germaine planted a sisterly kiss on pretty Frida's forehead, as the general's daughter continued.

"Upon our return to Berlin I told my father everything. He declared I was still much too young to get married. He added that even if this officer belonged to an excellent Prussian family and even if he were gifted with certain military aptitudes, his lack of wealth had to deny him any hope of marrying me. So, Wilhelm Ansbach, desperate, demanded a leave of absence. He left without telling me where he was going.

"After his departure, I heard nothing more from him. Sometimes I tell myself, 'he is suffering',

sometimes I think 'he has forgotten'. And then
suddenly I learn that he has disappeared, that perhaps
he has killed himself through despair. It's terrible,
miss, and if such a tragedy has come to pass, I feel I
shall never get over it!"

"Nothing proves that your terrible presentiments
are justified."

"Even so, my dream is doomed for all eternity, my
father will never go back on his decision."

And standing up, to distract from her pain, Frida
took her tutor by the hand and said to her. "Come, I'm
going to show you my relics."

Leading Germaine to a little Louis XV bureau, a
true work of art which again evoked France in this
pretty floral and perfumed corner that Frida had
created in the middle of the huge dark mansion, she
opened a secret drawer and drew out first a rose from
Nice, faded, but keeping even in death a little of that
radiant scent which seemed to have been born under
the sun's kisses.

"It was Wilhelm," the young girl continued, "who
gave it to me."

"This," she added, pointing out a sparkling little
gold star surrounded by a flood of multi-coloured
rubies, "is a souvenir from a cotillion at Nice carnival."

Finally taking a photograph from an envelope, she
passed it to the young French girl, showing it to her.

"This is him!"

Germaine stifled a cry.

In the handsome Uhlan officer with a blond moustache, she had just recognised the man who had stolen the combat aircraft plans, Jacques Müller, the false Alsatian, the infamous spy!

Germaine shuddered. "If this man returns here," she thought, "if he finds me in this house, with the Chief of Staff, he will recognise me, he will unmask me, and all will be lost."

But the valiant Frenchwoman rallied her thoughts instantly. "No," she told herself with implacable resolution, "all will not be lost because as I told my father, I will kill him if I have to, without pity!"

"Isn't he... isn't he handsome?" the young Berliner asked timidly.

"Yes," Germaine replied, cursing herself inwardly, "he's very handsome."

But just as she mastered her emotions, the Frenchwoman felt a whirlwind of thoughts invade her brain.

Now she could be sure that the aircraft plans were not in enemy hands and, ready for sacrifice and even martyrdom, she reasoned, "Now that I am in position, supposing that this Wilhelm Ansbach, delayed *en route* for unknown reasons, brings the documents he stole from us, who knows if I might not be able to prevent him from handing them over to his superiors? No, a thousand times no, I will not flee from him. Let him come, the wretch. I'm waiting for him!"

While Frida talked about her Wilhelm in a pained voice, Germaine said to herself, "And I who would wait upon this young girl. I who while caring for her, forgot the reason for my presence in this abode! What point is there in pitying myself in this way? Once battle is joined, I must not weaken. After all, it is not this young girl that I'm going to fight. It's my country that I'm defending! We don't get to choose our enemies and we will strike, whoever they may be."

The door opened, making way for General von Talberg who, worried, had come to enquire as to his daughter's disposition.

With a quick gesture, Frida had thrown the photo in the bureau drawer.

The general, as though he had seen nothing, approached his child and taking her in his arms, he said to her, "Be consoled, my gentle Frida. I understood, just now, how unhappy you were. I promise that if we can recover Lieutenant Wilhelm Ansbach, you will be his wife."

"Father!" the young girl cried in a movement of distracted recognition.

Standing, unmoving, the Frenchwoman watched and a terrible frisson shook her.

"No, no!" she thought wildly, "this angel will not be given to that demon! Because I'll have killed him first!"

CHAPTER SEVEN:

The Secret

Wearing a dark tailored suit, Germaine Aubry kept an alert pace as she walked down Leipsigerstrasse. Alone, as though lost in the crowd, she became herself again, freed for a few moments from the constraints her role imposed on her.

But on approaching General von Talberg's mansion, the inventor's daughter composed herself instantly with a physiognomy completely different from that to which she had reverted in those few moments of liberty.

She copied with great accuracy the attitudes, gestures, deportment and intonation of Berlin tutors, as she had done since her arrival. During the long visits that she had previously made to Germany's capital, she had been able to observe and to retain their slightest mannerisms, without considering that she would one day have to make use of the fruit of her observations.

Nevertheless, in spite of all her talent for assimilation, Germaine had been unable to wipe from her that natural grace and distinction with which she was gifted; and under her cold and voluntarily stilted attitudes, she remained essentially female, conquering in spite of herself all those who approached her from her gentle pupil, the blonde Frida, and General von Talberg, to his aides who also submitted unconsciously to the Frenchwoman's charm.

It was only Ulrich, the general's famous orderly, the mastiff ceaselessly on guard at his master's gate, who did not incline himself with a sort of tender respect before the adorable creature who, when she passed, left the world behind her as though in a wake of sunshine and spring.

Locked in her room, Germaine deciphered slowly the four pages of the coded letter that she had been to fetch at the post office on Spandauerstrasse. Captain Evrard told her of his pained surprise when he had learned of her sudden departure, and his admiration for the work that she had undertaken.

She learned that her father had tested his great moral energy and had completely recovered his spirits, especially once he had learned that the stolen plans for his combat aircraft had not reached the Chief of Staff in Berlin.

The Minister for War, touched by Germaine's brave devotion, had swiftly engaged the inventor to get back to work, assuring him that a genius such as he would not take long to reconstitute a new combat aircraft, thanks to which there would be no more to fear from the consequences of the enemy's theft.

The officer gave Germaine in particular, in finishing, some prudent advice, regretting he was unable to meet her and join in her struggle, and he expressed the hope that soon she would be returned to her father and to him.

No sooner had it been read than this letter was burned; and banishing to the depths of her heart the tender sentiments inspired by thoughts of those two dear people, her father and her fiancé, the tutor rejoined her pupil.

That day, Frida and the Frenchwoman had to eat alone, General von Talberg having been called out for official duties.

More and more, the young Berliner treated her tutor as a friend.

Since she had given her confidences and she had received the most delicate consolation from her, she had promptly arrived to consider her as both an older sister and the closest of friends.

For her part, Germaine felt herself grow more attached each day to the gentle young girl. She had to fight hard against this feeling which overpowered her, telling herself that she had no right to love this child, whose father symbolised the enemy, but the mind's reasoning could not hold against the heart's instruction, and she too felt for Frida a fraternal affection.

That evening, the general's daughter had been particularly melancholy. During the meal, she had barely uttered a few sentences.

Germaine had respected this silence, feeling herself the need to be withdrawn and to let her thoughts go out towards those from whom she had been separated, when, abruptly, Frida rose from the table. The girl approached her and, putting her arm under her tutor's, she whispered in her ear, "Come to my room. I have something to say to you."

Docile, Germaine followed her pupil and, as soon as the door was closed behind them, the young Berliner began. "Promise me, miss, never to reveal what I'm about to confide in you to anybody, and especially not my father."

"You can rest easy, my dear child," the Frenchwoman replied, intrigued by this mystery.

Frida continued. "When, five years ago, my poor mother left us for the heavens, my father, in his despair because he adored my mother, gave the order to hermetically seal the doors of her rooms and to leave them in the state they were in, so that no one other than he could enter. On each anniversary, he went there with flowers, and locked himself inside for long hours. Several times I asked to accompany him and he always refused. Doubtless he didn't want me to see him crying.

"But I, who loved my mother so much, felt that it would do me good, especially at that time when I had so much pain, to spend a few moments in the room which I had barely left when I was a child and where I heard such gentle words, received such tender caresses."

Lowering her voice, a little embarrassed, as though she was going to confess a fault, Frida declared, "For a long time I looked for the key to this apartment; but father had hidden it with such care that I could never manage to discover it. Just now, before dinner, having gone up to my father's room to say goodnight to mother's portrait, I saw a shiny key on the chimney. I recognised it immediately. It's very bad of me, but I took it, here it is!

"Tell me, Miss Bertha, would you like to come with me to the bedroom? I would be scared, on my own."

Germaine hesitated and tried to dissuade her pupil from this project; but Frida kept up such a gentle yet pressing insistence that she ended up giving her consent.

In the silent house the two young girls embarked together, with a thousand precautions, on their pious pilgrimage.

Frida showed her all the mementos of the dear deceased lady, the room where she had lived, today a true sanctuary of piety and pain.

Germaine tried to cut this painful trip short, and was trying to drag Frida away when the general's daughter, stopping suddenly, lifted a drape which hid a door garnished by an old wrought iron lock.

"This door leads to my father's office," she revealed.

At these words, Germaine shuddered; but repressed her reaction instantly. Still breathless with curiosity however, she listened to Frida who continued, "It's by this door that mother would go to meet my father when he was working late in the night. So I often pretended to sleep, then I got up and, on tiptoes, I went to open the door gently. I went out on the gallery which goes around the office, I leaned on the balustrade and I could see father before a huge table, leaning over his files, while mother, sitting close to him on an armchair, did some embroidery. I stayed there for a moment watching them, and suddenly I shouted out, 'Good evening, father! Good evening, mother!' They both raised their heads at the same time. Father groaned, 'little demon!' while mother smiled, saying, 'my darling angel!' and I quickly escaped.

"Today this door is abandoned," the young Berliner concluded, "no one comes through there any more, just as no one comes through here."

"Come along, let's go!" the tutor said feverishly. "That's it. Enough, my dear child. You're going to make yourself ill. What will I tell your father tomorrow, if he questions me?"

With one last look, one kiss blown towards the portrait of the dead woman, Frida let herself be led away.

One week later.

It is two o'clock in the morning. All is silent in the Chief of Staff's house, which General von Talberg left the day before to go on an inspection tour of the French border.

In the antechamber which leads to the great leader's office, Ulrich, the huge Uhlan, keeps watch from a cot, a revolver within arm's reach, ready to leap up at the first suspicious noise.

On the top floor, Frida sleeps peacefully.

Alone in the house, Germaine Aubry is not shut up in her room. She examines two keys by the light of a lamp, one of ordinary dimensions, the other very large and bizarrely shaped.

She slips them into her pocket, takes out a revolver hidden in a pile of clothes, and slips it in her blouse. She extinguishes her lamp, lights another small electric one, and prepares for her chosen course of action.

But she stops, hesitant. She is pale. A terrible conflict rages inside her.

"Have I really the right to do this?" she asks herself, seized by scruples. "General von Talberg has welcomed me to his home. He trusts me. He seems loyal, even generous. His daughter is so charming and so gentle, and it was she who, by choosing me in whom to confide her pains, by leading me to enter this locked sanctuary, showed me the path that I must follow to reach the general's office. Isn't it she who opens the door for me today, as it's through her that I had the idea to take a wax impression of the first lock, to go and find that secret agent with whom the French Secret Service put me in contact and ask him to make a key for me, thanks to which I can access the Countess's rooms and this time take an impression of the second lock blocking the door which gives access to the general's office?

"Now that I have almost reached my goal, now that I am on the point of getting into that room which hides so many secrets which may be useful to my country, I feel something lurking inside me. Not fear, but remorse. I have to ask myself if I have the right."

But suddenly, nervously, Germaine Aubry raises her head. A terrible vision has just struck her eyes. She sees again the terrifying scene in the Saint-Mandé villa where she could have been murdered. She sees Jacques Müller entering the house, tearing the bureau key from her and trying to strangle her, the infamy!

Then that desperate father, that great honest man who, believing he had finally achieved his goal, exulted with joy and who now despairs and collapses in the ruins of his happiness, forever ruined. It seems to her that a voice shouts to her, "What good are these scruples? Did Jacques Müller have them, when he ransacked your home, and duped your father shamelessly? And then, does there not lie behind you an entire nation that must be defended, a whole country that must be saved?

"France first! As the poet said. Courage! You are not the spy who betrays and lies. You are the soldier sent on reconnaissance, seeking to surprise the enemy. You are at the vanguard of an army who is waiting for you to give them the intelligence which will light their path! Onward, Frenchwoman! Ever onward, come what may!"

The die is cast. She leaves her room, slips into the corridor. She enters the forbidden apartment silently. One after another, the two keys, executed so skilfully, fulfil their function. The Frenchwoman stands in the German Chief of Staff's office.

There she is, leaning on the gallery balustrade from which she looks at the huge office. She makes her way down the staircase with a firm, assured step. Her whole being feels nothing more than a single desire to take her revenge.

She puts down the lamp which lights her way and she looks around her, on the table. The important files are locked away, doubtlessly.

Nothing. The large strongbox in front of her hides anything which might be precious or secret.

Germaine is irritated by her impotence. She rummages in the waste paper basket, discovering only a few scraps of paper covered in writing, which she picks up and hides in her blouse.

But there, on the desk blotter covered with blots, she sees some traces of letters, printed backwards. She picks it up and walks toward a mirror. The characters reverse, the words become clear, she reads:

"Order to Colonel Hoffmann, Chief of Intelligence, to send Captain Kefnerr to France as soon as possible with the mission of studying the equipment of heavy field batteries."

Then Germaine, radiant, notes this name in her memory, and tells herself triumphantly. "At last, I have one of them!"

With infinite precautions, she returns to her room, not without casting a last look over the office and saying to herself, "I'll be back! Oh yes, I'll be back!"

CHAPTER EIGHT:

The Three Champions

It was nearly midnight when the three infantry majors entered the famous Alt-Bayern tavern, situated on Potsdamerstrasse, which was choked with customers.

They were regarded with deference, for it was astonishing to see them in uniform, contrary to their habit.

They moved forward slowly, heavily, looking for a space, when a lively, alert waiter hurried towards the officers and moved to install them at one of the tables which had become available.

"Speaking for myself, I can go no further, let's stay here," one of the majors accepted immediately, thick, heavy, moon-faced and with a tiny moustache shaved almost to the skin.

His two comrades, one tall and strong, with a fat red moustache and with a rubicund nose, and the other potbellied, stumpy, with a prickly hedgehog beard, sat down either side of him, groaning.

"Of course, Major Schlaffen is always tired!" one of them said.

The other agreed. "It's amazing!"

But Major Schlaffen, without hearing his companions' reflections, ordered in a pasty voice, "A *halb*, and a pillow."

The waiter was astonished. "A pillow!"

"Yes, a pillow. To sleep."

"For me, a *ganz*," ordered the major with the red moustache.

"I'll have some sauerkraut and a half pint," said the officer with the pre-eminent stomach.

Then, yawning, Major Schlaffen spoke slowly. "Let's hope that tomorrow our luggage will finally be found, and that we'll be able to wear civvies to go to the tavern."

And, almost aggressively, he added, "It's your fault, Major Tourchtig. You were in charge of registering the baggage and you stayed at the buffet at Dantzig Station to drink beer!"

"I beg your pardon!" the accused officer clarified, "It was Major Hunguerig who was in charge of the luggage, and if he hadn't stayed to eat sausage right until it was time to board the train…"

"I'll stop you there," the third major interrupted. "It wasn't me who had to take care of the trunks. It was Major Schlaffen, and if he hadn't fallen asleep in a waiting room . . ."

"Sorry, sorry!" Schlaffen protested, "I assure you it was Major Tourchtig!"

"No, it was Hunguerig!"

"Not at all, it was you, Schlaffen!"

The discussion was halted by the waiter's arrival, carrying a pillow under his arm, in one hand two *halb* and the *ganz*, and finally the sauerkraut in his other hand.

Schlaffen, after having immediately drained half of his beer, took the pillow, propped it up behind him on the bench's seatback, leaned his head on it and, closing his eyelids, said in that pasty voice of his. "Major Tourchtig. Wake me up when I'm thirsty."

"How lucky he is to be able to sleep at will like that!" Hunguerig sighed. "I find I need ten sauerkrauts in my stomach."

"And twenty *ganz* in the stomach for me," Tourchtig agreed.

At that moment, a huge fellow, dressed in a grey suit on which lay a red cravat, and wearing a bowler hat which was too small for his flushed head, made his way towards the three officers, holding a magnificent mastiff on a leash, almost as fine as one of Bismarck's, and which, beneath the muzzle constraining its huge jaws, displayed a sufficiently ferocious attitude.

Standing at the booth's entrance, the newcomer cried, "What are you three all doing in Berlin?"

"Oh! Captain, Schmidt, the German army's professor of aerial locomotion!" Major Tourchtig said, rising automatically and holding out his large hand brusquely to the officer in civilian clothes.

"How goes Bavaria's invincible champion of Munich beer?" the newcomer asked, shaking the major's hand energetically.

"Very well, Captain Schmidt."

And Captain Schmidt, equally holding out his hand to Major Hunguerig, asked: "And Hesse Nassau's incomparable champion of Frankfurter sausage?"

Major Hunguerig could not answer: he had his mouth full. He contented himself with nodding in an affirmative gesture.

Then, looking with an eye full of admiration at Major Schlaffen who had not moved, the captain professor titular, etc, etc, asked: "And the German Empire's immortal champion of sleeping at will?"

"You see?" Tourchtig said, "He's at it now! But sit down. Will you take a half with us?"

The captain sat down immediately between the two majors, while the mastiff lay down under the table while making some prolonged growls.

The waiter was sent to fetch a fresh *halb*.

"So," insisted the captain-professor, "are you passing through Berlin?"

"No," declared Tourchtig. "We have been summoned for a fixed post."

"On a secret mission," Hunguerig added.

"My compliments!"

"We have been appointed by General von Talberg, Chief of Staff, to guard the mobilisation plans locked away in the War Office, in the armoured cabinets B. M. and W. in the Moltke Room."

"Taking turns," Tourchtig added, "one of us must stay in the hall, revolver in hand, with orders to fire on anyone who presents themselves without an order signed either by the Emperor's own hand, or that of the Minister for War or the Chief of Staff.

"We will relieve each other every six hours. No leave throughout the entire year comprising our mission, but a salary increase of one third, then leave for three months, and a nomination for the Iron Cross."

"Very good, congratulations again," Captain Schmidt said.

"So, to your health!"

"Major Schlaffen!" called Hesse Nassau's incomparable Frankfurter champion.

"Major Hunguerig?"

"You're thirsty!"

Then, seeing the captain, Schlaffen, raising his half, he groaned in a more and more pasty voice, "To your very good health, captain-professor of locomo . . ."

He could not manage the recital of the officer's lengthy title, gulping down three quarters of his glass, already refreshed, so he could rest his head on the pillow immediately.

The other three officers continued to drink and argue until closing time, holding forth particularly on the subject of military aviation which interested them greatly, in spite of the numerous setbacks encountered up to that point by the inventor of aerial war machines.

When all the drinkers had retired and the lights had been extinguished, the waiter with the alert eyes, who had put on a brown overcoat and fedora, was one of the last to leave.

With his hands in his pockets, and his collar turned up, he walked along Potsdamerstrasse at a brisk pace, crossing Leipzig Square, to reach the street of the same name, and turned right into Wilhelmstrasse.

Then he paced the hundred steps in front of General von Talberg's house, throwing a quick glance from time to time at a third floor window, that of the false Bertha Stegel.

The street was deserted.

The mansion's façade was plunged entirely in darkness.

But the window that the waiter was watching lit up suddenly, then fell into shadows, in order to shine again. Certainly a signal. Because he said to himself, when the darkness had become encroached again, "She'll come tomorrow. Let's go to bed."

The next day, around ten o'clock, on a beautiful sunny October morning, a fairly corpulent man, with his face framed by a grey beard, a pair of golden spectacles riding his fleshy snub nose, dressed in an iron grey suit, topped with a black cap with leather visor, and giving a good impression of a member of the Berlin bourgeoisie, an officer in the Landsturm (reserve force) was sitting on one of the benches in Sièges-Allées, the large shady avenue which crosses the prosperous district of Thiergarten.

He seemed to be reading the *Cologne Gazette* attentively, while peacefully smoking a large and ornate porcelain pipe.

From time to time, his alert and penetrating gaze passed over his spectacles and darted with a quickly repressed expression of impatience in the direction of Bellevue-Strasse.

Suddenly, he had a small shiver at the sight of a young girl with a slightly stilted allure and dressed like a governess in a grand house. Her beauty was not attenuated by a severe hairstyle of flat bands. She advanced without haste, with the calm air of a person going for a constitutional stroll.

Without giving any sign of knowing the man with the porcelain pipe, she came and sat down on the bench he occupied, in such a way that she found herself back to back with him. She slowly drew a German brochure from her leather handbag, and began to read.

After a moment, without turning and while inhaling long puffs of tobacco smoke, the man in the cap, his eyes still riveted to his newspaper, began in a low voice. "How are you, Miss Germaine?"

"Very well, Mr Chantecoq. And yourself?"

"Marvellous. Do you have anything interesting?"

"Yes. Yesterday, General von Talberg spent almost two hours locked in his office with Colonel Hoffmann. I don't know what was said during this long meeting; however, having found a way to slip inside the antechamber just as the colonel was leaving, I heard him say very clearly to his commanding officer: 'I shall follow your orders, general; but nothing will dissuade me from the idea that all our searching will be useless and that Wilhelm Ansbach will never return to us.'

"You see then that the German Chief of Staff has decided to recover this missing man at any cost! We must therefore redouble surveillance."

"You may count on me," the secret agent promised.

"If we have enough warning, we could prevent this man from presenting his commanding officer with the plans he stole from us for the combat aircraft."

And although, behind his gold-rimmed spectacles, his eyes were glittering with malice, Mr Chantecoq replied. "We could even take them from this individual ourselves and send them back to Paris, thanks to a little trick by which you will alert me. But I truly believe that we will not have this good fortune. If Wilhelm Ansbach was to return, he would already be there. In any case, my precautions have been taken; if this wretch ever sets foot in Berlin again, you will not need to kill him, I shall take care of him in my own little way."

"I have confidence in you," said Germaine.

"Now, let me bring you up to date with what I've been up to," Chantecoq continued, "I have some intelligence for you. Yesterday evening, at the Alt-Bayern inn, frequented by the Chief of Staff's officers by the War Ministry, where I have succeeded in securing a job as a waiter, I learned that the mobilisation plans are locked in the Moltke Room, in three armoured cabinets which bear the letters B. M. W., and that these cabinets are going to be put under the guard of three majors who struck me as being perfect imbeciles. They're undoubtedly devoted to their commission, but easy to fool, they go by the names of Schlaffen, Tourchtig and Hunguerig. They must report from tomorrow for one full year and their duty will consist of mounting an alternating guard before the armoured cabinets.

Her eyes still glued to her book, Germaine asked with a voice full of sharp decisiveness. "Do you know where this Moltke Room is?"

"In the part of the War Ministry's buildings which adjoins General von Talberg's house," Chantecoq specified.

"It won't be easy to get in there."

"Then let's get on with it! What you have already done proves that you are capable of accomplishing miracles."

"You forget, Mr Chantecoq, that it was you who forged my papers and who introduced me to the Friedmann agency. It was also you who provided me with the false keys which allowed me to get inside the general's office."

"Possibly, but you certainly knew how to make use of them," said the secret agent. "Twenty-two German agents burned in France, and according to what I have just read in the *Cologne Gazette*, Captain Keiffer arrested on the outskirts of Verdun just as he was on the point of stealing the map of a fort. All that is your work, Miss Germaine, and you can be proud of it. It was fast work."

"It's nothing compared to what I want to do," the young girl replied. "If I could get my hands on the documents locked in these three famous cabinets, I would have done a proud service for my country, and I would have taken a fine revenge! As such, I shall reflect, study, plan. I have to do this."

"Bravo, miss!"

"For your part, spin a tight web around the three majors and keep me informed about their actions."

"That's just what I'm proposing."

"This evening the general is going to the Emperor's grand reception. From ten o'clock until midnight, I will therefore have complete freedom to work in the office. There is a strongbox which I really want to investigate, because I'm certain I'll find the key in there which will open all doors to us. Tomorrow morning I shall doubtless have news, will you come?"

"As always, between half past two and three o'clock, but on Unter den Linden this time."

"How will you be dressed?"

"As a maid, a plump Berliner who is going shopping in town. A pale blue dress and a hat decorated with pink feathers. I'll be holding a parcel wrapped in grey paper with red string. We'll greet each other as if we've known each other a long time."

"Yes, that will make it more convenient to speak."

"So, until tomorrow, Miss Germaine, and good luck!"

"Thank you, Mr Chantecoq."

And after having closed her book carefully, the inventor's daughter stood up and, without any haste, retraced her path from the Chief of Staff's home.

That evening, around eleven o'clock, with the security and sang-froid given to her by several previous successful missions, after checking that

General von Talberg really had gone to the Imperial Palace, that Frida had retired to her bedroom and that the servants could not surprise her, the young Frenchwoman entered the Countess's apartments and got into the general's office.

She locked herself in, pushing the bolt, to ward herself against any surprises and, her electric lamp in her hand, she came to the table. The harvest promised to be abundant: contrary to his custom, von Talberg, surprised by the time, had left some documents on his desk which appeared to Germaine, after a rapid examination, to be of great importance.

Being unable to take them away, she took hasty notes in an exercise book, while throwing a rapid glance from time to time towards the strongbox, her true mission, when suddenly it seemed to her that, in the antechamber, she heard a footstep.

She ran to press her ear to the door.

She was not mistaken. It was the general who had returned, and who woke Ulrich, his orderly.

Germaine had a moment of terrifying anguish; but she did not lose her head.

She slipped the bolt from its catch softly and, on tiptoes, she ran to hide behind the huge red damask curtains which framed the window; and there, her little lamp extinguished, struggling to quieten her heart's thumping, curled up in the window, covered by the thick drapes, she waited.

The general appeared with a young officer of the guard.

While this last – an aide-de-camp for the Emperor – stopped straight away, immobile, von Talberg, after having turned on the electric light, went to the strongbox and unlocked it, bringing to light the secret letters within. Then, having drawn a small key from his pocket, he fiddled with one of the trunk's doors, removed another larger key which carried a label and, after replacing the heavy armoured door which shut with a clang, he returned to the aide-de-camp, saying:

"If you would follow me, Lieutenant von Limbürg. We will go to the Moltke Room to fetch the documents his majesty is waiting for."

Heading towards the huge oak table, the general bent down slightly and pressed his thumb on a secret spring hidden in one of the carved wooden chimeras which curled down the length of the Gothic furniture's legs.

Without the slightest noise, a cordovan-lined panel parted on a wall backing on to the Ministry buildings, slipping on invisible railings and revealing a narrow dark passageway into which the Chief of Staff stepped, followed by the lieutenant.

Germaine, from her hiding place, through the gap between the curtain and the wall, had missed nothing of this scene.

When she had heard their footsteps grow distant, she darted to the strongbox.

A cry of triumph burst from her.

The lock's letters had remained in the unlocked position, forming a name, that of the Countess von Talberg. "ELSA."

The young girl did not need to learn more. She reached the gallery and disappeared into the dead lady's private apartments.

CHAPTER NINE:

Enter Chantecoq

Lieutenant Wilhelm Ansbach's mysterious disappearance was not the Chief of Staff's only problem.

Serious leaks had been observed by Colonel Hoffmann, Chief of Intelligence Services; and that disoriented him completely, because all his policeman's flair couldn't begin to suspect the origin.

One recent piece of news had just reached him, more crushing still, transmitted by the international spy, Emma Lückner, whom he had put in charge of counter-espionage operations in France: Captain Keiffer, on a special mission, had just been arrested on the outskirts of Verdun.

"This is truly a calamitous day!" he said to himself. "Captain Keiffer, such a good officer, so valiant, and brave too! How could he have been burned in this way, even before his arrival?"

And the Chief of Intelligence Services, rubbing his forehead with his tense hands, seemed to be trying to jolt a spark from his brain which would illuminate this unbelievable mystery.

He stayed there a long time, hunched over his reports, truly confused, when an orderly came to warn him that the Chief of Staff had summoned him.

General von Talberg could not accept the young Uhlan officer's unbelievable disappearance and, faced with Frida's dull pain which was torturing his father's heart, he had resolved, whatever the cost, to expose this dark enigma.

"Still no news of Lieutenant Wilhelm Ansbach, Colonel?" he asked with visible discontent.

"None, unfortunately, general," Colonel Hoffmann responded piteously.

"This is unbelievable! What are your agents in France doing! What use are they, I ask myself!"

"I assure you, general, that all possible investigations have been carried out. Lieutenant Ansbach has been traced from his departure from Saint-Mandé, where he was able to remove the plans for the combat aircraft from the inventor Aubry, as I already had the honour of telling you. But the trail goes cold on the road from Lunéville, some kilometres short of the border, and, in spite of all our searching, it has been impossible to recover either his tracks, or those of the car that he was driving."

Von Talberg grew irritated at this inconvenient news and, glaring, he explained severely, "I tell you we must know, no matter what the cost, what has become of this officer. We must not, by leaving a mystery in the shadows, cast hesitation and discouragement among these people whose spontaneous devotion has given us such powerful results. Because don't forget, Colonel Hoffmann, that what gave us our superiority in 1870, was that we knew where we were going and that among the leaders who carried our troops to victory, there was not one of them who did not know by heart, both the map that they held in their hands, and the ground that they invaded."

"You are right, general," said the colonel, "I shall write again, in the most pressing manner."

"It's not a case of writing," Frida's father interrupted harshly. "You will head this enquiry in person, and go to Paris yourself, if needs be."

"As you order, general, but I fear that at the moment such a step would be futile, and even dangerous."

"Why so?"

"For some time, we have observed at the Intelligence Bureau that not only have there been some important leaks, but even that the French Chief of Staff has been aware of almost everything that takes place within the German Chief of Staff's headquarters."

"That's not possible!"

"That's the truth, general," the Colonel vowed with consternation, and added, "I have even just received a report which advised me that Captain Keiffer, who you have yourself described as one of the most capable agents, had been arrested by the French authorities."

"This is too much!" von Talberg burst out.

"That's not all, general. In the last six weeks, more of our men have been arrested in France than are normally arrested in a whole year."

"To what do you attribute this state of affairs?"

"General, my whole service is completely perplexed. Never, I assure you, have we carried out more rigorous surveillance. Never have our agents expended more activity, more energy, and I am obliged to confess to you that we have discovered nothing."

"This must stop!" the Chief of Staff cried, "Be aware, Colonel, that you are responsible for your service, and it's not up to me to teach you your job!"

"I assure you, general, that I am not guilty of any negligence," protested the Intelligence Chief sharply but humbly. "I will not allow myself to remind you of the services I have rendered . . ."

The general interrupted. "Past services," he said drily, "do not excuse present faults. Therefore you should know, Colonel Hoffmann, that if Lieutenant Wilhelm Ansbach has not been found in forty-eight hours, dead or alive, I will submit your replacement's nomination to the signature of his Majesty the Emperor."

"As you wish, general."

All while appearing absorbed in reading of the book she held, Germaine Aubry developed her plan.

The armoured cabinets' keys, she knew, were in the general's strongbox whose secret now belonged to her.

Thanks to the information that Chantecoq had provided for her, she also knew that the guard of these famous cabinets had been entrusted to three officers who knew only that their commission consisted of watching, revolver in hand, and to fire on whoever did not come on behalf of the Emperor, the Minister for War or the Chief of Staff.

That was hardly reassuring.

In effect, to enter the Moltke hall by surprise, thanks to the secret passage she had discovered, was to send herself to a death as certain as it was useless.

But Germaine also remembered that while giving her all this information, Chantecoq had added:

"These three majors are three imbeciles."

Therefore there was some resource, especially for a brain as fecund and a mind as agile as that of the Frenchwoman.

The heroic creature had reflected.

Her meditations had undoubtedly brought good results because, that evening, on returning to her bedroom, a satisfied smile wandered over her lips.

After closing her door, she sat down at her table and set to writing a letter to her father which began with these words. "Dear father, I believe that I am finally near the end."

Germaine was right to speak in this way; because if she succeeded in her undertaking, if she managed to delivered to the French Chief of Staff all these plans which formed the very basis of German mobilisation, her mission would be terminated and she could return to France, even without awaiting the return of Wilhelm Ansbach. It would indeed be impossible for her to remain.

Her missive completed, Germaine lay down peacefully and fell asleep almost immediately.

Since she had been in Berlin, the inventor's daughter had not enjoyed such restful sleep.

The next morning, Major Schlaffen received an order signed by General von Talberg, directing him to leave immediately for Stettin, where the local commandant ought to give him an envelope sealed in the name of His Majesty the Emperor.

At the same moment, the German Empire's

immortal champion of sleeping at will took his best pen and, in his thick heavy hand, he wrote the following note to Major Tourchtig:

"My dear comrade,

Having been sent by His Majesty on a special and confidential mission, and not knowing how long my absence will last, I come to beg of you, as specified in section III, article 21, paragraph 79, of the special regulations concerning the watch over the three armoured cabinets B. M. W. in the Moltke Room in the War Ministry, to take up the guard in my place until you receive new orders.

Yours, my dear comrade, in all faithfulness,
Major Schlaffen"

But Major Tourchtig, for his part, had received an order from General von Talberg directing him to go immediately, dropping everything, to Magdebourg, where the local commandant ought to give to him an envelope sealed in the name of His Majesty the Emperor.

So, jumping on his pen, Bavaria's invincible champion of Munich beer, exulting from vanity, had addressed this letter to his colleague Hunguerig:

"My dear comrade,

I have just received an order from the Chief of Staff directing me to report immediately to Magdebourg, in the name of the Emperor. I write therefore to ask you, as specified in section III, article 21, paragraphe 79, of the special regulations concerning the watch over the three armoured cabinets B. M. W. in the Moltke Room in the War Ministry, to take up the guard in my place until you receive new orders.

Yours, my dear comrade, etc,
Major Tourchtig"

Now, some moments before receiving this missive, Major Hunguerig had been touched by an order, again signed by General von Talberg and directing him to take the first train to Frankfurt, where the local commandant would give him an envelope sealed in the name of His Majesty the Emperor.

So Hesse Nassau's incomparable champion of Frankfurters, had seized his penholder, and stuffed with glee, he had written this note to Major Schlaffen:

"My dear comrade,

I have just received an order from General von Talberg sending me on a secret mission to Frankfurt. I write therefore to ask you, as specified in section III, article 21, paragraph 79, of the special regulations concerning the conservation of the three armoured cabinets B. M. W. in the Moltke Room in the War Ministry, to take up the guard in my place until you receive new orders.

Yours, my dear comrade, etc,
Major Hunguerig"

This letter remained sealed on its recipient's desk; because Major Schlaffen had already left for Stettin, with his soul tranquil and his conscience resting easy.

No less calm and no less assured, Tourchtig and Hunguerig had for their parts set off in the direction of Magdebourg and of Frankfurt.

In agreement with Germaine, Chantecoq was charged with watching the three majors.

Certain that they had taken their respective trains, he returned, towards midnight, under the windows of the governess who waited impatiently, her forehead pressed to the panes, and by a pre-arranged signal, he let her know that she could operate in total safety.

The beautiful Frenchwoman gave a sigh of relief.

Certainly, her precautions had been well taken. Thanks to the ease with which she could now reach the Chief of Staff's office and open his strongbox, she had been able to forge the orders which sent the three majors in three different directions while giving them the aspect of the most perfect authenticity.

She was therefore certain that none of these officers would have the slightest suspicion, and, even supposing that one of them had the unbelievable idea of going to find General von Talberg, whether to have the written order confirmed in person, or to solicit some extra explanatory details, there was nothing to fear there, the general having left with the Emperor to oversee mobilisation tests on the Eastern frontier and not being due back in Berlin until the following evening, at the earliest.

However Germaine had feared that at the last moment an unforeseen incident might occur, that for example Schlaffen might meet Hunguerig, or Tourchtig meet Schlaffen and that there would be an exchange of news between them, capable, in spite of the three champions' well-established intellectual shortcomings, of sparking some revelatory light in their shadowy brains.

Thanks to Chantecoq, however, she knew that everything had turned out for the best.

The Frenchwoman therefore only had to act.

Much as she had already done for her numerous nocturnal expeditions, Germaine, after having equipped herself with her electric lamp and having slipped inside her dress a revolver of feeble size but more than sufficient to defend herself in case of discovery, returned, again through the countess's rooms, to the general's office where, having opened the strongbox, she removed the keys to the armoured cabinets. Then she revealed the practically secret door in the wall adjoining the War Office, and she entered the corridor reserved for the Chief of Staff, reaching the threshold of the Moltke Room with no further obstacles.

But there she found herself facing a second door, or rather a sort of smooth iron panel, on which there was no keyhole or lock.

Germaine then felt a moment of uncertainty.

"It would really be too stupid," she said to herself, "to get stuck here, at this barrier, without being able to cross it, and to fail so pitifully, just as I was about to achieve my goal."

But the heroic Frenchwoman was not a woman to be discouraged when faced with an obstacle, however difficult it might be to overcome.

"There has to be a way of opening this door!" she reasoned with all the calmness she could muster.

With the aid of her lamp, she began to examine the panel's surface, which was polished like a mirror, not noticing anything which might provide a clue.

Then she examined the posts on which the panel was fixed. Still nothing.

There was nothing on the surrounding walls, either.

Germaine grew desperate. A cold sweat gathered on her buzzing temples when her handkerchief slipped from her hands and fell on the floor.

The young girl bent down to pick it up.

She was about to straighten up again when, by the light of her lamp, she noticed one of the floorboards which was slightly warped, giving the impression of having given way to the influence of humidity.

This was a beacon for the beautiful governess.

She looked closer and, in one corner of the plank she saw a minuscule nail head almost entirely hidden beneath the dust which had accumulated in the groove where it had been planted.

Without hesitation, the young girl pressed on this nail which gave way instantly.

Slowly the iron door swung open in the opposite direction from the Ministry side. Germaine had discovered the secret.

Three seconds later she was in the Moltke Room, which was deprived of its guardians.

Then, prudently, to avoid any surprises and manage her retreat, the inventor's daughter blocked the panel with a huge chair, to prevent it from closing again.

Then, resolutely but without noise, Germaine opened the B. M. W. armoured cabinets and began exploring them immediately.

It took her very little time to make an ample harvest of the documents.

Very judiciously she chose the most important pieces of which Chantecoq had given her a more complete picture.

Then she returned to the secret exit, letting the iron panel close behind her, walked down the corridor, re-entered the general's office, returned the keys to the chest, replaced the secret letters and went back through Countess Elsa's rooms.

The next day, towards eleven o'clock, carrying a fairly voluminous parcel in her hand, the governess left the house and met Chantecoq, who was waiting for her on a bench in Sièges-Allées.

This time, the Protean agent had created a new personality for himself.

It was no longer the brave Berliner who smoked his pipe while reading the *Cologne Gazette*, nor even the excellent bourgeois Chariottenberg lady who returned to do her shopping in the most select quarters, but rather a sort of shrivelled old man with a sickly appearance, swamped by a greatcoat, his head crowned with a cap with earflaps and his face overgrown by a grey beard, unkempt and dirty.

His head lowered, his stick between his knees, his body afflicted by incessant trembling, spitting and giving every impression of an asthmatic gout which would keep him seated to breathe, Chantecoq was waiting for the Frenchwoman's arrival with impatience.

"She succeeded," he said to himself on seeing her with the parcel under her arm.

Then, feigning an even more violent coughing fit, he let Germaine Aubry install herself behind him.

Having placed the parcel on the bench, the captain's fiancée said simply, in French:

"When I leave, I shall forget my parcel."

"So, it is done?" the agent asked between two coughs.

"Yes."

"Everything I asked of you is really there?"

"Yes."

"The covering troops, the graphs?"

"Yes."

"The invasion plan via Belgium?"

"Yes."

"Perfect! My congratulations."

And coughing more, Chantecoq continued.

"Allow me to tell you, my dear child, how happy I am with your success, both for my country and for yourself; because you can now return to Paris. With this lot we have the upper hand!"

"I believe, indeed," the young governess admitted, "that I kept my word and that I have given to France ten times more than was stolen from her!"

"A hundred times more!"

"However, I still have a duty to fulfil," replied Germaine. "I told you that General von Talberg left with the Emperor to help with mobilisation exercises which were both extremely important and even more mysterious. The plans will be, as usual, in the hands of the Chief of Staff who, on returning from his travels, will not fail to put them safely in his strongbox. I must take possession of them, because it could be that these plans bring some modifications to those here."

"You are right," agreed the secret agent. "You think of everything. Only permit me one simple objection. That's all very well, but perhaps it is not prudent."

"Why?"

"The three idiots will return. They are going to have to explain themselves. Everything will be known, and then…"

"Assuming that the affair blows up before I've left," Germaine objected in turn, "why would they suspect me?"

"Believe me," Chantecoq insisted, "don't go any further, this will become dangerous. You have not been suspected up to now, because you played your governess role admirably and, in addition; you have not made anything disappear. You have been taking notes, making copies. But today, what you have brought me, this will plunge Europe into fire and blood."

"It's your turn to listen to me, Mr Chantecoq," Germaine riposted, a little nervous. "If, one gloriously victorious evening, it was announced to a general that the leader of the troops who had just been routed was hiding out in a nearby house, and if this general replied: 'I'm not going, that's enough for today. I don't fancy taking a bullet!' What would you say? You would say that he was a coward."

"This is not the same. You have a father, a fiancé."

"And this general might have a wife and children."

"What good will it do playing with fire?"

"I wasn't the one who lit it."

"That's no reason for you to burn in it."

"Relax, I won't be burned. In three days, I'll be in France with the new documents. Nothing will deflect me from my goal. My father did the impossible to prevent me from leaving; I left all the same. Today, I am staying all the same!"

"Then, miss, I bow to your judgement, you are a true Roman."

"No, a Frenchwoman!"

And Germaine stood up, leaving behind her parcel, while murmuring: "Goodbye, Mr Chantecoq."

"Goodbye!" responded the agent, who had already put one hand on the precious package. "When shall we see next see each other?"

"I'm not sure. The signal will tell you."

And without even a glance at the old man who had hidden the parcel under his greatcoat under cover of a coughing fit, the governess left in the direction of Bellevue-Strauss.

CHAPTER TEN:

The Armoured Cabinets

The Intelligence Bureau in Berlin had finally received news of Lieutenant Wilhelm Ansbach.

It was Emma Lückner herself who had just sent it to Colonel Hoffmann.

Discovered by some country people in a ditch by the Lunéville road, insensible, bloodied, unrecognisable under the frightful contusions which had swollen his face, the false Alsatian had been transported to the nearest hospital, where he had remained unconscious for a long time and in a critical condition.

In the painstaking search that had been carried out, nothing that was found on him or around him, had been able to establish his identity.

Pictures of his camera, with the grey duster in which he was dressed in order to escape in the car, had been published in the papers, and witnesses had come forward, believing they recognised him as one of a gang of bandits, car thieves, whose exploits had been attracting a lot of attention for several months.

Specifically, a few days before the discovery of the mysterious wounded man, a grey car, which was later reported stolen, had been seen by night, driving at a crazy speed, by peasants who had been alarmed by gunshots.

It was thought therefore that the wounded man could be one of the bandits, left for dead so as not to delay their flight.

When Wilhelm Ansbach finally recovered consciousness and found himself in a hospital room, under the surveillance of two men that he recognised immediately as security agents, he was careful to conceal the improvement in his condition, wanting first to hear what was said and to learn what opinions had been formed on his account.

In this way he knew the suspicions about him; but, far from protesting, he responded evasively to questions that were put to him by the judge, so as not to lock himself in obstinate muteness.

For the authorities, the question was no longer in any doubt, they really held one of the famous car bandits; and the security agents' visits increased, with the aim of establishing the identity of this mysterious wounded man.

Emma Lückner, whose attention had been sparked by the noise around this business, soon recognised in the injured man the Uhlan lieutenant who had acquired the combat aircraft plans.

But an anguishing mystery strained her.

What had become of the precious papers belonging to the engineer Jean Aubry?

They had not been in Ansbach's possession when he had been discovered inanimate on the road.

No mention was made of them anywhere.

Wilhelm Ansbach, before succumbing to the wounds from his mysterious assassin, had had time stow them safely. Or would not these documents, to which Germany and other powers attached such a high price, have returned to France's possession?

It had been impossible for Emma Lückner to discover anything. While waiting, the Uhlan officer benefited from the error committed by the police who viewed him as a member of the gang of tragic bandits. However the truth could be discovered at any moment.

It was therefore vital to pull Wilhelm Ansbach out of this terrible situation at the earliest possible opportunity, and it was to help him escape that Emma Lückner, seconded by her agents, was going to employ herself.

She announced this to Colonel Hoffmann and he responded that she should succeed with no delay.

The Intelligence Bureau chief went straight afterwards to General von Talberg to communicate this important news to him, but he had barely finished reading the spy's report than Colonel Skoppen, Chief of the Mobilisation Bureau, appeared in the Chief of Staff's office, his face shaken and in a state of indescribable agitation.

"What is it?" von Talberg asked immediately.

"General," the Colonel announced in a shaky voice, "an important theft of documents has just been discovered."

"A theft of what?"

"File B., containing details of our troop deployments from Sarrehourg to Ribeauvillé, has vanished from the armoured cabinet W."

"That's not possible!"

"And yet it has happened, general."

"When did you discover this disappearance?"

"Just this moment, general. Needing to consult certain pieces for the work that you ordered me to do yesterday, I went to the Moltke Room; and you can imagine my stupefaction on realising that the File B. in question was no longer in the armoured cabinet W. where I had replaced it myself two days earlier. I looked and I found nothing so, I came to give you an account without wasting an instant, general."

"Do you hear this, Colonel Hoffmann?" cried the general in a hard voice.

The Intelligence Bureau chief seemed, for a moment, absolutely flummoxed.

"Yes, general!" he said piteously.

"This is alarming!"

"Indeed . . . alarming . . . but will you permit me, general, to put a few questions to Colonel Skoppen?"

"Do it!"

Then turning towards the Chief of the Mobilisation Bureau, Hoffmann continued. "You say, Colonel Skoppen, that this file was locked in the armoured cabinets?"

"Yes, Colonel Hoffmann, it was I who locked it in cabinet W."

"Who has the key to this cabinet?"

"There are two of them: one never leaves me. Here it is! As to the other, it is in General von Talberg's possession."

"And I am sure," the Chief of Staff declared instantly, "that it has not left this strongbox, to which I alone know the combination."

Heading towards the furniture, he pressed the secret catch, opened the iron panel, plunged his hand in the interior and soon drew out a key marked by a label which he showed the two officers, saying: "Here it is!"

While von Talberg replaced it and locked the strongbox, Hoffmann continued. "Do the armoured cabinets show any traces of a break-in?"

"None," responded Skoppen.

"Is there not a permanent guard in the hall where the mobilisation plans are locked?"

"Indeed. This guard was entrusted to three officers, Majors Schlaffen, Tourchtig and Hunguerig. Three brutes, but three dogs who watch in turn, day and night, over the cabinets."

"And they saw nothing?"

"No, for the simple reason that yesterday evening they had each individually received an order bearing the Chief of Staff's seal and telling them to depart, on state business, in three different directions."

"But I signed nothing, and I ordered nothing!" General von Talberg cried, striking a huge blow on his desk with his fist.

"These officers are there, general," Skoppen continued, "if you want to interrogate them."

"Go and find them," the Chief of Staff ordered.

Colonel Skoppen reached the antechamber.

Meanwhile, von Talberg, more and more furious, unleashed invective at Colonel Hoffmann:

"Truly, you deal in misery, Colonel! Not only are our agents in France arrested, but now our plans are stolen from us, here, in the War Office, in the offices of the Chief of Staff, just two paces from my own home. It's enough to make one wonder what you are good for! For retirement, Colonel Hoffmann, for retirement!"

"General," stammered Hoffman, "permit me to say . . ."

"Shut up!"

The door had just opened, making way for Colonel Skoppen, followed by Majors Schlaffen, Tourchtig and Hunguerig.

The three champions made a rather pitiful sight.

They stepped forward as though on parade, chests thrust out, mechanically projecting their legs forward, but with dazed, bewildered and confused expressions.

"Halt!" Von Talberg commanded the three brutes who stopped simultaneously, all pronouncing the sacred phrase. "Yes, general!"

Eyeing them disdainfully, the Chief of Staff attacked. "It appears that certain important items have been stolen for which you had the responsibility of guarding?"

"Yes, general," the three friends responded at the same time.

"And you were not there?"

"No, general."

"You had abandoned your post?"

"No, general, we had received... an order..."

But, stamping his foot, von Talberg interrupted. "Don't all speak at once! Which of you three was on duty the night when the theft was committed?"

"Me, general," Schlaffen responded.

"Then, Major Schlaffen, where were you?"

The German Empire's immortal champion of sleeping at will spluttered lamentably. "General, I was, I was…"

"Come now, explain yourself!"

"General, I was in Stettin, where I had received orders to report for a secret mission."

"And you, Major Tourchtig?"

The Kingdom of Bavaria's invincible champion of Munich beer responded immediately. "I was at Magdebourg, where I had also received orders."

He said no more.

Shrugging his shoulders, von Talberg then turned straight to Hunguerig. "And you?"

"General, I was in Frankfurt where I had also received . . ."

"And not one of you," the Chief of Staff cut in, "had any idea that this ridiculous coincidence was only a piece of misdirection?"

"No, general," the three champions swore in chorus.

"You are nothing but three idiots, three imbeciles, three baited asses."

"Yes, general."

Turning to Skoppen and Hoffmann, the general added: "I ask you why I would have sent these three morons to Stettin, Magdebourg, and Frankfurt for secret missions."

"General," Schlaffen hazarded, "I believed it was a mobilisation exercise."

"After all, general," Tourchtig offered, "The order did bear your stamp."

"And your signature," Hunguerig added.

"Did you keep these papers?" von Talberg asked, alert.

"Yes, general."

"Show me!"

"Yes, general!" the three majors said, at the same time taking out the forged documents and handing them with the same automatic gesture to von Talberg, who took them.

After examining them with care, he looked up. "It's exact. It's very skilfully done, even! I accept that anyone would have been mistaken."

"So, Major Schlaffen, once you were in Stettin, what did you do?"

"General," explained the immortal champion of falling asleep at will, "I went to the garrison, where the commandant told me that there was nothing there for me."

"Afterwards?"

"I went to have supper, go to bed, and I took the first train back to Berlin."

"And you, Major Tourchtig?"

The invincible champion of Munich beer declared: "General, as soon as I arrived in Magdebourg, I went to the garrison where the commandant told me there was nothing there for me. Then I did as Major

Schlaffen did, I went to have supper, went to bed, and I returned this morning."

"And you, Major Hunguerig?"

"General, when I arrived in Frankfurt, I went to the garrison where the commandant told me there was nothing there for me. So I did the same as Major Tourchtig . . ."

"You went to have supper, and went to bed," von Talberg interrupted brusquely, his patience at an end, "and you returned this morning. And you didn't realise that you had been duped? You didn't even have the idea to telegraph Colonel Skoppen to warn him about your misadventure."

Turning towards the two colonels, he added with contempt: "Drink, eat, sleep, that's what these three are good for!"

And addressing the three discomfited majors, in a furious voice he decided. "Go and reflect on this while I make my decision, don't breathe a word of this to anyone."

"As you command, general."

The three majors exited at a parade ground pace, stiff, moronic, and more and more stupid.

When the door was again closed, von Talberg, who had followed the three champions' exit with a contemptuous and furious gaze, continued immediately. "Ah! Colonel Skoppen, what an idea to entrust to such cretins the duty of watching over the secrets of our national defence! They would not even be up to the job of guarding the square, or a museum. I will not offer you any congratulations."

"General," the Mobilisation Bureau's Chief tried to defend himself, "we thought that, precisely, these three majors, incapable of rendering and active service, but fiercely disciplined and absolutely incorruptible, were completely designed to guarantee this guard."

"That's possible, but while waiting for me to order their retirement, pack them off to some fortress. I don't want to hear anything more about them."

"Permit me, general, to observe respectfully that the unfortunates have an excuse. They acted in good faith."

"On that matter, general," Colonel Hoffmann then said, "may I cast an eye over the bogus orders to which these three officers fell victim?"

"Take a look," von Talberg said, passing the papers to the Chief of the Intelligence Bureau. "It's certainly my stamp, and my signature is imitated perfectly."

"Indeed," observed the military policeman.

And, with a serious air, he added: "This is evidently the work of someone having complete access to this house."

Then, stopping, he said, as he turned to his colleague.

"Colonel Skoppen!"

"Colonel Hoffmann!"

"To reach the Moltke Room, it would have been necessary not just to remove the officers on duty, but also to evade the exterior guards?"

"Assuredly," the mobilisation bureau chief declared. "However, it is most likely that the guilty party, familiar with the building's topography, hid themselves in some corner during the day."

"But to get out?"

"Short of having wings or intelligence about the room, I can't explain even to myself how the thief or thieves could have got away."

Colonel Hoffmann, once again sure of himself, spoke to von Talberg, who had been listening with close attention to the dialogue between the two officers.

"General," he said, "you have lately established a corridor which leads directly between your office and the Moltke Room?"

"Indeed, Colonel," responded Frida's father. But this corridor serves only for my use, and it was not I who took the files."

"Oh! General, I simply wished to know if the door to this corridor . . ."

"Was locked tight?" the general finished.

Activating the spring hidden in the sculptures decorating one of the table legs, the Chief of Staff, indicating the opening which appeared in the wall, said, not without irony: "I believe, Mr. Intelligence Bureau Chief, that in spite of your flair, you wouldn't have thought to look for this corridor there."

"Indeed, general," admitted the policeman.

While the secret door swung itself closed, as if by magic, the general said to the Mobilisation Bureau Chief:

"Now, Colonel Skoppen, you can leave. On your way out, you will immediately telephone his Majesty's aide-de-camp and instruct him to come immediately to the Chief of Staff."

"Yes, general!"

Skoppen, after having snapped off a salute, left the office. At the moment where he crossed the threshold, he stood aside in order to allow the general's daughter, accompanied by her governess, to pass.

"You can see that your father is busy!" said the voice of Bertha Stegel.

"I only have a moment, indeed," said von Talberg, whose face had just lit up slightly at the sight of his daughter. "But it doesn't matter, come in."

"I just came to kiss you before going out," said Frida who went to her father and then responded to the greeting addressed to her by Colonel Hoffmann.

The military policeman's gaze now fixed itself on the young governess who, clad in her black dress, her hair coiled under her dark bonnet, had stopped at the entrance to the office.

"Where are you going?" the general asked, addressing both Frida and her governess at once.

CHANTECOQ AND THE AUBRY AFFAIR

It was Germaine who replied. "We are going to Thiergarten, general, where we will make a practical application of the natural history lesson that Miss Frida has just had."

"And which was so interesting, father!" the young girl added. "Miss Bertha made me study sea lions, polar bears and animals from the Arctic regions. It's fun."

"Very good! Don't forget, Miss Stegel, that tomorrow it's Thursday and that you must take my daughter to see Countess Richter."

"I won't forget, general."

"Well then, until this evening, my dear," said von Talberg as he kissed his daughter, "and have a good walk!"

The door had barely closed behind the two girls than Colonel Hoffmann, who had continued to fix his gaze on the governess, said, "General, a word, I beg you."

"Speak!" said von Talberg.

"This Miss Bertha Stegel…"

"My daughter's governess?"

"Yes, general. She is German, isn't she?"

"As German as they come."

"Are you sure of that, general?"

"Absolutely sure!" the Chief of Staff replied, visibly taken aback. "Ah! Do you really imagine that this young lady . . . ?"

"General, I abjure you to listen to me with all the patience you can muster," implored the Colonel over his superior's lively tone. "I beg you, see in me only a servant of his country who has but one desire, that of seeing a swift end to the atrocious nightmare in which we find ourselves."

"So be it! Speak!"

"In particular, general, don't take from my questions that I am permitting myself to put any stain on your personal dignity or any intention to cause you the slightest worry, the slightest pain."

"Speak, I tell you!"

"May I ask you how this young person comes to be in your household?"

"On the recommendation of the Friedmann agency who have furnished the best families in Berlin with governesses for many years. I'd add that Stegel came armed with the most praise-worthy references and, anyway, I can only congratulate myself for having chosen her."

"How long has she been in your service, general?"

"Around three months."

"Could you specify the precise date of her arrival with you?"

"Very easily."

And von Talberg, who began to feel the stirrings of a terrible anguish, took a notebook from the table, leafed through it and declared: "Miss Bertha Stegel commenced her employment last September 15th."

"That's strange!" the Intelligence Bureau chief could not prevent himself from murmuring as he fixed his eyes on the general's face.

"What do you mean?" the general started, frowning.

"I wonder, general."

"What, you suppose . . . ?"

"I suppose nothing, general. I repeat, I observe."

"And what do you observe, then?"

"That the arrest of our French agents and the theft of our documents in Germany coincide, to a troubling extent, with the entry of this person in your service."

"What are you telling me?" The Chief of Staff was incapable of controlling the indignation which stirred in him an equally painful suspicion for she who had earned both his sympathy and esteem. "Come now, you are mistaken! To mask your own incompetence, you would ask me to believe that this young girl is a spy? Since she has been here, I've been able to observe her, study her at my leisure. She is incapable of such an abominable act."

"In that case, general," Hoffmann riposted, "if this Miss Stegel is innocent, it must be one of your most intimate colleagues, one of your closest officers."

"Oh! Don't say that!"

"Yet, general, to have seized your stamp, to have imitated your signature with such perfection, to have discovered the secret of your strongbox, it would have to be someone completely *au fait* with all your actions and habits."

"That's true, but I can vouch for my officers."

"Permit me to insist, and let me follow the path that I believe I have found. If I am wrong, I will be the first to admit it."

But the general continued, with anger, walking behind his desk. "It's ridiculous! It's odious! To accuse this young girl! How could you prove that she had succeeded in opening my strongbox, forging orders, seizing the list of counter-agents, finding the confidential note that I wrote to you on the subject of Captain Keiffer and whose draft I took care to destroy! How do you imagine that she could have entered my office? How could she have entered this room before which Ulrich mounts an incessant guard day and night, and of which, each time I go out, I carefully lock all the doors?"

"Even that one up there, general?" The policeman insinuated softly, pointing at the door which led to the gallery.

"That one up there?" von Talberg said, raising his eyes in the direction indicated. "It leads to the Countess's rooms . . ."

And, his voice suddenly darkening, he continued. "It was down this staircase that my poor wife often came to keep me company when I worked very late in the night. Since her death, I have abandoned the rooms. It's a sanctuary for me whose solitude no one may violate."

"I beg your pardon, general," apologised Hoffmann, "for reminding you of such painful memories."

"You must make your enquiries. So you persist in believing that my daughter's tutor is to blame?"

"General, permit me not to respond yet on this subject. The only thing I ask of you, is to allow me to act."

"Act! You can in any case, count on me to throw all light on this matter. Anything, sooner than suspecting an innocent!"

"In that case, general, you can put me at ease by kindly granting me a great service."

"What service?"

"It would be indispensable, if you could order me to take over for a short period while you pretend to leave Berlin for some time. This departure would be nothing extraordinary, as you are often obliged to travel. But, this time, instead of leaving, you would remain hidden nearby."

And as the Chief of Staff made a gesture of protest, almost of disgust, Colonel Hoffman continued immediately. "I know, general, that such an attitude is barely compatible with your character and that it must be profoundly repugnant to you to use such means to discover the truth, but, unfortunately, we have no choice. Do what I ask of you, I beg you, and I'll deliver the guilty party to you before forty-eight hours have passed."

General von Talberg reflected for a few moments. "Whatever the outcome of this terrible adventure," he said to himself, "I have no right to stand down. I must do my duty to the end!"

And in a voice which trembled lightly: "Colonel Hoffmann," he added, "you are right. I will do what you ask of me."

"Thank you, general! Thank you on behalf of Germany and from myself!"

"Soon," decided Frida's father, "I will announce that I am leaving to visit a stronghold in the West. Tomorrow, a notice will appear in the papers signalling my presence in an important town, in Strasbourg or in Metz. In reality, I shall stay in Berlin."

"In a discreet and secure retreat, which I shall prepare for you myself, general." Hoffmann added, now beaming radiantly.

But von Talberg concluded, "If, as you promise, you deliver the guilty party to me, I will ask the Emperor that you receive the highest reward. But if you are wrong, I shall strike you down without pity!"

Hoffmann bowed, saluted, and took leave of his chief, who he left confused and consternated.

CHAPTER ELEVEN:

Into the Storm

Through Chantecoq, Germaine Aubry had learned that Wilhelm Ansbach was still alive.

The escape prepared by Emma Lückner had succeeded completely, and cheating his guards' surveillance, thanks to the intrigues set in motion, the spy had saved himself from the hospital where the judge had consigned him.

For the judge as for the general police, it was one of the tragic bandits who had escaped, because the Uhlan officer's identity had not been established.

He was therefore going to return; the inventor's daughter knew. Now, having been promised that Chantecoq would redouble surveillance, she awaited events with calm, an intrepid stoicism, ready to face all the terrible consequences which could arise from this development.

But one question repeated itself ceaselessly in her mind.

Did the traitor have the combat aircraft plans in his possession?

If he had kept them, he would have to be prevented from handing them over to General von Talberg, or they would have to be taken from Ansbach before he had the time to make use of them.

Indeed, though Germaine could trust to Chantecoq's zeal, ingenuity and devotion, she could not deny that in spite of all his finesse and courage, the German spy, who must be on his guard, might escape him.

It was equally important that she knew the exact moment of the arrival of Frida's fiancé; but she dared not interrogate her.

"In the general's office," she thought. "There I will perhaps find a clue; a police memo, or a secret report."

This plan was so much easier to execute as Germaine, who had not seen the general since the day before, had just learned from Frida that, suddenly called to the border, he had had to leave without having time to take leave of anybody.

So, sure of herself, at around one in the morning, the Frenchwoman left her bedroom; and taking her habitual precautions, she reached the Chief of Staff's office through Countess von Talberg's rooms.

As on previous occasions, she slowly descended the steps which led from the gallery to the office. She padded across to the door, closed the interior bolt, approached the table, set down the lamp, looked in the waste paper basket to see whether she could find some fragments of torn papers.

The bin was empty.

"The strongbox!" she thought.

She went towards it, adjusted the combination, slipped one of the false keys that Chantecoq had procured for her into the lock, and opened the panel.

No sooner had she reached out her hand, when the room was suddenly flooded with light.

Germaine turned brusquely.

A cry died on her lips.

Von Talberg and Colonel Hoffmann stood before her.

Apparently very calm, but pale, his lip shaking, the Chief of Staff, who had just appeared suddenly with the policeman from the doorway of the secret passage, cried, "Colonel, go and find the guard!"

While the officer carried out this order, the general stared fixedly at Germaine who, ready to stagger, leaned against the strongbox.

"Thief," he pronounced in a flat tone.

"I forbid you to insult me," said Germaine, raising her head.

"Yes, thief!" Frida's father repeated, advancing towards her.

At the end of her strength, succumbing under a weight too heavy for her shoulders, the unfortunate collapsed next to the table murmuring: "It's true . . . you don't know . . . you can't know . . ."

"How, could you, a German," said von Talberg, "have done this?"

"I'm not German!" Germaine protested, already trying to regain self-control. In a jerky voice, she continued. "I'm not a thief, but a Frenchwoman who fights for her country!"

"So be it!" the Prussian officer roared. "You're a thief, a miserable spy who, no doubt for money . . ."

"Ah! Don't say that, general," Captain Evrard's fiancée cried instantly with violence, having completed recovered her vigour and energy which had been slaughtered just moments before.

And standing up, facing the storm bravely, she continued. "It is enough for me to tell you who I am to convince you that I have not acted for money. I am the daughter of Jean Aubry, the French inventor of the combat aircraft, the plans for which were stolen by Lieutenant Wilhelm Ansbach, who you are now waiting for and who I would have killed by my own hand, if I had faced him! Will you still call me a thief?"

"So what?" said von Talberg, who felt confused before the haughty attitude of the Frenchwoman. "What you can't deny is that perfidiously, in a cowardly fashion, you have abused my trust, playing out under my roof the most infamous drama and pushing your hypocrisy to the point of making yourself loved by my daughter. Oh you have been subtle, truly and infernally cunning!"

And, advancing towards Germaine, his fists threatening, von Talberg, seized by a violent fury, shouted. "I really must remember you're a woman or I'd . . ."

He stopped, as though frightened by his rage.

"Strike me, general!" Germaine threw the words in his face. "You would not be the first German who has raised a hand to me."

"What does that mean?"

"I promised myself to remain silent if I was arrested, but I want you to know, general, that I am not in anyone's pay."

And as Frida's father raised his shoulders, she continued in a vibrant voice. "Yes, you must know what anguish I have felt. I have suffered, believe it, because I was sincerely attached to your daughter, so sweet, so good, because you have inspired in myself the most respectful esteem. Several times, I have been on the point of running away, because it was repugnant to my conscience, I swear, to lie to you, the loyal soldier that you are, and even more perhaps to your daughter, whose regard so pure appeared to me like a constant reproach. I've needed to remember what happened there, my father's misery, stolen, ruined by that wretch Ansbach. It's been vital above all that the image of France appeared to me, bearing on her chest the bloody wound that one of yours had just inflicted treacherously, for me to continue my work and for me to say to myself: 'All that you will do will be nothing next to what they did to you!'"

"That's all a fiction!" said von Talberg.

"I swear to you, general!"

"I don't believe you!"

"Look me in the eyes . . . do I look like a woman who's lying?"

"Even if you were acting in obedience to some exasperated patriotic sentiment, that excuses nothing. It is still true," replied von Talberg, "that to achieve your goals you used shameful expedients and infamous tactics."

"And yours?" the Frenchwoman riposted fiercely.

"Ours?" said the general, stamping his foot.

"Oh! It suits you well enough to scorn espionage, when you sent burglars and assassins to our house!"

"Assassins!"

"You reproach me for having abused your trust, for having made myself loved by your daughter, for having inspired some sympathy in you. But what would you say, general, of an individual who, passing himself off as Alsatian, as a patriot, infiltrated a French family, received the most loyal hospitality, constructed the most fervent friendships, and profited from this so that when one evening the young girl of the house was alone, he could slip over to her, half strangle her and flee after having robbed her father's secrets."

"I would say that he was a wretch!" the Chief of Staff could not stop himself from declaring.

"Well! This wretch exists! He's called Wilhelm Ansbach, and it is I who he wanted to kill!"

As the general fell silent, the inventor's daughter went on. "Ah! If you had not begun, I would never have had the idea of coming here. It's not I who chose the battlefield."

"Oh, come on!"

"No, general, we French, we love frankness and light too much to deliberately become spies, and I astonish even myself at what I have done here, of what I was still ready to do. Ah! There must really have been more than hatred in me, something indefinable which rendered me completely different from my nature and which made me feel lying was a right, subterfuge a virtue, and vengeance a duty!

"Yet, sometimes, I returned to my senses. When you spoke to me with generosity, and above all when your daughter presented her forehead to be kissed in the evening. Then I felt myself weaken. I was almost ashamed. I was unhappy, yes, sincerely unhappy.

"But I suddenly thought of all that I had left

behind, of my father: despoiled, ruined, aged ten years in one night of anguish. Think, therefore, the labours of his brain lost for his country and profiting you, you against whom he was working! Was I not right to try and take something back from you?"

There was a moment of silence.

Germaine, upright, breathless with her hand leaning on the table, looked into the void, as if she had perceived a distant vision of a corner of her country where the people she loved appeared.

"Just now, you inspired nothing but hatred in me," the general finally replied. "Now that I've listened to you, I begin to feel nothing but pity for you."

"I don't want your pity," replied the Frenchwoman proudly, "I played, I lost. I therefore accept the consequences of my actions, without seeking to attenuate their severity in any way."

"How you hate us!" said von Talberg with a profound melancholy.

"Whose fault is that? You who, for forty years, after all, still work to dig a trench full of the blood which separates us. You who have never missed an opportunity to humiliate us, reminding us ceaselessly that you were the victors! You who have never ceased to say that France is nothing more than a tired, spent nation, at the end of its race! You finally who, slyly, hypocritically, seek to depict us to the eyes of the world as a decadent people, without morals, having lost all vigour and languishing in the most abject corruption!"

"I have never held such views!" von Talberg protested.

"True, general," Germaine conceded, "because you are an honest man and especially because you have French blood in your veins! But the others? It is enough to listen to your officers' conversations, to read the venomous articles in the majority of your newspapers, to observe the bad faith of your diplomacy and the emphatic speeches of your pan-germanists, to be convinced that those who are charged with leading your people dream and wish for a new and imminent crushing of France!

"Ah! You can send men like Wilhelm Ansbach there. They will see, general, that my country is not in the state you think, say, write. Never has our army been more valiant, more disciplined, better commanded, more ready for victory. Never have we been less provoking because never have we been greater masters of ourselves."

Strongly impressed, General von Talberg had to let this ardent exaltation of patriotism pass.

"Yet you knew, in coming here, what you were exposing yourself to?" he said finally, while the French woman breathed with superb indignation.

"Yes, I knew," Germaine riposted. "You can send me to prison, general. I will not be alone, because when my story is known, there is not one

Frenchman who will not send me his consoling
and gentle thoughts, and to feel loved by all these
faithful hearts, that will be sufficient to soften the
ordeal. It is so good, when one suffers, to know that
one has many friends. And I will have thirty-eight
million of them, general! That will be my pride and
my reward."

At that moment, the door opened with a crash; and
Colonel Hoffman, whose smooth face was lit up with
an expression of ferocious joy, said in a vibrant voice.
"General! General!"

Von Talberg returned to his senses. "What is it?"
he asked.

"Lieutenant Wilhelm Ansbach is here!"

"Lieutenant Ansbach!" Frida's father repeated.

A noise was heard in the antechamber.

Almost immediately the false Jacques Müller,
in civilian clothes, and pale with tired features,
appeared on the threshold, supported by the
aide-de-camp.

Then, raising his hand to his forehead, he said
simply, in a voice broken with emotion and exhaustion.
"At your service, general!"

"Him! Him!" Germaine growled between
her teeth.

The spy officer continued. "General, if you knew
what I have suffered. I believed that all was lost. I can
no longer stand!"

He tottered, indeed, as though he was about to pass out.

But calling on all his energy, he approached the table and threw down a parcel that he took from beneath his clothes, saying: "There are the plans for the combat aircraft. There they are!"

As the general made a movement to take them, Ansbach tottered again, his strength exhausted, and von Talberg caught him in his arms.

Germaine had followed the whole rapid and moving scene with an alert gaze.

Then, profiting from the Chief of Staff's trouble, while Colonel Hoffmann also moved to help Wilhelm Ansbach, she launched herself at the table; quick as lightning, she swept up the papers and threw them in the wood fire which burned bright and sparkling in the huge chimney.

"The swine!" Hoffman shouted, grimacing in fury.

Quickly he hurried to the chimney to try and pull the smouldering plans from the brazier.

Then Germaine, picking up a revolver which lay on the general's table, pointed it in the direction of Wilhelm Ansbach, saying: "If you take one step, I kill him!"

At this terrible threat, von Talberg, Hoffmann and the aide-de-camp remained as if petrified, not daring to move a muscle, to speak a word. When the combat aircraft plans were no more than a blackened mass, ready to fall into cinders at the slightest shock, Germaine, calm, proud, smiling, threw the revolver on to the table and said simply:

"I have saved my country! Do with me what you will!"

"Take this woman to Spandau Citadel," the general ordered.

The heroic Frenchwoman followed the aide-de-camp calmly.

But as she passed in front of Lieutenant Ansbach who, trembling with rage and seeming to have recovered his strength, gave her a look charged with fury and hatred, the young girl stopped and, regarding the spy with supreme contempt, she offered him a single word.

"Blackguard!"

CHAPTER TWELVE:

Spandau Citadel

Germaine had been led to a room in the War Ministry, where, in the presence of the Chief of Staff and of Lieutenant von Limbürg, his Majesty's aide-de-camp, she had been subjected to a first interrogation from Colonel Hoffmann.

But the Frenchwoman, after having declared that she would add nothing to what she had said to General von Talberg, remained absolutely mute.

In vain did they try, by every method, by the most pressing abjurations, by the most tempting promises, to make her name her accomplices. She proudly refused to respond.

The orders given concerning her were carried out immediately.

Before daybreak, Germaine Aubry was escorted under guard to Spandau Citadel, whose commandant had been warned by telegraph, and was immediately incarcerated in a room situated at the top of Julius Tower, at the bottom of which Germany's war reparations from the Franco-Prussian war were stored.

Air and light entered the room freely through a window decorated with three solid iron bars.

A huge heavy door, pierced by a spyhole, locked her in.

In terms of furnishings, there was an iron bed, on which had been laid a mattress, with a woollen blanket and some burlap sheets. Then a white wooden table, furnished with indispensable toiletries, and two chairs.

Broken by emotion and fatigue, the prisoner fell down on the bed.

Earlier, facing her enemies, the heroic Frenchwoman had not had one minute of weakness; but now, alone in this lugubrious prison, her moral and physical strength finally betrayed her.

She thought of her father, of her fiancé who would not take long to learn the news of her arrest, and burning tears sprang to her eyes and flowed slowly over her face.

But Germaine soon got a grip on herself, in a vigorous appeal to her energy.

"I don't want to despair," she told herself with courage. "As long as there is a breath of life in me, as long as my blood flows in my veins, alone against everyone, disarmed prisoner, between the thick walls of this fortress, I must still keep my head against my enemies, if only to show them that a Frenchwoman is capable of seeing her task through to the end!"

Commandant Fürsner, Spandau Citadel's governor, was a man of fifty, tall, corpulent, his face framed by a reddish beard, with a character that was obtuse, stubborn and above all cast-iron honest. He was considered by his superiors as a living rulebook and they were sure that with him, the prisoner would be well guarded and watched over.

"Germaine Aubry," he announced in a brutal voice, "I am going to fill you in straight away on the rules to which you will be subject here throughout your detention. That way, you will get to know them so as not to risk violating them. You have been placed, pending your trial, in complete isolation. As such you will have time to meditate, and when you have decided the best path to take, you will doubtless adopt another attitude."

After waiting a moment, seeing that the prisoner maintained an indignant silence, and did not even raise her eyes to him, he shook his head and muttered between his teeth. "We will get through it all the same."

At the same time he turned on his heel and left the cell, whose door he carefully locked behind him.

Immediately after Germaine Aubry's arrest, General von Talberg returned to his office.

A truly emotive spectacle awaited him.

A man knelt before the chimney where the combat aircraft plans had just been consumed, as the inventor's daughter had succeeded in throwing them into the flames with such an audacious move.

It was Wilhelm Ansbach who observed the young Frenchwoman's act of annihilation with bleak despair.

Desolate, dazed, he was still there, eyes fixed on the brazier, contemplating the charred fragments of paper which still fluttered in a column of black smoke.

He had not heard his superior, whose steps had been muffled by the thick carpet which covered the floor, and he watched, still watched, like a madman, waiting for he knew not what miracle which would bring him the treasure he had won at the cost of so much pain, and which had been torn from him by the vengeful hand of she whom he had tried to murder.

"Lieutenant Ansbach!" the Chief of Staff called.

The Uhlan officer turned; and seeing the general, he stood, an apple ripened by Spring.

But almost immediately he staggered and had to lean on the enormous table.

"Sit down," Talberg said simply, witnessing his weakness.

"But, general," the spy stammered.

"Sit down!" the general insisted, "I have to speak to you."

"Yes, sir," Ansbach obeyed, at the end of his strength, letting himself fall on the seat that his superior pointed out.

Frida's father remained silent for a moment, pacing his office with jerky steps, occasionally releasing tatters of phrases from his trembling lips. Some of these were pained, some were angry, and some were ashamed. Then, having succeeded in calming himself down a little, he returned to Ansbach and, holding his gaze, he asked point blank.

"These papers, which earlier this young woman, this Frenchwoman, threw in the fireplace, were they indeed the inventor Jean Aubry's plans for a combat aircraft?"

"Yes, general."

"Could you reconstruct them?"

"No, general. First, I have not had time to study them sufficiently. Then, even if I had been able to, I would need to be a genius of the first order, and I am only a soldier."

"Then the disaster is irreparable?"

"Irreparable!"

After making a spiteful gesture, von Talberg went back to walking up and down, keeping, this time, the deepest silence.

Ansbach followed him with feverish attention. He felt that at that moment his future and his whole life were being decided in Frida's father's mind, and he asked himself with anguish if, now that the papers had disappeared and he had failed to complete the mission, the Chief of Staff would have the same reasons to reward him by granting him his daughter's hand in marriage.

His soul being narrow, petty, self-interested, and judging all characters according to his own, to the extent that he said to himself "success justifies everything!" he thought, "failure forfeits all your rights." And he no longer dared to hope.

"Did you know this Frenchwoman?" Von Talberg asked suddenly in a clipped voice.

"Perfectly, general."

"Is she really the daughter of the inventor, Jean Aubry?"

"Yes, general."

"She succeeded in infiltrating my home, as my daughter's governess, introducing herself under a false name, passing herself off as a German and producing the best qualifications. She spoke our language perfectly and she was skilled enough to gain both my trust and that of my daughter. I was a hundred leagues from suspecting her true identity as well as her criminal intentions, up to the point where Colonel Hoffmann, suspicious of her, helped unmask her, just a few minutes before your arrival. This is what you need to know! Now, lieutenant, tell me what you did over there."

While the Chief of Staff fixed him with a strange look, Frida's fiancé began.

"General. I will not seek to raise my value in your eyes by recounting the tale of achievements I did not accomplish. On arrival in Paris, my first concern was, as I let you know, to get close to Jean Aubry."

"As Germaine Aubry got close to me!" Frida's father punctuated quietly.

Wilhelm Ansbach stopped, taken aback.

But the general said to him in a dry, authoritative tone. "Continue, lieutenant, I'm listening."

"After quite some time," the spy continued, "I discovered that the combat aircraft plans were to be found at the inventor's house, locked in a bureau, and I resolved to snatch them. That very day, the War Ministry had decided to adopt the plans, and Jean Aubry was to deliver them the next day. I therefore resolved to hurry things and during the inventor's absence, I returned to his home. I knew that his daughter wore the key to the bureau where the documents were locked on a chain round her neck, and so . . ."

"So," von Talberg cut in drily, "you threw yourself on to this young girl, and you tried to strangle her."

"Who told you that, general?"

"She did."

"It's true, general, because in order to snatch these plans, I was prepared to do anything, even to kill this woman!"

With sudden energy, the Uhlan added: "Why didn't I do it? You would now have the plans for the combat aircraft! I was so happy, so proud, to have brought you those documents. I had escaped such dangers, if you only knew what I endured . . .

"Just as I was about to cross the border, I was attacked by bandits who left me for dead on the road and who fled with my car. I still had the strength to hide my papers in a ditch, and I lost consciousness. When I came to my senses, I found myself in a hospital bed, in Lunéville. A frisson of horror shook me. I asked myself: 'Have I been recognised?' No. I breathed again, because I had been mistaken for a highway bandit. Then I resolved to be silent and I refused to respond to the questions posed to me by a magistrate.

"But my wounds healed. They talked about taking me to Nancy prison. Luckily, a woman who you know, Emma Lückner, was watching over me and with the help of her agents, she managed to arrange my escape.

"Oh, general! You can not imagine my joy when I recovered the documents from the hole which I had dug with a knife and enlarged with my nails. This car journey, to Berlin, we were going fast, very fast, and yet I had an impression of desperate slowness, so keen was I to reach the goal.

"And just as I was about to give you those papers, that young Frenchwoman had to appear before me to destroy everything, to wipe out everything.

"Ah, general, forgive me from expressing myself in this manner before you. Just now, it seemed to me, from the severe tone with which you spoke to me, that not only did you disapprove of my conduct, but that you almost pitied this young girl."

"Lieutenant!"

"Do not be annoyed, general. Already, I am sure, you have forgiven me, understood, approved, and you have told yourself: 'there is above all one unfortunate thing, this simple officer, this young lieutenant who arrived with a heart beating with hope, and who, on the threshold of realising an admirable dream, has been struck twice in that which he holds dearest, in his country, and in his love."

At these words, General von Talberg shuddered.

He had just remembered the promise made to his daughter which, in his disarray, he had forgotten for a moment.

Then coldly and without any trace of benevolence, he spoke.

"I see, lieutenant, that you wish to broach an intimate question which is particularly close to your heart and which touches me in regard to that which

I hold dearest in the world. When you asked me for my daughter's hand, I told you simply: 'Deserve it!' It is with that aim that you have risked your liberty, your life. And if you had not succeeded in rendering an eminent service for your country, this is not your fault, I am sure. But at the moment, I am still too shaken to speak with you of such a serious matter. Return tomorrow morning. I will await you here, in this office."

"Yes, general."

"Until then, give me your word of honour that you will not show yourself anywhere or speak to anybody. To anybody, do you hear me?"

"I promise you, general."

"Dismissed, lieutenant. I need to be alone."

The Uhlan officer saluted his superior, turned on his heels and left.

Then General von Talberg gave free rein to his tortuous thoughts, murmuring,

"After the abominable treason of this woman, she ought to be an object of horror for me, but I feel that I pity her to the extent I am ready to forgive her, almost to admit she was right. It's Wilhelm Ansbach, who by acting so odiously, prompted her to come to us. She has only taken a just revenge!

"Certainly, she has caused me pain, she has broken my career, because I do not want, after what has just happened, to remain in charge of the Army.

"On the other hand I promised Frida that she would marry Wilhelm Ansbach. I am engaged. I do not have the right to break my word with my daughter. Yet this man is a thief, almost a murderer. I know this is war, but do I have the right? Do we have the right?"

Stricken by doubt, General von Talberg, still incapable of mastering his brain, which was overexcited by the combat raging in him, remained undecided until daybreak, fighting himself, accusing himself, not knowing what part to take.

Suddenly, at dawn, he heard the rhythmic sound of a troop marching. He approached the window. A violent shock struck his heart.

"A soldier must never be weak," he murmured. "If I have committed a fault, my duty is to make reparation!"

CHAPTER THIRTEEN:

Escape Plan

The news of Germaine's arrest, transmitted by Chantecoq who had quickly learned of it, had produced the most painful atmosphere in the little house in Saint-Mandé where, that very day, Jean Aubry had received a visit from Captain Evrard and from the young aviation officer's mother.

These ardent patriots needed valiant souls indeed not to be broken by the unspeakable catastrophe striking the person who was most dear to them.

The heroic woman's fate could not be in any doubt for them.

The Tribunal before which the young governess would appear, under the serious accusation of espionage, would certainly condemn her to a long detention, if not perpetual.

But far from letting themselves be weakened by the horrible pain which afflicted them, at the thought of all that Germaine would have to endure, at the mercy of the brutality of her gaolers and her judges, one lone thought shot through the minds of the Frenchwoman's father and her fiancé.

They instantly resolved to put everything at stake to effect her escape.

Quickly, they agreed and, resolved to act without the slightest delay, while the inventor prepared the necessary instruments for this audacious project, a special saw and a fine, strong rope ladder, Captain Evrard reported to the War Ministry.

Always respectful of discipline, the young officer wanted to be in line with his military obligations.

The Minister having immediately granted him the audience that he solicited, Maurice Evrard loyally brought him up to date on his intentions and on those of Mr. Aubry.

There was no risk, however, in this noble and energetic attitude; because his part was taken, and he had formally decided, should the Minister forbid him from quitting his homeland, to ask to be demobilised in order to be able to carry out the plan that he had assigned himself freely.

But much to the contrary, after having listened to him with the most perfect benevolence, the Minister declared to him that far from opposing this project which he considered hardy but natural, he was prepared, within his means, to facilitate the plan's execution.

However, in order not to implicate the government of which he was part, he declared:

"Officially I must ignore what you are going to do; also you will go immediately, on leaving here, to draft a request for leave of two months on family business. During this time, I will close my eyes to your actions and I can guarantee you that all your superiors will do the same.

"But promise me that you will be careful, very careful; and give me leave to wish that you will return promptly with your fiancée and that dear Mr. Aubry, to resume in our France the place that you occupy so well. Because we need you, my friend."

"Minister," said Captain Evrard, carried away by emotion, "I thank you with all my heart for your generosity towards me."

"Goodbye for now, captain, and good luck," wished the Minister of War as he shook the aviator's hand cordially.

And leading him to the door of his office, he added:

"As soon as you see Miss Aubry, tell her that not only do I wish to be a witness to her marriage, but that I'm also reserving for that day a surprise which, I hope, will undo some of the damage of all the trials that she has endured for her country."

"I thank you again, Minister, your commission will be carried out."

"Then you are hopeful?"

"Very hopeful, Minister."

"Until that happy hour!"

Some days afterwards the escape plans were stopped completely.

"The special saw that I have prepared," Jean Aubry could say to Germaine's fiance, "makes no noise. You can go and try it out yourself. In one hour, a twelve year old child could saw through an iron bar half as thick as my arm. As to the ladder that I am in the process of constructing, it is composed of a whole system of metallic links, and it will combine solidity with lightness. Of completely reduced dimensions, it will not be difficult to pass it to Germaine at the same time as the saw."

"But once Germaine is at liberty, what will we do?" Captain Evrard asked then. "We will have the whole of Germany to cross. We can't dream of the railway, and a car, however fast it may be, still presents dangers; because even granting that the Citadel's garrison could not run to our pursuit there is the telephone and the telegraph. The alarm will be raised quickly in every direction and we will pass several checkpoints before reaching the border."

"We will not have recourse to the railway, nor the automobile," declared Aubry, whose eyes had just lit up with true pride and focused strength. "The Germans have stolen the plans for my combat aircraft Mark I, but with my new plans, we have built the Mark 2 combat aircraft. It's with this that we will go to fetch Germaine and we will carry her back to France!"

Then, electrified in his turn, by this gigantic project, the aviator captain cried. "Yes, father! And it is I who will drive your new aircraft to victory!"

Mrs Evrard who was present at this meeting, could not hold back a stifled cry.

"Mother, understand me," the valiant aviator said immediately, taking her in his arms. "It must be done. It would be an act of cowardice to leave the care of going to deliver our dear prisoner to another. And then, am I not completely ideal to be Mr. Aubry's right arm in these circumstances? I was his collaborator when he acted to defend his country. I must play the same role now that he acts to save his daughter, that is to say she who must be and will soon be my wife."

And then, in these maternal anguishes, Mrs Evrard asked Jean Aubry to join her to dissuade her son from exposing himself to the dangers she apprehended.

Tenderly but energetically, the officer interrupted her by saying:

"If war broke out tomorrow, would either of you have the courage to prevent me from doing my duty? No, right? Ah well! Are we not in open war? And by what reckoning do we not have business with these disloyal enemies who have come to our home, provoked us basely, hypocritically, and who, sheltering behind the sacred laws of hospitality, have profited from them in order to dupe us in the most undignified way? Oh! Mother, dear mother, remember the beautiful story that you often recounted to me, a long time ago when, in the evening, before putting me to bed, you perched me on your knees.

"It was during the war of 1870. A great French writer, a poet, found himself in Geneva, sick, at the point of inspiring the gravest worries in his friends. As soon as he learned of our first retreat, he showed an ardent desire to return to France.

"His friends objected: 'What will you do? You are incapable of camping, of holding a rifle, of burning a cartridge!'

"So the poet, in a fit of admirable patriotism, cried, with a voice full of sobs, 'Mother is under attack. I am going to her aid!' And straight away he left to do his duty.

"Well! What this poet did for his country, I can do for my fiancée."

This admirable mother, this woman for whom the heroism of this son that she loved had already cost her so many tears, said simply, stretching her arms out as though to bless him, "You are right, my son, I have no right to keep you here."

The inventor and the officer had soon finished their preparations.

The dismantled new aircraft was sent with all necessary precautions by the care of a special commissioner of General Security, Mr. Ernest Gautier, who was assigned to accompany them and to help them in their perilous task.

Then all three of them left separately, admirably camouflaged, absolutely unrecognisable under their disguises, and they arrived with Chantecoq who had been warned by his superior.

The news that awaited them on their arrival forced them to adjourn the execution of their plans.

Chantecoq, who had the safest methods of being well-informed, had just learned that Wilhelm II, following a meeting with General Staltenheim, Minister for War, General von Talberg, Chief of Staff, Colonel Hoffmann, Chief of the Intelligence Bureau, and Councillor Ritchel, charged with the transfer of the detainee from the Julius Tower, had decided that Germaine Aubry would appear at nine o'clock the day after next before a secret tribunal appointed especially for this serious business.

Time was running seriously short to break out the valiant young girl before her appearance before these judges.

It was impossible to successfully deliver the instruments of escape to her!

The aircraft which was so indispensable to the

enterprise's success had not yet arrived and as a consequence could not yet be ready.

When reverting to the classic method, consisting of corrupting one of Germaine's gaolers with the bait of a large sum of money which there was no time to procure, it was vital not to think of more in the presence of such a short delay; because this negotiation demanded precautions, improvisations, the precise choice of the man who should be addressed.

What methods remained to them?

"To try a show of strength?" Chantecoq suggested. "However strong our ardour, our courage and our will to succeed, I doubt that the four of us would manage to storm Spandau Citadel and put the garrison to the sword."

"So, in your view, Mr. Chantecoq," the young aviator asked avidly, "what must we do?"

"Await events," the French agent responded cleanly, "and ready ourselves for all eventualities."

"I will not hide from you," he added, "that when I learned that the trial had been brought forward in such an unexpected way I was, no, not discouraged – because this is a sentiment that I affect not to understand – but very emotional, pained, and even tormented by this unforeseen *contre-temps*. All the same, thinking about it hard, all is far from being compromised. Effectively one of two things will happen: after her conviction, which is inevitable, Miss

Aubry will either be held in Spandau Citadel, and then things will remain in the same state, or she will be sent to another prison.

"Well! If this last alternative comes to pass, I guarantee that the prisoner will not arrive at her destination. We will have snatched her before! At that moment, an assault will be possible. If four people can not take a citadel by force, they can still stop a train and even disperse an escort. When one has with one a genius inventor such as Mr. Aubry, an officer as valiant as Captain Evrard and a detective as skilful as Mr. Ernest Gautier, the battle is already won!"

"Bravo!" the special commissioner applauded.

"You forget just one thing," said Maurice Evrard, "that is to say that when one is led by a general such as you . . ."

"I am not a general," Chantecoq interrupted. "I am just a good Frenchman and your devoted friend."

CHAPTER FOURTEEN:

Secret Tribunal

Germaine, from her prison, had no idea of what was afoot in order to save her.

Held in the most rigorous secrecy, narrowly watched by vigilant guards, no news from outside could reach her.

Without doubt, she thought, her arrest was known in France. Her loved ones, her father, her fiancé and that good Mrs Evrard, who loved her like her daughter, must be plunged into profound misery.

In absolute secrecy, she had no news from outside.

Beyond Commandant Fürsner, who particularly watched over his prisoner and who had only hateful and brutal words for her, she saw only the sentry stationed at her door and a woman who brought her food under the surveillance of an officer and who never addressed a word to her.

One day, the Citadel Commandant entered Germaine's cell, and, without any preamble, declared in the angry tone to which she was accustomed from him.

"I come to warn you that at nine o'clock tomorrow morning you will appear before the Empire's secret tribunal charged with pronouncing a verdict on your case. Consequently you have time to prepare yourself to appear before your judges. Here's a list of lawyers from whom you may choose a defence counsel. Finally you are authorised to designate the names of witnesses that you would like to be heard."

"You see," he added, "that the intention of the government is to surround your trial with all possible guarantees. I therefore engage you to take a different attitude to that which you have adopted up to this point."

Germaine, slowly, with an assured voice and looking her gaoler straight in the face, said simply, "I believed that in Germany spies were tried before the court in Leipzig. Why this exceptional treatment with regard to me?"

"I am not here to discuss with you!" said Fürsner coarsely.

"So be it, then you may leave, Mr. Governor; whatsoever the special jurisdiction that is imposed on me, I am ready to present myself before those that you call my judges."

At these words, the commandant's face turned purple with rage; but he contained himself, and in this gruff aggressive tone, which never left his voice, he said, "You have not given me an answer on the subject of your defence counsel."

"I have no need of one," the Frenchwoman responded proudly. "I shall defend myself."

"That's your affair. As to the witnesses that you wish to call?"

"I need only one," declared Germaine in a firm voice. "Lieutenant Wilhelm Ansbach."

"All right! I will transmit your wish to the authorities."

Commandant Fürsner left, leaving the prisoner a little relieved, because she preferred struggle to the inaction into which she had been plunged.

Germaine spent the whole day reflecting on the line of conduct that she would hold.

Her methods of defence would be extremely simple; because she had resolved to recognise the facts such as they had happened, having no other preoccupation than not to speak a word capable of compromising Chantecoq.

She had understood that this agent had not been discovered, as they had obstinately tried to make her denounce her accomplices.

As to her, she would not appeal to the judges' compassion; she would tell the truth, that was all!

For the first time since her incarceration, the inventor's daughter slept all night, peacefully.

She awoke the next morning around six o'clock, her brain extremely free and her heart beating out that generous bravado which she had already proved so many times in such perilous circumstances.

At half past eight, Commandant Fürsner appeared, accompanied by four armed infantry soldiers.

"Follow me!" he commanded the prisoner.

Germaine obeyed.

"The final battle!" she murmured between her teeth. "But whatever happens, show no weakness! I hold the French flag in my hands."

She was led to a small waiting room, where she remained under the Commandant's exclusive guard.

Through an oak door garnished with solid iron bars, she heard a confusing sound of voices, an indistinct murmur revealing to her the presence of several people in the neighbouring room.

Soon this door opened, making way for Colonel Hoffmann who said simply, "Commandant, bring in the accused!"

Germaine entered a huge Gothic hall illuminated by huge stained-glass windows.

Councillor Ritchel, an insipid figure in a uniform too large for him, flanked by a colonel from the Horse Chasseurs of the Imperial Guard, and on the left by a colonel of the White Cuirassiers, were seated at a table.

Parallel to them, Lieutenant von Limbürg, his Majesty's aide-de-camp, was sitting in an armchair, beneath a large portrait representing Kaiser Wilhelm II.

Beyond that, nothing. Not a single other thing. Not even a sentry.

It was the most complete, the most absolute closed session.

Commandant Fürsner led the Frenchwoman to a simple wooden stool placed in the middle of the room, opposite the tribunal. Germaine seemed almost lost in the immensity of this hall.

Colonel Hoffmann had disappeared.

Without any preamble, the debates began.

Commandant Fürsner, who filled the functions of both prisoner's guard and court clerk, read the imperial decree by which this strange special High Court had been convened, before which the young Frenchwoman had been called to appear. With an incomparable cynicism, the decree justified the constitution of this secret tribunal by alleging that the facts were much too serious not to remain absolutely hidden, that even before Leipzig's supreme court indiscretions could be committed, and that these indiscretions, in signalling the outrages and misdeeds committed by Germaine Aubry, risked provoking worse than anguish, that is to say discouragement, throughout Germany, etc, etc . . .

Germaine listened to the reading of this document with haughty impassivity.

Two or three times, she shrugged her shoulders, reflecting, "Why have they not thrown me straight into an oubliette?

"In any case, the only thing that interests me at the moment," she said to herself with implacable resolution, "is to find myself again face to face with that Wilhelm Ansbach and to spit upon him before everyone, once again, my contempt and hatred!"

As soon as Commandant Fürsner had completed his reading, Councillor Ritchel, who was presiding, attacked with a nasal, quavery voice.

"Are you the person named Germaine Aubry?" the President questioned.

"Yes, sir."

Desirous to conduct the proceedings with judicial correctness, Councillor Ritchel continued.

"You were born in Paris on January 6th, 1891?"

"Yes, sir."

"I have to put an opening question to you. Are you disposed to respond frankly? I must, actually, warn my assessors that during the investigation which has been entrusted to me, I have been able to obtain nothing from you, other than words imprinted with the most odious insolence."

At these words, Germaine declared, "Sir, I shall respond to you first by protesting with all my energy against the parody of justice which is being conducted now with regard to me."

The President immediately interrupted her by hitting the table with a copper paper-knife.

"Enough! I see that you persist in your attitude. You are wrong. You are here before magistrates who are enamoured of justice and of truth, conscious of the duty which is incumbent upon them and not, as you seem to believe, incapable of pity! I'll even go so far as to warn you loyally that our verdict will be influenced by your attitude. I do not need to say anything more of this to you; you are too intelligent not to have understood me.

"I now enter the depths of the proceedings. Do you accept that you introduced yourself, with the aid of false documents, into the home of General von Talberg, Chief of Staff of the German Army?"

"Perfectly."

"And that you did that with the aim of engaging yourself in the most intense espionage?"

The Frenchwoman replied with an incomparable sang-froid, "With the aim not only of getting my hands on documents that had been stolen from my father, but also to take from you, in my turn, as much as I could remove."

"There's a declaration which will singularly abridge your cross-examination," highlighted the President, leaning in turn, with dislocated dancers' gestures, towards each of his assessors.

"Do you really believe," replied Germaine, "that I intend to try, through hypocritical denials and lies, to conceal an act which will be the proudest of my life?"

"Enough!" Councillor Ritchel interrupted again, shaking with comical anger.

And, turning successively towards the White Cuirassiers colonel who was curling his moustache belligerently, and towards the Chasseur colonel who was drumming out a military march on the table, he exclaimed with indignation, "There! What did I tell you? Intractable. I believe that we have only one thing to do, and that is to hear the witnesses. Ah! However, one final question. Accused, have you decided today to tell us if you had accomplices?"

"I have nothing to say to you," Germaine said disdainfully.

"So, let us continue. Commandant, bring in Colonel Hoffmann."

Commandant Fürsner opened the door placed at the back of the room and the Chief of the Intelligence Bureau appeared.

He no longer had that cold, stuffy air, that wooden face with an indecipherable expression; instead a sort of contentment was visible on his features, and his gaze showed at once both triumph and hatred.

"Colonel Hoffman," said the President, "I am charged to congratulate you in the Emperor's name for the zeal, intelligence and subtlety which you have demonstrated in these circumstances."

Hoffman automatically raised his hand to the top of his helmet and let it fall pronouncing, "At your service, Councillor."

"Please describe to us the circumstances in which you were led to discover that the accused was a spy in the employ of France."

Colonel Hoffmann's declaration was dry, as if he were reading a police report.

"For some time, my attention had been drawn by leaks which occurred not only within my service, but even within that of the Chief of Staff; I immediately established surveillance and I was first struck by the fact that these leaks coincided in a striking manner with the arrival at General von Talberg's home of a certain German governess named Bertha Stegel. Discreetly, I gathered information about her and it was not long before I was certain that the information that had been provided about her was absolutely false, that she had not been born in the town from which she pretended to have originated, no more than she had practised her profession in the families by whom she was recommended. I was certain.

"There remained nothing more than to catch the criminal red-handed. That is what I did. I immediately warned General von Talberg and we surprised Germaine Aubry rummaging in the Chief of Staff's strongbox."

"Is that all, Colonel?"

"Yes, President."

"Thank you. Go and sit down."

Hoffman took a place on a chair next to von Limbürg's aide-de-camp, who was appearing to follow the proceedings with a feverish attention and never ceased, with a fountain pen, taking notes in a pocket book.

"Accused," said Councillor Ritchel, "have you heard Colonel Hoffmann's deposition? What do you have to say?"

"Nothing."

"Introduce the second witness," the President ordered.

It was Colonel Skoppen who appeared.

"Tell us what you know on the subject of the Aubry affair," Councillor Ritchel invited him straight away, as if eager to be finished.

"President, having received the order from General von Talberg to fetch various documents concerning mobilisation from the armoured cabinets, I was stupefied to observe that a certain number of them had disappeared. I immediately reported to the general. That is all I know, it is all I may tell you."

"However," the inquisitor asked, "these cabinets were the subject of a very special and most serious surveillance."

"Yes, President. The three officers charged with this mission had been the victim of the most subtle piece of misdirection that one could imagine."

"They are here," interrupted Councillor Ritchel, "and I believe that the best thing would be to hear them immediately.

"Commandant, bring in Major Schlaffen."

The German Empire's immortal champion of sleeping at will appeared, piteous, disconcerted and still trembling at the thought of the imminent retirement which threatened him.

He only repeated what he had already said to General von Talberg, humbly vowing that he had been duped and declaring that, from that moment, he had lost that faculty of which he was so proud, of being able to sleep whenever he wished.

Major Tourchtig succeeded him.

The Kingdom of Bavaria's invincible champion of Munich beer confirmed his comrade's declarations and expressed the same regrets.

Then it was the turn of Major Hunguerig.

The province of Hesse Nassau's incomparable champion of Frankfurter sausage gave a third rendition of the account already offered by Majors Schlaffen and Tourchtig, declaring that he too had been heartbroken, desperately sorry for what had happened, and how much he also congratulated himself to see the guilty party under lock and key.

But the proceedings which had dragged until then, were to take a different tone with the deposition of General von Talberg.

When Germaine saw him close to her, majestic, superb, imposing in his grand uniform, she felt that the duel had only just begun.

Councillor Ritchel, full of deference towards he whom all considered as one of the Empire's military glories, said as graciously as possible, "General, the floor is yours."

With a voice in which one could feel a deep bitterness, von Talberg spoke:

"Sirs, I must first make honourable amends before you, as I have done before my Emperor, before my master. You represent my country to which I owe an account. I am going to give it to you. Interrogate me, I shall answer you."

"General," the President asked, "can you first explain to us the precise importance of the documents taken by Germaine Aubry?"

"The list of our counter-agents, the formula for a new explosive, our military convention with Italy and the mobilisation plans for our troops covering the Western front."

"Hell!"

"The act of accusation affirms that you surprised this woman in the act of exploring your strongbox."

"That is true."

"How did she come to possess the key and the secret?"

It was Germaine who answered.

"I had the key made on the outside. As to the secret,

I do not have to reveal to you the manner in which I managed to discover it."

Then, addressing the general, Councillor Ritchel added:

"In all probability, Germaine Aubry would have taken the key to the armoured cabinets in the Moltke Room from your strongbox?"

"For me, there is no doubt on that subject," agreed von Talberg.

"And once she discovered the secret of your strongbox, she was also able to discover the secret passage running between your office and this room."

"It could not be otherwise, President."

"All that seems perfectly clear to me. I thank you, general; you may sit down."

Addressing himself this time to Germaine, Councillor Ritchel said in the implacably severe tone of an impassive inquisitor:

"You have heard the witnesses?"

"There is one missing," replied the Frenchwoman, "the most important of all, Lieutenant Wilhelm Ansbach, otherwise known as Jacques Müller. I can't believe that Commandant Fürsner has not made you aware of my desire to confront him."

Then drily the President declared, "Lieutenant Wilhelm Ansbach has provided us with a certificate from the doctor at the military hospital affirming that he has not sufficiently recovered from his injuries to appear before the tribunal."

"That's a real shame!" Germaine replied, "because I could not have a better advocate."

"What do you mean by that?" Ritchel asked, narrowing his eyes.

"I mean that it would have sufficed for the spy Jacques Müller to tell you what he did at my home to justify entirely what I came to do at yours. But he is afraid to stand in my presence. He is even more cowardly than I thought!"

"I forbid you," yelled the President, "to speak in such a way of a German officer."

"A German officer who, having robbed my father, tried to assassinate me . . ."

"We are aware of your arguments," the President cut in, who had received orders to avoid all talk on the subject of Ansbach. "The daughter who avenges her father, the patriot who defends her country, it's obviously very touching. The tribunal will appreciate it."

At that moment, Colonel Hoffmann rose and, approaching the tribunal, said, "President, I would like to know if it was really Germaine Aubry who fabricated the false orders thanks to which Majors Schlaffen, Tourchtig and Hunguerig were far from their posts on the night of the theft."

"You hear that?" the President asked the accused. "What do you have to say?"

"It was I who forged these items," Germaine declared simply.

"In that case," insisted the Intelligence Bureau chief, "I am keen to know if it was the accused herself who entered the Moltke Room in the War Ministry."

"Since I attest that it was I who stole the plans," replied Germaine, staring proudly at the military policeman, "what does it matter to you knowing how I managed it?"

"You had accomplices, because you won't convince us that any woman, as skilful and as audacious as she may be, could, alone and with no help from anyone, have forced the locks, opened the strongbox, and passed through the walls. You must have had intelligence in place."

Then, Germaine spoke simply in a voice which struck all these fierce men before her full in the face, "So you have the habit of seeing traitors everywhere, to assume that there was one among you."

"Silence!" yelled the President.

"So be it! I'll say nothing more."

"The existence of accomplices is undeniable. These false certificates in the name of Bertha Stegel, it wasn't you who forged them, any more than the false key with the aid of which you opened the strong-box. Will you not respond?"

"You told me to shut up, so I'm shutting up."

"Germaine Aubry, even as I told you earlier, you are here before judges who have only one aim: to know the truth. But however great your crime, believe that we are not immune to pity. So I declare to you that if you decide to make a full confession, instead of striking you with final severity, we will be able to reduce your sentence's duration considerably."

"You're offering me a deal."

"If you like!"

"I understand," said the noble Frenchwoman with indignation, "this is not only in the interest of your national defence that, not content to demand that the proceedings take place in the most absolute closed session, I have been dragged before a special jurisdiction, before an exceptional tribunal to whom the verdict has been dictated in advance. No, it is again and especially because it is hoped, by frightening me with threats or by winning me by promises, to obtain from me some revelations which I do not want to make!

"Oh well! Yes, it's true. I had some people on the outside who helped me, who facilitated my task, who procured these certificates for me, these keys that I could never have forged myself. As for telling you their names, for delivering them to you, never!"

"So," remarked Ritchel, "you expose yourself to the maximum sentence."

"So what?"

"Once behind bars, you will regret your silence, but it will be too late: speak while there is time."

"Never!" Germaine resisted stoically. "To buy my freedom at this price would be an act of cowardice, and I am revolted at the thought that these are officers who dare to counsel me to such an infamy!"

At these words, everyone, with the exception of General von Talberg, always serious and pained, stood up, furious, threatening.

"This is too much!" groaned the Cuirassiers colonel.

"She insults us!" the Chasseurs colonel vociferated.

"Convict her!" Skoppen cried.

But Ritchel struck the table with his paper-knife. "Silence, gentlemen! Silence!"

And addressing Germaine: "Your cynical and provocative attitude would have been sufficient to attract to you the tribunal's extreme severity. However, out of pity for your youth, I want to try one last effort."

"It's useless!" the young girl responded bravely.

"Germaine Aubry, the only emotion that you have displayed in the course of this trial, and since your arrest, is when you spoke of your father and of your fiancé. I say to you only one thing: *think of them!*"

These words fell in an imposing, tragic silence.

Germaine, with an accent of touching faith and limitless heroism, declared:

"My father, sir, would renounce me as his daughter, if he learned that I had weakened for a moment! As to my fiancé, Captain Evrard, he too would renounce me if he knew that I owed my liberty to a base act!"

"Imagine," replied Ritchel, thinking to soften this indomitable energy resonating filial love in her, "yes, imagine that you could be separated from them for many long years, that your father could die without seeing you again."

"Courage!" Germaine said to herself without wavering.

But the inquisitor continued. "Imagine that your fiancé may grow tired of your attitude."

"Him? That's impossible," the inventor's daughter said drily.

"Twenty years of separation, that's a test any attachment can hardly resist, however powerful it may be. How do you respond to that?"

Then, grown more admirable through resigned sorrow and boundless sacrifice, Germaine cried, "I have only one thing to say to you: I am French!"

"Gentlemen, let's deliberate," Ritchel concluded, feeling that the game was lost for him!

While the three judges conferred in low voices, von Talberg approached Germaine who waited impassively, and quietly he said to her, "You unlucky woman, all is lost for you!"

"I know, general."

"When it would have been so easy for you to . . ."

"Don't go on," the Frenchwoman interrupted, "From the bottom of my heart, you give me reason . . ."

But already Councillor Ritchel was calling for silence.

The officers present immediately took the regulation attitude. Germaine was left standing in the middle of the hall.

The President stood and solemnly he recited this sentence:

"In the name of His Majesty Wilhelm II, King of Prussia, Emperor of Germany, by virtue of the decree of January 22nd, 1912, which constituted us in a secret court of supreme justice, after having heard different witnesses, collected the explanations of the accused and listened to her defence, we declare in our soul and conscience that the Frenchwoman Germaine Aubry is guilty of espionage, abuse of trust, forgery, use of forged documents, theft with burglary, etc. After having deliberated, considering that Germaine Aubry deserved an exemplary punishment, the court, refusing her the benefit of attenuating circumstances and judging her without possibility of appeal, condemns the said Germaine Aubry to twenty years of reclusion in a fortified place which will be given an ulterior designation by the military authorities.

"Germaine Aubry, do you have any observation to make on the application of the sentence?"

Then, taking in the tribunal with a gaze of admirable dignity and sublime bravado, superb, radiant, as must have been the martyrs who, while walking to their execution, sang the glory of their God, the heroic inventor's daughter cried with a vibrant voice, "*Vive la France!*"

CHAPTER FIFTEEN:

Chantecoq Plays the Guard

The secret tribunal's audience, in the course of which Germaine Aubry's fate was decided, had lasted barely more than an hour.

No sooner had the condemnation been pronounced, but Commandant Fürsner led the prisoner back to her cell, and left, after locking the door himself with perhaps greater care than customary.

"Twenty years!" the young girl murmured when her guard had left. "Nearly quarter of a century locked between these walls, deprived of all communication with the outside world, without news of my loved ones! The most beautiful years of my life spent in the most absolute isolation! Because these people will never disarm any more than I will weaken.

"In the end, as it is necessary, I will see it through and I will hold my head to the fatalism until it crushes me. My energy will fade only with my existence! It must never be said that a Frenchwoman failed in the task!

"And then, don't I have the very noble and powerfully comforting thought to console me that, not only have the combat aircraft plans not fallen into German hands, but that I have been able to remove documents that we had every interest to know about at home? I know that my father and Maurice are alive. Certainly, they must suffer bitterly, but they must also be proud!"

The fortress cook's wife presented herself at that moment with the prisoner's meal.

Commandant Fūrsner accompanied her, watching closely.

At the same time as the food, she was also brought an enormous pile of rough sheets, of coarse thick cloth, that was deposited on the table.

"Here is some work," said the fortress Commandant. "Condemned, you are henceforth required to work. These sheets must be hemmed."

And, drawing several bobbins of wiry thread, and a packet of enormous needles from his pocket, he added, "Here is everything you need. It is now your task for twenty-four hours. Your work must be completed tomorrow at midday; because if I saw that you show ill will, I would not hesitate to punish you!"

Without adding anything, he retired.

Germaine took one of the rough, thick sheets and, after a moment of hesitation, she set herself to work courageously.

Her fine and delicate hands were hardly trained for such a hard exercise. And then, be it from forgetfulness, be it from a truly inexcusable refinement of barbarism, she had not been given a thimble.

However, despite the stinging pricks, Germaine was not discouraged; and when her evening meal was brought to her, she had done half of the chore.

"Twenty years!" the poor prisoner repeated to herself in dejection.

But the discouragement barely persisted in this valiant soul. She got a grip on herself and, as if she was ashamed of her moment of weakness, a breath of a hope passed over her face, and she thought:

"Who knows? Perhaps I will be free earlier. Yes, I know I have not been abandoned. I have intuition, what can I say? The certainty that Chantecoq is working for me, that my father and my fiancé are going to consecrate all the energy, activity and strength that they possess to my freedom. And, an extraordinary thing, it seems to me that I am not far from them, that they are nearby, that they will come to see me and help, that they will take me away, that I will get out of here!"

Disoriented for a moment by Germaine Aubry's unexpectedly sudden judgement, Chantecoq had quickly come to his senses.

It had been understood between him, Mr. Ernest Gautier, the inventor and the captain, that they would wait to know the verdict before acting.

The four Frenchmen, who no longer left each other's company and hid themselves carefully in a fake retreat, had learnt the same evening of the unfortunate young girl's fate, by a laconic note that the government had finally decided to communicate to the press.

It was a titbit composed like this:

"This morning, a secret court, presided over by Councillor Ritchel, condemned a French governness arrested and charged with espionage to twenty years of solitary confinement in a fortified compound.

"Perhaps people will be astonished that the criminal was not deferred to Leipzig's Imperial Court; but in view of the gravity of the facts revealed and the necessity of acting as quickly as possible, the Imperial Council decided to divest this jurisdiction; and it will be the same in future each time that the Council judge it necessary."

"Twenty years of solitary confinement," Mr. Aubry despaired.

"The poor child!" Maurice Evrard murmured, his throat dry.

"It's frightening," said Mr. Gautier.

"Oh! Wait and see," replied Chantecoq. Anyway, this isn't the time to lose hope, to the contrary! I guarantee you that Miss Germaine will not serve her twenty years, or I will lose not just my name, but my hide!"

"You can tell that these people don't like the light," shouted Jean Aubry. "Why, really, did the Court of Leipzig divest this case?"

"They had a whole heap of reasons for that," replied the policeman. "First, I believe that it would have been strongly disagreeable to the government to bring Wilhelm Ansbach's conduct to light. Then, the Emperor was determined not to lose his Chief of Staff by the wayside. Finally, he must have been opposed to the list of documents that Miss Germaine took being divulged."

"It's very likely," approved Mr. Gautier, "but at the Court of Leipzig, closed sessions are generally ordered."

"Oh the closed sessions at the Court of Leipzig!" Chantecoq railed, "Three years ago, when the business of the Russian captain accused of having stolen the secret of a new powder, I heard from a certain source that the Russian government and even the French government got their hands on the trial's complete transcript, and I am sure, my dear Mr. Gautier, that you will not contradict me on this subject."

"It's true," confirmed the special commissioner who immediately suggested:

"Could we not profit from this brutal, illegal trial, by organising a campaign in France in favour of Miss Aubry?"

"Beware of that!" Chantecoq intervened brightly. "At the moment it is crucial that at all costs public opinion does not focus on our dear prisoner. It must be, to the contrary, that the French government gives the impression of disinterest and even to the need of disavowing her, so indispensable is it that it is believed that Miss Aubry's friends are completely discouraged. It is the first condition for us to be able to operate safely.

"Furthermore, my dear Mr. Gautier, it will do no good to write an epilogue for what has passed. We face a problem which can be summed up in four words: break out the prisoner. Let's not stray from that; and as you wanted to entrust the mission's leadership to me, I ask you to trust me."

"We trust you completely!" Mr. Aubry declared.

"We are ready to march under your orders," said the captain.

"And me," added Mr. Gautier, "I make abstractions of my situation, of my personality, in order to submit myself entirely to you."

"Very well!" said the French agent. "In these conditions, we are going to do excellent work."

"Tell us what we have to do," Germaine's impatient fiancé demanded.

"Nothing for the moment," replied Chantecoq. "It is vital that I go on reconnaissance and that I take an exact account of the situation. Therefore stay here quietly, where you are safe. It will not be long, I promise you; and I hope from this evening to bring you information interesting enough to allow us to embark on our campaign immediately. All right then, until this evening. If I return a little late, don't be anxious."

"Until this evening!"

A few moments later, Chantecoq left his home mysteriously, absolutely unrecognisable under the German infantry major's uniform that he had taken, all while transforming his face with rare agility into that of Major Schlaffen.

He took the train and went to Spandau, entering the fortress without difficulty, in front of the guard on the gate who saluted him.

Before anything else, it was important to orient himself.

The night was quite clear. The moon bathed the Citadel's ramparts with its discreet and soft light.

Chantecoq immediately looked all around the side of Julius Tower. He noticed that this tower was linked to the main part of the fortress by a rampart in the form of a round path, on which was stationed a guard, wrapped shivering in a limousine cloak, letting a helmet's tip and a rifle's bayonet emerge.

"It's just as I thought," Chantecoq said to himself. "I was not wrong in my predictions. That will work as on the roulette wheel."

The French agent took a lit lantern from beneath his coat, climbed the paths which joined the courtyard to the round path and went straight to the sentinel who must have been asleep, because he didn't move. It was only when Chantecoq was only a few steps from him that, deciding to come out of his torpor, he stood to attention heavily and asked in a thick voice.

"*Wer da!* (Who goes there?)"

"Major's rounds!" the audacious character replied imperturbably. And then the false major, approaching the soldier, said to him familiarly:

"Are we asleep then, my lad?"

"Oh! No, major."

Chantecoq said to himself, "I'm dealing with a brute. Providence is definitely on our side . . ."

And straight away he replied:

"It's cold tonight."

"Oh! Yes, major."

Then, drawing a small bottle from his pocket, the French agent who had put his lantern on the ground, uncorked the vial and pretended to drink several mouthfuls from its neck.

"That does a body good, a few drops of old kirsch," he said, smacking his lips. "Nothing like it to warm you up."

And brusquely, in a gruff tone, he asked the sentry, while holding out the bottle to him, "Fancy a drink, to my health?"

As though surprised, not believing his ears, the soldier hesitated to take the flask. Chantecoq almost forced it into his hand, saying, "Drink, and hurry up. You're going to give me some news."

This time, the sentinel dared not resist any longer, particularly because the most enchanting odour of cherries was escaping from the bottle.

Stimulated by the fake major who said to him, "Just drink it, you beast!" the German soldier swallowed several swigs and gave the flask back to Chantecoq, saying, "Thank you, major."

"It was good?"

"Oh! Yes, heats up the body."

"So much the better!"

And resuming his authoritative military tone, the fake major asked, "Nothing new?"

"Nothing new, major."

"And the prisoner?"

"The prisoner?" repeated the sentinel while stifling a yawn.

"Yes, the prisoner in Julius Tower."

"Earlier, she opened her window."

"Ah! She's not asleep, then?"

"No, major."

This time, the soldier not only yawned once more, but he tottered while saying: "I think I'm in trouble. Everything's spinning around me."

As though he had not heard this reflection, Chantecoq replied. "Was it long ago that you saw her, the prisoner?"

"Barely ten minutes, ma . . . major."

"You know your orders?"

"Yes, major. To pull . . ."

But the poor devil could say no more. Folding up on himself, he would have fallen on to the flagstones if, swiftly, Chantecoq hadn't held on to him.

"For a good half hour he will rest in a sleep heavier than lead," he said to himself, lowering the man gently on to the parapet.

Then, propping up the soldier immobilised by the old kirsch which contained a powerful narcotic, the French agent followed the round path to the foot of Julius Tower.

He picked up a piece of fine gravel, placed it in a slingshot with which he had equipped himself and, taking several steps back, he aimed at the prisoner's window.

After several moments, the window opened and Germaine's head appeared anxiously through the bars.

Seeing the silhouette of this German officer, which was picked out in a ray of light, the inventor's daughter drew back.

But, with a prompt gesture which verged on prodigious, Chantecoq, who had put a little rubber ball in the slingshot, sent it skilfully through the window.

On the ball, these simple words were written:

"We are working for you, your loved ones are well. Be brave. You will soon get out of here."

Chantecoq waited.

As soon as Germaine had read this message, her heart filled with unspeakable joy.

Immediately, tearing a shred of fabric, she pricked her arm with a needle and, wetting a hairpin in her own blood she wrote this answer.

"I was able to destroy the plans. All is saved. Reassure my loved ones."

Chantecoq was beginning to wonder how long he would have to wait, when he saw a pale white arm appear in the window's opening, and a ball of thread came to rest at his feet.

He picked it up and put it in his pocket carefully.

Then, recovering his lantern calmly, he said to

himself, "Now, let's try to find out what goes on in this tower and learn how Miss Aubry is guarded."

The French agent crossed a kind of medieval portcullis which gave access to the interior; then he walked down a corridor leading to the central staircase which was vaguely lit by some old-fashioned oil lamps, hanging from the ceiling here and there. But he soon encountered a thick cast iron grille, which obstructed the corridor's full width and height.

Behind this grille, a machine gun, its muzzle turned towards him, seemed to await all indiscreet visitors.

On the floor above, Chantecoq heard the sound of boots walking on flagstones; it was the sentries who held watch day and night, under orders to march constantly, to avoid being lulled into sleep.

"I really suspect," thought the French agent, "that it would not be possible to reach Miss Aubry from this side, which gave me the idea of the sling shot and the balls. But what luxurious precautions! I understand why the German gentlemen chose Julius Tower to lock up their captive. It benefits from defensive measures which protect war plunder; it's both very wise and very economical at the same time. But it's a tricky problem for me."

Judging that it would be unwise to use his Major disguise much longer in this place, he returned in the direction of the Citadel, passed back in front of the sentinel who was still sleeping, his head leaning against the parapet and his rifle at his side; he went down into the courtyard, extinguished his lantern, and headed towards the postern.

He needed to pass the postern unchallenged. The skilful agent was not unduly worried; he knew that the officers lodging in the fortress had permission to go out at all hours. It would only take one question from the duty officer, however, to embarrass him somewhat; so he took the option of walking quickly.

It was a good choice. No one left the post and he passed through saluting the sentry, who stood to attention.

In a few seconds, he was outside.

He hurried, because there was only one train left to get back to Berlin.

Great was the surprise of Jean Aubry, Captain Evrard and Mr. Gautier who, unable to sleep, were smoking cigars and cigarettes while awaiting their friend's return, when they saw Chantecoq appear in this costume around two o'clock in the morning.

Straight away, they bombarded him with questions.

"It's going very well," said Chantecoq, "I'm doing my best work."

"You saw Germaine?" Maurice Evrard asked.

"Yes, captain, I saw her."

"Were you able to speak to her?" Aubry questioned him impatiently.

"No, but I was able to correspond with her with the help of a stratagem that I will describe to you in a moment. I was able to let her know that we are watching over her and that we are going to put everything in place to rescue her, and here is her reply."

While speaking, Chantecoq had drawn the ball of thread from his pocket, under the stupefied eyes of his friends.

"I wanted to give you the pleasure of revealing the message."

Breathless, Germaine's fiancé unwound the thread and, when he had finished, he found a little piece of batiste cloth on which the dear prisoner had written, with her own blood, these simple words which he read with a voice trembling with intense emotion:

"I was able to destroy the plans. All is saved. Reassure my loved ones."

"Is this possible?" Jean Aubry, the captain and Mr. Gautier all cried at once.

"She is admirable!" Chantecoq said.

"Miss Aubry must be free in a week!" the special commissioner said energetically.

"She will be, I swear!" the French agent assured.

"Or I will be dead," he added between his teeth.

"And me too," said Maurice Evrard, who had heard him.

CHAPTER SIXTEEN:

Unworthy

Faithful to his word, though it went against his heart, General von Talberg had recommended to the Emperor that Wilhelm Ansbach be promoted to the rank of captain.

While waiting to rejoin his Uhlan regiment at Colmar, the espionage officer had been admitted, officially, to see Frida.

One day when they found themselves alone, the general's daughter said to him point blank, "Now that we are going to be together, you must no longer keep secrets from me."

"But I don't have any, my dear Frida."

"Don't say that," the general's daughter persisted, while giving the Uhlan officer a look which revealed a heavy worry. She added, gently disengaging her hand which he had just seized, "It's not good for you to be so defiant with me!"

"I assure you I'm hiding nothing," protested the burglar of the combat aircraft plans.

But as the young girl hung her head, incredulous, disabused by his account, he continued: "Frida, you cause me a great deal of pain. Since my return, I can see that you are no longer the same with regards to me."

"What do you mean?" the pretty young Berliner replied. "It seems to me that there exists between us a sort of strange and mysterious constraint. Don't blame me for speaking to you like this."

"I'd much prefer it if you told me the truth. Anything rather than this uncertainty."

"Certainly, Wilhelm, I have nothing to reproach you for. Since your return, as before, you have not ceased to show your affection, your attachment. And yet this irritation that I see in you, I force myself in vain to understand it, I can not, at least . . ."

"At least . . . ?" repeated the false Jacques Müller, who seemed truly anguished.

As the young girl kept quiet, the Uhlan officer continued, "You weren't unaware that I was in France."

"I'd like to know what you did there."

"Nothing bad I suppose, as on my return your father, who knew the whole truth, didn't hesitate to grant me your hand, fulfilling the most ardent wish of my life as he did so."

"It's just," said the young girl, "I have followed this reasoning twenty times . . ."

CHANTECOQ AND THE AUBRY AFFAIR

"But what do you want?"

"I'd like to know the truth too. I won't go so far as to tell you that your refusal to reveal it distances us. No, but it puts a kind of shadow over my mind, over my heart. It's not female curiosity, either. My soul is incapable of such a sentiment."

"Doubt has entered your mind, I see that only too well."

"No, not doubt."

"What, then?"

"I don't know. Something like constraint, sadness."

"Believe me, if I could speak, I would. Because although you keep for France a sympathy that I can explain only by your distant origins, I would be very proud to tell you everything that I did over there. But I am bound by my word. Your father has forbidden me from revealing anything of my mission. Ask him to relieve me of my engagement, and I would be all too happy to break a silence which now weighs heavier on me than on yourself. For all the world, I would not want to prolong a situation which I truly feel may diminish your affection, which is less armed than mine to defend itself against the traps that life sets for it."

"Well! Let's go and find my father!" said von Talberg's daughter with an impressively grave voice. "I will ask him to relieve you from your oath. He will do it, I'm sure, because when I tell him what is going on with me, perhaps he will scold me; but he will certainly understand my worries and he loves me too much not to want to appease them immediately."

"So be it!" the officer accepted. "Let's go and find the general."

Wilhelm Ansbach, sombre, worried, brows knitted, mouth contracted by a crease which gave his face an expression of savage hardness, followed his fiancée.

They both reached the antechamber where the immutable Ulrich stood guard.

"Is my father alone?" Frida questioned.

"Yes, miss," replied the giant.

"Please let him know that Captain Ansbach and I wish to speak to him."

The orderly disappeared, only to return a few moments later, announcing with his usual impassivity, "The general will see you now."

Frida and the officer went into the Chief of Staff's office.

On seeing his daughter, the general gave a smile full of melancholy tenderness.

"My dear child, doubtless you are coming," he said, "to ask about preparations for your marriage? Oh well! Speak quickly, I have a formidable amount of work to finish before this evening."

Then the young Berliner, fixing her father in her gaze, with that frankness which was so young, so candid, which characterised her, said with such a firm tone that the general was immediately impressed:

"Father, I would like you to release Captain Ansbach from his promise."

"What promise?" von Talberg asked, surprised.

"Not to reveal to anyone in the world what he did during his travels abroad."

"What!" the general snapped with a certain vivacity, addressing the officer, "you told my daughter . . ."

"No, general," explained the false Jacques Müller, "Miss Frida so insisted that I tell her the whole truth, that I was forced to admit to her that it was on your orders that I was obliged to be silent."

"Why, my daughter, are you so determined to know the details of your fiancé's mission?"

"Because, father, I am not at peace."

"Not at peace!"

"I don't want there to be any secrets between Wilhelm and me."

"And if I told you that the State's will opposes him speaking?"

"I would answer that the State's will is a truly cruel thing, as it creates an obstacle between my fiancé and me which, I won't hide it from you, risks weighing heavily on our destiny. He went to France. For several weeks, we waited with no news of him. Oh well! I want to live those few weeks with him, I want to know where he spent them, in what circumstances he was wounded . . .

"Perhaps I am wrong, I admit! I ought not to be so demanding, so indiscreet. I ought to be proud of him. I ought to defer to you. However there is in me almost an obsession which pushes me to claim instantly from you both an enlightenment that I judge to be indispensable to our happiness. I have struggled with myself, it's strange! At the moment where my brain tells me 'you are wrong!', my heart answers. 'You are right.'"

And turning to the captain, the general's daughter added:

"Don't blame me for speaking like this. I assure you, I have no suspicion against you. I am obeying a sort of instinctive force completely independent from my will. I don't want our union to be tarnished by this mysterious shadow that I feel hanging over our heads."

Von Talberg had not stopped listening to his daughter with the greatest attention.

He reflected, hiding as best he could the emotion which was provoked in him and which grew in strength as Frida spoke. "Without knowing it and without anything precise in mind, the dear child has a clear intuition that her fiancé is unworthy of her. This sort of mysterious warning dictates my duty."

Then he replied in a firm and assured voice. "I suppose that there must not be any obstacle between two hearts which are on the point of being united. I therefore authorise you, captain, to reveal to your fiancée - but to her alone, you hear – what you did in France."

"Thank you, general," replied the Uhlan officer. "I will reassure your daughter straight away!"

And addressing Frida, he continued:

"What I did in France, any good German would have done in my place. I learned that a French inventor had just finished the plans for a combat aircraft which would have been very dangerous for us, and I resolved to get hold of them.

"I got hold of them, in fact, but at the moment where I was returning to Berlin with them, an accident happened a few yards from the border that immobilised me for several weeks, and that's what prevented me from giving you any news of me, because that would have lost me for sure.

"Oh! If you only knew what a trance I was in! It's unimaginable! I told your father all my patriotic concerns. Let me tell you now those which tortured me while thinking of you. I lived through hours – what am I saying – *weeks* of agony. It was only by keeping you close in my thoughts that I managed to forget the dreadful situation in which I found myself, in the French hospital at Lunéville in which I found myself, where I risked being recognised at any instant.

"Finally I managed to escape this strange nightmare. I had secured my liberty, I had escaped the dangers that I faced, I was in possession of the plans for the combat aircraft, I was bringing them to your father. At the end of my strength, exhausted, almost in agony, but triumphant all the same, I arrived in General von Talberg's office and as, defiant, I threw these precious papers on the table, a woman lunged forward suddenly. She leapt on the documents and cast them into the fire, so destroying all my efforts and compromising all my hopes."

The pretty Berliner had listened to her fiancé with every appearance of absolute impassivity.

When he had finished, she asked, with a cold tone which struck the German officer as disagreeable, even painful. "So, which woman is this who was found in my father's office and who, as you say, destroyed your effort?"

With a look, Wilhelm Ansbach questioned General von Talberg, who followed this moving debate with intense attention.

"Speak, captain!" the Chief of Staff ordered. "I told you, you are free from all secrecy. I trust my daughter. I know she will hold her tongue, when even . . ."

But, fearing to show his thoughts too clearly, he did not finish the sentence he had on his lips. He added, "Answer the question that has just been put to you!"

"Oh well," replied Ansbach, "that woman was your governess, Bertha Stegel, the French spy that a High Court just condemned to twenty years' detention."

"Germaine Aubry!" Frida cried, growing pale.

"Yes, Germaine Aubry!" Wilhelm Ansbach insisted, as his eyes glinted with hatred.

Then, mastering the disquiet which had taken hold of her, the general's daughter replied, "Why did she do that?"

"But . . . to accomplish her spying mission."

"So she knew the value of the documents you were carrying?"

"She knew them better than anyone," said the Uhlan officer, "as it was her father from whom I stole them."

"From her father?"

"Yes, from her father."

There was silence.

The pretty Berliner's pure, noble soul had done better than uncover the truth, to raise a corner of the veil. The curtain had been lifted entirely, revealing to her eyes, the ambitious upstart officer, torn from his pedestal, not recoiling before any method to achieve his goal.

Suffocating with pain and shame, holding back the tears which were torn from her by the horrible disappointment that overwhelmed her, she said in a trembling, broken voice, "You did that?"

"Yes, I did that!" replied the spy, affecting a pride he was no longer feeling, because he read in Frida's eyes how much his revelations had just dug an uncrossable chasm between them.

Slowly, as if she wanted to give a capital value to each of her words, Miss von Talberg declared, "Germaine Aubry only did her duty by trying to take back what you took from her father!"

"What, Frida!" exclaimed the officer. "You defend this woman who infiltrated your house traitorously? You take this spy's part!"

"This spy!" the general's daughter cut in. "What were you, yourself, when you were over there, in France, in order to take possession of something which didn't belong to you?"

"How cruel you are!"

"I'm fair! In wartime, that's different; one fights however one can, but to act in this way in times of peace is unworthy of an officer."

"Still with your French sympathies!" Captain Ansbach let this escape his lips clumsily.

"My French sympathies have nothing to do with all this!" the young girl yelled with a vehemence that managed to flummox the fake Jacques Müller and plunged von Talberg into frank astonishment. "Germaine Aubry could have been Swiss, English, Spanish, Italian, it doesn't matter! Whatever the consequences of her act for my beloved father and for my country, I could not prevent myself from not only pitying her with all my heart, but still to say to myself, 'after all, she did her duty!'

"And now, let's leave it there! I am too frank, Wilhelm, to hide from you how much you are diminished in my eyes. Until now I saw you as a noble and loyal officer. I was wrong, I was under an illusion on your account."

Ansbach's spite transformed into a cry of rage that only the presence of his superior prevented from bursting out.

Yet, in a cutting voice, he said, "And yet it was for you, to obtain your hand, that I accomplished this act that you judge so harshly and that I persist in finding worthy of approval from all good Germans who are truly attached to their country!"

"And I persist in finding it unworthy," Frida riposted. "Anyway, let's finish it! It's useless to prolong a conversation which, I won't hide it from you, is deeply painful to me. You have broken my heart, to such a point that I can no longer love you. I understand now why, on your return, I did not feel transported with joy. I had an intuition that you had something truly evil on your conscience. That was all too true!"

No longer capable of containing the fury agitating him, Wilhelm Ansbach cried out, "And so to the end, I find this Frenchwoman in my way! From the depths of her prison, she pursues me, defies me still. Ah! Frida, how happy she would be if she learned of your decision! But I don't believe that it is irrevocable."

"You should know me better, Wilhelm. I have taken back my heart from you, it's not for you to give it."

"Ah! The swine!" squeaked the officer.

"Don't take it out on this woman," protested the general's daughter, "better to blame yourself, because it was you who did all the damage."

But, pale with rage, Ansbach replied, "When I asked General von Talberg for your hand, he answered me: 'You want my daughter, deserve her!' I sought to accomplish some spectacular action which would allow me to realise my dream, and now see how what I have done has turned back on me, it's too unfair!"

"No, it's not unfair," responded Frida with an almost religiously serious tone. "You had no need to conquer me; it was just a question of obtaining my father's consent. Do you believe therefore that, to attain this goal, there was no other way than that which you chose? Do you believe, in place of burgling a French inventor and unleashing a whole storm which will have the result of enfeebling your country and condemning an unfortunate to twenty years in prison, yes, do you believe that it would not have been more glorious to leave for the colonies for a year or two and to accomplish there one of these exploits which make it said of a man: 'he is a hero' and not: 'he is a spy!'

"I waited for you, Wilhelm; and I am sure, when you would have returned, I would not have had my heart wrung by unknowable anguish and I would not have been prey to mysterious worries: 'Why am I not happier to see him again?'

"One last time, Wilhelm, on leaving here, bear no rancour against anyone. Follow the path that you have chosen for yourself. I can no longer follow it with you. Farewell!"

"Farewell, miss," said the officer, bowing, his heart thumping with rage, before she who had just displayed so much tact, dignity and nobility.

Then, saluting his leader, he pronounced in a different voice, "Farewell, general!"

Von Talberg responded with a characteristic coldness to the Uhlan officer's salute, as Ansbach reached the door at a nervous, jerky pace.

Then, when he had disappeared, the Chief of Staff, opening his arms wide to Frida, cried:

"Come and kiss me, my daughter! I am proud of you."

CHAPTER SEVENTEEN:

Emma Lückner

Obliged to leave Paris suddenly, and even France, Emma Lückner, henceforth burned in this country, had returned to Berlin, and at length she had recounted her long list of grievances to her boss, Colonel Hoffmann. Now, for her, there was revenge to be taken. Instructed on all the circumstances of the acts which had motivated the arrest and conviction of Germaine Aubry, she had employed herself with all her ardour, all her astute judgement, to discovering the accomplices that the Frenchwoman had not wanted to denounce.

It was to this task that the spy had resolved to dedicate herself.

She knew that she was dealing with a powerful opponent; but thanks to her feminine cunning and to the ruses that she used, with the competition above all of the agents under her orders, she flattered herself that she would triumph and revenge herself on those who, by signalling to the French authorities, had forced her to clear off in order to avoid an imminent arrest which she had been able to foresee in time, and which had put an end to the agreeable time she had spent in Paris, with the generous grant awarded her by the Chief of the Intelligence Bureau.

Emma Lückner had given a different mission to each of her agents. Through them, she hoped to discover all those who had aided the combat aircraft inventor's daughter in her work.

How great was her surprise and joy when the first, Jean Lenoir, one of her agents, a miserable Frenchman, arrived with his eyes shining, his stride confident, and announced, "I found the locksmith who made the fake key to General von Talberg's strongbox."

"You've been blessed by an incredible stroke of luck!" said the spy.

"No, I just had to have a bit of savvy. I said to myself, 'As it was a Frenchwoman who used this key, there's a ninety-nine percent chance that it was another Frenchman who was charged with the work.' I was right. It was a Parisian like me who carried out this bit of work! I had it confirmed this very morning."

"He gave you a description of the person who ordered this key?" Emma Lückner asked.

"No chance was I going to question him about that. I'd have put him on the alert immediately and I wouldn't have got anything else."

"So this locksmith?"

"He's called Louis Brunon. He's an honest man but he's still in one of those deep messes which it will be difficult for him to get out of. I did a little digging, and that's how I knew he was on the verge of bankruptcy. What's more, he has an anaemic wife and a consumptive daughter on his hands, so he no longer has the means to buy steel and iron in order to work. I'm also sure that, crafty as you are, it will be a game for you to tweak his nose, while coming to his aid."

"What's more," added the informer, "as I thought you'd be keen to make his acquaintance, I brought him with me, under the pretext that you had an urgent repair to order from him."

Pointing at a huge trunk with a strong copper lock, Jean Lenoir insinuated, "Such as opening this thing for which you have supposedly lost the key. What do you say to that, boss?"

"All my compliments! Admirable manoeuvring."

"Is it worth a little bonus?" sneered Lenoir, pointing out a chequebook which was lying on the desk. Without answering, Emma Lückner opened the book, wrote out a cheque and, having detached it, she held it out to her colleague.

"Fifty quid!" said the agent with a grimace. "It seems to me it's worth a bit more than that!"

"We'll see, when I've chatted with this locksmith," replied the spy. "Go and bring him in."

Jean Lenoir went to the door, opened it and brought in Louis Brunon.

He was a man of thirty years whose sickly face revealed long fruitless struggles. In his eyes, there was an expression of sadness that had very nearly become despair.

"Leave us!" Emma Lückner told her agent, who went out immediately.

She pointed out the trunk to the artisan who had brought his working instruments with him in a black leather sack that he wore on his shoulder, and in German, in a very good-natured tone, she asked, "My friend, could you open the lock of this trunk for me, for which I've idiotically lost the key?"

"Gladly, madam."

While the worker was starting to take out his tools, the spy, in French this time, asked, "I'm told you're Parisian?"

"Indeed, madam."

"I'm Russian, that is to say I love your country greatly, where I spend the largest part of my time. So when my assistant said that he knew the address of a French locksmith, I immediately gave him the order to go and seek you out."

"Madam is too kind."

After a moment, Emma Lückner replied, in the most natural tone: "Did you leave Paris a long time ago?"

"Seven years, madam," sighed Louis Brunon, seeming upset.

"What gave you the idea to come and set yourself up here?"

"In Paris I'd made the acquaintance of a young lady from Berlin. We both had a bit of money, and we got married. Then she wanted to return to her country, because of her mother. I couldn't refuse.

"I decided to establish myself here. At the start it wasn't going too badly. And then next door to me they set up a large hardware and metalwork company which took away three quarters of my clientele at a stroke. My wife fell sick, my little girl too . . ."

"Ah! You have a little girl?"

"Yes, madam. Only the poor little thing, she is like her mother, she's not hardy. If I could only send them both to the countryside! But no way of doing it. When bad luck is involved, you know, there's nothing to do."

"My poor boy."

While they had been speaking, Louis Brunon had succeeded in opening the trunk.

"There, madam, that's it."

"How much do I owe you?"

"A mark."

"That's not enough, my friend. Here's five."

"No, madam. That's too much."

"Even so. Keep it. It will be for your little girl."

"You really are too kind, madam. Thank you again."

"You've really interested me. Your language, so simple, has sincerely moved me. I would like to do something for you."

"You don't know me, madam."

"I have judged you, straight away, to be a very honest man."

"Yes, madam. I may say that I have always done my duty, and I assure you that it's hard for me to think that I owe money to my suppliers and that I will doubtless be unable to pay them."

"You are you going to think, my friend, that I am very indiscreet. How much do you owe?"

"Around twelve to fifteen hundred marks."

"No more?"

"That's a large sum for me!"

"Do you have no one who might be able to help you, to advance you that money?"

"No, madam. My wife's parents are dead; and in Germany, we other Frenchmen, we have no credit. Anyway, it would do no good! My house is lost and it would only be taking a step back in order to take a running jump. To get me out of this pickle, I'd need at least double that sum, so that once my debts were paid I could return to Paris and find a little corner to establish myself quietly, but securely this time. In

Berlin, I feel that for me there is nothing left and I shall never pick myself up."

"Would your wife agree to return with you to France?"

"Ah! I believe so! Nothing holds her here any more and she knows all too well that the climate of my country would be better for her than that of her own, as well as for our child, and that there I would have more heart in my work."

"That can be arranged."

"Who do you think would be interested in my fate?"

"Me, if you will let me."

"You, madam?"

"I can't repeat it enough, Brunon, you interest me greatly. Rightly, fate put me here at this moment to pull you out of the mess you find yourself in so unhappily."

"Is this possible?"

"Listen to me, my friend," said the spy, "this morning you received a visit from my assistant, who showed you a strong-box key, asking if it was you who had made it. You responded affirmatively. Now, for reasons I can't make you aware of, I have the greatest interest in knowing who this person was that placed this order. Do you know them?"

"Yes, I know them," the locksmith admitted very sharply.

"Their name?"

"I'm sorry, madam, but I may not give it to you."

"Whyever not?"

"Because I swore never to reveal it."

"If I told you however that the man for whom you have worked is a dangerous bandit, actively sought by the police, and that the keys he ordered from you have served him to commit the most serious burglaries, and even worse than that?"

"I would reply, madam, with all due respect, that there must have been an error. You really think so?"

"I'm sure of it!"

"I have been in contact with this person for a very long time and I know him to be incapable of committing the slightest indiscretion, let alone the crimes to which you are alluding."

"So, you won't tell me his name?"

"Not at any price."

"And if I didn't give you the four or five thousand marks which you need, but ten thousand, fifteen thousand, twenty thousand?"

"Useless, madam."

"It's fate, the very existence of your wife and your child which are at stake."

"I can only respond to you in one fashion, madam. I am an unfortunate boy, but I am not a dishonest man."

And, gathering his tools, Louis Brunon put them back in his bag that he slung over his shoulder and gave back to Emma Lückner four of the give marks that she had given him.

Then he saluted coldly and left.

"You have no idea, imbecile," snarled the spy, "that you just saved me twenty thousand marks, because your wife will speak to me, I promise you, without it costing me a pfennig."

Calling Jean Lenoir back in, she told him in this brief, imperative tone that she adopted when she was in an angry mood: "You are going to arrange things so that Louis Brunon's wife is here in an hour, and without her husband's knowledge."

"So it didn't work with the locksmith?"

"I don't have time for your questions. Go!"

"Oh!" said the informer to himself. "It's not the time to ask for an extra gratuity. The boss looks on edge."

But he knew all too well that he only had to carry out her orders and wait for the right moment to ask again for his reward.

Less than three quarters of an hour later, he brought Mrs Brunon into Emma Lückner's room.

The locksmith's wife, who had entrusted her little girl to a neighbour's care, had freshened up in order to be introduced to this great lady who, Jean Lenoir had told her, had important news to give her.

Mrs Brunon was quite a pretty lady of around twenty-eight. Very blonde, slim, pale, fragile, simply but properly dressed, she seemed to be a shy character; fearful, easily impressionable.

Emma Lückner had understood her from the start.

"Sit down then," she said with a certain haughtiness.

"Thank you, madam, I'm not tired," refused the poor woman, blushing.

"You are not carrying yourself well," insisted the spy, "and as we have to talk at quite some length, I would not want to keep you on your feet."

Mrs Brunon obeyed.

Then, having fixed her with one of those raptor looks that came naturally to her, Colonel Hoffmann's associate asked, "Has your husband filled you in on the conversation I had with him?"

"No, madam."

"Above all, speak frankly. It concerns very serious things. I won't hide from you that the fate of your husband and your child is in your hands."

"Oh! Madam . . ."

"Keep calm. Nothing is lost, everything can turn out differently, that will depend on the way you will answer me, hide nothing from me."

"Believe me, madam, that I am completely prepared to . . ."

"We shall see!"

Emma Lückner, holding her gaze and giving great emphasis to each word she spoke, continued. "Are you really up to date with everything your husband does?"

"Oh! Yes, madam, he is the best of husbands. Never has he hidden anything from me."

"Even in his commercial dealings?"

"No, madam. He trusts me completely, just as I have absolute faith in him. I know everything that happens in the workshop . . . unfortunately, not much does happen there."

"Yes, I know."

And with diabolical perfidity, the spy observed, "That's doubtless why Mr. Brunon became guilty of certain imprudences."

"What imprudences?"

"Perhaps you don't know about them."

"I assure you, madam, that my husband is the most honest man in the world, and that he is incapable . . ."

"Even of providing fake keys to burglars?"

"That, madam, surely."

"Then, as you are so up to date with his slightest activities, you are doubtless going to tell me the name of the individual for whom, several weeks ago now, he forged three fake keys, of which this is one?"

And the spy showed the locksmith's wife, now totally pale, the strongbox key that Jean Lenoir had given back to her.

Mrs Brunon, visibly appalled, remained silent and trembling.

I have her! The spy thought, and continued.

"I will not ask again. I simply want to warn you that I know from an absolutely certain source that the man who ordered these keys is no less than a spy in the pay of France. I know from an absolutely certain source that your husband may be arrested under suspicion of complicity in espionage and in burglary. That will mean the High Court, with five or six years of prison. Now, your husband will not talk; he is French in his soul, he won't betray one of his countrymen."

"It's true," the locksmith's wife acknowledged, in tears.

"But you, now you don't have the same reason to keep quiet. You are German."

"No, no . . . I am no longer German."

"Legally . . . but morally . . ."

"Legally *and* morally, I am Louis Brunon's wife. And by giving you his friend's name, that would betray him unworthily, and I don't want to!"

"So, you would prefer to see him thrown in prison?"

"He would prefer that than my consenting to talk to save him from arrest."

"And your child?"

"My little girl . . ." the poor woman murmured, completely shaken.

"She is sick, very sick, as are you."

"The poor darling!"

"In one word, you can condemn her or save her, because if you continue to hold your tongue, misery and death await you both. If you speak, it's a blessing for you; because I will arrange it so that not only will your husband not be bothered, but he also won't know that it was you who informed me. I add that, following this, I will do whatever is necessary to extricate you as soon as possible from the critical situation in which you find yourselves and that too, I promise you, without ever bringing your husband's suspicions on you.

"I have a long arm, very long, longer even than you can think. I know how to use it as much to strike those who oppose me without pity, as to reward generously those who serve me. I am giving you five minutes to reflect, no more! It's for you to decide, if for a miserable question of vain righteousness and conventional honour, you must allow an irreparable storm to devastate your home."

Emma Lückner fell silent.

Mrs Brunon, her head in her hands, was thinking.

Without doubt, the struggle within her was the most painful, the most tragic; because between her half-parted fingers, fat warm tears began to flow.

Then, clapping her on the shoulder, Colonel Hoffmann's auxiliary dropped this phrase which echoed like a funeral bell in the unfortunate's ears. "You have just one minute left."

The young girl stood up, reaching supplicating hands towards she who, implacably, tortured her. "Have pity," she moaned, in a voice broken with sobbing.

"His name?"

"But this is horrible! I can't . . ."

"His name, will you tell me?"

Mrs Brunon still hesitated.

But suddenly, a terrible vision struck her. She seemed to see her husband chained at the bottom of a dark dungeon. She heard him call in a desperate voice to save his daughter, his treasured little girl. Then, in the cradle towards which she was hurrying, the tiny thing that she took in her arms was cold, the child was dead . . .

Then, collapsing at the spy's knees, she cried, "I can't stand it any more, you want to know the name?"

"Yes, I do!"

"All right! It's . . . it's Mr. Chantecoq."

"Chantecoq! Good! Where does he live?"

"In Moabit, on the junction of Volberg and Steolver Street, between a bar and a bric-a-brac shop."

"Thank you, that's enough for me. You may leave."

And, getting to her feet wretchedly, the locksmith's wife moved towards the door.

Emma Lückner watched her leaving, murmuring, an infernal smile on her lips, "I think that this time Colonel Hoffmann is going to be happy with me."

CHAPTER EIGHTEEN:

A Difficult Rôle

Chantecoq!

The German spy knew the famous agent by reputation. She knew with what prodigious ease he transformed himself, changing personality with a virtuosity unequalled, and she knew that he was also gifted with herculean strength, incomparable audacity and unimaginable agility.

It could be said of him that he was untouchable.

Seizing him would not be an easy task; but difficulties didn't hold back Emma Lückner.

She knew the price that the Chief of the Intelligence Bureau would attach to this important capture, when he knew who they were dealing with.

She also knew that she could count on the three agents in her pay, Jean Lenoir, a Frenchman, Kouraguine, a Russian, and Elrick Maus, a German, who had already served her so well in France.

Emma Lückner intended to keep for herself all the merit and benefits of the operation and to seize he whom she considered to be Germaine Aubry's principal accomplice, without involving Colonel Hoffmann's police in the arrest.

She pointed this out to her affiliates while showing them in advance the difficulties in their task.

It was Jean Lenoir who suggested the plan of attack.

"As Chantecoq lives in Moabit," he said, "there's only one thing to do. Once his house is recognised, we will set ourselves up in the surrounding area, softly, discreetly, in such a way that no one would suspect a thing, and we will wait for the gentleman, choosing the right moment to fall on him and just stab him in the back."

"That's all very well," Maus objected, "But it's important not to be mistaken in this, and if Chantecoq metamorphoses to the point of being unrecognisable . . ."

"In spite of all his disguises, I would know him out of a thousand," the Parisian assured them. "It's enough just to have a bit of patience, to keep your eyes open and there. We hold the bird, it's up to us to prepare the blow."

"You are right," nodded the spy. "It's the best way to get hold of this man. All three of you go and get to work immediately. It's crucial that the attack and the abduction take place at night. Each evening, from ten o'clock, I will be permanently in an agreed place, close to Chantecoq's lodging, so that as soon as you have got hold of your man, you bring him to me and we'll head to the Colonel at top speed. Is that understood?"

"Yes, understood," the three bandits replied simultaneously.

"So, until this evening!"

"This evening," said Lenoir, "might be a bit too soon. But in any case, boss, you can be sure that this won't drag out!"

While the spy plotted in this way with her accomplices, Chantecoq, a hundred leagues from suspecting the danger that threatened him, continued to occupy himself actively with Germaine's escape.

According to him, after having reflected at length, there was only one way of delivering the ladder and saw created by Jean Aubry to the prisoner, and that was to corrupt Mrs Fürsner, the Citadel Commandant's wife, who alone had close access to her.

Towards this end, the French agent had succeeding in completely documenting the characters, habits even the mannerisms of the Commandant's wife. He learned that she had an unrestrained love of tapestries, and it was from this angle that he proposed directing his energies.

After having conferred with Mr. Gautier, Germaine's father, and Captain Evrard, Chantecoq had taken on the clothes and appearance of an old Jew, he had procured a whole range of patterns for tapestries, needles and wool samples of all colours.

Armed with this cheap junk, he went to Spandau one Sunday morning, rented a room in a modest hotel and left his merchandise there. Then with just a few articles in his hand, he went to lurk around the Protestant church where he knew that Mrs Fürsner was going to go and make her devotions. At the moment when the faithful were starting to arrive, Chantecoq placed himself ostensibly in the middle of the temple steps, holding a pattern for slippers in one hand, which were at once fantastic, and yet of deplorable taste.

Mrs Commandant was not late to appear, much as he had seen her in a cafe in the town, that he knew was frequented by the governor and his wife and where, with his skilful costuming, he had been given the most detailed information.

He kept himself facing front, contenting himself to attract her attention by using a long-prepared sales pitch.

He hadn't spoken three sentences before the huge lady came to a halt.

Chantecoq asked for no more.

Placing himself opposite 'Mrs Governor' and putting his pattern almost under her nose, he waited for the offers which did not take long in coming.

Indeed, Mrs Fürsner shouted out almost instantly:

"Oh what beautiful things one could make with that!"

And immediately, she asked, "How much?"

"Three marks, for the pair."

"That's not too expensive . . ."

"I have more much prettier patterns," insinuated Chantecoq.

"Show them to me," the embroiderer demanded.

"I don't have them on me. I've already sold quite a few this morning. The ones I have left are back at the hotel . . . If madam wants, I could go and fetch them and bring them to her home?"

"No, I'd prefer to go with you," said Mrs Fürsner. "Is it far, your hotel?"

"No, madam, a few yards from here."

"At least is it an establishment in which a lady such as myself might enter without compromising herself?"

"It's no palace, but it's very clean, very well kept, and I have some very well-to-do clients who come to make their choices in my room, because I can't carry everything on my person, more so because I'm old, not very good at carrying things, and I can barely lift anything."

Chantecoq who, as always, played his role admirably, started to sputter while whining painfully.

"On top of that, I'm asthmatic. I have trouble breathing."

But he didn't need to insist, the argument was won.

Indeed, Mrs Fürsner, who had taken hold of the pattern and hidden it in her immense bag, declared in a decisive tone, "My dear man, lead me to your lodgings. I'll follow you."

Enchanted at seeing his ruse succeed with such ease, the French agent led 'Mrs Governor' to the hotel he had chosen.

Still complaining, still sputtering, he climbed the staircase which gave access to his room, situated on the first floor. He opened its door and stood back saying, "This way, madam."

Hardly had she entered when the good German let slip a cry of admiration and cheerfulness.

On a table, a whole heap of the most diverse patterns, and wool in shimmering tones, was spread out, carefully presented.

The embroiderer hurried over.

Chantecoq had closed the door.

The moment was serious, because he was going to play one of the most difficult games of his life; and he, usually so calm, so self-controlled, felt his heart thumping violently.

"Sit down then, madam," he invited, offering his client a chair. "You'll be better able to make your choice. And then, I have only what you see there."

He was at a small table in black wood, placed near the window, and pulled out a whole series of catalogues and samples of wool that he placed under the commandant's wife's eyes.

Briefly, after quarter of an hour, she had not only bought all her merchandise from the old Jew, but she had again placed on a catalogue an order of the most important and the most expensive things.

And when, on her request, the improvising merchant had finished adding everything up, she perceived with fright and indescribable disappointment that the bill came to nearly seven hundred marks.

"It's not possible!" she cried. "Seven hundred marks?"

"Everywhere else," insinuated the fake Jew, "you would pay a thousand marks, and perhaps more."

"I don't doubt it, my friend, but my resources don't permit me to make such a purchase."

"Madam says that," Chantecoq flattered skilfully, "but I am sure that if madam wanted to, madam does not seem to be a person of frustrated circumstances, to the contrary."

"It's just that I have a husband," sighed the fat Teutonic lady, "and he would never let me spend so much money on embroidery. He treats it as an obsession, he knows only his pipe and his orders."

"Ah, your husband is military, no doubt?"

"Governor of Spandau Citadel, and as I am constantly locked in, this work is my single distraction."

Then, pretending deep stupefaction, the nimble actor repeated:

"Governor of Spandau Citadel? But he ought to be happy to see you apply yourself to such a serious, useful, beautiful art! That's more worthwhile than spending your money on toiletries, on lunches, on cheap ornaments. Well, it's none of my business; I can only sympathise with you with all my heart. If you don't want to take everything today you can always make a choice. I am entirely at your disposal."

"Everything that I chose is so beautiful that I no longer know what I should leave."

Then, gripped by an idea that she no doubt thought was brilliant, she added, "Perhaps there's a way to get around this."

"Tell me, madam."

"If I made an arrangement with you to give you, let's see, fifty marks a month, what do you think?"

"Believe me, madam, that I would be happy to please you but, unfortunately, I can't. I pay for all my merchandise in advance. I have no credit. It's impossible for me to do that."

"What a shame," lamented the brave woman, unable to tear her eyes from all the stock that had taken on for her the proportions of the treasure of Golconda. "Ah! If I only had a thousand marks with me!"

Chantecoq said to himself, "Here we are! Let's chance our arm! If I don't win now, I'll never win!"

And out loud, "A thousand marks! It seems to me that you would find it very easy, in your situation, to borrow them?"

"I don't think so. And then, if my husband learned that I was running up debts . . ."

"And if I, without your husband knowing anything of it, were to procure for you not only this thousand marks you need, but a true small fortune which would make you independent and permit you to buy not only everything you see here, but still more to deliver to you much more considerable works of tapestry, such as wall hangings, furnishings, door coverings, in the Aubusson style, or Beauvais or Gobelin . . ."

"This is an impossible thing and these are chimera to which a woman like myself, walled up in a fortress and almost the prisoner of a man who doesn't understand and who only tries to oppose my artistic tastes, has no right to consider them, if only for a moment! So my friend, it is useless to raise such hope in my eyes. Better that I leave. I will become mad before all your treasures."

"Stay, my good woman, stay!" the fake salesman advised gently. "As I tell you that I can give you the means to satisfy your noble passion for embroidery."

"What! You?" the astonished 'Mrs Governor' exclaimed, who had only brought a relative attention to the proposition that the fake Jew had made her an instant before.

"Yes, me," Chantecoq confirmed.

"I don't understand. Just now you told me you couldn't offer me credit and now suddenly you're offering a small fortune, and all that with no hope of a guarantee?"

Seized by a doubt, Mrs Fürsner, while giving her interlocutor a look charged with suspicion, added in a singularly cold voice, "I'm beginning to see your game all too clearly."

"I don't believe so, madam," replied Chantecoq, not without a note of irony. "Listen. I can put twenty thousand marks at your disposal immediately."

"Twenty thousand marks!" the Commandant's wife exclaimed.

"I'll even go as high as twenty-five."

"But you're mad!"

"I'm perfectly sane, believe me. In exchange for this sum, I ask you for no interest, no signature. You'll pay it back to me when you're able."

"I'll never be able to."

"That doesn't matter."

"I've no idea what's going on."

Then, lowering his voice, the French agent slipped these words into the fat German's ear:

"In exchange for these . . . thirty thousand marks, I'll only ask you for one thing, that's to deliver a little parcel that I'll give to you to the prisoner in Julius Tower, if you agree."

"Never!" cried 'Mrs Governor', red with indignation.

And staring at the fake Jew, whose eyes burned strangely. "Who are you to make such an offer to me?" she demanded.

"Haven't you guessed?"

"A French agent?"

"Bang on!"

"And if I called? If I had you arrested?"

Then, drawing a revolver from his pocket, Chantecoq, standing up, said in a firm voice:

"Then in spite of the sympathy that you inspire in me, madam, I would have the honour of blowing your head off, and the advantage of escaping before anyone arrives; because having foreseen your refusal, all my arrangements are made, and I have prepared a retreat.

"Anyway, let me insist. You are, I know, Germaine Aubry's warder; consequently you must know what a courageous and amazing being this admirable girl is. But perhaps you didn't know what events led her to come to Germany? Ah well! I'll tell you!"

Briefly, Chantecoq told the Commandant's wife the tragic account that we know.

"You who, I am convinced, already pitied this unfortunate girl," he concluded, "you who, I see in your eyes, have been moved, brave woman that you are, by everything I've just told you, you can do no less than help us to save Germaine Aubry."

"Sir," replied Mrs Fürsner with a grave air which banished everything ridiculous about her appearance, "I truly want to believe everything you've told me is true, and I loyally accept that you have the right to do the impossible in order to remove Germaine Aubry from her prison. But you will agree I'm sure, that I, I have a duty to oppose anything which might aid her escape. You are French! Myself, I'm German, an officer's wife. I don't need to say anything more. You understand me and you can only approve."

"Well! Yes, I approve," said Chantecoq in a quiet voice. "I chose the wrong door, madam. I'll leave in order to knock on another."

"I doubt it will open. But, as you're interested in this young girl's fate, let me advise you in her interest, not to try anything to break her out at this particular moment. Commandant Fürsner is a terrible man. If he notices that anyone is trying to take his prisoner away from him, he's quite capable of plunging this unfortunate into a dungeon in the depths of the fortress's cellars. That's why I shan't tell him what has happened here."

"Thank you, madam."

"I don't want to know who you are, nor where you came from, nor where you're going, but take this one thing. Germaine Aubry has in me, I can't say a friend, but someone who is looking out for her. Who knows? A day may come where she'll go without me knowing about it, without me being involved, and I'll hope that it was you who saved her," finished the brave woman with real emotion. "But by heaven, nothing for the moment. Nothing!"

The good fat Teutonic woman headed towards the door.

Turning back, she spontaneously held out her hands to Chantecoq, who hid his emotion badly.

"You're her father, perhaps?" she asked.

"No, madam."

"You know him?"

"Yes, I know him."

"Ah well, tell him that I pity him with all my heart."

"And you," replied the French agent, "tell Germaine: 'Courage!'"

CHAPTER NINETEEN:

Ambush

Chantecoq was completely disoriented.

The only method that he'd thought up to deliver to Germaine the tools that were indispensable to her escape, had just fallen apart in his hands.

But what caused him especially cruel anguish, was the warning given him by this woman whose sincerity he couldn't doubt.

"All that you'll do to help this prisoner escape will turn back on her!"

For the first time in his life, the skilful agent was beginning to hesitate, not knowing what approach to make, nor which path to stop.

He thought of the despair that news of his failure would cause for Jean Aubry and Maurice Evrard.

"The poor wretches!" he said to himself. "And I who had so promised to succeed! I who even yesterday, affirmed to them that Germaine's rescue was only a question of days, perhaps of hours, so sure was I to succeed with this fat German! I've cudgelled my brains, I've got nothing. When I'd spent whole hours pacing this room like a squirrel in a cage, I'd be no further advanced! I'd risk everything just to burn myself like an imbecile."

And looking at his suitcase, where he had ranked by value the objects which had so pleased the governor's wife, he mumbled:

"After all, I'm not going to embarrass myself with this junk. I only have to return as soon as possible to Berlin, where I've quite a bit to do before going home. I've got a meeting with all my agents, because there's also the citizen Emma Lückner that mustn't be forgotten."

And his gaze suddenly lit up with an expression of intense joy.

"Oh! What an idea!" said Chantecoq, "Gautier promised his boss to deliver him this spy bound hand and foot, but while waiting, she could perhaps give me some good ideas to deliver the ladder and saw to their destination. With that one, I think we'd get there much easier than with mother Fürsner! Anyway, if we must, we'd use methods which are hardly resisted! There we go, all is not lost . . . Quickly! To Berlin!"

One hour later, Chantecoq disembarked at Lehrte Station in Germany's capital.

All day long, in the most diverse areas in the city, and always in this same costume which rendered him completely unrecognisable, he had long and important conversations in the course of which he learned Emma Lückner's new address. He also learned of her trio of agents: Elrich Maus, Kouraguine and Jean Lenoir, who had become her bodyguards as well as her colleagues.

"Oh!" he thought, "the minx has walled herself in; but on that terrain, she can't measure up to me.

"I believe," he added with a strange smile, "that I won't need to unpack a whole stock of tapestries in order to make her talk, because, thanks to certain little papers that we have in our power, I can lead her to a hard life."

It was among the papers stolen by Germaine Aubry that General Security had found proof of the identity of she that Colonel Hoffmann held tightly under his dependence, following her conviction for her husband's poisoning, which Emma Lückner had suppressed in order to get her hands on his fortune.

Chantecoq established his new campaign plan that he prepared at length while dining in a tavern, then, around half-past ten, he went back to his district. He was walking, absorbed in his thoughts, when, having arrived in front of his door three men coming out of the shadows where they were hidden, Elrich Maus, Kouraguine and Jean Lenoir suddenly surrounded him.

"You're toast, friend Chantecoq!" the Parisian said to him.

But the French agent was already on the defensive.

As Jean Lenoir advanced to grab him by the collar, Chantecoq sent him rolling to the ground with an incredible hook to the jaw. Then, finding himself facing Kouraguine, with a double swing he brought him down before the Russian had time to recognise him.

And he was looking for his third attacker when a cry of pain burst from him: a steel blade had just stabbed him in the back.

It was Elrich Maus who, realising that he'd be dealing with a man of exceptional strength and incomparable audacity and scared for his skin, had drawn his knife in advance and had plunged it between his adversary's shoulder blades.

Chantecoq still had the strength to turn, however, and seizing the frightened German in his iron fist, he slammed his head against the wall; letting him fall like a rag to the pavement he pivoted, staggered and managed to enter the house reeling, after having slammed the door behind him.

Then he was struck by a blinding idea.

"Courage!" he said to himself, "or all is lost, I must get up there at all costs!"

He began climbing the stairs wretchedly, clamped to the banister, stopping at each step, half choked by the blood which obstructed his throat.

Finally he reached the first landing.

He still had the strength to press three times on the button of the electric bell, and giving out a long sigh he sank to his knees and fell unconscious.

Steps sounded from the other side of the door, which soon opened, making way for Mr. Ernest Gautier who had a lamp in his hand.

On seeing his colleague, the special commissioner could not repress a cry of anguish.

Immediately, Jean Aubry and Maurice Evrard came running.

They picked up Chantecoq and took him to his bathroom.

His bloodied clothes revealed one part of the truth.

But already the injured man was returning to his senses. His first word was:

"Fly!"

"Why?" asked the special commissioner who, as well as Germaine's father and fiancé, was plunged into the deepest anxiety.

"Because I'm discovered!"

His voice gasping, his breathing ragged, Chantecoq added:

"I was able to rid myself momentarily of three individuals who had come to seize me – doubtless Colonel Hoffmann's watchmen – but they'll certainly know that I'm still here. They might come at any moment. By staying, you'll be lost, without saving me."

"But we can't abandon you," Jean Aubry cried.

"We will try anything to save you," the captain declared.

"I'm staying!" said Gautier energetically.

"Us too! We're staying!" the inventor and the captain spoke with one voice.

"No, my friends," Chantecoq insisted, who was making superhuman efforts not to pass out. "Wait, all is not yet lost . . . First, give me quickly a cordial of my own composition, that you'll find there, in that little cabinet, a brown flask, on which there's a blue label, which reads '12'."

Mr. Gautier hurried over.

Two seconds later, he returned with the flask, which the wounded man seized with an already feverish hand and from which he drank a few mouthfuls.

"Now," he said, "I have a few minutes of respite before me. That's enough to give you my instructions. You'll try to get these clothes off me in order to make a field dressing. Everything you need is in the cabinet. And then you'll dress me as best you can, but quickly! Very quickly! There are some clothes in the wardrobe, it doesn't matter which.

"During this, one of you will disguise yourself as a coachman, and go to the nearest station. At this hour, Berlin cabbies are almost all busy drinking and smoking in the surrounding establishments, you'll only have to choose a carriage with a good horse, jump on the seat, and return that very second."

"That's my job!" Mr. Gautier said, resolved.

"Above all, go gently, completely naturally. It's a trick that's always worked for me."

"Don't worry!" the commissioner nodded, as he was already looking in the wardrobe for the outfit necessary for the part he was going to play.

"When you return," continued Chantecoq, as Jean Aubry and Maurice Evrard started to undress him, "we'll be downstairs. As soon as we're up in the carriage, you'll take us to the address where I sent you the different pieces of the aircraft. Then I'll be reassured, because we'll be sheltered. There is room to hide all of us, and Colonel Hoffmann's police won't go there to look for us!"

But Jean Aubry gave a strangled cry. Undressing Chantecoq, he'd just noticed the terrible wound that Maus had inflicted on him.

"I'm really hurt!" agreed the French agent. "Yet the blade must have slipped on one side; because the bleeding has stopped. I'll recover from this, without that slip it would already be over."

Then, feeling himself weakening again, "That poor Miss Germaine!" he added. "This will delay us a bit. In the end let's hope all the same. As I haven't succeeded this afternoon, I have another plan that I'll outline to you when we've arrived at our destination. Emma

Lückner . . . I can't tell you now. I've already spoken too much . . . and I feel that . . ."

"Rest," advised the inventor.

"Ah, my dear friends," said Chantecoq, "those people are true wretches!"

He stopped, choking again. Then he settled himself and, in a weak voice he begged, "Gautier, my friend, go quickly, quickly. In quarter of an hour it might be too late."

At the end of his strength this time, Chantecoq let his head fall back on to the sofa where his friends had placed him.

Jean Aubry and Maurice Evrard, with many precautions and real skill, made a provisional bandage for the wound, solid enough to await the surgeon's intervention.

Then, after passing him a very thick pair of trousers, they dressed him in an Ulster coat, put an otterskin cap on his head and wrapped him in a woollen blanket.

All this time, the poor man had not given the faintest sound of complaint.

Finally Maurice Evrard went down to see if the carriage had arrived.

Gautier was there, sitting on the seat of a fairly comfortable carriage. The trick had worked.

The aviator went straight back upstairs; and Jean Aubry and he carried Chantecoq, still unmoving.

Around half an hour later, the car stopped in front of a small building encased in a courtyard planted with lime trees and neighbouring large industrial workshops.

Gautier jumped down from his seat and rang the bell of a low door practically in the surrounding wall, next to a huge cast iron gate. He waited for a moment and rang again nervously.

This time a sort of concierge whose face was already bleary with sleep decided to answer the door and asked in a rough voice, "Who's there?"

"Is Mr. Laumann at home?" the special commissioner asked, his disguise giving him every appearance of being a coachman for a great house.

"Yes, he's at home," said the guard dog, "but don't think that he's going to be bothered for all that! This isn't a time to call on civilised people!"

The concierge was going to shut the door, when Mr. Gautier, placing himself resolutely between the panel and the door-frame, said, with an authoritative voice that impressed the building's guardian immediately.

"We didn't ask for your opinion, this is a business of the greatest importance. Go straight to Mr. Laumann and tell him that his friend Chantecoq is here and wishes to speak to him, and to drop everything."

"Mr. Chantecoq?" the concierge was still hesitating.

"Yes, Mr. Chantecoq," insisted the special commissioner energetically, adding with the most threatening tone to bully his opponent, "If you don't want to disturb yourself, I'll go and find your boss myself! But I warn you that he will not thank you for it."

The intimidated guardian, grumbling the whole time, went to the house where Mr. Laumann, Alsatian originally and French by heart, was celebrating his wife's birthday with his family.

At Chantecoq's name, he jumped up and ran to the gate, leaving his guests.

At first he didn't recognise Mr. Gautier in the shadows. But he immediately whispered in his ear, "Something very serious has happened!"

"Are you burned?"

"No, it's Chantecoq."

"Arrested?"

"Seriously injured. He's there in a car with Jean Aubry and Captain Evrard. We've come to ask you for asylum."

"You're welcome here."

"Chantecoq told us that in case of danger, there was always a safe retreat at your home."

"He was right. And this unfortunate? Grievously wounded?"

"We don't know yet."

"The doctor, my brother, is dining with us this evening. There he is! You know that he can be counted on as much as myself, but we must not waste a moment. Bring Chantecoq, I'll lead you to the hideout."

"It would perhaps be better not to pass before the concierge."

"He's as French as us and I guarantee that we have in him the most vigilant of sentinels."

"Then let's go!"

While Jean Aubry and Maurice Evrard, guided by Mr. Laumann, carried Chantecoq into the property, Mr. Gautier climbed back up on the seat and left at a moderate pace.

After having reached a distant area, he stopped, got rid of his hat and his coat, dumping them in the cab, put on a cycling cap that he had taken the precaution of putting in his jacket pocket; then, simply abandoning the horse and the carriage in a deserted street, he headed towards the nearest tramway station and went back to Mr. Laumann's house.

The concierge had, this time, received orders, because not just content to open the door to the nocturnal visitor, he led him to the villa at the bottom of the garden, to which Chantecoq had been transported.

Mr. Laumann was waiting for him on the threshold.

"Well?" the special commissioner asked feverishly.

"My brother is not very reassuring," replied Mr. Laumann. "If the poor boy escapes this, he fears it will take a long time, a very long time, and that will not help your business."

"That's very unlucky!"

"Everything had gone so well up to now! The machine is there, locked in a garage for which I have the key on me and where no one goes. I'm afraid you might not be using it too soon."

The two men entered the villa, where Mr. Aubry appeared, coming out of a bedroom from where there came a bitter smell of ether and carbolic acid.

"Hush!" he said. "He's resting."

"And you, gentlemen," Mr. Laumann advised, "I hope that you're going to do the same?"

Then, with a smile full of bonhomie and finesse, he concluded, "Here, we sleep peacefully! I'm watching over you!"

CHAPTER TWENTY:

A Little Lady Who Goes Too Fast

Emma Lückner, who was sure of holding Chantecoq, had vainly awaited the return of the three bloodhounds with their prey, hidden in a car.

After an hour, seeing no one come and boiling with impatience, she left her car and went to enquire herself.

The spy almost immediately noticed, at a junction, some passers by who had stopped in front of a pharmacy. She approached, and was shocked to see Jean Lenoir, Kouraguine and Elrich Maus behind the window, laid out on stretchers and seriously wounded. The pharmacist had bandaged them, and was preparing to send them to the nearest hospital.

Forgetting all caution, she entered the shop terrified, and went to interrogate the pharmacist and the agents who were there. Kouraguine, who was beginning to come to his senses, opened his eyes and groaned.

"You! What happened?" the spy asked him in Russian.

"We had our man. But we were dealing with a true demon."

"He was the one who put you in this state?"

"Yes."

"What happened to him?"

"I don't know. He must have reached his bolt hole."

Without bothering any more with the wounded men, Emma Lückner signalled to one of the policemen to approach her and, having taken him over to a corner, she showed him a special card which displayed her photograph in one corner and the words "Secret Intelligence Service" followed by Colonel Hoffmann's signature.

"Go and find me ten men," ordered the policewoman, "we have an important operation to carry out in the neighbourhood."

As the agent seemed to hesitate, she showed him the other side of the card, on which was written in the Security Bureau Chief's own handwriting: "Public forces are ordered to obey all requisitions."

The agent bowed and left immediately.

"Where are these men being taken?" Emma Lückner asked the pharmacist.

"To hospital, of course!"

"Good, thank you."

The spy went out into the street, and while tapping the asphalt nervously with the sole of her shoe, she waited for the policeman to return.

Soon their group appeared in the night, they were led by a brigadier to whom Emma Lückner made herself known.

They exchanged a few words in low voices; then, followed by agents, they reached Chantecoq's house.

"Knocking would be pointless," said Emma Lückner, "they won't open up. The only way is to kick down the door."

The brigadier called one of his men, a true colossus, and on the third attempt, the door gave way under his formidable weight.

The spy, full of ardour for battle, wanted to be first to enter, but the brigadier held her back; it could have been dangerous.

On the order of their leader, the agents lit their electric lamps; and the policeman, revolver in hand, entered the apartment.

It was quickly obvious that it was empty. In the dressing room, the fake Jew's discarded costume lay on the ground, all stained with blood.

"He was wounded too, then?" Colonel Hoffmann's collaborator observed. "But where could he have gone? Perhaps he's hidden somewhere."

They looked, but after rummaging everywhere, turning over furniture, knocking on the walls, nothing was found, other than the second exit leading to the street by which Chantecoq and his friends had beaten their retreat.

Then appeared the clues establishing the evidence that the French agent was not alone.

A black felt hat bearing the initials A. G. and the milliner's address: Paris, Vincent, 27 Boulevard des Capucines.

Emma Lückner needed no more than that, as she knew the special commissioner and had even been arrested by him, to shout, "What? Ernest Gautier? He's in Berlin!"

And she continued immediately. "Look! Look everywhere! We're going to discover some interesting things, I have no doubt of that."

The exploration resumed more carefully, the investigations were still more painstaking.

In one room, near a tiny iron bed, was found, on a nightstand, a photograph pressed against a vulgar little porcelain vase.

"Her!" the spy shouted, who seized it with a surprised cry.

She had just recognised a highly accurate portrait of Germaine Aubry, whose picture Hoffmann had shown to her on several occasions.

At the bottom of the portrait, the simple dedication 'To my fiancé' attested to the presence of Captain Evrard.

"He too was here!" said Emma Lückner. "And the father too, no doubt!"

She had hardly pronounced these words when the brigadier showed her a quite beautiful gold watch he'd just found in a neighbouring bedroom and whose case bore this engraving:

"To Mr. Jean Aubry. Presented by the University of Faubourg Saint-Antoine."

"All! They were all here!" the spy roared. "Ah! What a superb prize I've just lost through the fault of my imbecilic three agents!

"But I see it, the battle has only just begun! I will triumph! Now that I have been warned, I shall find them again, and this time, I swear, they won't escape me!"

Then, quickly making a parcel of the watch, the photograph and the hat, she said to the brigadier, "Send one of your men to fetch my car."

Then she continued her search, but in vain; because, apart from the wardrobe containing Chantecoq's innumerable disguises, there was nothing to find.

Before leaving, she recommended.

"Brigadier, though it's unlikely that the man we're seeking will take the chance of returning, you would do well to keep an eye on this place.

With such individuals, one can never take too many precautions."

The spy went back to the street, pressing the evidence against her, then gave the order to her motorman to drive her to Colonel Hoffmann.

She knew that the Intelligence Bureau chief, very busy with his service's reorganisation, completely disturbed by the 'capture' of Germaine Aubry, no longer left his office before midnight or one o'clock in the morning.

Emma Lückner was admitted almost immediately.

From the expression on her face, Hoffman immediately guessed that serious events had just taken place.

"Well!" he demanded. "Is there news? Germaine Aubry's accomplices?"

"I found one of them," replied the spy, "and I failed to bring him to you this evening. I discovered that he had taken the name Chantecoq. I knew he was living in Moabit, that it was he who had forged the fake keys which this woman used. As time was against me to warn you and as I feared that this man would slip through my fingers, I wanted to act myself. I posted my three agents on this Chantecoq's street, who were ordered to take him and to bring him to me in the car where I was waiting nearby. I don't yet know what could have happened, I found my men half unconscious at a pharmacy, from where they were taken to hospital."

"He did well, Mr. Chantecoq!"

"I called the police immediately; we forced the door of his lodging, but having observed numerous bloodstains which indicated that Chantecoq, before his disappearance, must have been seriously injured by my men, I conducted a minute search. And this is what I found," concluded Emma Lückner, placing the parcel she was holding on the table. "Open it yourself, Colonel!"

Hoffmann did so.

"Hold on!" he said, "A hat, a watch, a portrait . . ."

"Look closer!"

"Miss Aubry's photograph."

"See the dedication."

"To my fiancé."

"That shows Captain Evrard is here. Look at the watch. Read the engraving. That means Mr. Aubry, the combat aircraft's inventor, is also here."

"Hell! And the hat?"

"It belongs to Mr. Gautier, special commissioner of General Security. I believe, Colonel, that you'll need to watch over your prisoner even more tightly than ever; because if these people are in Berlin, it's only with the aim of rescuing her."

"As long as we don't send them to join her!" said the military policeman. "This discovery is precious and I congratulate you for it. I will put my best bloodhounds on the scent, because if in one stroke we get hold of this Chantecoq, the Commissioner, Mr. Aubry and especially this famous aviator, we'll have succeeded in what one might call a very nice haul!

"But I won't hide my view," continued the Colonel with a furrowed brow, "that you would have done better to bring me up to date with your discoveries without delay. You wanted to assure yourself alone of the glory and the benefits of this business. You see what good that did? To put an individual on his guard, who we could otherwise have arrested very easily."

Emma Lückner chewed her lip and kept quiet.

More than ever, she saw herself in the power of this terrible soldier and she felt that this wasn't the moment to rebel against a man who held her fate in his hands.

"You're right," she said in the end, quite humbly. "Forgive me to have let myself be led by my overpowering zeal to serve you. I was wrong not to warn you, to have acted independently. From this point, I'll be more circumspect. Please give me your instructions and I will carry them out to the letter."

"Until you receive new orders," said the Intelligence Bureau chief, "you will keep quiet."

The adventuress gave a little start.

"In a little while, I'll no doubt have need of you," continued Hoffmann imperturbably. "But right now it's useless and it would be imprudent to bring you to the attention of this Frenchman who, aware of your plots, would be perfectly capable of luring you into an ambush and repaying the trick you played on him."

"I'm not afraid of them!"

"Your courage does you much honour, but it doesn't convince me."

"As you wish, Colonel!" said Emma Lückner in a strained voice.

"I'll not keep you. After such a busy day, you must be very tired. Myself I still have work to do."

While she retired after having saluted, the military policeman mumbled between his teeth, "There goes a little lady who's going too fast and too far, to make us miss such a coup!

"I believe, anyway," he reflected, "that she's rendered us more services than she will render us henceforth. And then, I will mourn it easily. Now that she's compromised in France, she won't be useful to me for anything important."

For her part, on reaching her car, the adventuress said to herself, "I see from the Colonel's attitude, that I'm almost being laid off. We'll see! We'll see!"

CHAPTER TWENTY-ONE:

Wilhelm II

Wilhelm II woke up in a bad mood.

The night before, he'd received a report revealing that the governor of Spandau Citadel had found one of his sentries fast asleep, under the effect of a narcotic which had been administered by a major, though it hadn't been possible to identify the officer in question.

There was something strange there that needed to be illuminated, and the Emperor had immediately summoned General von Talberg, as well as the Intelligence Bureau chief and the Citadel's governor.

While waiting for them, he sent his aide-de-camp, Lieutenant von Limbürg, to whom he accorded a particular affection and trust, to fetch the whole dossier on the Germaine Aubry affair, and he had studied it with the greatest care.

General von Talberg was first to arrive.

The Emperor received him with great affability. He knew to what great labours this officer had been forced in order to reorganise the mobilisation compromised by the Frenchwoman's thefts; and he paid tribute to the character of this honest and loyal man who knew how to recognise his mistakes and to put every effort into repairing them.

"Sire," said von Talberg, "I am at your command."

"I have two important pieces of news to communicate to you," said the Emperor, pointing out a seat benevolently to the man he called his 'right hand'.

"A word first on the subject of Ansbach whom I promoted to captain on your recommendation. I know today the important role that this officer played in the Germaine Aubry business. Certainly, Ansbach showed energy, intelligence and audacity; but not everything that he did is to his credit. I have just read the file on this business and I congratulate you heartily on having prevented him from making a deposition before the Empire's secret tribunal. While it is good that our young officers are up to date with what is happening in France, and keep us informed of their observations and of their discoveries, there are certain methods that they ought never to employ. Ansbach's ploy is among that number."

"Sire," said the general, "you can't imagine how happy I am to hear you speak in this way. The words which have just fallen from your imperial mouth, I have spoken them myself to this officer."

"And yet it was you who asked this reward of me for him?"

"Yes, sire, because if he had succeeded we would no longer have anything to fear from this fourth weapon with which the French threaten us and with that we must consider . . . I blamed him as he deserved, for the methods used. But the effort remains, and it's only just that we should reward this. He was raised according to a certain school of thought."

"The Bismarckian school!" Wilhelm II interrupted with a strange smile.

"Wilhelm Ansbach is completely convinced," continued von Talberg, "that when he's acting in defence of his country, all methods are acceptable, even crime!"

"It's a theory, perhaps, but if everyone reasoned thusly the world would quickly revert to a wild state."

And with a fervent glint in his eye, the Emperor added, "That's not how I dream of a greater Germany!"

Then, after a brief moment of silence, he said:

"You will send Captain Ansbach far from here, to the Russian frontier or to the French frontier. I would prefer not to have him around me."

"At your command, sire."

A chamberlain announced, "Colonel Hoffmann. The governor of Spandau."

The two officers entered the Emperor's office and immediately, with no preamble, Wilhelm II attacked, addressing Commandant Fürsner, "What have you found to complete the report that I read? This Major who did a round, who spoke with the sentry, who offered him some kirsch containing a soporific, has he finally been discovered?"

"Sire," the citadel's governor responded humbly, "I questioned the sentry. I brought him before Majors Schlaffen, Tourchtig and Hunguerig, and he did not recognise them."

"Three brutes!" said the Emperor. "How did it come about that the prisoner's guard was entrusted to these officers precisely?"

"Sire," von Talberg intervened, "you gave the order to send these majors back to their regiment. An unfortunate chance had it that they actually made up part of the Spandau garrison. But I took care myself to send a confidential note to Commandant Fürsner to warn him of their intellectual inferiority."

"Three 'Ramollots', as they'd say in France," said the Emperor, shrugging his shoulders. "They're everywhere. But when they are uncovered, that's half the problem solved. Anyway, let's move on!"

"It's certain at any rate," replied Fürsner, "that this fake officer – because this can only be a man in disguise that the men on the gate let pass, fooled by the uniform that he was wearing – could not get into

Julius Tower. But it's no less certain that an attempt has been made and that, if it has failed, it's only thanks to the secure measures that I have taken in the fortress."

"I don't doubt it, But stay sharp!" the Emperor recommended. "Let's talk about Germaine Aubry's accomplice, because that's what particularly interests me. You wrote, Colonel Hoffmann, that you know his name?"

"Yes, sire, or rather his codename, they call him Chantecoq."

"That is indeed a policeman's nickname."

"He lives in Moabit."

"What are you waiting for, that you've not arrested him?"

"It would have been done, sire, but the fellow who, as you're going to discover, is perhaps the most dangerous French spy against whom we have ever had to fight, took to his heels quickly."

"What!" Wilhelm II cried, stamping his foot. "You let him escape!"

"The house had two exits!"

"Didn't you know that?"

"No, sire."

"That's a grave error."

"I humbly accept that."

"He's a skilful man, this Chantecoq, and I fear that now it will be a long time before you manage to get your hands on him. Feeling exposed, he must have already left Berlin."

"Sire, allow me to express a different opinion," Colonel Hoffmann hazarded respectfully.

"Let's hear it!"

"First, Chantecoq was seriously wounded in the fight that he had with my men."

"Ah! There was a fight!" Germany's ruler said, not without ill humour. "You didn't tell me that in your report."

"Sire," replied the military policeman, a little disconcerted and, inwardly, cursing Emma Lückner more than ever for her excessive zeal, "I didn't think that these details could possibly interest Your Majesty."

"To the contrary, they interest me greatly. So this Chantecoq was wounded?"

"Yes, sire. Drops of blood were found in his apartment where, after having escaped my agents, he took refuge."

"How many agents did you have?"

"Three, sire."

"Too few! When one is dealing with a person of this strength, one mobilises the necessary number of men."

"Sire, I had no idea that this Chantecoq was such a redoubtable adversary."

"Continue."

"I was telling Your Majesty that Chantecoq, wounded, can not have gone far."

"That's only a hypothesis."

"Another fact supports what I say. Various objects found at this spy's lodging revealed to me that, some minutes before, Mr. Gautier, Paris's special commissioner; Jean Aubry, Germaine's father and the combat aircraft's inventor, as well as Captain Maurice Evrard, were all together there."

"Captain Evrard . . . the aviation officer!"

"Yes, sire."

"Well! Colonel, You are dealing with a strong adversary."

"I don't delude myself, sire."

"Have you discovered these people's route?"

"Not yet, I confess."

The Emperor, his brows furrowed, fell silent. He reflected, coordinating his ideas, assembling all the elements capable of putting him on the track of the truth.

Immobile, serious, preoccupied, General von Talberg, Colonel Hoffmann and Commandant Fürsner respected this imperial silence.

Soon, Wilhelm II, very calm, replied with a completely lucid mind and perfect self-control, "It's beyond doubt that the events which are occupying our attention have a powerful link between them. Hoffmann, you have seen correctly in attributing, as you signalled to me in your report, the incident of this man disguised as an officer who succeeded in entering the Citadel, to an escape attempt.

"Like you, I believe that Chantecoq must not have left Berlin. Indeed, these four Frenchmen must be resolved, even at the cost of their liberty and their lives, to save our prisoner.

"Not only must we not be exposed to ridicule by letting this spy escape, but we must also get hold of Chantecoq and the three others."

"The first point is Commandant Fürsner's concern."

"Your Majesty can count on my zeal," the governor affirmed solemnly.

"The second point concerns Colonel Hoffmann."

"Sire, I shall neglect nothing in order to pick up the trail of this French agent and his friends."

"It's evident," replied Wilhelm II, "that they are hiding themselves in some retreat where it will hardly be easy to discover them, so much more so if, as you say, this Chantecoq is seriously wounded. The others will try nothing without him. But, fatally, one day or another, they will pick up their plotting. It's therefore crucial to get ahead of them and consequently to discover their bolt hole before they have the time to resume their mission.

"But I'm thinking, could I transfer Germaine Aubry to another State prison . . . What do you think, Colonel Hoffmann?"

"Sire," responded the Intelligence Bureau chief, "as you do me the great honour of asking my opinion, I'll permit myself to humbly remark to you that, in none of your fortresses or prisons will Germaine Aubry be more secure than in Julius Tower. And I'm persuaded that, whatever his desire to be relieved of such a heavy responsibility, the governor shares this opinion."

Commandant Fürsner nodded.

"So be it, we wait!" the Emperor concluded. "But redouble your surveillance and activity. I hope that shortly Hoffmann will have discovered Chantecoq's trail and that these four Frenchmen will be arrested; because I don't want to live much longer in such uncertainty."

The Emperor stood.

The audience was at an end and the three officers were going to leave when Wilhelm II said simply:

"General von Talberg, stay!"

Responding to Fürsner's impassive and Hoffmann's concerned salute, he waited for the door to close on them to yell, striking his fist on the table. "I don't know what I would give to be free of this nightmare!"

Then, turning to von Talberg, he asked, staring straight into his eyes, "General, do you know Germaine Aubry well?"

As the officer showed a certain awkwardness at this memory evoked so directly, the Kaiser continued immediately. "Don't see any recrimination in this question. I'm incapable, once I have forgiven, to reproach anyone for a previous error. I would simply like to know your very clear and sincere opinion on our prisoner. Respond to me frankly, von Talberg, as if you were speaking to your best friend."

"Sire," responded Frida's father, "Germaine Aubry is no venal adventurer, as a certain section of the Berlin press has tried to represent her. She's an exalted patriot. Excessively courageous, admirable, intelligent and profoundly honest, I believe her capable of every heroism and of every sacrifice. For us, she is a noble enemy; to them, she is a heroine."

"From the transcript of the trial, that's very much the opinion that I'd come to myself," Wilhelm said. "Thank you, general, that will do. I don't want to abuse your time further. I know what an immense labour you have undertaken. Return to your task, my friend, and know once more that your Emperor holds for you all his trust and all his friendship."

The general bowed, deeply moved; and as he reached the door, Wilhelm II murmured, "How pleased I would be to exchange this Chantecoq for this Frenchwoman!"

CHAPTER TWENTY-TWO:

Gautier

After eight days, Doctor Laumann declared to Jean Aubry and Maurice Evrard that Chantecoq was out of danger; but he didn't hide from them that his convalescence would be a long one, because of the abundant loss of blood that he had suffered and his extreme weakness.

"And Germaine?" the inventor had murmured miserably in Maurice's ear.

"We'll save her without him!" the officer responded resolutely.

"In any case, count on me," Mr. Gautier promised.

The wounded man, who was gifted with extremely sharp hearing, had grasped this dialogue, though it had been exchanged at quite a distance from his bed.

"Come here, then!" he asked with a smile. "First because I don't like eavesdropping, and also because I think I have something very interesting to tell you."

"Don't tire yourself by speaking," Germaine's father recommended, approaching the bed.

"Oh! It would tire me much more to keep quiet," replied Chantecoq. "Anyway, I feel better. This excellent soup, followed by a glass of champagne, that the doctor allowed me to take this morning, has completely restored my spirits. Even if I'm not yet ready to take on Spandau Citadel, I am perfectly able to discuss with you the subject that interests us above all, that is to say our dear Germaine's escape.

"Now sit down. Listen to me without interruption, and you'll see that your friend Chantecoq, though he's on the periphery, can still be very useful to you."

"We're sure of that, my dear friend," the special commissioner protested.

As soon as the 'three conspirators' had taken their places on chairs, the expedition's chief, whose face began to take on a little colour and animation, said, raising himself gently on his elbows:

"All right! I'm happy! The trunk is good and the Germans haven't caught my hide this time! At the very moment when I was assailed by these three individuals, that by the description that I gave him our friend Gautier recognised, not, as I'd believed, as Colonel Hoffmann's agents, but really as three bodyguards of the spy Emma Lückner . . ."

"Maus, Kouraguine and Lenoir," the special commissioner interrupted.

"There had just come to my mind one of those luminous ideas which comes to a man once in a lifetime."

"My dear captain," Chantecoq interrupted himself, "without ordering you about, could you give me a mouthful of champagne."

"Gladly!" Maurice Evrard replied, immediately taking a bottle placed on the nightstand and half-filling a Bordeaux glass with the sparkling liquid, which he gave to the convalescent.

After having drunk, Chantecoq, more and more on form, continued.

"I had just had a lamentable failure with Mrs Fürsner, the fortress governor's wife, who I had thought to seduce by playing on the passion she has for embroidery. But when, after a thousand circumlocutions, I ended by declaring that I wanted her to pass to the prisoner the little trinkets necessary for her escape, she sent me away with masterful force, and I must count myself fortunate that she had the generosity not to have me arrested."

"The fact is," said Jean Aubry, "that you escaped her."

"Certainly! And then, I was rudderless. I was asking myself how we would proceed to reach our goal when suddenly I had this inspiration which, you're going to jump, consists simply of bringing Emma Lückner into our game."

"Emma Lückner!" the inventor, the captain and the policeman all cried.

"Yes," smiled Chantecoq. "I didn't doubt I was going to surprise you. But you'll see that my suggestion isn't as absurd as it first appeared to you."

"Well, for example," Gautier cried, "I'd be curious to know . . ."

"You're going to be satisfied, my dear friend. I told you, did I not, that among the papers that Miss Germaine succeeded in acquiring from the German Chief of Staff, there was one which was of the greatest importance. It was the irrefutable, manifest proof that Emma Lückner, who is of Russian origin, and who is in reality called Princess Tchernikoff – did you know that, Gautier? - poisoned her husband to get her hands on his fortune. Now this document, instead of addressing it like the others, to Paris, where the director of General Security would have had nothing to do with it at this time, I kept it on me, in the conviction that one day or other I would have the opportunity to make good use of it. I was right, as today we're going to be able to use it with advantage.

"I truly regret being unable to deliver myself to this lovable princess. But this good Mr. Gautier, who knows her and who, he's told me, has a little revenge to take since she slipped through his hands by leaving France, will no doubt not be reluctant to pay her a visit."

And, taking a wallet from under his pillow, from which he drew a bundle of letters, he gave them to the special commissioner, saying, "Here's the parcel! You will only have to show this to the lady in question and, I am sure that will instantly become as meek as a lamb. I don't need to teach you the lesson. You have already understood the way in which one can use such a weapon. I'm convinced that you will use it masterfully and that we will soon have in Emma Lückner the most devoted collaborator; because it's easy for her to get in and out of Julius Tower."

"It is clear," agreed Jean Aubry, "that now this woman is in our hands, just as she was in those of Colonel Hoffmann."

"She'll certainly prefer that," said Gautier.

"I agree with you," Germaine's fiancé said in his turn; "but I ask you with the greatest insistence not to reveal our escape plans to this woman, and especially not to give to her the ladder and the metal saw, that she will have to pass to Germaine, until after she has proved herself and when you are sure that she is on our side in this game."

"Be calm, captain," said the special commissioner, "I could not act otherwise."

"Above all," the captain recommended again, "return immediately to tell us the result of your visit."

"That won't take long! I have some assets on my side and, for a king's ransom, I undertake to bring back the lady!"

Emma Lückner had just returned home.

She felt weary, discouraged.

Indeed, after having visited the hospital that morning, where she had observed that the state of her three bodyguards was far from satisfactory, she had set to work to uncover Chantecoq's trail. But she had not taken long to realise that it was a task beyond her capabilities.

She could no longer count on any support. Colonel Hoffmann had taken on the case himself, and from the characteristic coldness that he had displayed in their last meeting, she understood that the Intelligence Bureau chief had decided to forego her services.

And then, she didn't know Berlin as she did Paris; she had only vague connections from whom she could draw no profit.

So, would she have to give up the fight?

After all, it was the wisest course to take, and the spy resolved, "Tomorrow, I'll go to see Colonel Hoffmann. I'll tell him 'I see that you no longer have any confidence in me, I ask you for my freedom!' Then, I'll go far away, very far, I'll recreate an existence for myself, and then I shall see . . ."

Feeling more and more weary, Emma Lückner was going to return to her room, when her chambermaid appeared, carrying a business card on a plate.

"What's this?" the spy asked, taking the card with a nervous movement.

She paled on reading the special commissioner's name.

"Him! That's not possible! It's a mystery," she said to herself.

She asked, mastering herself to dominate her emotion, "Where is this man?"

"There!" replied the maid, pointing to the door of the antechamber.

Hardly had this girl retired after a gesture from her mistress than Emma Lückner ran to the door and opened it.

She remained on the threshold, frozen in shock. It really was Mr. Ernest Gautier, the special commissioner of General Security.

"What do you want with me, sir?" she asked, mastering her unease, while her heart pounded in her chest.

"My visit surprises you?" said Gautier, entering. "I need to have a serious talk with you."

"You are extraordinarily audacious," said the spy, letting him come in.

"Why's that, then?" the magistrate asked, affecting complete serenity.

"You don't know then that your presence in Berlin is known to the highest authorities?"

"I know."

"It didn't occur to you then that by coming to my home I would need just one word, one gesture to have you arrested?"

"I did think of that, and I came all the same!"

"Really? Well! We shall see . . ."

The spy headed towards the window in order to call for help; but resolutely Mr. Gautier blocked her way.

"No silliness, Princess," he declared, "because in getting rid of me you'd lose yourself too."

"What do you mean?"

"I mean that I'm here quite simply to free you from Colonel Hoffmann's clutches."

"You!" Emma Lückner cried. "Go on then! That's impossible."

"I'm asking for five minutes to convince you," said Mr. Gautier, with the determined air of a man preparing for a serious discussion.

"That he dared to show himself like this at my home, alone," thought the spy, "and he speaks to me in this way, he must be sure both of himself and that he has nothing to fear!"

And she sat down in turn.

Calmly, the special commissioner began. "As I just said to you, far from wishing to cause you the slightest worry, which would not be easy for me here in any case, I have the project of ridding you of an impediment which must weigh on you heavily. That's quite nice of me, isn't it? After the trick you pulled on me back there. But I am of excellent character and I forget these things quickly.

"You have greatly intrigued me, I must confess; and when I discovered who you were a . . . forgive the expression but I can't find another word . . . spy in the service of Germany, I said to myself straight away, I who know your social situation, 'For such a woman, a true princess, Princess Tchernikoff, to consent to play this role, she must have been led there by circumstances independent to her wishes and constrained by a force which she has been unable to resist.'"

Extremely surprised, Emma Lückner listened, not without emotion, to the special commissioner who continued with the best grace in the world. "So, the day when you succeeded in escaping me, and putting the border between my agents and you, I had only one desire, to pierce the mystery that surrounded you, that is to say to inform myself of the circumstances, certainly very troubling and totally special, which must have brought you to the attention of the German high police. I looked, and I discovered the truth!"

"Truly?" the adventuress asked, affecting the greatest calm.

"You'll see. Several years ago, Prince Tchernikoff, your husband, died suddenly at a banquet which you attended. It is said that he was struck by a lightning attack of apoplexy."

"That's the truth!"

"Wait! He was interred with great pomp and, by virtue of a will set down in sound mind and body by the deceased with his solicitor, you immediately came into possession of his immense fortune."

"You have been admirably informed!" the spy tried to scoff.

"That's my job, and I was so admirably informed that I learned that, contrary to the opinion of the doctors called to him, your husband didn't die a natural death. He had been poisoned!"

At these words, the adventuress shuddered. "Poisoned?"

"Yes, with a concoction that a medical student, called Kouraguine, had poured into the beverage of the incorrigible drinker that was your noble husband, during the course of the meal."

"Who could have told you such nonsense?"

"Oh! Princess, you know perfectly well there's not one word which is not the absolute truth in everything I've just told you. Anyway, I'm not here to play at refinement with you. We don't have any time to lose and I prefer to lay my cards before you directly.

"Colonel Hoffmann, Germany's great spymaster, came into possession, I don't know how, of several of your letters, written by the Kouraguine in question and in which your accomplice, reminding you of his participation in the premature opening of the opulent succession of your husband, claimed the reward you had promised him. Hoffmann summoned you to his office. That was exactly three years, two months and six days ago; the date is on the file. Now, this lofty civil servant used pretty much this language, as said La Fontaine in the admirable fable 'The Fox and the Crow', which your perfect knowledge of our literature suggests you won't be ignorant of . . .

"He said to you: 'My dear lady, this is what I have in my power. I ought to have you arrested this moment. Then I would immediately send these letters to the Russian ambassador. The next day a note would appear in our Berlin newspapers and would be reproduced instantly in all the broadsheets of Europe. The Tsar would immediately demand your extradition, and would obtain it straight away and . . . I don't need to tell you any more.'

"That's right, isn't it? More or less how things went?"

And as Emma Lückner fell silent, petrified, Mr. Gautier, more and more triumphant, continued. "Faced with these unexpected revelations, you literally collapsed. But Colonel Hoffmann went on: 'Princess, there is a way to sort everything out. Become a spy in my pay and these documents will remain forever buried in the special strongbox where we keep secrets even more important than your own.' You accepted and you became a remarkable collaborator for Hoffmann. I understand that; because however ungracious and even repugnant the role of spy might be for a woman of your quality, it is still preferable to being exiled to Siberia, or who knows? After having been cruelly beaten, a hanging in a prison in Saint Petersburg or Moscow!

"Now, by an extraordinarily prodigious stroke of fortune, it just so happens that the letters from this imbecile Kouraguine have wandered from the German Chief of Staff's strongbox . . . guess where?"

"Into your pocket?" the adventuress murmured.

"Here they are!" Mr. Gautier riposted and, with a theatrical flourish, brought out the Russian's dreadful correspondence and waved it in the Princess's face, adding: "You recognise them? Good! So I put them away again quickly, because there are objects which must not be aired."

"Get to the point," shouted Emma Lückner, rising, "what do you want?"

"Simply this," the special commissioner responded drily, "that henceforth you provide me with the same services that you provided for Hoffmann."

The spy, foreseeing this step, had had time to regain control of herself.

"My compliments, Mr. Gautier!" she said with a haughty irony. "You are taking a pretty revenge! But you must understand that before giving you a reply which will engage me in such a serious fashion, I need to reflect."

"Reflect! Why?" the special commissioner pretended to be astonished. "Your conduct is all traced. You no longer have anything to fear from Hoffmann, and you have everything to fear from me. You must therefore position yourself on my side."

"And if I refuse?"

"I'll act."

"In what way?"

"Let's see, you are intelligent enough to guess what use I might make of the weapon that I have in my hands."

"You forget, dear Mr. Gautier, that you're in Germany now, and that in Germany, if the police were to take an interest in you, it would be more likely that they would arrest you, rather than collar the people that you'll be denouncing."

"That depends," said Mr. Gautier. "I suppose that tomorrow the French, Russian and even German papers, recounting your little adventure with Colonel Hoffmann to their readers, while publishing Kouraguine's letters as proof . . .?"

The spy shuddered.

"I know Hoffmann," she said to herself. "He has an overwhelming fear of the press. He would drop me immediately. Oh! I'm truly in this Gautier's power, and just at the very moment when Hoffmann seemed ready to grant me my liberty. I must get out of this pickle by getting hold of Kouraguine's letters. Then I'll be able to face not just the French police, but also the German police, becoming myself again and no longer fearing anyone. As to Kouraguine, I'll deal with him myself!"

Then, aloud, she responded, "Who said I'm declining your proposition or refusing to serve you? What if I told you that, to the contrary, you have come at the perfect time?"

"Is this possible?"

"If I'd had enough of being in Germany's service? If I preferred to work for France? Because I love your country as much as I hate the other. All the same I wonder, when I'm an ally, will I be able to return to Paris?"

"Yes, but on one condition. First you will prove to us your sincerity and indeed devotion by rendering us one of those services which will erase at one stroke all the nasty tricks you've played on us. Then you'll be able to retake the sparkling place that you once occupied in Parisian high society, without anyone knowing what has happened; because the secret has been kept well and I would be sorry as much for you as for ourselves, if you would force us to reveal everything and expose your name to a sensational global scandal."

"My dear Mr. Gautier," replied the spy, "there's no point in making threats. You have taken your revenge. I won't make recriminations against fate. I acquiesce and I accept your propositions with so much more readiness than I could possibly express to you. I'm nostalgic for France, for Paris . . ."

"That's all for the best, then!"

"Earlier you told me, and it's completely natural of course, that first I would have to give you a blazing proof of my loyal attachment. I'm entirely prepared to do that."

"Well, that's interesting! Let's see!"

Then, slowly, giving each word its full weight, Emma Lückner said, "What would you say, for example, if I helped you break out the prisoner from Julius Tower?"

"Oh! Oh!" exclaimed the special commissioner who, despite the attitude of his redoubtable associate, had not yet lost all suspicion, and judged it prudent to remain on his guard. "That's a perilous adventure!" he added, twirling his moustache. "Do you believe yourself to be in a position to take on such an audacious project?"

"Yes," replied the spy, "especially with the help of Mr. Aubry and Captain Evrard, for whose presence in Berlin there can be no other explanation."

"I really don't know what you mean," said Mr. Gautier, a little disconcerted.

"Come on, come on!" protested the adventuress, who had regained all her assurance. "If you want us to work together usefully, it's vital that we both put our cards on the table. What do you have to fear from me? Nothing, as you own me, and you can hurl me into the abyss. I know that Aubry and Evrard are here, as I also knew that you were here. I guess that their cooperation is absolutely necessary to us and that the first thing to do is to unite our efforts in the common goal."

Approaching Mr. Gautier, putting her arm on his, she let slip, "If you only knew how happy I am to be removed from the yoke of these Germans, without any education or delicacy, who sometimes browbeat me like a simple agent in their secret brigade! I'm sure at least that with the French, relations will be agreeable and that you will never put aside the respect that is due to a lady."

"Consider the further services that I can offer," continued the spy, becoming animated and with a passion whose sincerity even the most sceptical and doubting person could not suspect. "Not only can I help you to break out Germaine Aubry, but I'm even ready to reveal everything I know, while pretending to stay on best terms with Colonel Hoffmann."

"That's precisely what I was going to ask of you," the special commissioner declared, radiant at the success of his mission.

"And I'm enchanted to get along with you!" said the adventuress whose face reflected a joy that she didn't even try to contain. Immediately, she suggested, "Let's speak a little of the prisoner. Some time ago, Colonel Hoffmann gave me the mission of obtaining enough information from her to track down her accomplices. I've been unable to tear a single clue from her, oh! She's a very fine character!"

"Yes, a very fine character!"

"I kept the pass which permits me to enter the citadel and to communicate with the captive. As a consequence, if you have something to be said to her, or some object to give to her, I can take care of that."

"That would be," replied Gautier, now convinced that he had in Emma Lückner the most devoted and precious of all collaborators, "that would be . . ." but the princess interrupted him.

"Excuse me, dear Mr. Gautier," she said. "At this time I usually take some tea, which I prepare myself in the Russian style. I hope that you'll accept a cup?"

"Gladly!"

"You'll excuse me for a minute, won't you?" said the princess, vanishing.

CHAPTER TWENTY-THREE:

A Double Revenge

The special commissioner was exultant.

"I'll do whatever I want with her," he said to himself, contentedly. "She is devoted to us. The director of General Security will pull one of his faces when I introduce the lady in question to him, saying, "Boss, I promised you that I'd bring Emma Lückner to your office, didn't I? Well here she is, not as an enemy, but as an associate!

"And this excellent Mr. Aubry! And Captain Evrard!" he reasoned. "They're going to be happy when I return and announce to them that Miss Germaine's deliverance is now just a question of days, perhaps hours! Because everything becomes extremely easy, thanks to the new asset that we have on our team. The time to transport the aircraft to Spandau and to construct it, that's one day's business! We'll give the famous ladder and metal saw to the princess, and all is done, it only remains to act . . .”

The door opened and the chambermaid appeared, bringing a smoking samovar that she put on the table.

The princess followed her with a tray on which two porcelain cups sat next to a silver sugar bowl.

The maid retired and the adventuress, with infinite grace, did Mr. Gautier all the honours of a tea ceremony, and the tea was excellent . . .

After having offered the special commissioner a second cup which he accepted readily, she took a cigarette, lit it, and stretched herself over the sofa, saying, “Why don’t we pick up our meeting where we left off?”

“Gladly!” Mr. Gautier accepted straight away.

But, getting up and taking on a suddenly distracted air, the Princess cried, “What am I thinking! I’m smoking and I forgot to offer you a cigarette. Please excuse me . . .”

And opening an ornate silver case, she offered it to the policeman. “Doubtless you’ll find my cigarettes a little weak. They’re the only ones I smoke.”

The special commissioner accepted and after having lit his cigarette, he said, “We were talking about Miss Germaine Aubry’s escape.”

“That’s it,” said Emma Lückner resuming her pose. “If you only knew how happy I am to be in this conspiracy, and to play one of those tricks which can demolish a man on Hoffmann. Such a repulsive, detestable man!"

"I agree!"

"What a shock to Germany when everything comes out! But I'm chatting away and it's time you let me know what I have to do."

"First," Mr. Gautier began, inhaling deeply the smoke from the excellent Russian cigarette, "here's . . ."

But he broke off, a little embarrassed.

Then he tried to begin again. "First, we ought . . ."

Mr. Gautier stopped again.

Emma Lückner, who for a moment gave him a strange look, immediately suggested, "Would you like a glass of liqueur, perhaps?"

The special commissioner, whose eyes had begun to flutter, shook his head. Feeling slightly dizzy, he wanted to move, and tried to rise from the armchair. But he instantly sat back down, as if a weight pressed on his shoulders and nailed him to his seat.

"Whatever's wrong?" asked the spy. "Are you indisposed?"

Gautier raised his arm in an evasive gesture; but it fell straight back down heavily, while his head fell against the back of the armchair.

A few seconds later, his eyelids shut, his mouth slightly open, the policeman slept deeply.

Emma Lückner waited a moment.

"Goodness," she sneered, while a wild light burned in her eyes, "my dear Mr. Gautier, you're not of a stature to face me! At least there's one game I've not lost! He wanted to take his revenge, the poor man! I rather believe that it's my own. A double revenge, one on him, and the other on Hoffmann!"

Then, leaning towards the sleeper, she slipped her hand gently into his coat pocket, removed the wallet where the special commissioner had hidden Kouraguine's letters, opened it and took out the papers.

Emma Lückner examined them with close attention and, satisfied, slipped them into her corset, saying, "They're all there, in full! Now, I'm free from this unbearable yoke. I'm free! I can finally hold my head high and retake my place in society. But most of all, I want revenge! Ah! It was Germaine Aubry who stole these papers from the Chief of Staff and who sent them to Paris, thinking to defeat me. Now, the Frenchwoman!"

Then with great care, the infernal creature proceeded to examine Mr. Gautier's wallet.

Doubtless, it contained nothing of interest for her; because Emma Lückner soon replaced it in the magistrate's pocket, without having disturbed the slightest object.

Then, sitting close to the table, she began to reflect. "If I warn Colonel Hoffmann that the special commissioner of French security has just fallen sound asleep at my home and has about another two hours before waking up? I think that he would be quite interested, Mr.. Intelligence Bureau Chief! That's what will rehabilitate me in his eyes! But I can do better. Through this imbecile, I may now discover Chantecoq's retreat, with Jean Aubry and Captain Evrard. What a haul! Not only will I prevent Germaine Aubry's escape, but I'll have them all arrested!

"What a great farewell I shall wish to Germany, and with what joy will I say to Colonel Hoffmann, 'See how kind I am to you! You're no longer in possession of my papers, and I could have purely and simply withdrawn my reverence to you; but I'm a dilettante and I hold to my reputation as an intelligent woman. As such I preferred to leave you with a good impression by doing you a small service, all while conducting my personal business.'

"I therefore just have to leave Gautier to sleep at his ease and sit in a car opposite my house. When he leaves, I'll follow him, and he'll lead me to the nest of conspirators."

Then, sitting at a small desk, the spy dashed off a few lines on an envelope that she pinned to the sleeper's waistcoat.

"Good evening, my dear Mr. Gautier," she sneered. "Sleep well, and happy awakening!"

Then she disappeared, still laughing, triumphant, diabolical.

Two hours later, yawning, stretching, rubbing his eyes, finally coming out of the sleep into which Emma Lückner's 'special' cigarette had plunged him, Mr. Gautier didn't manage to take account at first of his state or of the place in which he found himself.

But on noticing the bit of paper fixed to his buttonhole, he said, "Hold on! What's this here?"

Suddenly returning to reality, he felt himself overwhelmed by a dreadful disquiet which translated itself immediately into a cold sweat and a racing heart.

"Ah! That . . . did that woman . . .?"

And with a haggard eye, in dread, he read:

"Thanks to you, I'm again in possession of the papers stolen from Colonel Hoffmann. It's therefore futile to count on me for Miss Germaine Aubry's escape, as well as the other conditions of which you spoke to me. I have regained my independence."

"I'm forever dishonoured!" moaned the unfortunate Commissioner, "I will never again dare to appear before my bosses. I have no choice but to end it all!"

And still under the narcotic's effect, incapable of reflecting for a moment, the unfortunate, panicked, discouraged, ran towards the window and with one leap, hurled himself through.

CHAPTER TWENTY-FOUR:

The Protean Man

Chantecoq, Jean Aubry and Captain Evrard had awaited Mr. Gautier's return anxiously.

The next evening, having received no news of the special commissioner, their disquiet grew further.

They were hardly in a situation which allowed them to seek out the latest news. Though they were safe for the moment in the asylum that the excellent Mr. Laumann had prepared for them, they were as good as immobilised within their hideout.

The inventor and the officer didn't know Berlin well enough to wander it unguided; on the other hand, Chantecoq was not in a state of health which permitted him to risk such a perilous adventure with impunity.

Indeed, though the French agent's wound was much less serious than first feared, the quantity of blood that he had lost had weakened him and it would take at least a week, perhaps two, before he could resume his exploits, and even then in a worryingly weakened condition.

So he was in a nervous state, which preoccupied Doctor Laumann.

"I'm sure," Chantecoq said to himself, "that this devil Gautier has made an error. It's my fault. I'd have done better to wait. This Emma Lückner is capable of anything."

And through pure thought, the ingenious policeman reconstituted the scene he feared.

"Gautier will have wanted to be clever," he imagined, "and he will have brought out his big guns straight away. His opponent will have appeared very gentle, very humble, and she will have easily drawn him into a trap which he will not have seen coming.

"I wouldn't be surprised if right now he is reflecting, in a dark dungeon, on the inconveniences of acting too confident towards a woman.

"Luckily, I took care to photograph the papers that Germaine Aubry lifted from the Intelligence Bureau chief; without that we would be completely disarmed."

As Jean Aubry and Captain Evrard, who hardly ever quitted his bedside, came to check on him, Chantecoq said to himself, "It's pointless to sow disarray in the souls of these brave men. Let's pretend to believe the game is not lost. But I fear this poor girl still has some time to spend in Julius Tower.

By one of those efforts of willpower to which he was accustomed, Chantecoq, mastering his nerves, succeeded in giving his face an expression of perfect calm.

So, when Germaine's father and fiance approached, they were surprised to find him sitting upright, a smile on his lips, and to hear him declare spontaneously to them, "That's much better. I hope that we'll be able to get back to work in a few days."

"Then," the inventor observed, "Mr. Gautier's disappearance doesn't torment you too much?"

"Oh, Mr. Gautier!" Chantecoq bantered. "He's a very brave man. But no one is indispensable. If he's been taken, too bad for him! We'll try not to do the same."

"What are your plans then?" the aviator asked feverishly.

"First, to cure myself, and I feel that the way things are going, I'll be back on my feet in a few days. Then, to rejoin battle. While taking care of myself I'm going to reflect, to delve. I'm convinced that I'm not yet at the end of the road, and that I've not said my last word! The only thing I ask of you is not to leave this house, and to commit no imprudent act until I'm completely recovered."

"You can count on us," Jean Aubry and Captain Evrard responded simultaneously.

But the days were going to drag by for the two men.

Their thoughts could not be deflected from Spandau Citadel, where the heroic Germaine was locked up.

Their inability to help her gnawed at them.

Their souls, so very valiant, revolted against this sort of claustrophobic existence into which they were forced; and they needed, with the authority that Chantecoq exerted on them, all the strength and willpower they possessed, and their obstinate desire to break out the dear prisoner, in order to prevent them from going outside, and the need to deliver them from these foolish acts which engender despair.

After a few days, Mr. Laumann, who had wisely maintained vital relationships in Berlin's policing world, learned that Mr. Gautier, found insensible and violently bruised in one of the city's main streets, had been taken to a military hospital where he had been held in secret, and he was being cared for and watched with the greatest vigilance.

"Now I'm calm," Chantecoq declared philosophically. "I know where he is, that's the main thing, and bearing in mind that he didn't get us caught along with him, I couldn't ask for any more.

"It would be prudent not to leave him to marinate too long in the soup that Colonel Hoffmann is preparing for him, however. One stray word would be enough to doom us all. The first thing to do is to get Gautier out from where he is, the second is to send him to Paris as quickly as possible, where he'll be able to recover at ease from his ordeal and his worries.

"We'll see! Let's make fewer monologues and let's think wisely. I still need three or four days to regain my strength. That's more or less all I need to compose with care the new character that I'm going to incarnate. Because this time, I've decided to risk all to win all, and I see no other way of finishing than to take over the direction of the German police myself.

"Who could deliver Mr. Gautier and Germaine Aubry to me at once? Who is all-powerful enough to open the prison gates for me? Colonel Hoffmann. Oh well! Why shouldn't I become Colonel Hoffmann for a time? He's a little taller than I, that's nothing. I'll grow, though I'm not Spanish.

"He has a smooth face, a clog for a chin and a bird's beak of a nose. It's an easy face to model. I've had much greater challenges than that.

"As to the uniform, that question is secondary.

"That just leaves the monocle, the gait, a few gestures, and there we are."

The same evening, Chantecoq had one of his sub-agents deliver a photograph of the Intelligence Bureau chief in secret, and a Saxon infantry colonel's complete uniform.

For several days while he convalesced, he studied Colonel Hoffmann's face and gaze, managing to identify him to such a point that, seeing himself in the mirror, he couldn't stop himself from crying out, "Truly I disgust myself! I want to stab me myself!"

But not content with the show of satisfaction that he'd just bestowed on himself, he resolved to try a test which would be a decisive guarantee of security and an encouraging promise of success for him.

Around four o'clock one morning, feeling completely fit – the evening before, Doctor Laumann, who had replaced the dressing with a simple band of cloth pressing the thoracic cage, had given him his all-clear, while recommending he try not to overdo things – Chantecoq got up quietly, transformed himself into Colonel Hoffmann and left the villa which had served as his retreat as well as that of his two companions; he reached the courtyard, walked the length of the factory buildings and, opening a small door which led to a deserted street, behind the workshop of Mr. Laumann, he returned to the main entrance by another path, and rapped on the grille.

Growling, the concierge got up and came to open up.

On seeing the silhouette of a German officer, the watchman, having become best friends with the three Frenchmen, panicked and fell backward.

"We're betrayed!" he said to himself. "I'm going to warn the boss before I open up."

As he was moving away, Chantecoq, wanting to push the test to its limits, drew a revolver from his pocket and said in German, in a dry, imperious voice:

"If you say one word, I'll blow off your head! Let me in!"

The concierge reflected for a second. "If I call out, that will do no good, other than getting me killed by this man. Let's be more subtle! Once he's in the courtyard, I'll lock the door, I'll bring him in with me, I'll keep him there, I'll go and find the boss, and if there are other Bosch in the street, while this one explains himself to Mr. Laumann I'll warn my friends and take them to a safe place. There are some empty barrels standing ready in the cellar."

And, executing his plan, the concierge unbolted the door, letting the visitor pass. He closed the peephole brusquely, then said to the fake Colonel, in the most markedly obsequious tone, while pointing him towards the threshold of his lodge, "Please enter, Colonel, and wait while I go and wake my boss."

Chantecoq, who was beginning to enjoy himself immensely, entered the little villa and allowed himself to be locked in without giving any sign of resistance.

A few minutes later the good Mr. Laumann, who had sent the concierge to warn Germaine's friends in all haste, ran over to the lodge, and recognising Germany's supreme police chief, asked him with a friendly voice and perfect assurance:

"Is that Colonel Hoffmann I have the honour of addressing?"

"Yes, Mr. Laumann," the Protean man responded impassively.

"What have I done to merit the grace of your morning visit?"

"Mr. Laumann, you're hiding three French spies here."

"Me, Colonel . . ."

"Yes, you!"

"I'd be curious to know who could have told you such nonsense?"

"That's no concern of yours, I know it! And the proof is that at this moment Chantecoq, Aubry and Evrard are hidden in a building attached to your home, and that they sent you a dismantled aeroplane which is there, in your home, in your courtyard, designed to break out the prisoner in Julius Tower.

"Well, Mr. Laumann, know this, if you don't deliver to me immediately these three individuals and their contraption, I'll arrest you on suspicion of espionage and the crime of lese-majesty."

"As you wish, sir," said Laumann coldly. "But in any case I can assure you that you are in error. Nevertheless, if you demand, I'm ready to follow you!"

Then, in his natural voice, Chantecoq, radiant, said in French, grasping the noble Alsatian's hand, "I beg your pardon, Mr. Laumann, to have indulged myself in this little joke; but it was necessary for the success of our undertaking. I needed to be sure that my latest creation was as successful as the others."

"What! Then you're not . . ."

"Come, my dear Mr. Laumann, don't you recognise me?"

"But . . ." the excellent man hesitated.

"I'll give you a clue," said his interlocutor. "I'm one of the Frenchmen to whom you extended, so many long days ago, such cordial and discreet hospitality."

"Chantecoq!" gasped the industrialist suddenly, completely bewildered.

"The very same! Now that I'm sure of my little effect, go quickly and reassure my friends who must already be hidden in your cellar's barrels, and tell your cook to prepare a good lunch for us at noon precisely. I recommend above all that your valet sets one extra place."

"You have a guest?"

"Exactly."

"May I ask whom?"

"It's a surprise."

And releasing the good Alsatian's hand, who had not yet completely left his state of bewilderment, he embraced him warmly, saying, "I believe that my health has been restored and I hope that before long the aircraft of which we just spoke, will fly towards the frontier, towards France, with a pretty passenger on board!"

CHAPTER TWENTY-FIVE:

The Military Hospital

Mr. Ernest Gautier had escaped death as if by a miracle.

Emma Lückner, who watched for his exit and intended, through following him carefully, to reach the place where the other Frenchmen were hidden, had seen him throw himself through the window and fall in the street.

Quickly, she had hurried over and arranged for the special commissioner to be picked up and taken into her home. He seemed in quite a pitiful state.

The adventuress was a woman of decision.

Immediately she said to herself, "It's impossible for me to keep this man at home, so much more so as the noise of the accident will quickly echo through the town and reach the ears of the police.

"As a consequence, it's wiser on my part to forestall this by warning Colonel Hoffmann.

"It's already a fair result to deliver to him one of the finest specimens of the French police. And as this brave Intelligence Bureau chief will not suspect for a minute that I am once again in possession of the documents thanks to which he had a hold on me, I'll be able to mock him most agreeably, all while having the air of serving him, which is not at all displeasing to me."

So while the unfortunate Gautier was being laid out on his enemy's own bed, she ran to the telephone, asked for Colonel Hoffmann and let him know that he had to come to her house, dropping all other business, to take delivery of a parcel which could not fail to interest him greatly.

This news came as no surprise to the German Vidocq.

Indeed, some moments before, on returning to his office to read over the evening reports, he had learned from an agent who had run there in all haste, that a stranger had tried to commit suicide by throwing himself from the window of an apartment occupied by Princess Tchernikoff, and he had considered making enquiries himself when the Russian's call made up his mind to go and see her.

Emma Lückner was waiting for him in her lounge.

"Colonel," she said, welcoming him with her most gracious smile, prepare yourself to learn something completely unexpected and original."

"You'll forgive me," Hoffmann said instantly, "if I'm not as surprised as you hoped, because nothing astonishes me when it comes to you."

"Truly?"

"Yes. Anyway, I already know a large part of what you're about to tell me."

"Impossible!"

"About an hour ago, a man tried to kill himself, at your home, by throwing himself in the street."

"My compliments, you are well informed!"

"It's my duty and my function to be so."

"So, Colonel, do you know this man's name?"

"I confess I do not, and I came solely in order to find out."

"Well! It's one of those I promised to deliver to you and who, alone, was caught in the trap."

"Chantecoq?"

"Ah! No, that would have been too perfect!"

"So . . . Evrard? Jean Aubry?"

"No. Mr. Ernest Gautier."

Colonel Hoffmann pulled a slightly disdainful face.

"Mr. Gautier," he said, "is a target only of secondary importance. It's something though, at the end of the day. Explain to me then how he got there."

"As usual, he had unlimited confidence in himself. He believed himself very bold by coming to find me suddenly to propose to me that I . . . guess what?"

"My word, I've no idea."

"To break out Germaine Aubry."

"What? He came to you, he dared!"

"He was very sure of himself."

And with a strange accent, and all while gazing obliquely at her redoubtable companion, the adventuress added, "Would you believe that he had the audacity to tell me that being in possession of the documents which have allowed you to force me to be your auxiliary, he gave me the choice to either facilitate the escape of the prisoner in Julius Tower, or to see myself dishonoured in the eyes of all Europe, and needfully the object of an extradition demand on the part of Russia?

"I laughed down my nose at him, and seeing that he was bluffing I replied first that I didn't know to which papers he was alluding; and as he detailed certain facts of a nature which showed me that he was quite aware of the event, I replied that while admitting you had a file in your possession that was compromising for me, you were too skilful to allow yourself to be robbed of it."

"Very good!" Hoffmann approved, listening to the spy with the greatest attention.

"Seeing that, I told myself I only had one moment to lose and that the best course was to assure myself of this imprudent and impudent Frenchman's capture. I locked him in my lounge, and as I was about to telephone, I was told that a man, trying to get down from my apartment by way of the balcony, had fallen to the ground.

"I hurried to intervene; and as Mr. Gautier was showing no further signs of life, I had him brought up here. I sent out for a doctor who is examining him now. It is now up to you to take any measures that you deem appropriate. I have delivered your man. I have only to busy myself with the others; because I hope that, with this new success, you will grant me again, Colonel, all your confidence."

"What game is this woman playing?" the Colonel asked himself, very perplexed. "In the end there's no time for psychological deductions; to the contrary this is the moment to act. She brings me one of the men I'm looking for, there's still that. It's up to me, through him, to get the others."

And aloud he asked, "Conduct me to Mr. Gautier."

"Follow me," said Princess Tchernikoff, who immediately led the Intelligence Bureau chief to her bedroom.

The doctor was sitting at the bedside of the injured man, who was beginning to regain consciousness.

On noticing Colonel Hoffmann, whose silhouette was legendary, not only in Berlin but throughout Germany, the practitioner who was a medicine-Major in the Landstürm, immediately snapped to his feet, taking the stiff stance of a wooden soldier, a true Prussian.

"Is he seriously hurt?" Hoffmann asked drily, with no further preamble.

"I don't believe so, Colonel," the medic replied. "Multiple contusions, but no fracture. Just a violent concussion."

"No internal injuries?"

"I can't yet say. It's only in a few hours and perhaps in several days that I'll be able to establish a certain diagnosis."

"Is he transportable?"

"Oh! Yes, Colonel."

"Good! Arrange an ambulance to come here immediately."

"Yes, Colonel."

"Go!"

"Yes, Colonel."

One hour later Hoffmann, who had not wanted to entrust the duty to anyone else, drove the unfortunate Mr. Gautier to Berlin's principal military hospital himself. Gautier who, returned to his senses and taking account of his situation, regretted bitterly and from the bottom of his heart that he'd escaped the death that he'd tried to give himself.

Following a confidential meeting between the Intelligence Bureau chief and the hospital's director, the special commissioner had been led to an isolated room and placed under the surveillance of two agents that Hoffmann had sent for with all haste and in whom the policeman could have absolute confidence. So Gautier was in the same situation as Wilhelm

Ansbach had been in Lunéville. But his case was seriously different.

First, he was in the hands of the military authorities.

Second, he had two colossi for guards, and it was impossible to disrupt their vigilance, whether by ruse or corruption.

Thirdly and finally, he was known, identified, and he could not for one moment benefit from confusion or an escape attempt.

So he was desolate, desperate. Indeed, not only had he found himself in the most dangerous position, but in letting the precious papers be recaptured by Emma Lückner, he fell into the German police's clutches, he had compromised that which he had undertaken to do and those who were associated with him in his goal.

Bruised, broken, twisted, he sought to recall if his wallet, of which he had been carefully relieved, had contained any items capable of putting Hoffmann and his agents on the trail of Chantecoq and his friends. But his poor brain, feverish, sick, distraught, was incapable of stitching two ideas together.

So he had moments of invincible anguish, after which, broken, spent, he remained stretched out on his bed, incapable of thought.

Several times, Colonel Hoffmann came to visit him.

With an affected courtesy, the German enquired after his health, asking him if he was satisfied with the care being given him, and if he had any complaints to make.

But he kept himself from making any allusion to the situation in which the special commissioner found himself, treating him much more as a colleague than an enemy.

By acting in this way, Hoffmann had his plan, which didn't lack a certain skillfulness.

Having found nothing interesting in the papers seized from the French policeman and possessing no other clue on the hideout of those for whom he would pay dearly to capture, he said to himself, not without logic, "Even though I've not seen this Chantecoq, I know him well. All the acts that he has committed against us bear their maker's mark too clearly for me not to have been completely edified as to his character for some time.

"Now, at this moment, he must have only one goal: to save Gautier, perhaps even before saving Germaine Aubry. The best thing, therefore, is to organise surveillance around the hospital which will be as discreet as it will be active. Then, facilitating Chantecoq's manoeuvres to a certain extent, will permit us to get hold of him and his whole team."

So, with this intention, the Prussian detective established one of those true police networks. Now, days went by and the Intelligence Bureau chief saw no dawn on the horizon.

For his part, Mr. Gautier began to find the days very long.

He was better, much better, and was growing bored and irritated.

One day, returning to this bluff which had not yet ever succeeded, he asked the hospital director when they'd sign his discharge papers, and the doctor replied, "That's not my business!"

"In that case," replied Mr. Gautier haughtily, "send me straight to prison!"

"You're already there."

"So allow me to write to my ambassador."

"That would give you a fever."

"But that's abominable! By what right do you hold me here?"

"Because we are very interested in you, and we want you to avoid a further accident."

"Enough taunting!"

"I'm not taunting. Allow me to prescribe you the greatest calm, to avoid the return of this hot fever, which failed to cost you your life."

Mr. Gautier did not insist further.

He felt that he would not be the strongest at this game.

He contented himself to grind his teeth and clench his fists in rage deep in his pockets.

Now, one morning when he had just got up and was pacing his bedroom as a tiger paces its cage, seeking in vain for a way in which he might communicate with the outside world, the door opened, making way for Colonel Hoffmann.

"Mr. Gautier," said the newcomer in the most perfect French, "I've come to give you some good news. The military hospital's director just told me that you don't seem to be very happy here."

"That's true."

"Ah well! As I basically try to be agreeable to you, I came to look for you to take you to a place where you will certainly be much more at ease."

"Colonel Hoffmann," cried the special commissioner, immediately on the defensive, "I trust to tell you first that I have had enough of all your misplaced jokes. Tell me frankly what you want to do with me, but stop this cruel game, so unworthy of both of us."

"Don't get angry, Mr. Gautier," recommended the German policeman. "This time, I assure you that I'm not joking. You're going to have the proof of that very shortly."

"I doubt that."

"Come now, Mr. Gautier, have a little more faith in a colleague who asks for nothing but to be agreeable to you."

"Leave me alone!"

"What a bad mood you're in this morning! If you've spent a sleepless night, I believe I can guarantee that you'll sleep better tonight."

"What are you doing here, Colonel, proving the extent to which you lack generosity?"

"Then you don't want to come with me?"

"Ah! Of course I don't want to!" shouted the angry French Commissioner. "I'd be crazy to want to go with you. Without doubt you'll have me stabbed by your cops, brutalised, maltreated . . ."

"Oh! Mr. Gautier, how you misjudge me!"

"In the end, it's futile to prolong a meeting which can only last too long. I beg you, let's stop this charade."

"Oh well, come along?"

"I'm following you."

The special commissioner, taking his hat and his overcoat that were brought to him after one having been ironed and brushed, and the other cleaned carefully, followed suit behind the German police chief who, once in the corridor, took hold of his arm in a friendly gesture.

"Don't touch me!" Emma Lückner's enemy recoiled.

"Be assured," said Hoffmann, "that I'm afflicted with no contagious illnesses. I simply feared that you were still a little weak."

The hospital director advanced towards them.

Hoffmann handed him a document which was none other than the receipt for the prisoner that the chief doctor returned to him.

The two Germans saluted each other.

As to Gautier; forcing his hat further down over his eyes, he headed towards the door, still flanked by the Intelligence Bureau chief, who did not take his eyes off him.

A closed car was parked before the military hospital gates, piloted by a soldier from the guards.

Politely, Hoffmann invited his companion to climb in.

Gautier obeyed, and as soon as the two men were sitting in the car it set off at a fair pace, soon heading towards Berlin's popular districts.

Mr. Gautier had taken a grave resolution a few moments before.

He had sworn to lock himself into a silence as contemptuous as it was absolute.

But after ten minutes, seeing that they were heading into the narrowest streets, he asked, "Ah, Colonel, where are you taking me?"

"To Moabit."

"Where we'll reach one of your main holding houses?"

"Where I'll provide you with a surprise which you'll never think to expect."

"What?"

"Oh! After all, I don't know why I should make you languish any longer. You're already very nervous."

"What's this?"

"I see. Well, dear Mr. Gautier, open your ears, widen your eyes, call on all your strength not to be overwhelmed. In a few minutes you will be in the arms of your friends Chantecoq, Aubry and Maurice Evrard."

"Ah! You've taken them too?" demanded the brave functionary.

And, incapable of mastering the fury bursting from him, Gautier, chancing everything, threw himself on Hoffmann crying, "So be it! Too bad! What will be will be, but I'm still going to smash your face in!"

Suddenly he felt himself paralysed by an iron grip.

"Mr. Gautier," the Intelligence Bureau chief declared placidly, "you're being unreasonable. What! I tell you that I'm going to reunite you with your best friends and you want to kill me?"

Disarmed, agitated, reduced to impotence, the special commissioner, who had believed himself gifted with a muscular strength that was not common, stammered unintelligible insults to which his adversary responded with an ironic smile.

The car continued now, at top speed. After having crossed Moabit, it reached the outskirts, driving down a beautiful avenue planted with trees and bordered with industrial buildings and powerful factories whose chimneys sent to the sky long plumes of black smoke.

Then letting out a gay peal of laughter, Chantecoq-Hoffmann cried out. "I pity you, my good Mr.

Gautier. You asked for the drama to end; well! You will be satisfied!"

And letting out a cock a doodle doo which made the car's windows rattle, he asked triumphantly. "Do you recognise me now?"

"Chantecoq!" the special commissioner exclaimed.

"Yes, Chantecoq! What do you say to that?"

"I say that you are our master in everything," Mr. Gautier confessed, "and I ought to thank you on my knees and beg your pardon."

And, his eyes full of tears, he added: "Certainly, I'm nothing but an imbecile!"

"No!" the French agent replied with a voice overflowing with the most benevolent sympathy. "You're not an imbecile, my dear friend; far from it!"

"However . . ." Taking hold of the civil servant's two hands affectionately, Chantecoq interrupted him to continue, with a voice that emotion made tremble slightly. "No, you're a brave man, too brave a man for a career as a policeman."

"Oh well! And you?" replied Emma Lückner's victim spontaneously.

"Oh! It's not the same thing at all with me!" said the mysterious character with a voice pierced with contempt and hatred all at once. "I have an old score to settle with these people!"

CHAPTER TWENTY-SIX:

The Order

Some moments later, Gautier fell into the arms of Aubry and Captain Evrard.

The excellent special commissioner, incapable of containing himself any more, collapsed in tears.

"To think that I almost lost you all!" he moaned.

In clipped, disjointed phrases, he told his friends of the remorse that gnawed at him.

But Chantecoq, always generous, put an end to his sincere lamentations by declaring in a joyous voice: "All's well that ends well!

"We have missed you a bit; but as you're back here now and the danger is behind us, it only remains for us to congratulate ourselves on finding ourselves reunited, intact, and ready to begin again."

"Not I!" said Gautier, sheepishly.

"Well! Dear friend," replied the Protean man, "do you want me to tell you something?"

"Speak!"

"In the end, and without you knowing, by being arrested you have done us a great service."

"Impossible!"

"I'll go further . . ."

"Say it!"

"You've helped Miss Germaine's escape, which up to now appeared to me to be the most problematic and even the riskiest thing, to become a child's game for me."

"I confess that I don't fully understand," said Mr. Aubry.

"Nor me," confessed the captain.

"Patience!" said Chantecoq. "I'm going to explain myself."

And, while installing himself at the abundantly stocked table that Mr. Laumann had prepared for his hosts, the mysterious policeman continued. "Follow my reasoning closely and you'll see how everything falls in place, everything is linked, and everything gives us practically certain success.

"Indeed, just as I was able to enter a Berlin military hospital under the guise of Colonel Hoffmann without being recognised, there's no reason why I can't enter Spandau Citadel just as easily. And, in the same way as I was able to get Mr. Gautier out of his room, who says that I'll not succeed, without any more trouble, to get Miss Germaine out from her prison?

"Only we must hurry, because it's essential that I try the adventure before the Intelligence Bureau chief is warned that there's a Colonel Hoffmann walking around the town and countryside, and granting liberty to the very prisoners that he most wants to keep under lock and key."

"You'd dare to go to Spandau, like that?" Mr. Gautier was astonished.

"As soon as I've dined and gulped down a cup of this delicious Moka coffee that Mr. Laumann's cook has excelled in preparing for us, I'll head for Spandau in the car which brought us here and I hope that this evening I'll beg our host's leave to return to France, by an aerial route, naturally.

"Therefore, Mr. Jean Aubry, and you, captain, while I'm away, prepare your aircraft and bring it up to the hangar that Mr. Laumann has put at your disposal.

"The rest is up to me!"

The lunch, rapidly concluded while Gautier remained prudently inside the villa, Aubry and Maurice slipped inside the building where they had left the different pieces of the machine which was going to serve to rescue Germaine.

A flat terrain, quite extended and surrounded with a palisade would permit the machine to launch itself into the air without any difficulty, carrying, with a vertiginous rapidity, the three people that its cockpit could contain: the fugitive, her father, and her fiance. As to Chantecoq, he had decided, his exploit accomplished, to return to Berlin; he estimated that his role was not ended and that his scores had not been settled.

While waiting, he drove at top speed on the road to Spandau in a top of the range car, piloted by one of his sub-agents in whom he had the greatest confidence.

He arrived at the Citadel around half past two.

The car which had was identical to that which the Intelligence Bureau chief habitually used, stopped in front of the sentry box.

Without the slightest hesitation, Chantecoq-Hoffmann got down: and, the living image of the policeman, he automatically passed the sentry who saluted him.

Right in front of the gate, he met Majors Schlaffen, Tourchtig and Hunguerig, who, standing to attention, heels together, one hand to their helmets and the other on their sabre hilts, seemed hypnotised by the arrival of one who they naturally took to be the all-powerful master of German high police.

Bold-faced and calm as he always was when he played for high stakes, Chantecoq advanced towards the three brutes and asked them in that simmering, aggressive, shrill voice with which Colonel Hoffmann habitually addressed his subordinates and which the skilful policeman had assimilated marvellously, "What are you doing there, you men?"

"Colonel," the three champions responded simultaneously in a comical chanting tone, "we are replacing Commandant Fürsner."

At those words, Chantecoq's heart beat a little faster, because he said to himself, "Indeed, Providence smiles on us! Only Fürsner was to be feared. With these three cretins everything will work out smoothly."

And taking on a suspicious, impatient attitude:

"What, you're replacing Commandant Fürsner yourselves?"

"Yes, we . . ."

Feeling an explanation was necessary, Schlaffen declared: "Colonel, this morning Commandant Fürsner was forced to report to Berlin, on the Emperor's orders."

"Do you know if he will be absent for long?"

"He ought to be back this evening."

"Good!"

Then Chantecoq, more and more reassured, ordered, "Lead me to the Frenchwoman's dungeon."

Major Tourchtig stepped forward. "Yes, Colonel."

But Major Hunguerig, desirous to bring himself back in favour, thought he could guess, "Doubtless, Colonel, you want to observe yourself that precautions were well taken?"

"Who is this asking something of you?" replied the fake Hoffmann, blasting Hesse Nassau's incomparable champion of Frankfurt sausage with a terrible glower.

"I said this, Colonel, because earlier we had a phone call from Berlin warning us that an individual, passing himself off as Colonel Hoffmann, had broken out a French spy from the military hospital where he was under observation."

"This is hardly news to me," Chantecoq riposted imperturbably. "It was I who phoned you."

"It did indeed seem to me, Colonel, that I recognised your voice from the machine."

"And it's precisely for that reason," the skilful policeman thought he ought to add, "that I have come to fetch the detainee myself, to transfer her to another prison where she will be more secure than here because, with people who employ such procedures and show such audacity, we must be ready for anything, and I won't rest easy until . . ."

But he stopped.

A guttural cry had just burst from the three majors' throats.

Indeed, a second Colonel Hoffman, identical to the first in every respect, was stepping briskly over the citadel's entrance. Chantecoq said to himself with an instant and energetic decision, "If I don't chance my arm, I'm lost . . . Let's do it!"

And pointing the handle of the whip he was carrying at the Intelligence Bureau chief, he cried to the three majors: "What luck! We have him! Apprehend this man, this imposter, because it is he!"

Without hesitating for a second, so happy were they to finally have the opportunity to prove their zeal and devotion before their all-powerful leader, the sleeping champion, the beer champion and the sausage champion leapt on the true Hoffmann who, bewildered and incapable of resisting the formidable charge of the three majors, was in a moment grabbed, seized, mastered and led into the guardroom.

At the height of his rage, he called out to Chantecoq, who, his eye staring from behind his monocle, watched him silently.

"But it's he who must be arrested!" the German chief of police shouted vociferously.

"Gag him!" Chantecoq ordered phlegmatically. "Then throw him in a cell to await my preliminary interrogation."

As the majors carried out his orders conscientiously, the skilful agent, approaching the man he'd just beaten with a rare mastery, said to him, sneering: "I have you, Mr. Chantecoq! No doubt you wanted to release your compatriot, Germaine Aubry? Ah well! It is I who am going to take her soon, and to a place where you won't follow her!"

Hoffmann was frothing with rage.

He fainted. It was more than he could bear.

While Schlaffen, Tourchtig and Hunguerig led the military policeman to a cell, Chantecoq, respectfully saluted by the guard post's officer and his men, set off at a jaunty pace towards Julius Tower.

"Now," he said to himself, "I only have to enter the cell and Germaine is ours."

He climbed the staircase and reached the round path.

But his steps had barely echoed on the flagstones when a sentry advanced towards him, his rifle aimed, and shouted: "Who goes there?"

Confused for a moment, the fake Colonel stopped.

It seemed to him that he recognised the soldier who barred his route. The man who, some time ago, he had drugged with a narcotic in some kirsch.

The French agent was not mistaken.

It was indeed the same man.

Now, this same sentry who, quite apart from the days in prison to which he had been condemned, was quite stiff from the abuse which had been administered to him copiously by the governor's order, had become suspicious to such a point that in peril of his life he would not have let the Emperor himself pass the gate which he was charged with guarding.

Chantecoq, nevertheless, continued to approach him.

"Who goes there?" the sentry repeated.

"Ah dear," said the mercurial man, "so you don't recognise me?"

And straight away, believing to vanquish the sentry's resistance, he added. "I'm Colonel Hoffmann, Intelligence Bureau chief! Let me pass!"

"The password?"

Chantecoq started.

He had neglected this detail, not thinking for a single moment that a simple soldier of the King of Prussia would show himself to be more demanding than the chief medical officer of Berlin's military hospital.

But having decided to finish it, and feeling that if the situation was prolonged it risked being compromised irredeemably, he replied immediately with virulence. "Let me pass, I tell you! I must! I order you!"

"You shall not pass, Colonel."

"We shall see."

And confident in his strength, Chantecoq attempted to take hold of the rifle and disarm the soldier.

But he was dealing with a strong opponent.

The sentry, a robust Saxon, resisted, pressing his weapon against his chest and crying, "Guards! Guards!"

The guard ran.

Chantecoq reflected only for a second.

"If I let the guard arrive, I'm lost," he said to himself. "I'll have to confess that I don't know the password, and that will be enough to stir their suspicions and lead them to think that I'm the fake Hoffmann. But how to escape?"

The French agent never hesitated when faced with danger.

It was said that to the contrary difficulties increased his intelligence and audacity tenfold.

Well aware of the Citadel's topography, Chantecoq leaned over the wall, measuring with a glance the height which separated him from the wide moat surrounding the fortress, and before the sentry, strongly jostled by him and pushed some distance away, had the time to intervene, he swung his legs over the parapet and let himself fall into the ditch full of water.

From the exterior, his accomplice who, from the car's seat, had been present throughout the scene which had just played out on the round path, understood what he had to do; and, putting the car in gear straight away, he drove around Julius Tower and arrived just in time to pick up the fake Hoffmann at the point where, soaked to his bones, he was climbing up the slope.

Jumping in the car which left at top speed, Chantecoq, furious to have failed in the attempt, grumbled: "Without that brute of a sentry, I'd have removed Germaine Aubry from under the garrison's nose and beard! It's to the despair of all and enough to believe truly that fate is against us!"

But the guard, having arrived on the battlements and been informed by the sentry, fired a salvo in the direction of the car which, luckily screened by a thick curtain of pine trees, escaped the German bullets and disappeared round a bend in the road.

Attracted by the shots, Schlaffen, Tourchtig and Hunguerig who, still proud of their exploit, after having locked the Intelligence Bureau chief in isolation, had gone to the officers' mess to empty a bottle of 'seckt' (German champagne) to the Emperor's health, hurried over to be informed about what had happened.

The sub-officer on duty explained to them that Colonel Hoffmann, after having attacked the sentry who blocked his way, because he refused to give him the password, had leapt from the top of the ramparts, had swum across the moat and from there had fled in the car which had brought him.

So, for the first time, doubt sprouted in the minds of Germany's immortal champion of sleeping at will.

And this doubt translated itself by a phrase which, pronounced in a lifeless voice, made his two colleagues tremble with no less anguish. "If we were mistaken . . . !"

"That's not possible!" Bavaria's invincible champion of Munich beer refused to believe it pre-emptorily. "Colonel Hoffmann telephoned us himself, he told us that!"

"And then, then that would be too extraordinary," Hesse Nassau's incomparable champion of Frankfurter sausage observed.

But Schlaffen scratched his ear, which was a characteristic sign on his part of the most intense preoccupation. "All the same," he said, "all this is not very clear . . ."

The junior officer, whose own perspicacity was otherwise relative, appeared as a blinding light next to the intellectual obscurity of the three majors, and replied in turn.

"I fear that there was an error; because the true Colonel Hoffmann, first, would have had the password. Then, if he'd forgotten it, he would not have attacked a soldier who was fulfilling his duty . . . and, finally, on seeing the guards arrive, unless he had suddenly become mad, he would not have thrown himself from the top of the ramparts, at the risk of killing himself, in order to run away like a malefactor.

These words were simple, but clear, and sufficed to cast dread in the three majors' souls.

"He's got a point!" said Schlaffen.

"I fear so," added Tourchtig.

"Ah well! Then we're in the doghouse," Hunguerig concluded piteously.

A heavy and measured step echoed across the courtyard; and soon Commandant Fürsner appeared with the air of a dog, ready to bite.

Very worried – because he had heard, the shots fired from the top of the ramparts from outside and he had seen a car which, driven by a Saxon soldier, heading at top speed in the direction of Berlin – he came forward, growling, "Ah! What's going on? Has the prisoner escaped?"

"No, governor," the junior officer responded.

"All right, explain yourselves," groaned Fürsner. "What's the meaning of this drama?"

In a few words, the junior officer gave his leader an account of recent events.

Then the governor, understanding the contempt in which Colonel Hoffmann held these three cretinous lackeys who, their eyes on stalks, mouths open and trembling in their breeches, were waiting for the next part and the end of the incident, started to yell: "You've left nothing out! As gaffes go, you couldn't have made a more colossal one!"

"The one time that I was absent, well, that's in order! Where did you put Colonel Hoffmann?"

"In cell no. 7," moaned Schlaffen.

"With the toads and rats!"

"Come on, follow me and let's hurry!"

And as they descended the stairs which led to the underground area in which the cell was located, where the unfortunate Intelligence Bureau chief had been chained and where no prisoner had ever been locked up since the reign of Frederic the Great, Fürsner, guided by the junior officer who had been to look for a lantern, continued to vociferate.

"I had no idea we were so daft, so limited, so bitten! Oh! But this time... when the Emperor learns of this, he who already considers you to be three 'Ramollots' – he said it in front of me – he's surely going to force you into retirement, if he doesn't put you in front of a court martial. People have been shot for less than this!"

They finally arrived in front of cell no. 7's iron-barred door in which Hoffmann, returned to his senses, after having yelled like a demon in a font, was now only making deaf pleas and pained moans.

"It's me, Colonel! It is I, Commandant Fürsner, who has come to save you," Spandau Citadel's governor shouted immediately.

But, as though at this announcement of imminent liberty, the military policeman responded only with feeble cries of despair, the Commandant, turning towards the three majors, cried.

"Could it be said that the Colonel is wounded?"

"We might have roughed him up a bit," admitted Schlaffen.

"We did take him down the stairs a bit quickly," acknowledged Tourchtig.

"He was maybe a bit bruised," specified Hunguerig.

"Cretinous cretins!" roared the frothing governor.

And sharply, he ordered, "Open this door!"

The three majors looked at each other, dazed.

"Well! What? What are you waiting for?"

"The key . . ." said the three champions simultaneously.

"What! The key?" Fürsner exclaimed. "You ought to know where it is, you locked up the Colonel."

An eloquent silence was the three friends' only response.

Then, in paroxysms of exasperation, Fürsner seized Schlaffen by the arm and shook him rudely, crying, "Answer me! The key? Let's see the key!"

The champion of sleeping at will decided to admit piteously, "The key, governor, I no longer have it . . ."

"What have you done with it?"

"I gave it to Major Tourchtig, so that he could put it back on the board, where Major Hunguerig took it."

"Then, Major Tourchtig?"

"Governor," replied the beer champion, "I gave it to Major Hunguerig so he could replace it on the nail where he took it down."

"Very well! Major Hunguerig?"

"I returned it to Major Schlaffen," replied the sausage champion in his turn, "thinking he would need it in order to take food to the prisoner."

"Right! Major Schlaffen?"

"I returned it to Major Tourchtig . . ."

"You didn't!"

"I did!"

"I assure you!"

"Let's see!"

"Enough!" Commandant Fürsner interrupted with authority.

And he ordered: "Go and find this key immediately; because it will take too much time to knock down such a door! No locksmith would come out here. We'd have to get an engineer to blow it up, and we'd risk killing the Colonel."

"That would do it!

"Ah! Clumsy!

"Why did the Emperor have to summon me today? Why especially did the rules oblige me to entrust the Citadel to these three dumb asses?"

Schlaffen, Tourchtig and Hunguerig had turned around.

Heavily, their heads low, they climbed back up the stone steps that brought them into the light.

All three headed towards the gate where the board full of the fortress's keys was to be found. The nail above which the number 7 was printed was devoid of any key.

"Perhaps," hazarded the champion of sleeping, "one of us dropped it on the way."

"Let's look!" the beer champion suggested philosophically.

"Let's look!" echoed the sausage champion.

After an hour, Commandant Fürsner, seeing nothing coming back, decided to climb back up himself, after having assured the Intelligence Bureau chief that his deliverance would only be a matter of minutes.

As to the three majors who had rummaged in vain through every corner of the guardhouse, they were in the process of exploring the round path.

Seeing them bent over, red, sweating, huffing, confused, Commandant Fürsner shrugged his shoulders and cried: "For goodness sake! They've lost it, and they're too daft to find it again. I need to resort to the engineer after all."

The Citadel governor immediately reported to the Hauptman's (captain's) office representing this option and explained the situation to him.

After a lengthy cordial, but contradictory, meeting, the two officers agreed to acknowledge that it would be extremely dangerous to make use of any explosive to blow up the door.

It was decided to appeal to the garrison's sappers.

The most robust were chosen who, armed with spikes, hatchets and heavy hammers, succeeded, after prodigious efforts, in breaking down the door and freeing the unfortunate Hoffmann.

The Colonel was in a pitiful state.

His head bore multiple bruises.

The blood he had lost from his nose was staining his tunic, and his badly torn trousers left his shirt untucked.

Incapable of speaking a word, he fainted for the second time in Fürsner's arms, and two men had to carry him up from the guardhouse.

At the moment when the cortege was crossing the courtyard, heading towards the governor's private apartments where he had given the order for the police chief to be transported, Major Schlaffen, sweating huge droplets, gasping like a seal and running as fast as his little legs could carry him, appeared, brandishing the key to cell no. 7 and crying: "Here it is! Here it is! I found it!"

"Where was it?" the Commandant asked.

"In my pocket," replied the German Empire's immortal champion of sleeping at will, triumphantly!

CHAPTER TWENTY-SEVEN:

The Promise

A new subject of preoccupation and cause of general anguish had come to join all those which were already assailing General von Talberg.

The Chief of Staff had noticed with a ceaselessly growing disquiet that his daughter, the gentle Frida, became more melancholy every day, and was dwindling before his eyes.

One morning, feeling herself suffering, she let her father know that she would not come down.

Shaken, the general who had lavished the most profound tenderness on this frail child, of which his excellent heart was capable, in spite of his cold appearance, hurried to his child, whom he found pale, feverish, her hair in disarray, her eyes red-rimmed, as if she had spent the whole night crying.

"My poor child," he cried. "What's wrong? Are you sick?"

"No. But I've spent a bad night."

Trying immediately to master herself and to hide the pain which seemed to gnaw at her, the exquisite creature added: "You must not bother yourself, father. You above all who are so busy at the moment. It's a simple indisposition, a light illness, which will have vanished in a few hours."

Hardly had Frida pronounced these words than her eyes rolled back and her head fell to her pillow.

In full emotion, von Talberg rang for the chambermaid who came running and hurried to help him to revive the young girl.

But he had to leave Frida almost immediately, called by the functions of his duty, after having given the order to seek the family doctor, Professor Swinemunder, with all haste. Then he declared several times that he must be telephoned at the arsenal to be told of the physician's findings.

One hour later, the doctor, who had a complete paternal affection for Frida, found himself at her bedside, and after the most attentive examination, he wrote out a prescription, however a very anodyne one, consisting of a simple sedative to take in the evening before going to sleep.

He recommended that the sick girl should eat well, allowing her whatever she liked.

As the chambermaid told him of the general's manifest desire to have news of his daughter as soon as possible, Professor Swinemunder declared, "I'll go to the arsenal myself."

Now, on quitting the young girl's bedroom, the doctor no longer wore that jovial smile which seemed to fit so naturally on his large kind face.

Preoccupied, he reached his car which drove him to the place where the Chief of Staff was found, who came running as soon as he was warned of the professor's arrival.

Immediately, from the doctor's concerned physiognomy, von Talberg believed that his daughter must be seriously afflicted; because he cried straight away, grasping the hand Swinemunder held out to him, "Is it serious, doctor?"

"I consider, general, that you are one of those men who is always owed the truth. Well, yes, it is quite serious, but mentally more than physically. Your daughter is suffering from a sort of nervous depression, which is surely the result of a great intimate sorrow. For the moment, there is no immediate danger."

"Ah! My friend," the Chief of Staff interrupted with a sigh of relief.

"But I must not hide from you the fact that, if this state becomes prolonged, that dear child could very well be prey to a consumption which would not fail to cause some troubles to her system, followed by ravages which science is incapable of repairing and even of fighting."

"That's terrible!"

"That's why I'm giving you the earliest possible warning."

"I'm ready to do the impossible to save my daughter. In any case, you'll be there to guide me, and I'm convinced that your intelligent and devoted ministrations . . ."

"Oh! I," interrupted Swinemunder, "I may only be a very relative amount of aid in all this. It's you, my dear general, who must be your daughter's remedy."

"Me?"

"Yes, you! Listen to me carefully!"

"Without wanting to penetrate the intimacy of your home too far, will you allow me to ask you a question?"

"With pleasure! I consider that one must hold no secrets, even moral ones, from one's doctor, because often, to recognise what's wrong with a body, it's necessary to read a soul like an open book."

"You are right a hundred times and you put me completely at ease."

"Then speak," said von Talberg, "and I'll respond with complete sincerity."

Then with a tone of affected friendship, professor Swinemunder asked, "Some time ago, this dear Frida felt a profound disappointment, a bitter chagrin, didn't she?"

"Indeed, my dear professor," von Talberg replied very drily. "You have not failed to read in the papers of my misadventure with that French spy?"

"Yes, and perhaps your daughter suffered from the attacks that certain wretched minds directed against you?"

"Certainly, but above all she felt much pain on the account of that Frenchwoman to whom she had attached herself so deeply. But, my dear professor, it's not that which might have plunged her into this state which worries us both so much."

"Heartbreak, no doubt?"

"Yes, heartbreak."

"Devil take it!"

"Frida was engaged to an Uhlan lieutenant. For a long time I fought this project of marriage, for completely personal reasons; but seeing how Frida held on to this young man, I gave in . . ."

"You were right."

"Unfortunately, recent events have intervened, disappointing my daughter about her future spouse to such a point that she herself, of her own volition, took back her promise to him."

"And she has regretted it ever since?"

"I fear so."

"The facts which motivated the dear child's decision are of a sufficiently exceptional gravity that they render any hope of reconciliation impossible?"

"That rather depends on one's point of view."

"By admitting that your daughter is going back on her decision, would you consent to follow her down this path?"

"If it would restore her to health, I would do it wholeheartedly!"

"There's no other way to proceed," affirmed Professor Swinemunder. "Now I have the key to the mystery, Frida still loves her fiancé. Doubtless she obeyed a moment of ill humour, of jealousy, perhaps, or of momentary disappointment. That happens every day. As under her very gentle, very shy appearance, she hides a proud temperament, as well as an ardent will, she won't have wanted, from self-respect, to appear weak and to give in by leading this young officer to understand that she regretted acting precipitously and that everything could still be resolved.

"Yes, that's it, that must be it! Don't doubt it for a moment. It's therefore up to you, my dear general, just as I foresaw, to put things back in order and to place again your daughter's hand in that of her dear lieutenant."

"I'm truly afraid . . ." von Talberg hesitated.

"What are you afraid of?"

"That my intervention might be useless. Frida is so proud . . ."

"Bah! Bah! As you say that the motives behind this rupture are not those which dig uncrossable divides . . ."

"For others, certainly not. But for her?"

"In the end, general, that's for you to discover. But remember what I'm about to tell you. Frida's nervous state must be calmed . . . if not, I won't answer for the consequences!"

On returning home, von Talberg went straight up to his daughter's bedroom.

During the journey from the arsenal to the Chief of Staff's headquarters, he had reflected. Very impressed by the medic's declarations, he had reached, in the disarray where he found himself plunged, the same conclusion that Frida was regretting having broken off so brutally with her fiancé who had known how to inspire such profound affection and such a sincere attachment.

And he reflected, "Doubtless, time has played its part! The dear child will have understood that she was indignant and acted a little quickly and, retaken by thoughts of her fiancé, she certainly now deplores that moment of sacrificing him for cavalier reasons.

"I'm going to have a heart to heart with her; and if it's that, whatever little sympathy that Ansbach inspires in me, I'll not oppose Frida becoming his wife. Above all, I want to save my daughter!"

Full of these thoughts, von Talberg entered his child's bedroom.

The pretty Berliner, making an effort for herself, and desirous above all to not worry her father, had left her bed. Reclining on a chaise longue, she leafed through an illustrated brochure distractedly.

Noticing her father, she tried to get up and welcome him with her most gracious smile; but her strength betrayed her and she fell back on the chaise longue.

The general hurried towards her.

"It's nothing," said Frida. "Don't worry, father. You see, I'm well, I'm very well! I was getting ready to go down. Anyway, good Professor Swinemunder told me I had to eat. I'm in haste to get to the table, because I feel my appetite is strong."

But while she was speaking, the paleness of her face grew, so giving a flagrant lie to all this reassuring verbiage, which all rang false in his paternal heart.

"Don't lie, my poor darling," said von Talberg, sitting near the young girl and taking hold of her feverish hands.

And, kissing her on the forehead, he continued. "I've just had a long conversation with Professor Swinemunder. He declared to me, and you know how much we can trust his gifts, that your physical health, at least for the moment, has not been compromised.

"But, without me making any confidence to him regarding you, he immediately added that your mental state was much less satisfying and that he attributed the very real depression with which he finds you afflicted to a profound personal sorrow that it's crucial that we treat.

"You will not want me, my darling, to speak to you with such abandon. If your poor mother were there, it would be for her to undertake the gentle and delicate mission of interrogating your heart. Certainly she would acquit herself better than I, who am nothing but a soldier . . ."

"Say rather the most loving and beloved father," the gentle young girl rectified coaxingly.

"Thank you, my child. You give me courage to see through the perilous mission that I've imposed on myself."

Drawing the frail creature gently to his chest, the father continued. "Frida, answer me sincerely, I beg you. You still love Lieutenant Wilhelm Ansbach, don't you?"

With a brusque gesture Frida, who an instant before, had seemed like a flower who would lean on a stem too weak to support her, had seemed to take refuge, to huddle in the paternal embrace, suddenly disengaged herself, protesting with energy, while a sudden redness coloured her face.

"Oh! Father! Father!"

And, with a tone of the most painful reproach, she added, "How could you have such a thought? Still love that wretch? After what he has done! I'd have to lose all feelings of honour, all self-respect!"

Strengthened by the courage grown by the cavalier heroism which poured from her whole being, Frida continued. "From the day I knew the means to which this officer had resorted in order to win me, my heart was broken, my love for him darkened. I have buried it in myself. I took it down to the tomb myself. I placed the cold and heavy rock over it, that nothing can shift; and, since that moment I swear to you, father, that it has not occurred to me once to go and pluck the flowers of my regrets."

Then, with a ferocious energy, she said again, "I beg you, speak no more of Lieutenant Ansbach to me. He's dead to me. It's over, truly over!

"And if I suffer . . . it's not for him, nor by him, certainly. It's . . ."

She stopped, suffocated by tears.

"Frida, my darling, tell me the truth. The whole truth," begged von Talberg, moved beyond all expression and a hundred leagues from suspecting what his daughter was trying to say.

Then Frida murmured, plunging her wet tear-drowned eyes in those of her father, "You haven't guessed?"

Suddenly a light went on in the Chief of Staff's mind.

"Germaine Aubry?" he said in a flat voice.

"Yes, Germaine Aubry!" the general's daughter repeated.

And regaining her strength little by little, as if an internal fire reanimated her and restored her intact will, she continued. "The more I think of what happened here, and especially over there, the more I understand that we have not done our duty towards that young lady."

"What do you mean?"

"I mean, father, that in this frightful drama which has shaken our house, before and above all, Germaine Aubry is innocent! I mean that there is only one guilty party, that's Lieutenant Ansbach! Consequently, if your soldier's duty was to arrest this Frenchwoman, your duty as a man, what am I saying? Your duty as an honest man, was to let her go."

"But, alas, to talk like this, you must have lost all reason!"

"It's not a question of reason, father. It's a matter of the heart!"

Then, revealing the depths of his soul, General von Talberg replied, in a tone of impressive gravity, "The fatherland before everything, my daughter! By acting as I acted, I only defended it!"

"The fatherland!" murmured Frida, her gaze unfocused as though looking towards a distant horizon.

And, suddenly bright, with an unprecedented vehemence. "Well, father, stop offending yourself, stop angering yourself, stop causing yourself pain, I may only give you one answer: Germany will never be my fatherland! Because the fatherland, the mother which brought you into the world, is the land where the family grew, it's the blood of our ancestors. And for me, the fatherland can only be France!"

As, struck by surprise, von Talberg remained silent, Frida continued. "Once, I could let myself be circumvented, I could make believe that my heart gave itself, but in the end it was only the compassion that I was feeling for a being who seemed to suffer for me. But how quickly am I restored! So, father, I demand to your face, would a Frenchman have acted like Lieutenant Ansbach? Would a German have conducted themselves like Germaine Aubry? Oh! I don't need to ask you which side is the better role.

"The traitor, is the German! The heroine, is the Frenchwoman who put everything to work to avenge her father, to avenge her country, to take back what was stolen from her, and on the day she was discovered, stood up proudly, and bravely admitted what she had done. Germaine Aubry is one of those fearless beings beyond reproach such as only France knows how to produce. So, as long as she's in prison, I'll be unhappy.

"Ah! If that only depended on me, how quickly the door of her dungeon would be opened before her! How I would sacrifice myself for her! How I would go to take her place joyously!"

"Calm down, dear little angel," replied von Talberg with an accent of infinite tenderness.

But throwing herself round his neck, Frida implored. "Father, save her! Save her, I beg you!"

"Why, my darling," the general said in despair, "why do you ask me for the one thing I can't grant you?"

"Yet, father, if you wanted . . ."

"But it's impossible. Understand this! I swore loyalty to my Emperor, to my country. And while I admit I share your feelings and that more than anything else, more even than you perhaps, I grant all the compassion of which I'm capable to this unfortunate, of whom I confess the thought haunts me, pursues me ceaselessly, like remorse, I am the last, you hear me? Yes, the very last who has the right to grant her liberty, the last who may aid in her escape. Think of who I am!"

"It's true, father . . . you're German."

"And you?"

"Me, I'm French!"

The father and the daughter now fell silent.

It seemed that all at once a wall had just been raised between these two beings who cherished each other tenderly and that an atrocious misunderstanding was now going to divide them irreparably.

But, gathering himself, von Talberg said, in a trembling voice, "Listen to me, my dear child. I still have a considerable task to accomplish, that of reorganising our mobilisation, which was compromised by Germaine Aubry. I promised His Majesty, and nothing, you hear me, can make me break my word! When I've repaired the damage, in a year, two years perhaps, but not before, because I'm certain you would blame me if I gave in too easily to your tears, I shall offer him my resignation.

"Then I'll do everything to save this woman; and it is I who will go and throw myself at the Emperor's feet to beg his pardon! And then . . ."

The general's voice darkened further and, with a true effort, he finished. "And then . . . we'll go there . . . to that land that you love so much."

"The land of our grandparents!" Frida murmured as though in ecstasy.

"But until then, you will swear to me, you will train yourself to resist this anger which undermines you and which could kill you in the long run. Trust me. I'm not asking you for resignation for your whole life, but simply a little patience for a while."

Then the pretty Berliner approached her father and, letting her gracious head fall back on his shoulder, she asked simply, "Do you believe the Emperor will want to?"

"Want to what, my darling?"

"Pardon Germaine Aubry."

"Yes, I don't doubt it. When I've shown him that I am wasted, broken, aged by twenty years to restore my country's compromised strength, I'm sure that Wilhelm II will refuse me nothing because he's very good, so much so that he too will understand that the time for clemency has arrived and that by sending this woman home, he will have made one of those gestures which count in history."

"Father, I thank you to have spoken to me like this. Thanks to you, I feel better. I'm delivered from a terrible weight which was crushing me. But one last word . . ."

"Speak, my child."

"Germaine Aubry must not believe that I've abandoned her. I hope above all that she might learn that soon . . . in a year or two, as you just told me, she'll be returned to her loved ones."

"What you're asking of me there is very delicate, very difficult."

"Father, go to the limits of your generosity."

Then von Talberg, contemplating his daughter whose face reflected like an angelic beam come from above, divine inspiration and supreme pity, said, "Doubtless you'd be very happy to tell her all that yourself?"

"Oh! Father!"

"Do you feel strong enough to come with me to Spandau this very day?"

"Yes, straight away! Straight away!"

"Very well! Be ready in two hours. I want it to be you who announces to Germaine Aubry that we will both save her!"

CHAPTER TWENTY-EIGHT:

A Huge Gaffe

How great had been Commandant Fürsner's astonishment, the day after the cruel misadventure involving Colonel Hoffmann, on seeing General von Talberg arrive at Spandau Citadel, accompanied by his daughter!

Indeed, on the firm request of the Intelligence Bureau chief who, deeply humiliated by the ordeal that he had endured, had asked to keep the most absolute secrecy concerning this whole adventure for the moment, the governor had not sent any report to Berlin;

"Here we go then, good!" he said on sight of the Chief of Staff, "sooner or later the event would have been known. After all, it's nothing extraordinary! In reality, I love it. Too bad for Hoffmann! As to me, I won't hide behind him if the Chief of Staff accuses me of wanting to stifle the truth, because I only carried out his instructions."

Straight away, advancing towards his superior, Fürsner stopped, stiff, frozen, bringing his hand up to his helmet's visor.

"Hello, Commandant," began von Talberg. "Any news?"

Persuaded that the general was there only in order to make an enquiry into Chantecoq's latest exploit, and to enquire after news of the victim of this latest, Commandant Fürsner responded spontaneously, "He spent an agitated night, general, but he's a little calmer today."

"Who's that?" Frida's father asked, understanding nothing of this impenetrable conversation.

Fürsner bit his lip. He could see that he'd just made a huge gaffe. But he was flexible enough to get himself out of it. Anyway, being of a frank nature, he was hardly trained to lie.

So he replied at once, "Colonel Hoffmann, general!"

"Colonel Hoffmann? What are you telling me?"

"That's right, general! You're not up to date."

Understanding that had no more room to hesitate, the governor gave the Chief of Staff an exact and detailed account of what had happened the night before, taking pains to remark to his leader that his responsibility was absolutely sheltered as, though he'd been absent from the citadel, it had been on orders.

Commandant Fürsner put the full blame on the backs of the three majors who were under arrest while awaiting the final sanction, and he finally declared that, if he hadn't immediately telephoned the Chief of Staff, it was only on the express order of Colonel Hoffmann.

Von Talberg listened to this report with the closest attention.

Frida, at his side, didn't missed a single word.

The general declared, "Decidedly this French agent is capable of anything. One of these days, he could put on a show in the Emperor's place and I would not be overly surprised.

"He's a cheeky jouster and an adversary of whom we must get hold of at any cost."

As to the young girl, she thought, "What an extraordinary being this Chantecoq is! What boundless devotion! What admirable courage! What a true misfortune that he did not succeed!"

"Commandant Fürsner," replied the general, "I hold you responsible for only one thing, that's to have acceded to Colonel Hoffmann's wishes in hiding the truth from me for so long. If I hadn't come here for a completely different reason, it's probable that you would have continued to keep quiet and that I would have been informed of these facts only much later."

"General, please excuse me, but I felt bound in obedience to the Chief of Police. He appeared to have a plan that indiscretion could have foiled."

"That's possible, I suppose," acknowledged von Talberg. And in a more benevolent tone, he asked, "So Colonel Hoffmann is rather ill?"

"He's not broken anything, general, but he's ground down, aching. Would you like to pay him a visit?"

"In a moment. First, lead me to Julius Tower. I need to speak to the prisoner."

"As you order, general."

And as Fürsner watched the pretty Frida with a certain amount of astonishment, whose presence at her father's side he could hardly explain to himself, the general continued. "I've asked my daughter to come with me. I even plan to leave her alone with Germaine Aubry for a few minutes. Miss Talberg," he explained, "will perhaps obtain what we want to know much more easily."

"Indeed, general," the governor approved, always ready to defer to his superiors' wishes.

And wanting to erase the bad impression that he was afraid he'd made on his superior by deferring too easily to Hoffmann's demands, he added, "Mrs Fürsner, who has been delegated to look after this prisoner, has also made every possible effort to persuade her to take the path of confession. She has been unable to make her say anything. But I'm convinced Miss von Talberg will have more success."

The general made no reply.

All these white lies were still repugnant to his conscience.

All three set off on the round path which led to the famous tower; they passed through the grille to which only Commandant Fürsner and the special guard had the key, passed the machine gun and climbed the staircase which led to the corridor where the junior officer on duty mounted guard before Germaine's cell door.

"Send the sentinel away for a moment," ordered von Talberg. "I'll take his place."

"Very well, general."

Fürsner made a signal.

The junior officer moved away.

Then, as the governor was returning to the Chief of Staff, the general ordered: "Open the door for Miss von Talberg."

The Commandant again carried out his leader's orders.

The pretty Berliner entered the cell.

"Regulations," observed Fürsner, "demand that I lock the door behind her."

"Do it, do it."

The governor turned the key in the lock.

"We wait," said the general simply.

On seeing Frida enter her dungeon suddenly, Germaine Aubry, occupied with the sewing which had been assigned to her, believed that a miraculous apparition had been sent to her by Providence in order to comfort her in her prison. She could not believe her eyes.

But the young girl's voice echoed softly in her ear. "Miss! Miss Germaine . . ."

"You!" the Frenchwoman cried then, full of emotion.

"Yes . . . me."

"How were you able to get in here?"

"My father brought me himself."

"General von Talberg!"

"Yes, let me tell you . . ."

"Oh! Yes, speak, speak!"

Then Frida continued in a very soft voice. "First, let me kiss you."

"Kiss me?" Germaine was astonished. "Oh! Miss Frida!"

"Call me Frida, as before, call me your little friend."

"Yes, yes, my little friend. If you knew how much good your tender words do me, and how happy I am to see that you have kept your affection for me."

"My affection. Far from being taken, it has grown larger still."

"Thank you! Thank you!"

"I learned everything. I suffered cruelly when I knew that you were a spy; but as soon as I knew the motive that you had to act in such a way, not only did I understand your gesture, but I approved of it to such a point that I scratched from my life the man, or rather the wretch, who provoked it."

"Oh! I'm so happy with what you are telling me! My dearest wish is granted! If you knew how miserable I was at the thought that such a pure and noble child as you could be the wife of such a miserable wretch! But you must have suffered, to be obliged to take such a brutal decision, also . . ."

"I suffer still more to know you are held captive. That's why I wanted to come to you, so that you knew that I will not abandon you. Certainly, your friends are working hard for your deliverance. Chantecoq failed to succeed in taking you away from your guards."

"That's why I heard gunshots," said Germaine. "I pray the brave man has not been hit!"

"Be assured. From what I just heard the Citadel's governor tell my father, Chantecoq succeeded in escaping those who were pursuing him. But this above all I want to tell you: assuming that your friends don't succeed in breaking you out, your captivity will not now be of long duration."

"How is that?" the prisoner asked, quivering.

"I obtained from my father a vow that he would petition the Emperor to obtain your pardon, and he told me himself that he's certain the Emperor would not refuse him."

"What admirable creatures you both are!" the Frenchwoman cried, full of admiration and gratitude.

"And then in around two years," finished Frida, "my father will submit his resignation. He agrees that following this we'll go to live in France which, I feel, is my true country. That's all I have to tell you."

"Ah! Let me kiss you again!" said Germaine. "Allow me to express to you, my dear Frida, all my profound gratitude. You have been the ray of light which suddenly penetrated my cold, sad, pathetic cell, adorned it with all the beauty of Spring, warmed it with all the sweetest hopes. Do also tell General von Talberg how touched I am by what he wanted to do for me instead of striking me, of overwhelming me without pity as he had every right to."

"Yes, I'll tell him. But we must leave."

"Oh! If only, while waiting for my liberty, I could see you from time to time!"

"I'll try, I'll do my best . . ."

"Oh! Goodbye, my dear Frida!"

"Goodbye, my big sister!"

"And see you soon!"

"See you soon!"

The general's daughter headed towards the door and raised the latch. Then on the other side, Commandant Fürsner worked the lock and Frida found herself with her father again.

"Well?" asked the general.

"Still nothing," declared the pretty young Berliner, mastering her emotion, "but with time and patience, I don't despair of arriving at my goals."

The governor summoned the junior officer guard.

Then, guiding his guests, he led them to his private apartments, and while Frida stayed in the company of Mrs Fürsner who, straight away offered to show her her embroidery works, the Commandant took von Talberg to visit Colonel Hoffmann.

CHAPTER TWENTY-NINE:

Serious Threats

The Chief of Staff had never felt a great deal of sympathy for the great master of the German military police.

A soldier of honour in every meaning of the word, he judged these functions to be incompatible with the military spirit.

Moreover, he knew very well that enamoured of his trade, Hoffmann would stop at nothing in order to obtain intelligence that he judged useful or a confession that he considered indispensable.

He found these procedures profoundly repugnant.

If he could not disavow them at the highest level, he nevertheless felt an instinctive repulsion and marked antipathy with regards to he who used them.

On seeing Hoffmann's head swathed in bandages, and his face covered in bruising, the general made this reflection. "After all, it's only what he deserved. He must count himself fortunate that those three brutes didn't knock him out completely."

At the sight of his superior, the Intelligence Bureau chief tried to sit up straighter.

But the curvature from which he was suffering tore a cry of pain from him.

"Relax," commanded von Talberg. And immediately he added, "You're in a fair state! I can't help but wonder when you'll be able to return to duty."

"Don't speak to me of that, general! I'm in despair at the thought! This Chantecoq has escaped me again. When I was so close! It would have to be those three imbeciles, again, who found themselves in my path, not only to prevent me from arresting this spy, but to immobilise me for entire weeks!"

"That's all very regrettable," said Frida's father without a great deal of conviction.

"During that time, my enemies must have a golden opportunity to retry their attempt. And who's to say they won't succeed this time? Because I must do them this justice, they are as cunning as they are audacious. According to what the governor told me, if a happy chance hadn't led to Chantecoq stumbling across the sentinel that he'd already tricked, this damned Frenchman would have had the dungeon unlocked by the junior officer, and by this time Germaine Aubry would have been in France. What would His Majesty have said?"

"That's precisely why I don't understand, Colonel," von Talberg riposted with no coaxing, "your forbidding the governor to make his report straight away. Your colleagues could have picked up the trail of this Chantecoq individual."

"General," replied the policeman, "you're right. I had a moment of weakness, I humbly confess it, I make all apologies to you. Yes, I ought to have sounded the alarm straight away. But I felt so confused, humiliated by the adventure which had just befallen me, that I feared ridicule, not for my own self, but for the office that I occupy. And then, please trust my long experience. My colleagues, would not have succeeded in putting a hand on this Chantecoq who was able, thanks to his car, to defy all pursuit.

"You understand that he had foreseen failure, his precautions had been taken, he had in his car all the necessary equipment to transform himself, and that he must even have changed car on the way."

"Then you're giving up the battle?"

"With Chantecoq, yes, because I'm certain that I won't come out on top. If I could take him, it would already have been done. One doesn't get an opportunity like that twice in one lifetime!"

"You acknowledge then that you are powerless to prevent Germaine Aubry's friends from breaking her out?"

"That, general, is another matter; and even while debating with you, I have just found to the contrary the means to put an end to their audacious attempts."

Von Talberg was sceptical. "Truly?"

"General, you'll see as it's hardly complicated."

"Explain yourself!"

"My method consists simply of an official communiqué to the press."

"An official communiqué?"

"In which we will reveal that for some time, several attempts have been made with the aim of removing Germaine Aubry from the punishment that she has so well deserved.

"We'll add that the precautions we've taken have been sufficient to thwart these reckless projects. Nevertheless, the imperial government has decided: 1) that in the event of another attempt, the twenty years of solitary confinement with which the prisoner was struck will be transformed into perpetual detention, 2) that the condemned woman will be transferred to a bunker in Breslau Citadel and submitted to a special regime."

And, a look of satisfaction in his eyes, Hoffmann asked, "What do you say to that, general? Do you not believe such a measure to be well taken to discourage our adversaries?"

"I'm sure of it," approved von Talberg who, despite all the disdain that this man inspired in him, couldn't help admiring the fertility of his ever alert intelligence.

Encouraged by the approval of his leader, Hoffmann continued. "I believe that it sends them a little show of force to the French gentlemen! They know that we're capable of carrying out our threats. Then they'll stay quiet, I'll wager! The only favour I demand of you, general, is to ask you, without delay, to communicate my idea to the Emperor, as you find it suitable, so that the note appears in the *Empire Monitor* from tomorrow morning and that it should be communicated to the other papers in the shortest possible time. The quicker we act, the quicker we will annihilate Chantecoq and his gang, while waiting for us to get them under lock and key, if that's ever possible."

"It will be done according to your wishes, Colonel Hoffmann," replied von Talberg.

"I thank you, general. Anyway, I hope not to delay taking up my duties. Tomorrow, I'll return to Berlin, and when I ought to rest on a camp bed in my office, I'll do my duty. I'm driven to it, general."

"I understand that," said the Chief of Staff.

And, taking leave of his subordinate, he added. "I wish you a prompt recovery, Colonel."

"Thank you, general."

Von Talberg retired and went to find his child, who Mrs Fürsner was making admire the most diverse works of embroidery, engaging her keenly to apply herself to this art, according to her, the finest which could be reserved for a woman.

Von Talberg and his daughter returned immediately to Berlin.

Throughout the journey, the Chief of Staff stayed lost in thought.

He reflected on what Hoffmann had said to him.

"He's right," he said to himself, "it's the only way, and my duty is to take his idea to the Emperor, as I promised him, and to press it strongly, as is my duty.

"Especially since this measure, dampening her defenders' zeal, doesn't prevent me from preparing Germaine Aubry's pardon. I engaged myself to ask for and to obtain her grace; I will ask for it and I will obtain it! If I could only make my intentions known to those who want to break her out of her prison at all cost. But it's impossible! Finally I leave to God, in whom I believe, the trouble of arranging things with all justice."

Calmed by these reflections, the general spoke out loud, addressing his daughter who had respected his meditation. "Frida, tell me what your friend said."

Slipping her arm under her father's, the little Berliner said simply. "She told me to thank you from the bottom of her heart."

Then the Chief of Staff, leaning towards his daughter, said, putting a paternal kiss on her forehead, "It's you, my adored child, that, from the depths of my heart, I thank."

CHAPTER THIRTY:

Eva Strelitzer

It was eleven o'clock in the evening.

The Alt-Bayern tavern, where we saw Chantecoq for the first time, dressed up as a waiter, listening with an attentive ear to the conversations of Majors Schlaffen, Tourchtig and Hunguerig, was stuffed with clients.

The pipe organ screamed the French tune which was so popular: *Returning from the Show*.

It was the same bourgeois, the same landlords, the same civil servants sitting in families, eating, drinking, stuffing themselves fit to make themselves sick.

In one corner, a man of fifty or sixty years, with a golden pince-nez perched on his flat nose, completely bald, shaven, dressed in a long black redingote, was drinking beer and watching the people who passed to and fro before him with a smile.

The waiters were everywhere. Under the eye of a straight-backed manager, stiff and formal, authoritative, like a junior officer in plain clothes.

A plump little woman with a vivacious allure, whose hair was disheveled and who looked like a Jew from Vienna, was sitting at the counter.

A fat gentleman and a fat lady, accompanied by their three fat young daughters and a fat little plump-cheeked boy, dressed as a cuirassier, entered the establishment; and, with the gravity of people who are entering a temple, they directed themselves towards an unoccupied niche and sat around the table.

The father, in a deep voice, called a waiter and, taking hold of a menu with the solemnity of a magistrate passing sentence, he ordered his family's supper and his own.

The organ had just stopped.

The old man with the pince-nez and bare skull called in a voice like a husky dog. "Waiter! Waiter!"

A waiter approached. "Does Professor Ostern require anything?" he asked with a certain deference.

"A half and a sauerkraut!"

The family installed in a neighbouring "box" were largely doing justice already to the copious dishes and numerous halves that had been served to them.

The child disguised as a cuirassier, who had eaten like a guardsman, demanded, still not satiated, "Food! I want more to eat!"

"Mr. Kosker," observed his mother, "your son Gunther is a glutton! It's colossal what he has already eaten!"

"Colossal!" the father repeated. "I was the same at his age."

And tapping his huge belly, he added, "I believe I didn't do too badly!"

"It's very pretty," remarked the oldest sister judiciously, "but while waiting Gunther is going to give himself indigestion again."

"That's not important," declared Mr. Kosker. "Indigestion. I've had it, I still have it, and I'll always have it. Do I carry myself any less well for all that? Does my business suffer? Am I not a good husband, a good father, and a good Landsturm officer? No, aren't I? Ah well! Waiter, bring another goose confit for Lieutenant Kosker."

"And drink!" bellowed the child.

"A half!" the father ordered.

"That's too much!" the youngest intervened in her turn.

"Too much!" said Mr. Kosker shrugging his shoulders.

And philosophically, he concluded, "What he can't keep down, he'll return soon enough!"

A tall, thin and angular married couple had just appeared, arms linked, giving, as much by their clothes which were tight and somewhat faded as by their embarrassed air, the impression of people whose purse is garnished quite lightly.

"Remember, Mr. Hochplatz," the woman murmured in her husband's ear, "no more than one sauerkraut and one half!"

"Yeah, yeah!" agreed the man.

"At the moment, our means do not permit us to give ourselves over to excess."

"Yeah, yeah! Yeah?"

Suddenly, seeing the Kosker family, Mrs Hochplatz cried, as though a good opportunity had fallen on her from the sky, "Oh! That dear Mrs Kosker!"

"Hello, Mrs Hochplatz," said the great eater's wife, coldly.

The two newcomers, not discouraged by this rather chilly welcome, took the best course which was to install themselves at the Koskers' table where there were still two places left.

"What a pleasure to meet you!" simpered Mrs Hochplatz.

And straight away, complimenting, expansive, affectionate, she added, while giving a friendly pat on the grease-stained cheek of the young cuirassier officer, "How well your little Gunther wears the uniform!"

"It's in the family!" Mr. Kosker said, full of vanity.

"The fact is," continued the lady, "that when Mr. Kosker puts on his Landsturm captain's uniform, he is a sensation throughout the neighbourhood.

"Yeah, yeah, yeah," agreed Hochplatz who had understood his wife's tactics.

"Don't tell me about it," Mrs Kosker derided herself, "all the women look at him."

But Mrs Hochplatz, feeling that she was gaining ground, added while looking with sympathy at the three young girls who were bundled like Nuremberg dolls and whose dull blonde heads were disappearing under ridiculously-shaped hats, "And these young ladies! How they have grown in taste! How elegant they are and how well they wear their finery."

"Even so!" beamed Kosker. "And these hats? There are none finer in Paris!"

"It's delicious!"

"Do sit down," insisted the Landsturm officer.

Mrs Hochplatz breathed.

She had earned her half and her sausage.

However she excused herself for form's sake. "I wouldn't want to be indiscreet."

"Sit yourself down!" Kosker invited.

And calling the waiter, he ordered them to set two more places.

Then, Mrs Kosker, in order to have something to say, expressed, a wrinkle of disdain on her lips, "I was truly sorry, Mrs Hochplatz, not to see you at my last reception."

"And us too," agreed the tall, dry woman. "We were obliged to absent ourselves, my husband and I. Did you have many people?"

"Don't talk to me about it!" simpered the little round woman. "We were obliged to make tea in the wash basin and punch in the bath."

"Colossal!"

The little cuirassier, who had gluttonously devoured the heavy goose confit that had been served to him just moments before and who had gulped down three quarters of his half, demanded again in an imperious voice: "Food! Drink! Drink! Drink! Food!"

"Heh! How fine he is!" the father swelled with pride. "You can see that all that's not doing him any harm! And your children, Hochplatz, how are they?"

"Very well, very well."

"You've got a whole regiment of them."

"Eleven!"

"Hoch, hoch! To their health!"

The organ launched into a military march.

Two officers had just entered the tavern, installing themselves quite close to the niche where could be found the Kosker family and the Hochplatzes.

The "lieutenant" stopped stuffing himself for a moment to stare with naïve admiration at the two new arrivals' uniforms.

"Go on then, Gunther. Salute."

The little boy hesitated. But his whole entourage invited him.

"Go on, go and salute!"

The child made up his mind and, taking up a parade ground step, he headed towards the two officers, then, camping before them, he imitated with a gaucherie already full of military stiffness, while saying, "At your command!"

"Very good, lieutenant," said one of the officers.

"Let's see how he manoeuvres a bit," cried the other.

And in a commanding tone he declared, "Attention!"

The young cuirassier took position.

The officer continued. "Head up! Hold it! Half turn, right! Straight ahead, march! Half turn, march! Attention! Halt! At ease!"

The kid carried out the movements with a precocious precision, which greatly diverted the audience. "He manoeuvres very well, this young sub-lieutenant!" said the first officer.

"As well as one of Frederic the Great's grenadiers," added his comrade, pinching the kid's cheek amicably. Then he added, "You're dismissed, lieutenant."

"At your command, captain!"

The little German, making a correct about-face, went, still at parade pace, to rejoin his parents in the middle of the "Hoch!" repeated by all present.

While this scene unfolded, two men had entered the tavern and sat down in a niche.

They were Jean Aubry and Captain Maurice Evrard.

Both spoke in low voices, without touching the drinks they had ordered distractedly.

An angry flame burned in the young aviator's eyes.

An expression of deep sadness was painted over Germaine's father's face.

He seemed beaten, discouraged, this time for good. In a voice trembling from emotion, the combat aircraft's inventor said, "My poor friend, what good is this supreme approach? You're risking your life, and why?"

"In order to punish a wretch, this Wilhelm Ansbach who has caused our misery," replied the officer. "Like me, you read in the papers the new measures that Wilhelm II's government have just just taken against Germaine? It's abominable!

"We can therefore no longer hope of freeing her, as, even in Chantecoq's opinion, everything that we try will turn back on to her. But we can still avenge her! And that's what I'm going to do! Ah! That infamous Ansbach, how I'm eager to insult him before his comrades, and to have him at last at the end of my sword!"

"You believe he's here?" Jean Aubry asked.

"That's what Chantecoq told me, at least."

"Perhaps you would do well to check."

"You're right."

Captain Evrard made a signal to the manager who hurried over, asking, "Would the gentlemen care for some champagne?"

"No, a simple piece of information. Do you know Lieutenant Wilhelm Ansbach?"

"Lieutenant Ansbach? You mean captain, because he's just been promoted to that rank."

"That's right."

"Yes, I know him! But he's one of our best customers. He's here almost every evening with his friends."

"Thank you, that's all I need."

Hardly had he spoken these words than a group of officers brusquely erupted into the hall.

They were accompanied by two strikingly pretty women, in evening gowns, and who were none other than Eva Strelitzer, the opera singer, and her friend, Paula Santi, the famous dancer in the imperial ballet.

The establishment was full.

The officers, insolently, headed towards a group of students who occupied a large table in the middle of the tavern.

"Make room!" commanded Lieutenant Limbürg.

"Go away!" threatened Captain Ansbach.

"Get out!" intimidated Lieutenant Bingerbrück, while the others, hitting their sabres' sheaths against the flagstones, repeated, "Go on, make room for us! Get out!"

The students stood up.

"No, we won't leave!" they protested. "We're at home here! We're paying for our drinks and you don't scare us!"

"Go away!" screamed Bingerbrück, a colossus who was always furious.

"Grunts!" riposted the students.

"Delinquents!"

"Mercenaries!"

"Socialists!"

"Thugs!"

The fight was inevitable. It happened.

The shock was terrible.

While the two artistes took refuge in the niche occupied by Evrard and Aubry, the officers, more numerous and and more solid than their adversaries, threw the students outside, in spite of their keen resistance and their indignant protests.

No one dared intervene, such is the respect for uniform in Germany.

Still simmering after their easy victory, the officers returned to the hall which was three quarters empty and littered with glasses and broken dishes, which the waiters rapidly cleared away.

"Oh the brutes! The brutes!" groaned Aubry.

"Wait a moment!" Evrard murmured, chewing his lip with impatience.

"Our apologies, ladies," said von Limbürg to Eva Strelitzer and her friend.

"Truly," Ansbach cried, "it's getting intolerable!"

"In a little while," added Bingerbrück, "these jokers will think they can get away with anything!"

"They arrogantly claim all rights," said von Mittel in his turn, a little sub-lieutenant with a nascent blond moustache which was already standing on end like an angry cat.

And the chorus added.

"They act as if they own the place!"

"They no longer respect anything!"

"They insult the army!"

"That can't last!"

"They needed correction!"

"They received it!"

"It's well done!"

"You did very well!" nodded Paula Santi. "And it's by acting in this way that you maintain the uniform's prestige."

"Some champagne, ladies?" Ansbach offered.

"Gladly," the dancer accepted.

"Which label?" asked the manager, who had just approached.

"Heidsieck Monopole!"

The officers sat in the exiles' places. Soon champagne sparkled in their glasses.

"Captain, is it then true that you're leaving us?" Paula Santi asked Wilhelm Ansbach.

"Yes," replied the former Jacques Müller. "I'm leaving tomorrow morning for Colmar to join my new regiment."

"To Colmar!" the dancer repeated. "How bored you're going to be!"

"Don't pity him," said von Mittel. "The captain is twenty-seven years old!"

"It's a great advancement," opined von Limbürg.

"In any case," said Bingerbrück, "you've never told us how you obtained it."

"I beg of you," Ansbach said evasively, "don't ask me about this subject."

"Didn't you go on a secret mission abroad?" asked Paula Santi.

"Don't press me!"

"And yet," replied von Mittel, "it's said that you did a great service to the Chief of Staff, in peril of your life."

"They exaggerate," the Uhlan officer said with a false modesty.

"You're very discreet," said the dancer.

"Too shy."

"To your health, all the same!" said von Limbürg.

They all stood, repeating the toast brought by the young aide-de-camp. "To Captain Ansbach and to his swift return among us." But Eva Strelitzer who had not taken her eyes from Ansbach for a moment, had taken a newspaper, and suddenly cried out.

"Oh! That's too much!"

"What's that?" she was questioned on all sides.

"What they're saying in the '*Worwaerts*'."

"What?" spluttered Ansbach, "you're reading that grubby socialist rag?"

"I assure you that it's very troubling," affirmed the singer gravely.

"What a joke!"

"However . . ."

"Read it anyway," von Limbürg intervened gallantly.

And Eva, aloud, read what follows. "We can even confirm that lately the French ambassador has addressed our Foreign Minister with very serious concerns about the procedures of the enquiry which was held over a young Frenchwoman accused of espionage and condemned to twenty years of solitary confinement."

"Ah! Yes," said Bingerbrück negligently, "the Germaine Aubry affair!"

The opera singer continued. "The new ambassador would equally have furnished proof that if this young girl had been guilty of espionage, her father, inventor of a combat aircraft, adopted by the French War Ministry, would have been the victim of a theft of important documents, on the part of a German officer who came him as an Alsatian and whom he had welcomed in his house."

"What's next?" Wilhelm Ansbach asked, nervous.

"That's all!"

"What do you say to that?" von Limbürg felt he had to ask.

"I say," replied Eva Strelitzer, "that the conduct of this German officer singularly attenuates the act of this young Frenchwoman."

Everyone around her was astonished. "How's that?"

"Doesn't it seem," reasoned the artiste, "that this Germaine Aubry only came to us because we went to her?"

"All that stuff," Bingerbrück declared pre-emptorily, "is just lies anyway!"

"Inventions by journalists short of copy," added von Mittel.

"What would you know about it?" Eva Strelitzer riposted.

Von Limbürg interrupted, angry. "You're not going to put faith in the words of people who are looking to Paris for their news!"

"It could be, nevertheless . . ."

"You're mad!" Paula Santi interrupted.

"Indeed, I have the right to an opinion!"

"Obviously!"

"Drop it!" Wilhelm Ansbach interrupted. "Everyone in Berlin knows that Eva Strelitzer is not German but an annexed Alsatian, and that she still misses her old country."

"And when would that be, captain?" the Berlin Opera singer replied energetically.

"Moreover," said Paula Santi smoothly, "we're not going to argue over this Frenchwoman."

"This woman is in prison," replied the singer severely, "she deserves our pity."

"Her! Pity!" groaned Ansbach. "Ah! If you only knew . . ."

"I only know one thing," claimed the Alsatian, "that's if *Worwaerts* is telling the truth, Germaine Aubry ought to be acquitted."

"Acquit her!" they protested.

"Yes, acquit her!"

"But that's unheard of!"

"I'll go further," said Eva Strelitzer, with a greater vehemence than ever. "I maintain that a woman who acts in this way deserves everyone's respect, because the villain's role does not belong to she who sacrificed herself in order to defend her country, but to the officer who, all to attain the goal he was pursuing, has played a sneaky trick!"

The officers were standing, red with anger.

Ansbach alone was pale with fury.

Then a voice echoed in the hall, dominating the tumult. "Bravo, miss! You are a woman of spirit, I congratulate you for it!"

It was Captain Evrard who, not having missed a word of this scene, was advancing towards the group of German officers, his head high, his eyes clear. French style!

CHAPTER THIRTY-ONE:

Defiance

At those words, Wilhelm Ansbach had shuddered.

Turning quickly, he recognised the inventor and the captain.

Unable to suppress his panic, he let slip, "Captain Evrard!"

"Yes," replied Germaine's fiancé, "the Captain Evrard who is finally going to spit his contempt in your face!"

The other officers were intervening already.

"What's that?"

"What does this mean?"

"Who is this individual?"

But with a sovereign authority which imposed on everyone, the young aviator replied, "Sirs, I beg of you, in the name of honour, listen to me!"

And with silence once more established, he continued. "Sirs, you don't know me! Presently, I'll tell you who I am; but in the meantime I have the honour, or rather the disgust, to introduce you to a German officer who, under the name of Jacques Müller, gained entry to a French genius's house in order to steal the secret of a combat aircraft."

He pointed out the spy.

"Well! Yes, it's true!" Ansbach dared to brave it out and, in the face of danger and his adversary, he was regaining a bit of his undeniable audacity and insolent arrogance.

"No doubt," the voice of justice continued, "you have been ordered from telling your comrades the methods that you employed in order to get hold of them?"

"That's enough!" von Limbürg interrupted.

"We ask you to withdraw!" summed up Bingerbrück.

"We're German officers!" yelled von Mittel.

"And I," Maurice Evrard replied proudly, "I'm a French officer!"

Then, turning towards Ansbach, livid with rage, he added, while seizing Jean Aubry's hand, in a tone at once of the most contemptuous irony and with the most fixed determination, "Mr. Jacques Müller, introduce us to your comrades, then! Don't you want to? Oh well! We're going to have to introduce ourselves. Sirs, here is Jean Aubry, inventor of the combat aircraft for which the plans were stolen by the lieutenant, or rather by Captain Ansbach. And as for me, I'm Captain Maurice Evrard, the fiancé of that young girl who failed to be murdered by this bandit!"

As murmurs went up among the officers, Evrard reiterated with force: "Sirs, I abjure you to listen to me."

"Oh well! Speak!" replied the aide-de-camp with an accent of undeniable loyalty.

And turning to his friends, he added in a tone full of conciliating dignity, "Let's listen to him, comrades!"

Germaine's fiancé picked up straight away, pointing a vengeful and menacing finger at Captain Ansbach, whose lips were trembling with anger. "To reach his goal, do you know what this man did? No! Because, I'm sure he's not flaunted it before you.

"Well! I'm going to tell you! Not content with infiltrating fraudulently a family of brave people who received him at their table, and who cared for him when he was sick, he had the infamy to return at night, knowing well that there was only in the house one young girl, ready to welcome him like a brother. Then, abusing her trust and her weakness, he threw himself on her, he struck her, he left her half dead, while he saved himself with the documents stolen from her father. Do you dare to say now, wretch, that this isn't true?"

"I saw only the interest of my own country," Ansbach defended himself.

But Evrard was already riposting with force. "No country demands that one dishonours itself in her service, as you dishonoured yourself!"

As the German officers, angry, saddened, didn't manage to hide the angry impression that these revelations, as sensational as they were unexpected, caused in them, the French officer, continued, addressing the false Jacques Müller again. "Look at your comrades. Read on their faces what they think of you! They all think you're a coward!"

"I demand satisfaction!" Ansbach blurted.

"Whenever you want!" Evrard replied. "Though you're disqualified in the eyes of all honest men, I consent to drawing my sword against you. I want to kill you; I don't want to murder you! We fight tomorrow!"

"Tomorrow is impossible."

"Are you afraid?"

"Afraid? Me? No! I leave tonight to rejoin my regiment at Colmar."

"Even better! We'll fight at Colmar! You facing your country, me facing mine!"

"So be it! In two days!"

Then, in a gesture full of simplicity, Captain Evrard raised his hat and saluted the officers who, pale, moved more than they would have wanted to appear, responded militarily, their hands at the visors of their helmets.

Then the two Frenchmen left.

As to Eva Strelitzer, she had disappeared.

Maurice Evrard and Jean Aubry followed Potsdamer-strasse for some time. After a few moments, the young officer took a deep breath.

"Finally," he said, "I was able to say to that bandit's face all that I thought of him! In two days, I'll have him at the end of my sword! Yes in two days, I'll have punished him as he deserves. At least, as we've been unable to save Germaine, I'll have the consolation of having avenged her!"

"My daughter!" Jean Aubry murmured.

Walking side by side, they now both fell into silence.

Their thoughts went at the same time towards Julius Tower where the dear captive was locked up, without it being possible at present to attempt anything to free her.

And tears appeared in the corners of their eyes, tears of pain and misery from her father, tears of anger and despair from her fiancé.

As they prepared to cross Potsdamerplatz (Potsdam square), Jean Aubry turned back brusquely.

"Attention!" he said. "I believe we're being followed."

"By who?"

"By a woman."

"A woman! Pray that it's . . ."

"Emma Lückner, yes?"

"You understand me."

"Hold on, look there, on the pavement, near the ground . . ."

"We shall see!"

Then, resolutely and without hesitating, Evrard set off at a firm, decided pace towards a young person enveloped in a rich fur cloak, whose silhouette stood out in the glare of the light from an electric lamppost.

But suddenly the young woman, as if she too had taken a sudden resolution, started to walk towards the captain, and he almost immediately recognised Eva Strelitzer, the Berlin Opera singer who, some moments before, at the Alt-Bayern tavern, had so spontaneously and courageously leapt to Germaine Aubry's defence.

"You, miss!" the French officer cried almost joyously, while signalling for Jean Aubry to approach, who had stayed several steps distant.

Then in a brief, trembling voice, the annexed woman said at once, "I have only a few moments to give you, because my absence must not be of long duration. That would arouse the suspicions of this odious Wilhelm Ansbach that in my quality as an Alsatian, I congratulate you, captain, to have acted with such vigour."

Then, plunging into her confidant's eyes a look full of loyalty and frankness, she added, "I have got it in my head to save the woman you love. I think I've found a way to do it, but I can't tell you anything yet. In any case, give me a place to meet you tomorrow in the morning, wherever you want. The only thing I ask is to have a blind, absolute trust in me."

The artiste spoke with such a loyal tone that immediately the two Frenchmen, enchanted, conquered, held their hands to her, full of gratitude towards this beautiful and good creature who devoted herself to their cause at the moment where it had appeared absolutely hopeless for them.

"Thank you with all my heart!" the inventor said with effusion.

"We'll put Miss Aubry's fate in your hands," agreed Maurice Evrard, who felt a ray of hope reborn in him.

"Choose the place yourself," Eva Strelitzer insisted, "but quickly, in heaven's name! I must return to the tavern."

"Very well!" said the aviator. "Tomorrow morning, nine o'clock, the junction of Unter den Linden and Wilhelmstrasse."

"Understood, I'll be there."

"So will we."

"Until tomorrow!"

"Till tomorrow!"

And while the singer returned to the officers, Jean Aubry, passing his arm under Maurice's, said in a voice trembling with emotion, "Who knows if this woman hasn't been sent by Providence?"

"I believe so," affirmed the officer, whose gaze shone with a strange flame.

CHAPTER THIRTY-TWO:

Last Chance

On arriving, after a thousand detours, at the retreat that the good Mr. Laumann had provided for them, and where, after their recent adventures, Chantecoq and Mr. Ernest Gautier had prudently gone to ground, Aubry and Evrard's first care was to bring their friends up to date with the evening's events, that is to say with the scene of provocation with Ansbach and the unexpected intervention of Eva Strelitzer.

After having commended the captain warmly for his noble attitude, the special commissioner, having become excessively prudent – and with reason – cried, "In your place, I'd have avoided that singer like the plague! You always have to be suspicious with women. What do you think, my brave Chantecoq?"

"I'm of a completely different opinion," the French agent declared categorically. "From what our friends have just told us, this person appears completely sincere to me.

"First, she's an annexee. She has French blood in her veins. Then, she's an artiste, and almost all artistes, who have their faults like everybody else, have nonetheless a heart full of elan which makes them capable of all devotion and generosity. And then, what the hell! I'm sure that Mr. Aubry and his future family will be of my opinion! It would be deplorable not to profit from the opportunity that presents itself; and if, truly, this Eva Strelitzer can save Miss Germaine we would be idiots not to profit from it."

"Bravo!" applauded Evrard.

"I don't deny," continued the skilful policeman, "that precautions are necessary. Also, without appearing to do so, I will accompany these gentlemen, and I will watch over the details. In this way, I'm sure that nothing irritating will happen to them."

"And me?" asked Mr. Gautier. "What am I going to do during this time?"

"You," replied Chantecoq, not without a note of irony, "you'll stay here safe and sound."

And, aware that this phrase could have been a bit injurious to the self-respect of the bumbling civil servant, Chantecoq who was ultimately a kind man, continued. "You will await news on the phone and you'll be ready in this way to carry out the instructions which we will transmit."

"Understood!" the magistrate accepted at once who, anyway, had lost all his beautiful self-assurance of former times.

And very cordially, he added, "Good luck, my friends! What joy if we could save this dear child, and if I could help you in some way! That would rehabilitate me vis-a-vis myself."

The next day, at the agreed hour, Jean Aubry and Maurice Evrard, watched by Chantecoq who, incorrigible, had put on a policeman's uniform this time, were at the rendezvous.

Eva Strelitzer, just as she had told them the night before, was waiting for them.

She was in a car.

On seeing them, she gave them a signal with her hand.

The two Frenchmen approached.

At once, from the singer's radiant face, they guessed that she had succeeded.

Jumping down from her vehicle, Eva Strelitzer ran towards her new friends, telling them, "I believe I have something very interesting to reveal to you."

Leading the two men under the lime trees which line the famous road through Germany's capital, the artiste explained everything to them. "I must first tell you that I'm on very good terms with an aide-de-camp of the Emperor, Lieutenant von Limbürg, who is a great admirer of my voice and who never fails to come and compliment me at the opera when I'm singing.

"I profited from the good disposition in which he found himself yesterday. I succeeded in questioning him skilfully on the subject of the prisoner in Julius Tower. It's from him that I learned that it was decided that tomorrow, or the day after tomorrow at the latest, Germaine Aubry would be transferred to Glatz Citadel.

"My God!" the inventor sighed.

"Wait!" Eva said. "This evening, around nine o'clock, a Protestant pastor, the venerable Mr. Schoenreck, must come to the so-called prison to bring her evangelical consolation, but in reality to make one last attempt to persuade her to name her accomplices."

"The wretches!" Maurice groaned.

"Do you speak German well?" the singer asked.

"Like my mother tongue."

"Then all will be well! I propose that in the place of this Protestant pastor it should be you, captain, who enters the cell."

"Oh! So," cried the young officer, "I answer Germaine's prayers."

"That's just what I was thinking," declared the annexee. "There's nothing simpler. At the last moment, the minister will be ill, I'll take care of that. I've gathered my intelligence: this worthy pastor is a true gourmand. A good pie sent to him by one of his flock will make it impossible – oh! Without causing him any great pain – for him to carry out his sacred ministry.

"And as he won't have time to nominate his replacement, you'll be able to, around six o'clock this evening, present yourself in his name at Spandau Citadel whose doors will open themselves so much better before you now that I've taken care to bring you a blank pass I acquired from Lieutenant von Limbürg's wallet and that you will fill in yourself, with your signature, of course, complete and conforming to the model.

"One last piece of advice. Disguise yourself slightly . . . Oh! Very slightly! Take on a timid, reserved air, of a young trainee in pastoral functions."

"Don't worry."

"Don't forget that you're called Pastor Jerkhein."

"Perfect!" the young aviator said, writing the pastor's name in his notebook.

"With you, I'm at peace," Eva Strelitzer concluded. "I'm convinced that tomorrow I'll read in the papers that the prisoner has escaped."

"I'm sure of it!" Germaine's fiancé affirmed, superb at once in resolve and audacity. "Certainly the plan is perilous . . ."

"I have absolute faith in it."

"Miss Strelitzer," cried Maurice Evrard, "I owe you more than life!"

"As to me," declared Jean Aubry in his turn, "I will never have enough recognition for you from the bottom of my heart!"

Eva Strelitzer gave the captain the pass, and having shaken the hands of the two Frenchmen who thanked her again, she went back to her car and left, all radiant at the good action that she had just accomplished.

Then, Evrard and Aubry rejoined their brave and precious collaborator who, an impeccable agent, had been within a hundred paces of them.

"Dear friend," said the aviator in his ear, "I announce to you an extraordinary piece of news!"

"What's that, then?"

"I'm going to play at being Chantecoq!"

"You?"

"Yes, me!"

In a few words, Germaine's father and fiancé gave their friend the complete account of their meeting with this providential woman; but when they'd finished, the two men noticed with a certain astonishment that the police pseudo-agent remained silent.

Then the worried young officer asked, "It could be said that you don't share our satisfaction?"

With a pensive, almost discouraged air, Chantecoq shook his head. The aviator asked again. "Do you have doubts over this singer's sincerity?"

"No," replied the French agent. "After all that you've just told me, this woman appears absolutely sincere.

And even if her attitude inspired the least suspicion in us, I consider that at this time we can't afford to hesitate. Eva Strelitzer indicates to us the only way of reaching that dear child. Let's go, then! Too bad if it's a trap! We'll soon see, and rather that than it being said of us that we recoiled before a danger which is no doubt only imaginary and in which, for my part, I refuse to believe."

"Bravo!" applauded Aubry.

"Then," Evrard asked, "why, my dear Chantecoq, instead of appearing excited by the prospect of a perilous adventure as usual, do you suddenly seem to be so preoccupied?"

"Will you permit me to speak frankly?" said the French agent.

"We graciously demand that you do."

"It's very simple! Without doubting you, my dear friends, you've just cause me a little . . . what am I saying? . . . a lot of pain?"

"Is this possible?"

"Believe that there's no bitterness in my recriminations. But, you need someone who transforms themselves into a pastor-in-training, to get into a prison, and it's not me that you're choosing?"

"But, my friend . . ."

"Wait! I who pass rightly or wrongly as a skilful master of disguise, I who know Spandau Citadel to the smallest detail, I who have already failed. But I see!

Perhaps you fear, since I failed by being discovered, that I would not fill my role sufficiently."

"How could you have such an idea?" protested the inventor.

"No," Evrard declared cleanly, "we still have complete confidence in you, and it's precisely because we consider you indispensable, because we consider that your arrest would be the end of all our hopes, and above all because we judge that you have run enough risks for us, that I have at once decided that it should be I who takes to Germaine the rope ladder and the metal saw prepared by her father.

"We must anticipate everything. If, against all hope, Eva Strelitzer had cheated us; if, more plausibly, an incident takes place in the course of which the herald of liberty would be unmasked, it would be better that it was I rather than you who ran the risk of being arrested.

"They wouldn't dare keep me in prison too long. I would be left for a few months of captivity. While you, they would make you disappear forever. And what would become of us without he who has been the soul of our expedition, our best protection, our most precious counsellor?"

Then Chantecoq, tears in his eyes, held his hands to Evrard, saying, "I can see there's nothing to be done. You want to save your fiancé yourself . . . Go! And God be with you!"

CHAPTER THIRTY-THREE:

The Decisive Moment

This time, the decisive moment was going to play out.

Germaine was either going to leave her dungeon, or it would all be over for her.

The French charged with her salvation knew this, so they had neglected nothing in order that the attempt should succeed.

On their return to Mr. Laumann's, they had deliberated and taken some important decisions in the greatest secrecy.

At the end of this conference, which had not lasted less than two hours, everyone, including the good Mr. Laumann, had a radiant face. Hope shone in all their eyes.

Chantecoq had insisted on presiding over the camouflage of Maurice Evrard as Protestant pastor. He had accomplished a true masterpiece.

The elegant officer was absolutely unrecognisable.

An hour later, Jean Aubry and Mr. Gautier, disguised as delivery boys, took their place in a lorry loaded with several hermetically sealed crates.

Chantecoq, as a Berlin tram driver, was taking the wheel and put the car in gear, while Mr. Laumann left for his part with a race car driven by his brother, the doctor, who was a driver as skilled as the most experienced professional.

Towards five o'clock in the evening, Maurice Evrard, or rather Pastor Jerkhein, a thick Bible under his arm, presented himself at the gates of Spandau Citadel and showed the sentinel the absolutely regulation pass that had been given to him, that same morning, by the brave Eva Strelitzer.

Since Chantecoq's last attempt, security had become even more rigorous. No one could enter the fortress without the governor's express authorisation.

So the soldier called a guard who he charged with warning Commandant Fürsner.

This last was in a very bad mood.

Indeed, he had only just been warned that General von Talberg was going to come in a few moments to make an inspection of the Citadel (on the Emperor's orders) and he had noticed that the courtyard was, according to him, insufficiently swept.

So he began by receiving the unfortunate guard like a dog at a game of skittles.

However, when the pastor was mentioned, he decided to lend a slightly more attentive ear. Indeed, he suddenly remember that, during the day, he had received word of an order emanating from the Chancellor himself, warning him that he would have to give a warm welcome to Pastor Schoenreck, charged with bringing the consolation of his ministry to the Frenchwoman Germaine Aubry.

"Damn," said the governor, "We'd better not mess this up."

He ordered the visitor to be brought to him at once.

On crossing the fortress's threshold, Maurice Evrard's heart certainly beat faster than usual.

Nevertheless, the aviator, while fully aware of the terrible responsibility which fell to him, was very calm, very sure of himself.

After having explained without stumbling, and in the best German, that Pastor Schoenreck had suddenly fallen ill and that he had been charged with replacing him, he gave the governor the pass which would open the prison gates wide to him.

Commandant Fürsner, a hundred leagues from suspecting the truth, decided, after having examined the papers, "I'll take you to the prisoner."

Some moments later, the two men found themselves at the cell door.

"Wait for me a moment," said the governor. "I must warn this woman."

Fürsner entered the cell, whose door he had unlocked himself, leaving it wide open.

So Evrard heard this conversation.

"By superior orders, Mr. Jerkhein, pastor in training, has come to bring you the comfort of religious thought. I trust you will receive him with kindness and grace."

"Why impose on me the presence of this man who I don't know, and whom I don't want to know?" replied Germaine's voice. "I warn you that I shan't say a word to him."

"I have orders to bring him in here, he will be brought in!" Fürsner declared.

Then, turning back towards the door, he called, "Pastor, come in!"

And as Evrard entered the cell, he added, "I'm going to leave you alone with the prisoner; I warn you that she's of a wayward character."

Germaine, turning her back on the newcomer, headed towards the window and stared obstinately at the dark sky.

The Commandant continued. "In line with regulations, I must lock you in here with the prisoner. When you've finished your meeting, you just have to call the sentinel, who will warn me, and I will come at once to get you out."

Evrard nodded his head slightly.

Fürsner went out.

There was a click-clack from the lock.

The officer and the young girl were alone.

Germaine, her gaze still fixed on the horizon, had not moved.

As to Maurice, he stayed immobile for a moment, his ears pricked. Then, only when he heard Fürsner moving away, the young officer, softly, murmured in French, "Germaine!"

Jumping, the inventor's daughter spun round. She stifled a cry.

She had recognised the friendly voice.

But, facing this Protestant minister, she still hesitated.

"Germaine!" the aviator repeated, "Germaine, it's me!"

"Maurice!" said the captive, sure this time that she'd not been mistaken.

And in a mad gesture, lost, she was going to rush towards him when, in one word, Evrard stopped her. "Silence!"

"You're here? But it's not possible!"

"Silence, I beg you!"

And holding the Bible, he said, "You'll find inside this book, which is fake, a metal saw prepared by your father."

Then, drawing from under his coat a parcel wrapped in grey paper, he added, "It's a rope ladder. Hide it quickly under your bed."

"My friend . . ."

"Listen to me carefully."

"Yes, yes!"

In a low voice Maurice continued. "This evening at lights out, attack one of the bars. Two hours of effort will do it. Here's a little wax to suppress the noise and to help the steel teeth grip the iron better. When you've detached the bar, the one in the middle, fix the ladder to the two others, solidly by the two carabiners. Then let yourself slip outside. We'll be below, your father, Chantecoq and I, to receive you. Trust in us. All our precautions are taken. Germaine, you're saved!"

"As long as you're not recognised before leaving the Citadel!" breathed the noble creature.

"The Commandant didn't stumble just now. I've a valid pass. The hardest part is done. Rest easy.

"I tremble at the thought of the dangers that you have braved, that you still brave . . ."

"I had no choice. I played the hand, I won it. Tomorrow, at break of day, we'll all be in France!"

"And my father?"

"He's as well as can be expected. You'll see him in a few hours. Courage and see you very soon!"

Then the captain seemed to change his mind. "One last word however."

"Speak!"

"Though I'm absolutely convinced that I'll leave this fortress as easily as I entered it, you're going to make me a promise."

"What?"

"It's that, whatever happens, do you hear me? Whatever happens, you'll profit from the escape tools that I just gave to you."

"What's this promise for?"

"Germaine, I want it!"

And as a footstep was heard in the corridor, Maurice added, "Quickly! I ask you, I beg you!"

"Very well! Yes, I promise you, but repeat again that you fear nothing for yourself, that you're really sure . . ."

The young girl did not have the time to complete her sentence.

A key turned in the lock and the door opened, making way for General von Talberg.

Instantly, Evrard had resumed his persona of pastor-in-training.

As to Germaine, overwhelmed by this unexpected apparition, she asked herself what was going to happen.

Von Talberg, cold, glacial, his brow furrowed, advanced towards the fake minister.

"It appears you're called," he began in a very hard voice, "Mr. Jerkhein."

"Yes, general," the officer replied imperturbably.

"You're a pastor in training?"

"Yes, general."

"And you're here to replace the suddenly indisposed Pastor Schoenreck?"

"Yes, general."

"That's not true!"

"General . . ."

"It's not true, I tell you! Warned of your presence in this cell and overcome with sudden suspicion, I myself telephoned Pastor Schoenreck straight away; he replied at once that he had indeed been indisposed, but that he had charged no one to replace him."

And threatening, in a superb tone, von Talberg asked, "Who are you? Answer me!"

The moment was terrible.

Evrard said to himself, "Now is not the time for lies. I'm taken. Let's pay with our own person!"

And in a flash, baldly, he replied. "I'm Captain Maurice Evrard!"

"Captain Maurice Evrard!" the Chief of Staff repeated, shuddering.

But, mastering the formidable emotion which had just taken hold of him, he replied. "With what aim have you infiltrated this prison?"

"I wanted to see Germaine Aubry, to speak to her," the aviator said simply, pointing to his fiancée who was standing pale, immobile, but with a torn heart, awaiting the end of this tragic meeting with unbearable anxiety.

And he added with a voice trembling with the most touching tenderness. "I wanted to bring to her the comfort of my tenderness."

The general was already heading towards the door.

Evrard understood what he was going to do.

"General!" he said.

Von Talberg turned back to him.

Then, taking one step towards the German officer, the aviator declared in a tone full of nobility and imposing grandeur, "General, you can't send me to prison."

"That's what we're about to find out!"

"Tomorrow I must fight on the border with Captain Wilhelm Ansbach. You have no right to make me miss that meeting."

"And why?" asked the Chief of Staff who seemed a little more conciliatory.

"Because you wouldn't want it to be said that General von Talberg prevented a German officer from claiming satisfaction from a French officer."

Frida's father fell silent.

This reply so proud, so haughty, had half disarmed him.

"Sir," he said after a moment of reflection, "my soldier's duty would be to have you arrested on sight, but my conscience as a man obliges me to acknowledge that you're right. You will leave here without being bothered and you will fight Captain Ansbach at the appointed time; but on one condition, however. That you give me your word of honour that as soon as the duel is over, you'll come and report here as a prisoner."

"I engage myself gladly," replied Maurice, "because if I return it will be because I've killed him, and so I will have accomplished my task."

"Very well! Come!" said von Talberg.

But the eyes of the two fiancés had crossed.

In those of the young girl, Maurice read very clearly. "I don't want to be free when you're going to be a prisoner."

And Germaine had read in Maurice's: "Keep your promise, you must! I want you to!"

"Come, sir," repeated the Chief of Staff.

A minute later, the door was locked behind the German general and the French captain.

Germaine remained, her eye fixed on that door.

It seemed to her that Maurice coming, and in going, had robbed her of all her courage.

Suddenly, one word exhaled from her mouth in a painful sigh. "My father! He'll be waiting for me! He waits for me! Two hours of effort and I'll be in his arms, free! Free! And then I promised my fiancé . . . No, I have no right to stay here!"

But soon her gaze met the Bible lying on the table.

Mechanically her fingers reached out to the book. They raised the cover.

A little handsaw, with steel teeth, pointed, was revealed.

"Yes, that's it," murmured Germaine. "Soon, when the lights out is sounded, I'll attack the bars of my prison. Maurice, you've saved me. But I'll save you in turn!"

CHAPTER THIRTY-FOUR:

Liberty

It was close to midnight.

A thick night enveloped Spandau Citadel.

Two men hidden in the middle of the reeds which filled the fortress ditches talked in low voices.

"So," Jean Aubry asked feverishly, "there's nothing to fear from this side?"

"Nothing to fear," reassured Captain Evrard.

"And General von Talberg?"

"I ostensibly took the train for Berlin in front of him. On arriving in the capital, I changed back into this aviator gear and then came to rejoin you with all haste."

"Are you sure you weren't noticed or recognised?"

"I hope so. The aircraft is ready?"

"It's waiting, ready to take flight, in the property that Mr. Laumann rented specially some time ago. Chantecoq and Mr. Gautier are keeping close guard."

"The motor?"

"Snoring marvellously. On that side, I'll answer everything!"

"And the car?"

"Hidden two steps from here, in the vegetation that lines the road. It's waiting for us, headlights extinguished, ready to drive us to the aircraft."

"Provided we have time to get away before the alarm is given, and provided the garrison don't leave the citadel."

"The garrison won't leave, whatever happens," the inventor affirmed categorically.

"Are you sure of that?" asked the officer.

"Absolutely sure. I can even tell you that if these gentlemen are recalcitrant, I prepared a surprise for them in my own way."

"All in good time! And Germaine?"

"I've already been able to send her some signals; she responded and I'm certain that, for two hours at least, she's working on her escape."

"Do you believe that she's succeeded in sawing the bar?"

"I hope so!"

"And from the side of the Citadel?"

"As you see, everything is quiet."

But suddenly, struck by a poignant worry, Evrard murmured, "Provided that once outside, the poor child isn't seized by a fainting fit."

"Our thought will sustain her," replied Jean Aubry.

Then, leaning on his companion's arm, the inventor added, "there she is!"

"God, protect her!" the young officer prayed.

By the light of the moon which was beginning to detach itself from the wind-chased clouds, the two Frenchmen had just glimpsed Germaine who, after having followed her fiancé's instructions, that is to say having sawn the window's central bar and attached the ladder to the other bars by its carabiners, had let it unroll down to the very bottom of the tower.

"Oh! That sentinel!" Evrard murmured, pointing out to Jean Aubry the soldier who was patrolling the round path, watching the whole zone that the prisoner would have to cross in order to escape.

"I'll make it my business," replied the inventor. "You, get ready to receive Germaine."

At these words, the young officer slipped into the ditch, through the reeds.

Soon he had water up to his armpits. But gripping the bottom of the ladder, he tugged it vigorously.

Then Germaine, passing through the window, began her perilous descent, slowly, with poise, calling on all her sang-froid and supported, as her father had foreseen, by the thoughts of those who were waiting below.

But the sentinel had just stopped.

A suspect noise had attracted his ear. The soldier leaned over. He saw, suspended in the air, a human shape.

He guessed everything.

It was the prisoner who was escaping.

Without hesitation, he shouldered his rifle, he had his finger on the trigger, he was about to fire . . .

A detonation echoed.

The sentinel, dropping his weapon, fell with a cry.

It was Jean Aubry who, after having succeeded in slipping up to the foot of the round path, had just wounded the unfortunate guard, with an excellent revolver of American manufacture with which he had taken care to arm himself,.

But the alarm was given. Rumbles were rising from the guard post.

Germaine slid down the few rungs which separated her from her fiancé with extraordinary agility.

Maurice caught her in his arms; and while holding her against his chest, he carried her out of the ditch; then, followed by Jean Aubry, he ran with his precious burden to the car, whose engine was running.

In a few seconds they were in the car, which left at top speed.

During this time Commandant Fürsner who, his rounds finished, was going to go to bed, had hurried, at the noise of the shot, to the Citadel courtyard.

The commotion was indescribable.

The soldiers, roused by the junior officer, had lost their heads.

Fürsner, noticing the rope ladder which hung the length of the tower, gave a howl of fury.

He understood.

His prisoner had just escaped him!

He ordered a mass sortie.

But the drawbridge had to be lowered, that took a certain amount of time, during which the governor swore, cursed, shook, and spoke of having the whole garrison shot.

Finally the drawbridge was down.

Fürsner, revolver in hand, wanted to go first.

But as he approached the gate, a formidable explosion went off.

A stick of dynamite had just blown up the drawbridge in the governor's face without injuring anybody.

It was the prisoner's parting gesture, and the inventor's calling card.

Meanwhile, the car piloted by Doctor Laumann had reached the property where the aircraft was waiting.

Mad with joy, Jean Aubry pressed his daughter against his chest.

"But there's no time for effusiveness. We'll catch up later."

Swiftly, the young aviator who was exultant, led Germaine and her father towards the aircraft which, like a sleeping bird, but ready to wake, was stretched out on the ground, wings open.

He helped Aubry and the young girl up into a sort of nacelle reserved for passengers and installed himself behind them.

A friendly salute to those who stayed behind and the aviator started the motor, which gave out a loud purr that augured well.

At once the aircraft leapt into life, trembled, slipped on its wheels, in order to raise itself soon on the flat terrain that Mr. Laumann had prepared carefully, and, driven by the admirable aviator Maurice Evrard, they disappeared into the night, while Germaine, tears filling her eyes and thinking she was dreaming, still had the strength to shout to those who were left behind, "See you soon, my friends! Again and always *vive la France*!"

"Yes, that's it, this time," sighed Chantecoq happily.

"Provided nothing happens to them on the way!" Mr. Gautier wished ardently.

"I'm at peace," Mr. Laumann affirmed. With a pilot like the captain, Berlin to Paris is nothing."

"No more than Paris to Berlin," added Doctor Laumann with an inexpressible expression of hope.

"And by dawn," Chantecoq finished, "they'll be at the frontier, where we will not be long in joining them. But while we wait, my dear Mr. Gautier, we have a little score to settle with a certain lady."

"Emma Lückner," shuddered the special commissioner, as if a viper had bitten his heel.

"Yes, Emma Lückner. If Mr. Laumann agrees, we will go to beg of his brother to drive us to Berlin and we shall report to the home of that excellent princess, Marfa Tchernikoff."

"What!" Mr. Gautier exclaimed, terrified at the thought of revisiting the perfidious adventuress. "How! You want to visit that woman?"

"Perfectly!"

"But aren't you afraid that . . ."

"I fear nothing, Mr. Gautier," replied Chantecoq. "Let's get underway quickly, because we must also be returned to France by tomorrow evening!"

Around half past one in the morning, two men dressed as good bourgeois gentlemen who were about to take quite a long voyage, rang on the bell of the house inhabited by Emma Lückner.

The door was soon opened before them.

A young maid, with an alert cherubic face, appeared, an electric lamp in her hand, ready to guide their way.

"Is everything in order?" the first traveller asked in excellent French.

"Yes, sir," the young maid replied in the same language.

"She's sleeping?"

"Like a baby."

"And the 'trinket'?"

"It's there, ready to function."

"Then all is well, my little Manette. Lead us to the lady's bedroom."

While, guided by the comely maid, Chantecoq and Mr. Gautier reached the spy's apartment, the protean man, leaning towards his companion, whispered in his ear, "I believe, my dear special commissioner, that you're going to get yourself a good pint of blood."

The chambermaid, a sly smile on her lips, pushed the front door and, after having shown the two Frenchmen into the antechamber, she led them into a brightly lit lounge.

On crossing the threshold, Mr. Gautier could not repress a cry of surprise.

Lying on the divan, in a charming negligee with a delicious pink robe, garnished with lace, divinely or rather diabolically beautiful, the Russian was resting peacefully.

"What a shame," Chantecoq said loudly, "that such a beautiful frame encloses such a villainous soul!"

"Take care not to wake her," Mr. Gautier, more reserved, intervened at once.

"No danger, my dear friend. We could fire a cannon next to her ear and she wouldn't falter. She has at least thirty-six hours before she wakes up."

Then turning towards the kind maid, the French agent added, "And that's thanks to our pretty Manette, who I introduce to you as one of my best collaborators in Berlin – French, of course – who, after eight days in the service of Lady Lückner, has succeeded in placing herself in her good graces – which isn't easy – and has put to sleep not only her defiance, but her whole person by making her, not smoke a dodgy cigarette, but to absorb a little glass of liqueur of my making. Now, let's make haste, we have work to do. Manette, where is the 'trinket'?"

"Here it is, Mr. Chantecoq," the maid replied immediately while folding a charming Japanese screen which was masking a huge leather trunk of the most comfortable appearance.

"Very good!" Chantecoq approved. "That's it exactly!"

And, raising the lid, he revealed a padded interior, in the shape of a sleigh bed and furnished with silk belt straps.

"We're going to put our exquisite princess in this modern style bed," announced Chantecoq. "She'll be surprised to return to Paris with us."

"But she'll suffocate in there," Mr. Gautier objected.

"Some invisible and marvellously arranged air holes permit her to breathe at her leisure. Come on, help me."

Chantecoq grabbed Emma Lückner by the shoulders, Gautier seized her by the feet and both, with infinite care, placed her in the trunk which they sealed after having secured the sleeper with the straps, in such a way as to avoid shocks and to protect her from potholes on the road.

"Now, Manette," Chantecoq ordered, "light our way, as we're going to take the package down. But before, let me thank you and offer you this small gratuity."

And, slipping a well-stuffed wallet into the chambermaid's hand, the French agent added, "This is nothing next to the service that you have just done me. But we'll meet again, my child, and you won't be dealing with an ingrate."

"Oh! If you only knew how happy I've been to play a trick on this evil woman!" the young maid declared, nevertheless slipping the wallet quickly into the pocket of her apron.

Then, raising the electric lamp, she said, "Now, sirs, come this way, and take care above all not to do yourselves a mischief on the staircase."

Chantecoq took the 'trinket' by one handle; Gautier took it by the other.

A Berlin car this time, but still driven by Doctor Laumann, waited outside.

In one swing – the two companions were robust – they loaded the trunk on to the car's roof and left at a good speed, while Manette, with her hand, bade them farewell and shouted after them a joyous, "Safe journey!"

At break of day, an aeroplane, after having crested the Vosges, descended in a graceful landing within sight of Epinal.

Three people soon climbed from the nacelle. They were Germaine, Maurice Evrard and Jean Aubry.

Then, falling to her knees, the heroic Frenchwoman leaned over the ground and kissed it, murmuring, "I kiss you, oh land of France that I believed I'd never see again."

The inventor and the officer were touched.

And as the young girl stood up again, she saw fat tears of joy rolling down their faces.

Then, she too, weeping with happiness, threw herself in their arms.

It was an instant of inexpressible happiness.

"My children," said Mr. Aubry with a tremble in his voice, "you have conquered your happiness nobly. You can now look our country in the face. It might be just as proud of you as you are of it!"

But suddenly Germaine cried out.

She had just remembered the oath that Maurice Evrard had made to General von Talberg.

The officer, with a discreet gesture, pointed to her father while murmuring, "Silence!"

Then, leaning towards his fiancée, he whispered in her ear. "Courage! I'll be back soon, I'm sure of it!"

And out loud, he carried on, turning towards the inventor. "I'm going to leave you, father."

"Yes, the duel."

With an expression of inexpressible hatred, Maurice Evrard added, "I have to kill this wretch. And I will kill him!"

CHAPTER THIRTY-FIVE:
Von Talberg's Dilemma

General von Talberg, after having left Maurice Evrard at liberty on his word, had returned to Berlin in a very understandable state of agitation.

He locked himself in his office, forbidding anyone from disturbing him.

Indeed, he needed to be alone in order to examine himself and to ask himself if his conscience was troubling him.

"No," the great honest man said to himself, "I could not keep this French officer locked up. I was right to let him fight Ansbach.

"But wouldn't it have been more generous not to demand that he return to turn himself in?

"And yet, thinking about it carefully, I could not act differently. Above all I am and I must be the

German Chief of Staff. Alas! For the last few months I've forgotten that a bit too often."

But the day started to appear behind the red tints of the tall windows.

Von Talberg prepared to retire to his rooms, not in search of sleep but simply to lie on a bed to rest for a few moments, when he heard a discreet knock on the large door to his office.

Unhappy to have been disturbed, the General frowned; but then he heard the rustle of cloth against the door, and at that moment three light blows rang out again on the panel.

It could only be Frida.

Von Talberg stood up and ran to open the door.

"What! Already up, my dear?" he cried, receiving the charming young girl in his arms.

Frida hid with her kisses the embarrassment that gripped her because she didn't know how to broach before her father the subject which was causing her disquiet and which had brought her here.

"You don't have your pretty rested face, like when you've slept well," said the father. "What's the matter then?"

"I've not seen you since yesterday morning."

"Well?"

"And you went there, didn't you? Did you see her?" Frida asked breathless.

The events of the day before, forgotten for a moment, replayed before the Chief of Staff's eyes.

"Yes . . . I saw Germaine Aubry in her prison yesterday," he said with pain in his voice.

And suddenly, febrile, nervous, almost vehement, he added, "Let's not talk about it, my child. I have serious concerns that I can't yet confide in you. Perhaps, quite soon, I'll have some advice to ask of you."

"Advice, from me?" Frida cried, surprised.

Never in the most tragic hours which had upset her existence had she seen her father so strangely troubled.

"Yes, from you, my dearly beloved child," repeated von Talberg.

And drawing his daughter into his arms, he placed a long kiss on her forehead.

At that moment, Ulrich knocked at the door.

As the general didn't respond immediately, the guard fell back.

"Who's there?" von Talberg asked, while Frida, disengaging from his embrace, was already heading towards the door.

"Colonel Skoppen, on urgent business," Ulrich responded.

Colonel Skoppen was currently running the Intelligence Service, with Colonel Hoffmann still unavailable.

"Let him in!" said the general.

The German officer appeared straight away. He was so upset that, not noticing his superior's daughter, he bumped into her.

Excusing himself immediately, he said, "Miss, I beg your pardon, but something so frightening has happened . . ."

"What's that?" the Chief of Staff demanded.

"General," said Skoppen who appeared to have completely lost his mind, "Germaine Aubry, Spandau's prisoner, has escaped."

At those words, Frida, who was on the point of leaving, stayed nailed to the spot, while a heavy cry escaped her throat.

"Escaped!" von Talberg exclaimed. "When was that?"

"Tonight, general."

"At what time?"

"Around midnight."

"In what circumstances?"

"Germaine Aubry, after having sawn through the bars over her window, climbed down to the ditches with the aid of a marvellously adapted ladder, that we have recovered, because it was still hanging down the height of the tower."

"How was she able to procure this ladder?"

"I don't know, general. Yesterday the prison received no visit to her prison other than that of Pastor Jerkhein, pastor in training, and your own."

Von Talberg bit his lip.

In a moment, he had understood. "It was Captain Evrard," he thought to himself. And he added. "I have no right to blame him, it was well played!"

Then, after having thrown a glance at the face of his daughter shivering with a joy that she could barely contain, von Talberg spoke. "Colonel Skoppen, was there no guard?"

"Yes, general. The soldier on patrol even saw the prisoner at the precise moment when she was halfway down the ladder, and he tried to fire on her, but he didn't have time. Instead, a man hidden at the foot of the ramparts and armed with a revolver, sent a bullet square into his chest. The unfortunate soldier has been injured, but not grievously. While the alarm was sounding, Germaine Aubry, carried by a robust man who had seized her in his arms, reached an automobile which was waiting near there."

"This car ought to have been pursued."

"General, just as the guard was going to set out, the drawbridge exploded, so immobilising the garrison inside the Citadel for a long time."

"How is it that it's been left so long to inform me of this?"

"General, as you're going to see, the people who helped Germaine Aubry to flee had taken the most minute precautions. All the telegraph and telephone wires linking Spandau to Berlin had been cut.

"That's it, at least?"

"I'll add, general, that one of our agents, who is operating from the French frontier at the moment, just signalled me by telegraph about the landing of an aeroplane near to Epinal, containing two men and one woman, of whom the description corresponds entirely with that of Germaine Aubry."

"Good, Colonel Skoppen," von Talberg said, impassive once again. "I'll lead the enquiry myself. You're dismissed!"

"Yes, general!"

Colonel Skoppen withdrew after having saluted his leader.

Then, in a blink, Frida had thrown herself into her father's arms, finally letting all her joy escape, crying, "Saved! She's saved! Oh, how happy I am!"

"And it's my fault," von Talberg said.

"Oh! Then father, tell me quickly. I will be so happy to know that it's to you she owes her freedom. It seems to me, if it were possible, that I'm going to love you even more!"

"For the moment, I can tell you nothing," the general replied.

"In forty-eight hours, you'll know everything. Thank you for your tenderness, my dear daughter, because I'm going to have great need of it."

"Oh! Father, you can count on me entirely."

"I know. Go back to your room. I'm going to be absent for some time, two days at most, at the end of which I'll send you a telegram to ask you to come and join me."

"And this advice?" Frida asked tenderly.

"It's only then, my child, that I will ask you for it."

Von Talberg, left alone, sat down at his table and began to write.

Then he tore up his letter and began another.

And finally standing up, he said in a serious voice. "Me, tender my resignation? No, not yet, because I've not finished my task!"

CHAPTER THIRTY-SIX:

The Duel

The sun was beginning to appear over the horizon.

A French officer, wearing the elegant and sober uniform of an artillery captain, was leaving a tavern placed on German territory, at the most extreme point of the French frontier.

Slowly he walked towards the border post and stopped there without crossing the line.

Then, his face grave, a fire in his eyes, he contemplated the horizon at length, that is to say France, while a bitter smile wandered over his lips.

After an instant, the tavern door opened again, making way this time for General von Talberg, in simple fatigues and whose temples, under his flat helmet, seemed much more greying than in previous days.

He took a few steps, stopped at a certain distance from the French officer, examined him at length with a strange expression in which there seemed to be

ARTHUR BERNÈDE

more sympathy than resentment, more admiration than anger.

"You're looking at your country," he suddenly said.

Surprised by the sound of that voice which had not entered his ears since the tragic scene in the prison, Evrard turned quickly and, courteously dashing off a brief military salute, he replied. "Yes, general, I'm looking at my country."

Then, with a voice which shook with emotion, he added, "And never have I found it more beautiful than this evening."

There was silence.

Evrard was going to turn back towards the West when von Talberg declared, pointing at the tavern that he had just left, "Captain Wilhelm Ansbach is there with his seconds."

"I'm waiting for mine," Maurice said simply, "Anyway, they're not late. It's only half past five, and the encounter is fixed for six o'clock."

"That's true," acknowledged the German Army's Chief of Staff. "Do you have your swords?"

"Yes, general. On that note, I must thank you for having authorised me to bring them into Germany, as well as this uniform. Let me also tell you how grateful I am to you for having avoided me during these last hours, a surveillance which, I won't deny, would have been very tough for me."

"I didn't need to put you under surveillance," replied the general. "I had your word. That was enough for me."

"I'm happy to see you attach such value to a French officer's sense of honour."

"I learned to know them and to appreciate them a long time ago," said von Talberg. "Also I was astonished to see one of them using a subterfuge that I don't dare to qualify in order to break a woman justly condemned as a spy out of prison."

Coldly, but firmly, Evrard replied. "Miss Germaine Aubry is not a spy. You know that as well as I do, general."

"Yes, understood," cried the Chief of Staff with nervous energy. "A young girl who avenges her father. A Frenchwoman who defends her country! The combat aircraft plans . . . Wilhelm Ansbach . . ."

Then, as though he was still grappling with his conscience, as though he felt, even without being accused, the need to justify himself before his adversary, he added, "But I too, don't I have the right, what am I saying, the duty, to defend my country? I've done it with all my strength and my conscience makes no reproach!"

"Not even for being associated with a parody of justice in order to condemn this unfortunate to a pain so cruel which, in the depths of your conscience, I'm sure you can't help finding undeserved?"

Then von Talberg, approaching Maurice Evrard, said to him in a halting voice, "But don't you then suspect what my life has been like since your fiancée infiltrated my house, since all those items entrusted to my care and to my soldier's honour have been overturned?"

"And you, general," the aviator riposted, "Do you doubt what ours has been like, for her father and for me, since this wretch, an officer from your army, entered under our roof?"

"Certainly, I understand your anger, but Germaine Aubry did not only take from me the most precious documents, for which I answered before my master and before all Germany. It was also necessary that she put in me frightful doubt, which makes you suspect your best friends. This way of conducting a war is abominable."

"Whose fault then? Was it us who began? Was it us who, fifty years ago, instituted this shameful system of espionage?"

"Ah! You speak of fifty years ago," cried von Talberg. "What were we then? A vague agglomeration of powers without unity, consequently without strength and still bearing the barely-healed scars of wounds that yours had inflicted, so well that when our fathers were labouring in their fields, their ploughshares were breaking the bones of our soldiers killed by your Bonaparte's grunts!"

"As today," replied the French officer, "our peasants find at the bottom of their fallow fields, the skeletons of our troops and our snipers killed by your Bismarck's soldiers!"

"How you hate us!"

"How we hate ourselves!"

"Yet," replied von Talberg, "other peoples have waged war on you cruelly, and you have since held out your hand to them."

"That's because they weren't so cruel as to amputate us!" said Maurice, pointing towards Alsace-Lorraine, "Because they understood that to destroy us would be a crime, and that France's existence is necessary for life, for the beauty of the world!"

"Who's talking about annihilating you? Isn't it fair, however, in the face of your colonial expansion, that we should seek to conquer new territories? Is it our fault if you no longer have enough men to populate your provinces and to defend your land?"

At these words, the French officer's face grew purple and, shaking, he replied, standing proudly before the German general. "Then come for us, general! You'll soon see if we have enough soldiers to bar your path!"

"I don't deny the valour of your troops," admitted von Talberg, a little taken aback by this virulent speech. "I also know the merit of those who command them . . . However, you are obliged to admit that the military spirit is dwindling in France."

"What an error!" the artillery officer cried. "Because five or six dreamers believe it's tasteful to espouse antimilitarism in a sort of international dogma, you assume our whole country is behind them? Then let's go! Perhaps one day you'll pass one of our regiments. Look at our soldiers: infantry, cavalry, artillery, all of them marching with a smile on their lips, and ask what they'd do in the hour of danger?

"You'll hear how they will answer. Oh! It will be brief. One word, one single word: 'to the border!' Stop in Paris one Saturday night, mingle with the crowd which escorts our military parades. Listen to all the cries of 'long live the army!' which burst from not only the robust chests of artisans, but from every floor of every house, from the balconies of the rich to the poor man's attic.

"And it's not, believe it, the puerile manifestation of an ephemeral chauvinism, it's the soul of a nation which is gathering itself, yes, of a whole nation which has never been more ready to fight, and to defend itself, because never has it felt stronger.

"And there is your work!"

As von Talberg shrugged his shoulders, Maurice continued. "Yes, this is what you did, with your pretension to invade us in all domains, and especially with your incessant provocations and your evil quarrels.

"The union of all Frenchmen, it's you who realised it! It's a result!"

"I admire your enthusiasm," said Frida's father. "In its favour, I really want to forget what might be injurious to my country in your words. But this union which you value so strongly, is it as solid as you think? Your France is divided by social passions. It's prey for politicians!"

"What's a parliamentarian compared to the flag?" interrupted Evrard forcefully. "Consider then our accomplishments in the last few years. This fourth weapon, our aeroplanes, which frighten you so much, and that you try in vain to organise yourselves! Ah, general, we can be content. We have worked hard. We have fewer spies than you, it's true; but we others, we do not crawl, we have wings!"

"We'll break those wings!"

"There will be others reborn, always and even so!"

This time, the German officer fell silent.

Profoundly moved by the officer's energetic attitude and noble ripostes, he felt being born and growing inside him, with a strange rapidity, the bitter regret of no longer being French.

The blood of his ancestors boiled in his veins, and up to that land of France that he could make out in the evening mist, all this contributed to revive, to awake in him a feeling which, up to then, had only been asleep in his soul and which, suddenly, in an unexpected fashion, overwhelmed, flooded him, enlightened him, leaving him unable to fight it.

And just as his daughter one day had declared to him, "I am French!" von Talberg was for a moment on the point of launching himself at Maurice Evrard, of seizing him and to press him against his chest crying: "I too am French!"

But Captain Ansbach, followed by Lieutenants Bingerbrück and von Kissingen who had accepted to serve him as seconds, left the inn.

Von Talberg contented himself with making a sign to Captain Evrard, and as on the French territory, two infantry officers appeared, Germaine's fiancé announced, "General, here are my seconds!"

Far away, on the edge of a pine wood, two shadows loomed.

It was Jean Aubry and Germaine.

The heroic young girl had stayed, indeed, to attend the battle.

To the end, she wanted to stay near he to whom she owed her liberty. If he succumbed, to give him the last rites, to close his eyes herself, and if he triumphed, to greet him at the moment when, faithful to his sworn oath, he would go to place himself in custody, with a comforting gesture, and the promise of eternal attachment.

The French officers were heading towards the German officers.

All, with perfect precision, a cold courtesy, impassive, set to the preparations for the duel, choosing the ground and brandishing swords drawn at random.

But at the moment when combat was engaged, a noise of fifes and drums sounded nearby.

It was a regiment which was returning to Colmar, to the sound of the retreat.

The combatants' swords struck sparks.

Both seemed of equal strength.

Both, animated by a matchless hatred, staked their life resolutely.

And those who were present at this terrible encounter realised that it was a true fight to the death, with no mercy, between these young enemy officers.

Suddenly, Germaine, who had stayed on French territory with her father, but quite close to the French border post, gave an anguished cry. "Wounded!"

Indeed, Wilhelm Ansbach's sword had lightly touched his adversary's shoulder.

Von Kissingen, who directed the combat, cried with authority. "Stop!"

The two combatants obeyed.

Straight away, Maurice Evrard affirmed, "It's nothing, a simple scratch. Let's continue, sirs!"

"Gladly!" Ansbach declared.

The German Major who was there observed, indeed, that the captain's wound was insignificant.

Combat resumed, more brutal, more furious still.

The German retreat had moved away.

All that could be heard, in the distance, was an indistinct murmur.

The dry echoes of little boxes and the sharp squeal of fifes.

Ansbach, a fencer of the first order, pressed Evrard again who, not wanting to break off, and, more aggravated than he thought by the sword's blow which had brushed his muscle, felt his wrist growing tired, his arm growing heavy.

Germaine was truly anguished. "Is he going to succumb? Am I going to see him die before me?"

Jean Aubry, pale, trembling, felt tears spring to his eyes. He couldn't stop himself from murmuring, "Poor child! He's lost! The other is going to kill him!"

But now some notes from the clarion burst out; joyous, vibrant in the air, accompanied by the vigorous rhythm of the tambours.

This time, it was the French who were advancing.

Suddenly Evrard felt himself reborn, galvanised by a prodigious strength, superhuman.

All trace of fatigue disappeared from him.

He attacked his adversary, forced him to break off

and pursued him with such ardour that, passing the border post, crossing the frontier, the two combatants now found themselves on French soil.

Then while, by a path running down the length of the hill, like a field of poppies, the red caps of the French infantry began appearing, Evrard laid a straight blow on Ansbach and struck him full in the chest.

"Touché!" von Kissingen cried, hurrying with the other officers.

Wilhelm Ansbach staggered, then fell in the arms of his seconds, saying to them, "I'm lost!"

A red foam stained his lips.

But stiffening, the German officer cried in a voice which rattled, "Yes, it's over! It's over! Ah! These drums, these clarions, payback! It's payback!"

And directing his haggard eyes towards Captain Evrard who, sword in hand, stayed straight, immobile, awaiting the end of this atrocious agony, he added, "Captain, you'll tell your fiancée that I beg her pardon? She was right . . ."

Then, resisting the death which was coming, Ansbach implored in a begging voice, "Comrades, bring me. I want to die on the soil of my own country."

He was dragged to the other side of the border post.

Clinging to his seconds, so as not to fall, he looked at the ground which stuck to his uncertain feet, then in a heavy voice he murmured, "Alsace, it's still France! Always France!"

A cough half choked him.

It was like a final sob.

"Farewell, my friends!" he said. "Farewell!"

His head fell back on his shoulder and, addressing General von Talberg who had approached him, he tried to speak. "General, will you tell . . ."

But he stopped, a stream of blood burst from his mouth, followed by a profound sigh.

He died.

Everyone crossed themselves.

Then Evrard, taking a step forward, said to von Talberg, "General. Faithful to my vow, I place myself in your custody."

"Stay, captain," replied the German Chief of Staff with a gesture full of nobility, "because if you cross the border, I'll be obliged to arrest you. You're on home ground, sir, stay there."

"And my word?"

"I return it to you!"

The French officer saluted him with his sword.

But a cry of joy made him turn. It was Germaine who was there, behind him, holding her arms to him.

And as he hurried to her, the little French troop left the path. The soldiers marched on happily.

Von Talberg, his arms crossed, watched them leave by the rays of the setting sun.

Epilogue

How great was the stupefaction of the director of General Security on seeing Chantecoq and Mr. Ernest Gautier suddenly enter his office!

From their triumphant faces, the top civil servant concluded straight away that they had come to give him good news, and immediately, hurrying over to them with his hands held out, he asked, "Germaine Aubry has escaped, hasn't she?"

"Yes," the two collaborators replied in unison.

"That's what I gathered from your telegram. I can't tell you how overjoyed I was! I was still afraid it was a lie or a trap. Now that you're here, I'm completely reassured. And I'm delighted, because it has truly been very wretched for me to know that this heroic young girl was a prisoner."

With the most sincere accent of joy, the director of Security continued. "As always, I'm sure, you must have accomplished some true miracles?"

"Oh, director, don't talk to me about that," Mr. Gautier declared spontaneously. "Our friend Chantecoq has been simply admirable!"

"I don't doubt it."

"But not at all!" the excellent agent protested with vehemence. "If Germaine Aubry was able to escape her gaolers, it wasn't thanks to me, but thanks to her fiancé, Captain Evrard, and to the extraordinarily resourceful man that is the inventor Jean Aubry."

"I'm sure, my dear friend," rectified the director, "that as always, you're being too modest."

"Don't worry, director," said Emma Lückner's victim, "I'll tell you everything our friend did out there. It was simply prodigious."

"While we're waiting," Chantecoq interrupted, "tell him a bit about what you did!"

"Me?" said Mr. Gautier, a little irritated.

"Yes, you! You don't want to? Ah well! Wait a bit, I shall be the one to tell all."

And Chantecoq, with his sunny day aplomb, continued with an engaging volubility. "Mr. Gautier, before leaving, promised you, director, that he would bring that terrible woman Emma Lückner to your office, tied hand and foot."

"Yes, what of it?"

"What of it? director, the special commissioner has kept his word!"

"Is that possible?"

"It's the truth."

Mr. Gautier intervened already. "You've forgotten to mention, good Chantecoq, that if we obtained this result, which I don't hesitate to qualify as prodigious, it's thanks . . ."

But the French agent interrupted him in a tone which brooked no reply, and, staring straight in the eyes of he whose professional honour he wanted to save at all costs, he declared, "It's thanks to your perspicacity, your courage, your audacity, because, I can't say it enough, repeat it enough, you were superb!"

Faced with such generosity, the excellent policeman could not control his emotion and, unable to speak a word, he took hold of his friend's hands and clasped them hard enough to break them.

At that moment there was a knock at the door.

"Come in!" said the director of General Security.

A hussar appeared, announcing, "There's a trunk which has been brought to the director's address."

"A trunk?"

"Yes, director, a large leather trunk which comes from Germany."

"Ah! Ah! Director," Chantecoq declared quickly, "this is a souvenir that Mr. Gautier and I have brought you from Berlin."

"You're really too kind . . ."

"We would be very happy," said Mr. Gautier, who was beginning to recover his aplomb, "if you would open this trunk in front of us."

"Gladly," accepted the senior civil servant who was guessing the truth.

And he told the hussar who was awaiting his orders, "Bring up the parcel to my office."

Some moments later, two men put down, in the middle of the office, a large leather trunk which seemed quite heavy.

Mr. Gautier took a key from his pocket, opened the locks, raised the lid, then said, "Director, if you would like to come and see? I have the satisfaction of announcing that the trinket that we have brought you has not suffered too much from the journey."

A smile on his lips, the director of General Security moved forward.

Then, on seeing the terrible spy whose capture he had yearned for so ardently lying at the bottom of the trunk and still sleeping peacefully, he couldn't help laughing, and said, "I don't mind seeing this pretty lady up close again! She's truly charming when she's asleep!"

"We're going to wake her," said Chantecoq, "because I can't wait to see her face when she finds herself facing us. My dear Gautier, could you give me a hand?"

"Very gladly!" the special commissioner responded.

They both took Emma Lückner out of the trunk and placed her in a leather armchair, opposite the director's desk.

Then, taking a small stoppered phial from a pocket, Chantecoq passed it to the director saying to him, "We're going to hide for a moment, Mr. Gautier and I. Meanwhile, you're going to make the beautiful princess inhale this drug."

"Understood!"

While Chantecoq and Mr. Gautier hid behind the curtains, the director, uncorking the phial, brought it delicately to the sleeping woman's nostrils, who, after ten seconds, after having breathed the agent sharply, opened her eyes, again conscious of all that was happening around her.

"Ah! Hello, Princess!" the director greeted her in a mocking tone.

As the spy gave him a dull look, he asked, more and more derisively, "Did you have a good trip?"

"Good trip . . ." Emma Lückner repeated, still not understanding.

"Of course," said Chantecoq, suddenly coming out from his hiding place.

"You weren't shaken about too much?" Mr. Gautier asked, revealing himself in turn.

Then a terrible cry burst from the adventuress's chest. Now she understood.

Without being aware of the circumstances of the ambush into which she'd fallen, she was no less conscious of the reality.

She knew she was lost.

But, a good player to the end, she sat up with a kind of fierce pride and, glowering at the three men disdainfully, she said, "You caught me, well done! But you won't keep me long!"

Before anyone had time to restrain her, the spy leapt towards the director's desk, grabbed a metal letter opener and tried to stab herself with it.

But Chantecoq was able to seize her by the wrist in time.

"Come, come! A little calm, Princess," he said. "You won't manage to kill yourself with a toy like that. You'll hurt yourself, that's all, and that would be a real shame. And you mustn't try to avoid your judges."

The director had already pressed one of the numerous buttons for electric bells available on his desk.

In moments, two stocky, solid agents appeared, in plain clothes.

"Take this woman to a safe place," the senior civil servant recommended, "and don't let her out of your sight for a moment."

While the two policeman dragged away Princess Marfa Tchernikoff, pale, her jaw clenched, her eyes flashing, and not daring to offer even the slightest resistance, the director of General Security said, "Now, I only have to phone Parquet and request, my dear Gautier, your promotion to the highest grade. As to you, my brave Chantecoq, who have always refused even the slightest recompense, let me tell you once more: you have truly served the country!"

Some weeks after the events that we've just recounted, Captain Maurice Evrard married Germaine Aubry.

The ceremony took place in the strictest intimacy.

The two young people had wanted to avoid curiosity, or rather the public's enthusiasm, because Germaine's adventure had dominated the news for some weeks, and the noble creature, since her return to France, had not ceased to receive, as well as her saviours, innumerable testimonies of the most sincere admiration.

However, among the guests, one great friend was missing, to the disappointment of the young couple.

It was Chantecoq.

Indeed, he had declared, that to his deep regret, he would be unable to attend the wedding, forced as he was to leave again immediately on an urgent and confidential mission.

At dessert, Mr. Aubry was about to stand up to raise a toast to absent friends, when suddenly the door opened and the hotel manager announced solemnly, "Representing the War Ministry!"

A man of around forty years, slim, elegant in his black suit with a red rosette flourishing in the buttonhole, his face framed by a carefully sculpted brown pointed beard, stepped forward and greeting the restricted assembly, he made an announcement. "Ladies and gentlemen I'm here today, in the name of the Minister for War, to bring to Captain Evrard and his charming wife the most agreeable wedding present that they could desire."

And, opening a case he was holding, in which there was a cross furnished with its ribbon, he added, "Dear Mr. Aubry, it gives me great joy to announce to you that you have been named a Knight of the Legion of Honour! Permit me, by attaching to your chest this decoration so well earned, to give you a fraternal accolade."

While a frisson of the softest emotion shook the guests, the Minister's delegate approached the inventor and decorated him according to the rites.

But instantly a cry of stupefaction burst from all their lips.

When he turned back, the delegate no longer wore a beard.

Then the same name escaped the lips of Germaine, Evrard and Jean Aubry.

"Chantecoq!"

"Yes, my friends, Chantecoq!" the protean man declared in a vibrant voice. "Or rather, Daniel Leroy, a former art teacher at Nancy college who transformed himself into the man you know to avenge his son, murdered ten years ago by a German border guard."

"A hero!" declared Captain Evrard.

While Mr. Ernest Gautier added, "The doubly greatest of men!"

But the champagne corks were popping loudly. Chantecoq, grabbing his cup frantically, raised it while saying, "My friends, it is I who am going to raise a toast! I drink to Germaine Aubry. I drink to the most valiant lady of all, as well as to Maurice Evrard her husband and to her father, because all three here represent the French family in everything she has that is great and beautiful, that is to say the soul of the land of their birth and boundless devotion to their flag!"

And as all eyes were fixed on this admirable trio, all vibrating with the same emotion, Chantecoq, whose voice trembled slightly, shouted, with a final crow, "*Vive la France!*"

FIN

The book you've just read has never been translated into English before. At first glance, that might not be entirely surprising, with the story's focus on conflict between France and Germany, not to mention a French agent who is *so* French that he drinks champagne to recover from a stabbing.

But Chantecoq and the Aubry Affair is a fascinating work when contextualised. At a time when Europe is commemorating the centenary of the events of the 1914-1918 War, commentators are still struggling to make sense of the conflict. Despite being published in 1912, two years before the outbreak of war, this book suggests very strongly that not only was war in Europe all but inevitable, but even that there was significant public appetite for the conflict.

Writing in 1912, Bernède offers very clear and raw grievances, that we sometimes overlook from our twenty-first Century perspective. War reparations from the Franco-Prussian War really were stored in Julius

Tower at Spandau Citadel, and our heroes freeing the patriotic Germaine Aubry from that very place can hardly be coincidemtal on the author's part. Names like Bonaparte and Bismarck are slung around by military characters in a pointed fashion. Chantecoq's motives for becoming a secret agent, tucked away in the epilogue like an afterthought, are remarkable. The behaviour of every French character in the book betrays a level of anti-German sentiment and paranoia that would seem absurd if the book had been written today.

In many ways, *Chantecoq and the Aubry Affair* reads like a propaganda piece for a war that had not yet started. And the imagery of poppies in the final chapter is poignant in its clairvoyance.

Elsewhere, I was drawn to this book precisely because of its charming obsolescence. The plans for Jean Aubry's combat aircraft, years before words like 'fighter plane' had been coined, place this book firmly in the realm of science-fiction at the time it was written. And with characters leaping into fast automobiles and worrying that the authorities will have been warned about their actions by telephone and telegraph, it's clear that Bernède wrote the 1912 equivalent of a high-tech thriller.

If Bernède's place at the cutting edge of science-fiction has been usurped, however, there is still one area where he was unfortunately ahead of his time. Germaine Aubry. This is a novel, written by a man in 1912, in which a young French woman leaves her love interest without hesitation, infiltrates German High Command as an untrained but highly effective secret agent, and smuggles secrets back to France. She is braver than Chantecoq himself, continuing her mission even after the German authorities are aware of a security issue. When she is unmasked, she remains hilariously unrepentant.

That the rest of the novel concerns the male characters' attempts to rescue Germaine from prison disqualifies the book from a positive feminist reading, but even within Julius Tower she resists interrogation, writes messages to her rescuers in her own blood, and is more than capable of breaking out of her own cell once she finally has the tools. In fact, while Germaine needs resources from men while planning her actions throughout the book, she then achieves everything she accomplishes on her own. Germaine Aubry is a genuinely 'strong female character' at a time when women didn't even have the vote, and I think she does the author credit.

Finally, I must thank Rachel Lawston for another incredible front cover, and Kath Middleton and Paul Lawston for invaluable proofreading and editing input. And of course my lovely wife Melanie for her constant love and support. *Vive la France*.

Andrew K Lawston, November 2015

ABOUT THE AUTHOR

Arthur Bernède was a prolific French writer who was born in Brittany in 1871. The author of more than two hundred novels, he created popular characters including Belphégor, Judex, Mandrin and Vidocq, as well as Chantecoq, the 'king of detectives'. Bernède died in 1937.

ABOUT THE TRANSLATOR

Andrew Lawston is a writer, actor and translator. He has published two collections of short stories and a satirical novella, as well as a translation of Casanova's *Histoire de ma fuite*. Andrew works as a publishing professional and lives in London with a black cat, a cocker spaniel, and his lovely wife Melanie, to whom this translation is dedicated.

Printed in Great Britain
by Amazon

41870024R00267